KT-478-083

Meier Susan cinderellas billion
dollar christmas

Also by Susan Meier

The Spanish Millionaire's Runaway Bride
Carrying the Billionaire's Baby
A Diamond for the Single Mum
Falling for the Pregnant Heiress
A Mistletoe Kiss With the Boss
Wedded for His Royal Duty
Pregnant with a Royal Baby!
Marriage Made in Monte Calanetti

Also by Brenda Harlen

The Sheriff's Nine-Month Surprise
Her Seven-Day Fiancé
Six Weeks to Catch a Cowboy
Claiming the Cowboy's Heart
Double Duty for the Cowboy
One Night With the Cowboy
Bring Me a Maverick for Christmas!
The Maverick's Midnight Proposal

Discover more at millsandboon.co.uk

CINDERELLA'S BILLION-DOLLAR CHRISTMAS

SUSAN MEIER

MAVERICK CHRISTMAS SURPRISE

BRENDA HARLEN

MILLS & BOON

First Published in Great Britain 2019
by Mills & Boon, an imprint of HarperCollinsPublishers,
1 London Bridge Street, London, SE1 9GF

Cinderella's Billion-Dollar Christmas © 2019 Linda Susan Meier
Maverick Christmas Surprise © 2019 Harlequin Books S.A.

Special thanks and acknowledgment are given to Brenda Harlen for her contribution to the *Montana Mavericks: Six Brides for Six Brothers* continuity.

ISBN: 978-0-263-27272-7

1219

CINDERELLA'S BILLION-DOLLAR CHRISTMAS

SUSAN MEIER

For Mikie.
I still miss you every day.

CHAPTER ONE

LENI LONG STARED out the big front window of the Family Diner in Mannington, Kansas, watching snow cover the sparkly gold Christmas bells hanging from the town's eight streetlights. With the breakfast rush over and the red-and-white-themed diner empty, a hush had fallen over the tiny town.

A black SUV pulled into a parking space a few feet down from the diner. A tall man in a charcoal-gray overcoat exited. His broad shoulders hunched against the snow-laced wind, but there was a strength, a power to the movement. Maybe because of his size. He had to be over six feet and was built like someone who'd spent time in the military. Snow dotted dark hair that had been cut in a sleek, sexy way that sharpened the angles of his handsome face.

A thrill ran through her. Mannington didn't have any men that gorgeous, that male, and he was heading toward the diner.

She raced behind the counter as his long strides ate up the sidewalk between his SUV and the door. It opened. He stepped inside, turning to close it behind him before he faced her.

His gaze cruised from her candy-cane-print blouse, red apron, short green skirt and red tights to her black patent leather buckle shoes.

Damn it! The first fabulous-looking man to come to Mannington in decades and she was wearing an elf suit.

Oh, well. That was life in a small town. Waitresses

dressed like elves. The cook sat outside on the back steps smoking. And her mom, the second waitress for the breakfast shift that morning, hadn't thought twice about calling to say she wouldn't be in until after ten. This was one of those mornings she needed to stay with Leni's dad, making sure he was okay because his head injury from a work accident was now causing small seizures.

Gorgeous Guy peered at the name tag on her blouse. "Leni?"

It wasn't unusual for an out-of-town customer to read her name tag and call her Leni to be friendly, but something about the way he'd said it hit her funny. As if he were disappointed.

"Yes." She smiled. "That's my name."

He ambled over to the counter. "You're the only waitress here?"

She grabbed a nearby cloth and ran it along the worn white countertop. "Yes. The other waitress is coming in later."

"How much later?"

That was a stupid question. Why would he care what time her mom came in? "She'll be here any minute now." She laughed. "But really, it's fine. I can take your order."

"Okay." He sat on one of the round red stools at the counter. "I'll have a cup of coffee."

"Sure." She turned to the pot sitting on a two-burner warmer behind her. "And you should know that it might be after ten, but the cook makes breakfast all day."

"Sorry. I had breakfast."

Drat. That was her only angle to keep him here. Now he'd drink his cup of coffee and race off—

She frowned. Unless he planned to wait for her mom?

Fears about insurance adjusters and private investigators sent by At Home Construction to spy on her dad raced through her. After two years, the company was arguing his workers' comp and questioning medical bills because they believed he could perform light-duty tasks and come back on the job.

But if this guy wanted to catch her dad working around the house to prove he was no longer disabled, he wouldn't come looking for her mother.

Would he?

No. He'd spy on her dad.

Feeling guilty for thinking the handsome stranger was a private detective, she swiped the cloth down the counter again. "Maybe you'd like a cinnamon roll?"

He laughed. "No. Thank you."

His words were kind, but precise. Leni smiled. He didn't need food and sometimes customers didn't want to talk. She would leave to him to his coffee.

She turned to walk away, but he said, "Nice town you have here."

She faced him again. "Mannington's okay."

His dark brows rose. "Only okay?"

Maybe he did want to talk? And maybe a few minutes of personal time with him would stop her from being suspicious? His brown eyes lit with a hint of amusement and this close he was so gorgeous it was fun just looking at him.

No harm in enjoying that.

"No. Mannington's a great place, but I'll be moving soon. I just finished my degree and I'm probably going to have to relocate to Topeka to get a job." She shrugged. "That's the way it is sometimes. If you want to work, you go to the big city."

"I'm from New York. My family owns a money management firm. I always knew where I'd be employed. Went through a bit of a rebellious phase, but I think everybody does, and here I am."

In Mannington, Kansas?

A guy who owned a New York City money management firm was in Mannington, Kansas, where no one had any money?

Her suspicions rose again. But at least they were talking. Maybe with a little good old-fashioned waitress chit-chat she could get him to tell her why he was here?

Especially if he was looking for her mom.

Nick Kourakis couldn't stop staring at the woman behind the counter. He'd been sent by the estate of Mark Hinton to find Elenore Long, probably the waitress who hadn't yet arrived, and instead he'd run into the most naturally beautiful woman he'd ever seen.

She had an exquisite face, a perfect figure that her goofy elf suit couldn't hide and big green eyes that shone with humor—

Until he'd asked when the other waitress would be coming in. Then she'd gotten quiet. But now that they were talking about her getting a job, things had perked up again. It didn't matter what he told her or what she told him. They'd never see each other again. That was the beauty of a conversation with a stranger. It was pointless. Exactly the diversion he needed while he waited for Elenore Long.

"So, you think you'll be moving to Topeka?"

She shrugged. "Probably."

He gestured at the candy-cane blouse. "Gonna take the elf suit?"

She laughed. "I doubt they let social workers wear them."

He loved her laugh. He loved her flowing hair. He loved that a little small talk had brought back her smile. "That's a tough job."

"I know."

"But it should be fairly easy to find work."

Her smile grew into a grin. "I know that, too."

"Well, there's just no fooling you, is there, Leni?"

She smiled again. Her full lips lifting and her green eyes sparkling.

He swore to God his heart turned over in his chest. He'd been single for so long that he couldn't remember the last time he'd had this kind of reaction to a woman. Not just an instant connection, but a welcome connection, as if the small talk he thought so pointless was a door to something—

Looking at her beautiful face, big eyes, high cheekbones, perfect nose, and lips just made for kissing, he almost suggested she search for work in New York, but that would be as pointless as a conversation about the weather. Why would he ask a beautiful woman to make such a drastic move for him, when he knew nothing would come of it?

The diner door opened and he turned. A woman in an elf suit just like Leni's walked in.

The other waitress. Most likely Elenore Long.

His eyes narrowed as he studied her. She was fifty, at least. Her chestnut hair curled around a square face and her eyes were blue. His heiress was the first of three children fathered by Mark Hinton, who'd died two weeks ago at the age of sixty. This woman was too old to be his child, even his firstborn.

He rose from his stool. "*You're* the other waitress?"

The woman began unbuttoning her coat. "Yeah."

"I think he's been waiting for you, Mom."

Nick swung to face Leni again. "Mom?"

"That's my mom. Denise Long, Mr. Owner-of-a-Money-Management-Firm. If you think we got a settlement to invest after my dad's injury, you're wrong. We can barely get the insurance company to pay his medical bills."

He fell to the round red stool again. "I'm not after your dad's money." He took a quick breath and caught Leni's gaze. "Your last name is Long?"

"Yeah."

Not taking any chances, he said, "And Leni is a nickname for something?"

He waited for confirmation but deep down he already knew the answer.

"Elenore."

He ran his fingers along his brow. "Elenore Long." He shook his head. If he hadn't been so blinded by her bedroom eyes, glorious mane of hair and sexy little body, he probably would have figured that out. "You're Elenore Long?"

She nodded. "Yes."

"Is there someplace private you and I can talk?"

She pressed her hand to her chest. "*I'm* the person you're here to see?"

"Yes."

"Why? I could barely get student loans. I don't have anything to hand over to a money management firm."

"Seriously. We have to talk someplace private." He caught her gaze. "Now."

Leni had never seen anybody's mood shift so quickly. He went from cute and flirty to serious in under a second. But that was fine since she was totally confused by him. First, he wanted to talk to her mom. Now he wanted to talk to her?

"The only people in the diner are you, me and my mom. George, the cook, is outside smoking." She glanced around. "We can just go to one of the booths in the back."

"Okay." He pointed to the last booth in the farthest corner. "We'll sit there."

He walked behind her until they reached the table. Then he slid onto the bench across from her.

"My name is Nick Kourakis. I work for a money management firm in New York City."

"So, you said. And I told you my family doesn't have any money to invest."

"I know."

His eyes darkened as he studied her. With all his attention centered on her face, she had to hold back a shudder. She had never seen a man this good-looking. But as she thought that, she noticed that his gray overcoat was stunningly made, and his white shirt and tie looked expensive. As big as he was, he wore both effortlessly, as if he was accustomed to luxury. Maybe even made for it.

She suddenly realized he wasn't gorgeous so much as he was a combination of the whole package. Expensive clothes. Sparkling clean. Handsome.

And wealthy.

Probably so rich, she couldn't even fathom the amount of money he had.

"I'm not selling anything. I'm not even here on behalf of the money management firm. I was sent here to retrieve you."

"Retrieve me?" His sultry brown eyes held her captive, sending warmth swimming through her blood, confusing her, almost hypnotizing her.

"Because I have some exciting news for you."

"Oh, yeah?" She fought the strange sensations assaulting her with sarcasm. "And what would that be?"

"First, what I have to tell you *has to* remain confidential."

Some of her equilibrium returned. "Okay."

He leaned back on the bench. "Have you ever heard of Mark Hinton?"

More of her confidence came back. Enough to put starch in her spine. "No."

"He's a billionaire…or was. We have reason to believe you are one of the people mentioned in his will."

"Oh…" Her composure took a tumble. Imagining herself getting as much as ten thousand dollars and paying off some of the bills that had accumulated since her dad's injury, she told her wishful-thinking brain to stop before she got her hopes up. "That's good. Right?"

"It could potentially be wonderful."

"Dude, wonderful to me is enough money to pay my dad's medical bills."

"It's more than that."

New thoughts scrambled around in her brain. Like buying her dad the service dog he needed because of his seizures, and not worrying about the company forcing him back to work.

But as quickly as her good thoughts set up shop, some bad thoughts came tumbling in. Adopted at eight, after a year in foster care when her biological mom gave her up, she'd always believed she was not a lucky person. The way she'd struggled for eight years just to afford her basic bachelor's degree backed that up. "What's the catch?"

"Before I say another word, I need your promise that you won't talk about this with anyone until I tell you that you can."

A laugh bubbled out. "You want me to take a vow of silence?"

"You are the first of three potential heirs to Mark Hinton's estate. A *huge* estate. You can tell your parents, but that's it. And they have to promise to keep this news to themselves. Frankly, it's a matter of *your* personal safety."

It all seemed to so preposterous that it couldn't sink in. As good as it would be to be rich, she was much too practical to believe in magic or miracles. It had to be a joke or a mistake.

When she said nothing, he sighed. "Do you have your phone?"

She pulled it out of her apron pocket.

"Search *Mark Hinton*."

She did as he said, though she mumbled, "Anybody can put up a fake website."

But her phone produced eight thousand results for Mark Hinton. Her gaze leaped to Nick's. "What is this?"

"Information on his life." He paused for a second before he added, "I was sent here by the law firm handling your dad's estate. The attorney in charge is stuck in court today. He's a friend of mine, and my family's firm manages your father's fortune, so I was picked to come in his place."

She barely heard anything after he said "your dad's estate." Her breath stumbled. "My *dad's*?"

She struggled to take it all in. Her biological mom hadn't told her anything about her father. She would always say he wasn't important, and they didn't need him. At seven, she'd known that wasn't true when her mom couldn't afford to keep her anymore.

"According to the estate lawyer, the paper trail says Mark Hinton is your father," Nick said. "But they'll be getting DNA."

She leaned back in disappointment and disbelief, her voice dull when she said, "My biological father was rich."

"One of the first multibillionaires." Nick shifted. "If you let this get out before the estate has a chance to protect you, you will be mobbed by people who want money. You'll be a target for scam artists and kidnappers. I came here not merely to tell you, but to take you to New York so the lawyer can make the process of vetting you easier for *you*."

Something Leni couldn't define or describe fluttered through her, tightening her chest, making her head spin. She looked at the eight *thousand* results to her search and saw the words *billionaire*, *reclusive*, *oil and gas prodigy* and *missing heirs*.

Her heart stopped then burst to life again with such a frantic beat she thought she'd faint. This would be more than enough money to care for her dad.

"You think this guy is my father and I'm one of these heirs?"

"The estate lawyer is fairly certain you're one of the heirs. He says the paper trail is solid. But they'll do a DNA test to confirm it."

Her voice came out as a squeak as she said, "Okay."

"For confidentiality purposes and for your safety, you have to go to New York now." He paused long enough to catch her gaze. "Will you come with me?"

Ten minutes ago, that offer probably would have scrambled her pulse. Now? The happy, flirty guy was gone. A businessman had replaced him.

She almost missed the flirty guy. But her brain had been captured by the idea that she might be wealthy enough that her parents would no longer have to worry about money.

Still, she wasn't going to New York with a man she didn't know, based solely on his word. "Give me a day?"

"The plan was to leave as soon as we told you."

She shook her head. "I want a day. Twenty-four hours to explain all this to my parents and to check you out."

"I can provide you with references—"

"No thanks. I'll find what I need on my own." She'd check every dark and moldy corner of the internet if she had to, to make sure he was for real.

There was no way she'd leave for New York with a stranger. And no way she'd get her parents' hopes up for nothing.

CHAPTER TWO

NICK KOURAKIS LEFT the diner, a mix of disappointment and confusion slowing his steps. He should have been focused on the fact that this unexpected trip was a chance to convince Leni Long to keep her dad's money with his money management firm. But Danny Manelli, attorney for the estate, didn't want him making a pitch to her. A clause in the will could give the estate trouble, and Nick could make it worse by talking about money before Danny could properly explain the clause to Leni.

Now that he had given her the basics that would get her to New York to start the process of vetting her, Nick wasn't supposed to talk about anything except the weather and football. Two things Danny was sure wouldn't accidentally tip them into talking about the estate.

That was good, sound logic. And normally Nick would be totally onboard with it. Instead, he was gobsmacked. Leni Long was the first woman he'd been overwhelmingly attracted to in a decade. But it was more than that. Something about her clicked with him. And that was so odd he couldn't shake the feeling.

Telling himself that was absurd, he walked down the sidewalk and jumped into the passenger seat of the SUV.

Behind the steering wheel, Jace MacDonald, owner of Around the World Security, said, "Where's the girl?"

"She wants a day to investigate us."

Jace shook his head, then shifted to face Nick, the gun beneath his black leather jacket visible when he turned. "It's going to be difficult to keep an eye on her here. Even for twenty-four hours." He motioned outside. "Not only are the houses and businesses spaced in such a way that an extra person sticks out like a sore thumb, but so do cars. You should have seen the people sniffing around the SUV while you were in the diner. A strange vehicle parked on a street where everybody knows everybody else's car? That's like a neon sign."

"I don't care. You heard what Danny said. That woman is worth more money than the gross national products of several small countries combined. If the wrong people find out, she'll be a target."

"Yeah, of banks that want to compete for her business." Jace snickered. "You do realize Danny's keeping you from an excellent opportunity to convince her to keep her share of the estate with you?"

Nick peeked at him. "You're not allowed to pitch your company either."

Jace raised his hands in disgust. "Got the same sermon you did."

"Then you know the problem with the will. After a few charitable bequests, Mark divides the remainder of his estate between his first child and any subsequent heirs. A good lawyer could argue that that gives Mark's first child half, with the other half split between the other two kids. Danny wants to be the one to explain it to Elenore."

Jace sniffed. "How the hell can pitching our companies' services affect that stupid clause?"

"He just wants to be sure we don't accidentally say something we shouldn't."

"That's ridiculous." Jace growled.

Nick totally understood his frustration, but he didn't want to do anything that could make trouble for Danny. "Look, you knew Mark. He was a good guy. Nine chances out of ten, he wanted that estate distributed equally among his heirs. I'm sure Danny has a plan to get all three of

Mark's kids on board with that. That's why he doesn't want us talking to her. Muddying the waters."

"Right." Jace pulled the gear shift out of Park and headed toward the interstate. "There isn't a hotel or even a bed and breakfast in this town. I'll drive you up the highway until we find one, then I have to get back here to figure out a way to hide myself and this boat of an SUV we rented so I can watch her tonight."

Nick winced. "Sorry. I couldn't talk her into leaving today."

"Not to worry. I'll deal with it. How are you going to handle the fact that she wanted time to check *you* out?" He laughed. "What's she going to find when she does a search on you?"

Nick faced the window. "Nothing."

"You're sure? The guy they call the New Wolf of Wall Street doesn't have a skeleton?"

Nick said, "No skeleton," but he lied. He'd talked his only brother into going out on a night when the roads were icy. A former Navy SEAL, he counted on himself to be one of the best drivers in unusual situations. But a combination of icy roads and other cars had bested him that night, and his only sibling had been killed.

But that was five years ago, and he didn't think the story even popped up in internet searches anymore.

"Come on. Nobody meets a guy like Hinton without a story."

"I did."

That part was true. He'd met Mark Hinton in Dubai. They'd gambled. They'd skydived. They'd talked money. Especially investment strategy. In Nick's world, there was nothing special about any of that. After Mark decided to trust Kourakis Money Management with most of his fortune, they'd had meetings on his yachts or while fishing in the Florida Keys. They drank tequila, talked about his financial goals and even about the kids who were now Mark's heirs. Though never while Mark was sober. Powerful men didn't admit weakness or failures without a nudge. Mark's nudge was alcohol. With enough tequila, Mark would talk about his kids—without mentioning their names—and Nick would nurse his regret and sorrow over his brother's death. *That* was why Mark was comfortable with Nick. Even with a thirty-year age difference, they understood each other. Understood mistakes. Understood regret.

Even now, it trickled from his subconscious to the front of his brain. He'd been too confident, cocky even. His brother hadn't wanted to go out that night. His parents hadn't wanted them to go. But he'd been so sure—

He was always so sure.

After Joe's death, he'd had to stop jet-setting, return to New York and take over the family business.

But he was still the same guy deep down inside. Instead of taking risks on the slopes or in the sky, he played with money.

And no one beat him.

Ever.

He'd gotten so good at what he did that he liked it. Until he recalled the reason why he was the "New Wolf." Even now, the grief of losing his brother sent guilt oozing through him.

He didn't understand what had happened to him in that diner that he'd forgotten Joe, forgotten his guilt and laughed with someone he barely knew. But when they returned to New York, he'd be focused again, diligent. If he was going to lose even part of the Hinton money when the estate was settled and one or two of the heirs decided to hire new money management, he'd have to find big investors to replace it.

He would not let his parents down twice.

Leni's mom only worked until two o'clock, but Leni's shift didn't end until three. Having evaded her questions about

Nick Kourakis, taking Nick's warnings seriously about the complications of people finding out she might be an heiress, Leni raced home and found her parents in the kitchen.

"Hey."

Sitting at the center island, her dad looked up from his newspaper.

Her mom glanced over from the stove. "Hey. Finally going to tell us what the guy in the overcoat wanted?"

Leni forced a smile. Denise and Jake Long had adopted her when she was in the gangly stage for a little girl. No longer an adorable infant or cute toddler, with a bit of a history of being difficult at school, most potential parents overlooked her. The Longs had given her a home, made her their daughter. Now she didn't merely know she had a biological mom out there somewhere who had given her up; she might have had a rich dad who hadn't wanted her at all.

Once again, she thanked God for her adoptive parents.

She took a seat beside her dad. "First, what I'm about to say is a secret. So, you can't tell anybody."

Her mom said, "Okay," as her dad nodded.

"The guy in the overcoat was Nick Kourakis. He owns a management firm in New York, and he told me that I might have inherited some money."

Her dad's weathered face brightened. A lifelong construction worker, he had wrinkles around his eyes that appeared when he smiled. "Well, that's great!"

Her mother gasped and walked over from the stove to hug Leni. "I'm so happy for you."

"Yeah, well, it's not assured. I have to go to New York. There will also be a DNA test to confirm my identity. Honestly, I won't quite believe all this is true until DNA says I'm an heir. So, our not mentioning this to anybody protects me from embarrassing myself if it doesn't pan out."

Part of her almost wished it wouldn't. If her biological father had been a struggling factory worker, she could have understood him not being able to take responsibility for her, but a guy who was rich and not paying child support, forcing her mom to give her up when she got sick? When it was a decision between the medicine she needed and feeding her child?

It was demeaning, insulting, infuriating.

She'd have to deal with that if Mark Hinton really was her biological father. Those feelings would all go away if he wasn't.

Her dad leaned back in his chair. "It's always good not to get your hopes up, Kitten. But maybe this family's due for some good luck?"

And that was the catch. Part of her would like to tell Nick Kourakis to take her biological dad's money and shove it. She was educated now. She had a career path. She would be fine.

But her parents wouldn't.

They'd never ask her for a dime, but she wouldn't make them ask. If she'd inherited enough money to care for her dad, she wanted it.

"Okay." She slid off her chair. "I'm going upstairs to do some investigating into everything. I'm not getting on a plane with a guy I don't know."

Her dad smiled. "That's smart, my girl."

The simple comment hit her right in the heart. She was his girl. *His* girl. Not the child of some sperm donor who'd never even checked to see if she was okay.

That was not a father.

Almost twenty-four hours from when Leni had met him, Nick Kourakis and a man she didn't recognize pulled into the driveway of the Long residence in the big, black SUV. Nick had looked up her parents' home phone number and called her the night before to say they'd be leaving at ten o'clock. He'd given her time to research him and his firm, to talk to her parents and to pack for a couple weeks in

Manhattan, but that was it. They needed to get her safely to New York.

Her breath frosty in the cold, last-day-of-November air, she hugged and kissed her short, curly-haired mom and balding dad, saying goodbye at the front door of their house, her conflicted feelings about Mark Hinton dogging her.

Nick handed Danny Manelli's business card to her parents, telling them that he was the lawyer in charge of the estate and if they had any questions, they could call him. Then he introduced her to Jace MacDonald, the guy in the black leather jacket who directed her to the back seat of the SUV. Nick got in beside her.

She frowned at the empty passenger's seat in the front.

"Jace owns Around the World Security. He'll be your bodyguard while you're in New York."

She gaped at Nick. "Bodyguard?"

Jace caught her gaze in the rearview mirror. "Trust me. If you're worth billions, you'll need one."

She huffed out a breath. "Billions?"

Nick laughed. "Yes. Mark Hinton had billions. With an *s*. Plural. As in many billions."

"I know. I researched him last night, too. It's just so hard to believe."

She shook her head and looked out the window. The guy had billions and he had left her mom so broke she'd had to put Leni into foster care.

The insult of it stiffened her spine.

Jace made a few turns and they headed north. Twenty minutes later, he pulled the SUV onto a private airstrip. When they drove up to a sleek red and silver jet, she gasped. "Holy cow."

Nick laughed. "That plane is nothing. I'm just a simple billionaire."

She knew that, too. She'd spent forty minutes the night before reading about how successful the investment arm of his family's money management firm was. What she hadn't expected was that they'd be riding in *his* plane. Not when her biological father was supposed to have so much money.

Something about that just seemed off.

She faced Nick again. "This plane is yours?"

"Yes."

He glanced over, catching her gaze, and her breath shivered.

Damn it. Now was not the time to be feeling that stupid attraction she had to him. Not only did he seem to be in charge of her, but she was too confused about her potential biological dad to add an attraction into the mix. Plus, there was something wrong with Nick using his own plane to get her. This was not the man to be attracted to.

Jace exited the SUV and came around to her door to open it. She climbed out at the same time Nick did.

Nick led her to the small stack of stairs and into the jet. She had to hold back a gasp when she stepped inside. Three small groupings of white leather seats were arranged around the large cabin. The little windows had elegant gray shades. A silver and black bar sat discreetly in a back corner. A rich red carpet covered the floor.

She took a slow, measured breath. She could not be a country bumpkin about this. She had to stay sharp.

Pretending a calm she didn't feel, she stopped by the first group of seats and slid out of her worn leather jacket.

Behind her, Nick said, "The flight's about three hours. Then, because we use an airstrip outside the city, we'll have about an hour-and-a-half limo ride."

"Limo ride?" She swallowed, picturing her blue-collar self, in her ancient leather jacket and worn jeans, getting into a limo.

He took her coat and handed it to the flight attendant who scurried to the back of the jet with it.

"Don't worry. You'll acclimate. After a day or two in

New York, you'll realize a limo's the easiest way to get around the city. Just like this jet is the most comfortable way to get from place to place."

He motioned to the rear of the cabin. "The first room you walk into back there is a kitchen. If you want a snack you just ask Marie, but she'll be serving lunch at noon. So, a snack might not be a good idea. Beyond that is an office-slash-den, complete with a pullout bed. Jace will probably go back there once we take off." He winced. "He stayed up most of the night keeping an eye on your house. He'll need the nap."

"He stayed up all night?"

"That's his job, remember?"

She did. She simply hadn't connected him being a bodyguard to him sitting in his SUV all night watching her house.

"You'll get used to it. For now, settle in. Get accustomed to the convenience that's your new lifestyle."

She couldn't fathom riding in a limo let alone owning a jet. "If I'm an heir."

"The lawyer for the estate all but said your DNA test is only a formality." He pointed to the rear of the plane. "I have some work to do, so I'll be back there if there's anything you need."

He turned to leave but she said, "Why are we in your jet instead of one of my dad's?"

Nick faced her again. "What?"

"Why are we using your jet instead of one of Mark Hinton's?"

"We're not using one of Mark's jets because we're not using anything belonging to Hinton Holdings."

"Why?"

He sighed. "We don't want to alert anyone that we might have found an heir before we confirm you."

"Because?"

This time he pulled in a long breath, obviously losing patience with her questions. "This estate is worth so much money that everyone in the world is curious about who you are. Danny devised a plan to find the heirs and keep you safe. Not using estate property is part of it. If we start using jets or houses and cars, people will know something is up and begin snooping. The longer we can keep the press and curiosity seekers at bay, the better."

She held the gaze of his dark eyes for a second, then she shook her head. She didn't think he was lying. But she did know he hadn't told her everything. Until her DNA results were back, she probably didn't have the right to push him. But she would watch him, pay attention to every word he said, because there was definitely something going on with him.

Nick breathed a sigh of relief as he headed to the seat in the back of the plane. He didn't mind her questions. They were generic enough that he could answer them. It was her nearness that threw him for a loop. He was smarter than this, more in control. His whole body shouldn't buzz just because they were standing close.

He reached the plush leather seat, but before he sat, he realized he'd forgotten his briefcase. He returned to the front and opened the overhead bin above the seat Leni had chosen.

She glanced up at him, her thick lashes blinking over her sultry green eyes, her long brown hair sort of floating around her.

"Forgot my briefcase," he explained, trying not to stumble over his words. "I kept it on the plane, thinking we'd be leaving yesterday."

She smiled in acknowledgment and his heart went from pitter-patter to a drum solo in one breath.

Stifling a groan, he headed to the rear of the cabin again, eager to return to New York to lose these crazy feelings he had around her. Part of it had to be surprise over how pretty she was. Mark Hinton wasn't even a five on a scale of one to ten, but apparently Leni's mother had been a twelve.

The other part was just plain attraction. Serious lust. Something biological that sprang up before he could control it.

So, it was wrong.

Had to be.

He didn't get out-of-control feelings and he sure as hell never let emotions rule him.

A movement in the front caught his attention and he peeked up to see Leni get out of her seat to put her purse in the overhead bin. Her head fell back as she reached up, sending all that thick, shiny hair bouncing.

This time he allowed himself an internal groan.

This was crazy.

For the first time since Danny had laid down the rules for Nick's trip to retrieve Leni, he was glad he'd been ordered to keep his distance from her. Because whatever he was feeling, he didn't want it. He had priorities, a company to run, parents to keep happy. He couldn't afford the weakness of a hellishly strong attraction.

He put his head down and went to work and didn't look up until hours later when the jet began to descend. Choosing not to go up to the overhead bin again, he secured his briefcase under his seat, fastened his seat belt and waited for the jet to slide onto the ground, relieved that he only had a little over an hour more in her company. He would leave her with Danny and never look back.

CHAPTER THREE

GIVEN THE TIME difference between Kansas and New York, it was almost three o'clock when they landed in New York. Leni had eaten a fabulous lunch, served by Marie, prepared by a chef hiding somewhere in the back. Leni hadn't seen her luggage since climbing into the SUV in Mannington, but she suspected someone had handled it. Nick had said to settle in and get comfortable with luxury…but, come on. A chef who had flown from New York to Mannington and from Mannington back to New York, just to make lunch? On a jet? For her?

It boggled the mind.

They boarded a limo and headed for the city, Leni feeling totally out of place in her worn jacket and jeans. Though Christmas decorations in shop windows, on streetlights and clinging to parking meters gave the area a familiar feel, she had never seen so many buildings in such a small place.

But she didn't mention it. She didn't want to be attracted to Nick or to mistrust him. But, unfortunately, she felt both things, and mistrust trumped attraction. She wouldn't say anything around him that she didn't have to.

When they pulled up to a building so tall that she couldn't see the top of it, Nick said, "Our first appointment… Your lawyer."

"My lawyer?"

"The lawyer for the estate."

She gasped. "I'm in jeans! You should have told me I'd

be meeting him this afternoon. I thought I was only flying here today!"

"You're fine. You're a blue-collar woman who's just been told she might be a billionaire. You don't have to put on airs."

"Lucky thing, since I hadn't given a thought to trying that."

The driver opened the back door. Nick climbed out first and extended his hand to help her exit the limo.

Light snow fell around him, and he pulled her out into it. The shiny white flakes collecting on his dark hair reminded her of seeing him getting out of the SUV and walking to the diner, huddled against the falling snow. All the feelings from the day before came tumbling back. Her attraction. Their small talk. Laughing together.

Close enough to kiss him, she fought the magnetic pull that tried to lure her in, but it was her mistrust that fluttered away. Before she'd known who he was, she'd told Nick about needing to move to Topeka and he'd told her that his family owned a money management firm and he'd had a rebellious streak.

They'd formed a connection and she felt it again, as clearly as if they were still in the diner.

She stepped back, trying to get rid of it and the fears that rushed at her when she realized where she was and why. It didn't work. All her worries tumbled out, even as the sense of connection to Nick held on.

"All I can think about is being embarrassed or scared when it's announced that I'm an heir. Doing something stupid, making a fool of myself—"

He stopped her by putting his hands on her shoulders and looking her in the eye. "You don't have anything to be embarrassed about. And as for being scared, from the couple of hours I've known you, I can tell you're strong. You can do this."

His dark eyes had sharpened with a strength that sent

a shot of attraction from her chest to her toes. This was the Nick she'd made a connection with. The nice guy. The guy she'd liked.

She had to swallow before she could say, "Okay."

He took her elbow and directed her toward the building. She swore heat from his touch seeped through her worn leather jacket and to her skin. She didn't know what it was about him that seemed to draw her in, but whatever it was, it was powerful.

A tiny part of her whispered that her feelings were right. That she could trust him. That she *should* trust him.

She really wanted to believe that, especially walking up to a building with so many floors jutting up to the sky she couldn't count them, fancy pillars carved into the exterior walls and a sophisticated medallion resting over the entry like a royal crest.

When they reached the revolving door, her knees wobbled and she was grateful for Nick's hand at her elbow. He released her when they stepped into a lobby with marble floors and red and white poinsettias scattered about. No plastic wreaths. No gaudy ornaments. No blinking lights. Just tasteful flowers. And twenty or thirty people dressed as sophisticatedly as Nick.

Her thoughts scrambled again. He only touched her when she needed help, barely spoke, had ignored her on the plane. He might be the guy from the diner, but he wasn't always nice. He had a job to do—get her to New York—and he was doing it.

She had to stop imagining good things about him.

They walked past a bank of elevators to another row hidden around a corner. These elevators had keypads and Nick had to punch in a series of numbers on the third one for the doors to open.

A man in a power suit came out of the second elevator, followed by a woman in a pencil skirt and silky blouse, visible because her fancy wool coat was unbuttoned. Like people on a mission, they bounded around the corner and off to parts unknown.

She sucked in a long breath, straightened her old jacket and smoothed her hand along the high collar of her turtleneck, hoping it looked newer than it was. Because, man, she was seriously underdressed.

When they stepped out of the elevator into an office, she didn't just think it. She knew it. A wall of glass behind the desk displayed a view of Manhattan that made her breath stutter. The buildings looked close enough to touch. And with so much glass surrounding the room she felt like she was walking on air.

A short, slender woman opened the door on the far left and peeked inside. "Hey, Nick. Could you come into my office for a second?"

Nick glanced at Leni and she forced a smile. "I'm fine. Maybe I'll go over to the window and try to see inside the office across the street."

Nick stifled a laugh, but just barely. Leni had to be the most naturally funny, most open person he'd ever met. He couldn't help comforting her when she'd admitted how afraid she was, but he'd kept his solace short and simple. Because in another ten minutes, he'd be back on that elevator, heading for his own office. His favor for his friend completed. His sanity restored.

He followed Danny's assistant, Mary Catherine, into her office. She pointed at the phone on her desk. "I have Mr. Manelli on the line."

Confusion stopped him where he was. "On the line? He was supposed to be here waiting for us."

She skirted her desk and headed for the hallway. "Why don't you let him explain?"

When she was gone, Nick picked up the receiver of the desk phone and said, "Where the hell are you?"

"Stuck in court. Remember the trial I told you I would be getting a continuance on? The reason I needed you to be the one to retrieve Elenore Long instead of me? Well, the judge didn't go for the continuance. I'm stuck here."

"Stuck there?"

"The judge thinks there's no reason to postpone a trial that won't last more than a few days. It's corporate stuff. Everybody's prepared to the max. It will take a day or two to get through it."

"Why are you telling me this?"

"Because we can't let Elenore Long sit alone in a hotel room this afternoon, tonight and all day tomorrow."

"Danny, I agreed to do this favor for you mostly because Mark was my friend and I knew how he felt about his kids' safety. But that was it."

"That was all I needed when I called you on Saturday, but through no fault of mine, things changed. That's life. You remember life? If something can go wrong, it usually does."

Understanding that a little better than Danny knew, Nick blew his breath out on a frustrated sigh. "What about Jace? He's the bodyguard. He should be with her. Not me."

"Jace had an emergency come up. He and most of his men are on their way to El Salvador."

He gaped at the phone. "El Salvador!"

"Yep. So, we're down to you. You know all the information about the identity of the heirs and potential heirs has to be kept as quiet as possible. The fewer people who know, the less chance someone will accidentally slip a name to their wife or girlfriend. Besides, you're the most closed-mouthed person I know."

"I'm not a bodyguard!"

"You don't need to be. As long as no one knows who she is, she's just another New York tourist."

"And what the hell do I do with her for the next day… or two?"

Danny's voice lifted with hope. "Anything you want. New York's a big city. As long as you stay away from talking about the estate, you could very easily entertain her for a week."

"A week!"

"Tops. I swear."

Nick squeezed his eyes shut. "You owe me."

"Big time," Danny agreed.

As his friend gave him the name of the hotel he'd booked for Leni, Nick looked through the glass separating Mary Catherine's office and Danny's. Leni stood by the wall of windows staring at the Manhattan skyline, obviously a fish out of water.

And she'd already admitted to being afraid.

He passed his hand down his face. The part of him that wanted to help her was the part he wanted to squelch, destroy, kick so far out of town he wouldn't even think about being attracted to her anymore. He'd planned on doing the eviction tonight with a bottle of scotch and four hours of work. Danny and Jace weren't the only ones with commitments.

Danny sighed. "Look, get her settled in the hotel and take her for a nice dinner."

Nick blew his breath out in exasperation. "I'm serious about this costing you one big, fat favor."

Danny laughed. "Why? Does she look like Mark?"

"No, I'm guessing she got the cocktail waitress's genes."

Danny guffawed. "That good, huh?"

Nick gazed longingly at Leni again. "Better."

"Okay. I've got to go. The judge is back from recess. And I swear I will end this trial as quickly as possible."

As Danny hung up, Nick took a long, slow breath. He didn't want to spend any more time with a woman he was already attracted to. Work was his life now. Besides, she was way too nice for him. Innocent. Sweet. He wasn't any of those. Still, he was helping Danny because Mark had been his friend. He resisted women all the time. This one would be no different.

He walked into Danny's office and straight to the private elevator. "Let's go."

Leni scrambled after him. "Where?"

"The lawyer is stuck in a trial. I'm taking you to your hotel and then to dinner."

They stepped into the elevator. "I can't go to dinner with you."

He peered at her. "You're ditching me?"

"No. I'm just not going out with someone dressed like you," she said, pointing at his black suit and charcoal-gray overcoat. "When I look like this." She motioned down the front of her jacket.

"We can buy you a dress before we go to the hotel. In fact, we can get you anything you want. There's a slush fund for vetting potential heirs. It's there to get you anything you need while you're in the city."

She gaped at him. "I'm not letting you buy me clothes." Though she almost wished she could. Her old jeans and jacket firmly announced her as someone not from Manhattan. Which made her stick out in the crowd milling about in the building lobby. The people who'd seen her walking out of the private elevator for a lawyer's office probably thought she was a petty thief.

"I can't pay you back if I'm not an heir."

"I told you, there's a slush fund. You're in New York at the estate's request. While you're here it's our responsibility to get you anything and everything you need. No paybacks. It's part of the process. We'll be putting the exact same amount of money into slush accounts for all potential heirs."

"You might have to pay for the hotel and the limo, but you're not buying me clothes."

A muscle in his jaw jumped as he motioned to the revolving door. "Fine."

She could see she'd aggravated him, but she didn't care.

She walked through the door, out into the snow and into the limo again. They took a short ride and exited the limo onto the busiest street Leni had ever seen. The jumbotron, lights and videos were the familiar backdrop of an early morning news show.

She reverently whispered. "Times Square."

Nick pointed to the right. "Your hotel is this way."

The only hotel she saw to the right was way down the street. She glanced back at the limo. "We're walking?"

"Traffic was backed up at the hotel entry. It's not far."

"Oh. Okay."

"You want to get back into the limo and wait out the line?"

Not really. Cool air massaged her warm face. The noise of Times Square and the crowded street took her attention away from Mark Hinton and money and the handsome guy walking with her who seemed to have gone from annoyed to angry. No sense poking the bear.

"Yeah. Walking's good." Shoving her hands into her jacket pockets, she peered around again. "I like seeing everything."

He pointed across the street. "My office is in that building there."

Gray brick with black slate accents. Long, thin windows. A doorman.

"Wow." She fought the question that automatically rose as she shuffled along beside him, but it bubbled out anyway. "What's it like to work here?" She gestured around her. "In all of this noise and people?"

"Our windows are soundproof."

She laughed. "Seriously? You know what I mean. You saw where I live. There are about fifteen hundred people in our entire town, and I'll bet there are three thousand on this street with us now. You can't know everybody. How do you decide who to trust?"

He peeked at her. "Reputation."

She skipped twice to catch up with his long strides. "Reputation? If you don't know someone, how do you know their reputation?"

He shrugged. "I always know somebody who knows somebody who knows them. And, if they are high enough in a corporate structure, there will be things written about them."

"Written about them?"

"In professional journals, but I do search the internet sometimes to find out things about them."

"Did you research me?"

He gave her the side-eye. "That was Danny's job."

"This Danny—the lawyer—is pretty important?"

"His firm is handling the Hinton estate. He's the boss. Any mistakes are on him."

Things began to fall in to place for Leni. Nick never lied to her, but she was beginning to understand why getting a complete answer out of him was close to impossible. *She* was the problem.

"Like mistakes you make with me?"

He stopped walking and studied her for a few seconds before he said, "Yes."

That ill-timed thrill ran through her again, and she knew why he'd stopped walking, why he was still looking at her. Their initial conversation at the diner had been flirty and fun and she wasn't a thirteen-year-old girl wondering in the boy next door liked her. She knew the signs. But he'd had to squelch those feelings. Because of the estate? Because of not wanting to make mistakes?

"You aren't allowed to get too chummy with me, are you?"

"No."

"And the reason you keep acting all stuffy is because we sort of already did make friends in the diner?"

"Yes. And that's wrong." He shook his head. "You're funny and you have a warmth about you that's very appealing. But there are things in my life that prevent me from even considering a relationship, and you could potentially be inheriting tons of money which will completely change *your* life. You shouldn't want to get involved with me any more than I want to get involved with you. Which means we shouldn't even try to get to know each other."

She'd thought the same thing herself. Except her thinking had run along the lines of not being able to trust him. And hadn't she already figured out he had secrets? Though, it did intrigue her that he'd *admit* there were things in his life that prevented him from even considering a relationship. That had to mean there was more to his backing off than keeping his professional distance. Which was good to know. A woman who had been a little girl in foster care, wishing her next set of parents would love her enough to adopt her, didn't need to be wondering why he ran hot and cold with her or why he sometimes downright ignored her. Insecurities like that ran deep and popped up when she least expected, but his explanation tamed them.

She was glad she'd asked. Knowing would keep her from worrying every time he clammed up or ignored her. "Okay."

A laugh burst from him. "Okay?"

"Yeah. Okay. See how easy that was? You told me the whole story and now I understand all the weird things you've done since you realized who I was."

"I didn't do any weird things."

She raised her left eyebrow as she gave him an "Oh, really?" expression.

"Name one."

"Well, when we met, you talked a lot. Once you found out I was the person you were looking for, you barely said anything. In the diner, you were also kind of funny."

He laughed again. "*I* was funny?"

"Not hysterical but…" She shrugged. "You know. Silly?"

"My parents would not believe you if you told them that." He turned and started walking again.

She raced to catch up with him. "Which means I have to tell them. If only because they'll get a chuckle out of it."

"You'll probably never meet them."

She sighed. He was back to being careful again. She understood, but if they were stuck together for the rest of the day and he didn't talk, their time together would be insufferably boring.

"Are we really going out for dinner tonight?"

"Yes. One thing about New York City, there are a million wonderful restaurants I can take you to."

She glanced down at her worn jeans. She did have one dress packed. She'd planned on using it for the meeting with the lawyer, though. "Just don't get too fancy."

"Maybe we *should* go look for a dress?"

"I don't take charity."

"There's an entire slush fund at your disposal. That's not charity."

"You see things your way. I see them mine."

"Look, the bottom line is I don't want any attention being called to you. Neither does Danny. Dressing to fit in is a good idea." He pointed ahead of them. "There's a shop a few blocks down. It's where I get my mom's Christmas and birthday gifts. I'm going to have Danny set up an account for you. That way, after tonight, if you feel like you want a dress or shoes or something, you can get what you want or what you feel you need while you're here. No pressure."

"You want me to shop where you get your *mom's* clothes?" She laughed. "No thanks."

He sighed. "It's a nice place. It's got things for younger people, too."

"If you expect me to shop there, it better."

"It does."

She quelled the flutter in her stomach. She longed to

look like the woman wearing the pencil skirt and silky blouse…but she also didn't have any money. Didn't have anywhere to wear something like that when she got home. Buying pretty things would be a waste. A waste of the money of a man who had hurt her. Money she didn't want—except to help her dad. She was only here on the chance she was an heir and she could help her parents. They were the ones who'd plucked her out of the system and saved her. She didn't need fancy clothes. Especially if she wasn't an heir.

"But don't get your hopes up. I'm not going shopping."

"You never know."

"I know."

"No. You don't."

She shook her head. For a guy who wasn't supposed to talk to her, he never seemed to let her get the last word.

CHAPTER FOUR

NICK TURNED TOWARD the entry of a grand hotel. Leni glanced up. A white facade was the perfect backdrop for the huge green wreath that sat above the portico. Red ornaments scattered around it glittered in the late afternoon sun.

The muscles around her heart tweaked. She was missing everything happening at home. Christmas parties, carolers, making cookies with her mom. Nick had told her to pack for two weeks and she assumed that's the longest she'd be away. She might miss the baking and extra-special holiday tips from regular customers at the diner, along with the occasional gift, but she'd be home over a week before Christmas.

There was no point in getting homesick. Everything was under control.

She followed Nick as he walked into the lobby, marched to the reservations clerk, gave his name and got a key card. Within seconds, they were in the elevator.

He continued the silence through the ride to the tenth floor and down a quiet hall. When they stopped at a door, he opened it by scanning the key card. She stepped inside the room and gasped.

A huge window ran along the entire back wall, bringing the sights of Times Square into her room. Two red sofas sat parallel, in front of a marble fireplace with a bar off to the left. A dining table and upholstered chairs had been set up near the window.

"All this is for me?"

"Yes."

She looked around in awe. "This has got to be costing the estate a pretty penny."

"The estate has lots of pretty pennies, so don't worry about it." He glanced at his watch. "I'll be back at seven."

She nodded.

"If you need anything…and I mean *anything*, call the concierge."

"I do wish I had a book."

"I'm sure they can get you one."

With that he turned and walked out of the room, closing the door behind him.

She glanced around again. "No television." She spotted the big mirror above the fireplace, saw the remote on the mantel and laughed. "Thank goodness I watch enough house fixer-upper shows to know how they hide televisions these days."

She carefully lowered herself onto one of the two red sofas, running her hand along the smooth leather, enjoying the luxury.

Was this how she'd live if she really was rich?

Even as she thought that, the silence of her suite enveloped her. She'd hate to think that all wealthy people were lonely. But Nick was rich…a simple billionaire he'd said… and he barely spoke. Of course, she knew why he didn't want to talk to her, but he didn't even speak to his driver.

That was what had bothered her. He never even said hello to his driver, the pilot for their plane or any of the ground crew scrambling to get their luggage into the jet's belly. He walked around as if he were in his own little world.

Which was a shame. Good-looking guy like that should be the happiest man around. And with all his money, he should realize he was one of the luckiest.

She thought of her adoptive dad. How he'd worked and

scrimped and saved and barely made ends meet. Yet, he considered himself one of the luckiest people on the planet.

Nick Kourakis should be swinging-from-the-chandeliers happy and if she got the chance, maybe she would tell him that.

Nick arrived at Leni's suite at exactly seven. When she opened the door to him, he almost stepped back. His former elf wore a simple black dress with a red sweater. Her eyes had been painted with shadow and liner and mascara—but only enough to make her pretty, not overdone—and her lips were ruby red. Her long brown hair had been caught up in a twist in the back, giving her face a look of sophistication that nearly stole his breath. Black heels provided at least three inches of height and put her right at his chin. The perfect place for a woman to be.

He shook his head to clear it of that stupidity. She might be beautiful, but they'd never get to test out why coming to chin level was perfect. He would never kiss her.

That registered oddly, way deep down in his soul, in a place he hadn't acknowledged for so long the ping was a hollow, empty sound.

Calling himself foolish and exhausted, he ignored the weird feeling and said the one thing that might get her to tell him if she'd gone to the boutique after all. "You look nice."

"Nice?" She spun around once. "I look fabulous. This is the dress I'd bought for my college graduation ceremony last week. I'd brought it to wear to meet the lawyer, but I can wear it twice."

The hope that she'd shopped was replaced by another ping of acknowledgment in his soul. Her simple pleasure in the dress was fun. Almost cute enough to make him laugh.

He'd forgotten what it was like to really enjoy something ordinary. Actually, he'd forgotten what it was like to enjoy *anything*. He'd snuffed out that feeling, but one laugh from her and he remembered it, longed to feel it again.

Even though he knew he wouldn't.

He cleared his throat. "You made a good choice with the dress—and shoes."

She extended her foot and looked at her black pumps with love in her sparkling green eyes. "I know. They make me feel like I'm tall enough to talk to you without having to stretch my neck."

He'd thought they made her tall enough to kiss easily, naturally.

He really needed to get some sleep. The well-rested New Wolf of Wall Street didn't care about enjoying things, didn't compliment a woman he wasn't dating, didn't notice anybody's shoes.

But when Leni put on her worn leather jacket, he remembered her real world again. Remembered why this dress was so important to her. And told himself that no matter how tired he was, he could be nice to her.

Then she spoke. "You look pretty good yourself."

He glanced down at his black suit. "This is what I had on this morning." And the day before. It was a wonder he wasn't a wrinkled mess.

She winked and headed for the exit. "I know. You looked fabulous then, too."

His brain scrambled. Had she just flirted with him?

Realizing she was almost at the door, he had to hurry to open it before she did, confusion and fear skittering along his nerve endings. They'd talked about this. There was no point in flirting.

He opened his mouth to remind her they'd already decided they shouldn't get chummy, which in his book included flirting, but as she stepped into the hall, she casually said, "I'm starving."

His brain stopped and then started again. She'd said he looked fabulous, but he hadn't confirmed that she'd flirted with him. And the "I'm starving" comment shifted them back to normal conversational territory.

Did he really want to bring up flirting?

Especially when they'd already discussed this?

Not in a million years. "Then let's get you some food."

Outside the hotel, at a time of day when the avenue should have been dark, it was lit by hundreds of thousands of lights from jumbotrons, video advertisements, scrolling newsfeeds and storefronts. Leni looked up and down the street, her curiosity and wonder evident on her face.

Nick suddenly understood why Danny had put her in Times Square. The place was filled with tourists and her interest blended with the curiosity of the people around her. Even if she couldn't control her reactions, she didn't stand out. Half the people on the sidewalk were gawking in awe at the lights and videos and shops.

"I hope you like Italian food."

Her eyes widened. "I love it."

"Great." He motioned to his driver that they were going to walk and headed down the street to the left. "I know a wonderful place. It's low-key. A favorite hangout of visitors to the city, most of whom are going to a Broadway play."

She huddled against the cold, sinking into her jacket, but her eyes were big, taking in everything in the exciting city he barely noticed anymore.

He slowed his pace, let her enjoy the walls of advertisements on the buildings, the vendors, the Christmas shoppers, and the cacophony of sounds from people and taxis and buses.

Seeing the city through her eyes, he felt the rhythm of it. The movement of tourists and vehicles in the brisk night air, all lit by thousands of colored lights.

The crowd thinned as they drifted away from Times Square. In another block they were at the restaurant. He gestured for her to walk down the black iron steps and opened the door for her when they reached the bottom.

Warmth hit him immediately, along with the shift in noise from a busy street to a crowded bar. After a clerk checked their coats, the hostess led them to a table in the middle of the dining area. The waiter poured wine for sampling. Nick almost told him it would be fine but realized he didn't even know if Leni liked wine. Mark had been someone who drank tequila with a beer chaser. Of course, her father hadn't been around to influence her decisions.

"Is wine okay?"

"Are you kidding? Wine would be great about now."

The waiter grinned, poured two glasses and scurried away, leaving them to read the menus.

She took a slow sip of the wine and savored. "This is fabulous."

He loved the way her eyes closed as she enjoyed her sip and slowed himself down as he took another taste from his glass. It *was* fabulous. "I think you're having a fabulous night."

She snickered. "That's pretty cocky of you to say."

"It's not me. It's you. You said you looked fabulous and I looked fabulous and now the wine is fabulous."

"Sometimes fabulous really is the only word."

He shrugged, but she was right. He'd known it when he took the time to savor the wine. He might not put himself or his clothes in the fabulous category, but her in that dress, with her green eyes and red lips? She was fabulous.

"Anything you recommend?"

He glanced up and saw her studying the menu. "Any of their pasta is—" he grinned "—fabulous."

She laughed. "You *do* have a sense of humor."

"No. I just took advantage of your love of fabulous."

"Nick?"

His brain stalled at the sound of his mother's voice, but he quickly gathered his wits and rose. "Mom!"

* * *

Leni glanced up at the pretty blonde with perfect makeup, wearing a bright blue dress, standing next to an older version of Nick. *His mom and dad?*

Nick's mom hugged him. "Sweetie! What a surprise."

"And what a surprise to see you," Nick replied.

Leni had to swallow a laugh. She'd bet it was a surprise…or a shock, from the horrified expression on his face.

He glanced at her, then said, "Leni, these are my parents, Amanda and Walt. Mom, Dad, this is my *friend*, Elenore."

She knew the emphasized word was for her. He wanted her to get on board with that description of who she was.

His parents looked at her expectantly. She didn't know if she should stand or stay seated or reach across the table to shake hands, and that lack of knowledge froze her.

His father nodded to her. "Nice to meet you."

"Nice to meet you, too."

His mother grinned broadly. "*Lovely* to meet you." She pulled in a satisfied breath. "You're here for dinner?"

Nick said, "Yes." He cleared his throat before cautiously asking, "Are you here for dinner?"

"We're done." His mother turned her big blue eyes on him. "You're lucky we're on our way to a play."

From the look on Nick's face, Leni would guess he did believe that made him lucky. But he said, "Too bad. We could have eaten together."

Leni almost snorted. She didn't think his parents bought that any more than she had.

His mother's gaze slid to Leni, then back to Nick. Her expression said she was putting one and one together— her son with a woman and not really wanting to eat dinner with his parents—and coming up with a very clear two.

"So, this is a date?"

Nick's mouth fell open slightly, as if he'd had to pause

to stop the denial that automatically sprang up because he didn't know how else to explain who Leni was. He wasn't allowed to tell them the truth. Nobody was supposed to know who she was or why she was in New York. But she and Nick could be friends. All he had to do was stick with that.

Finally, he said, "I told you we're friends."

His mother laughed. "Friends could be on a date."

"Well, we're not. We're *friends*, having dinner together."

His mother turned to Leni. "He can be a real grouch sometimes."

The devil got into Leni and she smiled at his mom. "Oh, I don't know. The day we met he was actually funny."

Nick's mom's forehead scrunched. "Really? Nick was funny?"

Leni grinned. "Yes."

Amanda shook her head. "That's amazing."

Nick sighed. "Come on, Mom. I'm not that bad."

"Yes, you are." She faced Leni. "I'm hoping this means you'll be at the annual fundraiser Nick hosts for the children's wing of the hospital."

She glanced at him. "You host a fundraiser?" She wanted to say, "By yourself? Really?" But she suddenly realized that what was impossible in her world was probably commonplace in his. He'd have assistants and party planners doing the work.

"It's a thing we've always done. My dad's the one who's on the hospital board. I merely volunteer for this."

He sounded old and tired. About something he'd volunteered for...or something he'd been pressured into volunteering for?

"There's a Christmas party in the ward itself," his mother explained. "And an absolutely breathtaking ball a week later."

"Sounds nice." It sounded like a lot of work. On top of

the job of running an entire company. A company that had clients like Leni's deceased dad who had *billions* of dollars. If he'd given only half of that to Nick's firm to manage, that was a lot, lot, lot of responsibility.

His mom smiled. "I can see we're making my son uncomfortable and I don't want to ruin your dinner. But I do hope you'll come to the party and the ball."

"Yes," Nick's father said, but his eyes zoned in on her, studying her, judging her. "We would love to see you there."

No, he wouldn't. His tone said it quite clearly. But his mother was so happy to think her son was dating someone—Nick's denial had been too weak to shift her away from her hope—that guilt tweaked at Leni's conscience.

Knowing she nonetheless had to play along, she found a way to answer the question honestly without making promises. "I'd like that."

His mom smiled. "Great." She turned and headed toward the door.

Nick's parents walked through the small room packed with tables filled with diners and Nick sat down again.

Wanting to ease the tension, she said, "I told you I'd tell your parents you were funny."

"You shouldn't have. Now they're going to call tomorrow and ask a million questions."

"Look at it this way. I could have told them you flirted."

He cursed. "You are so lucky you didn't say that."

"Why? What are you going to do? Lock me in my hotel room?"

He rolled his eyes, but she could see she'd shifted his focus, and if she kept teasing him maybe he'd relax.

"Your mom sure likes the idea that you might be dating someone. Have all your other dates been shrews or has it been so long since you've dated anyone that she all but did a dance of joy?"

"It could be a combination of both."

She chortled. "My mom and dad do the same thing. Except they tried to set me up with every eligible guy on my dad's construction crew." She took a breath. The last two years had been so difficult with her dad being injured that she'd forgotten that, and the memory sent a wave of sadness through her. "But he hasn't worked in two years." She sucked in another breath. And she hadn't had a date in two years.

She was in no position to tease Nick.

The waiter arrived. They ordered. As he'd said, the food was better than anything she'd ever eaten. Preoccupied with enjoying every bite, she almost didn't notice that they didn't talk. They finished a bottle of wine and refused dessert, which meant the night was over. And she would go back to the hotel now.

Stepping out into the quiet end of the street, she let herself enjoy the city. She didn't mind returning to her room. It was cold and she had warm pajamas in her suitcase. Plus, she was tired. It had been a long day.

But with Nick silent beside her, she thought about his parents again and her guilt over deceiving them returned. His mom was expecting "Nick's friend" to show up at a hospital event when technically she was in hiding.

Because he hadn't told them the truth.

"Do you lie a lot?"

His voice jerked with surprise. "What?"

"I understand keeping your distance from people and not talking to your driver and pilots and such, but you seemed to lie really easily to your parents."

He shook his head. "I did not lie. I led them to draw their own conclusions. And what my dad ended up thinking is going to cost me a lecture because I can't tell him who you really are. But I did try to steer them away from thinking we were dating."

"Yeah, but you did it a little too late."

"I had to leave a little doubt in their minds because

we're hiding you, remember?" He sighed. "It's just better if I keep my distance."

Complete disbelief overwhelmed her. "With your parents?"

"Especially with my parents."

She glanced over at him, but he was staring straight ahead. No expression on his face. No remorse. No sadness. No sign of guilt.

"Now, see? To me that is just plain odd. After a year in foster care I was so grateful to get parents that I'd never want to be distant."

He pulled in a heavy breath. "Have you forgotten we decided it would be better if we didn't get to know each other?"

"We're not talking about ourselves. Technically, we're talking about our parents."

"That's worse. That could be construed as me trying to get your sympathy."

"Because you don't date?"

He dropped his head to his hands. "My not dating isn't reason for anyone's sympathy. This estate must be handled carefully. Danny wants to be the one who explains all this to you because there's a lot at stake."

She mumbled, "I suppose," and shut up. The beauty and noise of Times Square were enough to take her attention for the rest of the walk. Ambling through the lobby of her hotel to the elevator, she didn't expect him to talk.

But when they reached her door, the silence seemed out of place. She said the only thing that popped into her head. "I had a great time."

"What? Not a fabulous time?"

And her Nick was back. The guy she liked. They might have agreed not to get too chummy, but his "fabulous" comment was definitely flirting, at the very least teasing. Still, what would a little flirting hurt? It wasn't like stoic Nick Kourakis would fall in love with her because she teased him.

"Just not going to let me forget that, are you?"

He laughed. "No."

Their eyes met and suddenly it felt like a date. Not the weird outings she had with guys her dad found, but one of the real dates she had the first few years at university. Dates with guys who thought her pretty, made her laugh and wanted to kiss her.

Her heart sped up. What if *Nick* wanted to kiss her?

He couldn't…could he?

Why not? He'd flirted with her. And before that he'd told her she had a warmth about her that was appealing—all but admitted he liked her when he explained why their getting to know each other was a bad idea.

The silence continued as they gazed into each other's eyes. He was gorgeous, funny sometimes, and he'd taken good care of her that day.

If he did want to kiss her all he had to do was bend forward a few inches and press his lips to hers—

Her heart nearly exploded just thinking about his mouth meeting hers. She could not let her thoughts run away from her like that! She couldn't forget that Nick wasn't her friend because he didn't want to be. It would be crazy to spin fantasies about someone who'd told her up front he didn't want to get involved with her. She'd had enough rejection in her life. When she chose a romantic partner, it would be someone who didn't have secrets, someone who'd trust her and love her, just as she was.

What it felt like to kiss Nick was totally irrelevant stacked up against the truth of what she needed. She shouldn't be probing into his life or, worse, spinning fantasies about him.

She turned and swiped her key. For the first time since she heard the no-talking rule, she realized it was a wise one. "Good night."

CHAPTER FIVE

LENI WOKE THE next morning totally disoriented.

In a fancy hotel, fighting a crush on a guy with secrets, she ordered eggs and toast from room service and a pot of coffee.

When her breakfast arrived, she grabbed her cell phone and called her mom.

Her dad answered. "Hey, Kitten."

"Hey, Dad. Feeling okay?"

"Fit as a fiddle." He always said that, not wanting Leni or her mom to worry. "How's the Big Apple?"

"Huge. Except it goes up to the sky instead of spreading out."

"Oh, it spreads pretty far. Your mother's tapping my shoulder. I think she wants a turn."

Before Leni could say goodbye to her dad, her mom said, "So? What's happening?"

She told her mom about eating on the jet, riding in a limo, seeing people dressed in fancy clothes, going to the Italian restaurant and how Nick didn't want to talk about the estate because the lawyer needed to explain it all to her. He couldn't.

She bit her lower lip. "It's all kind of strange and confusing. Like I'm in a dream."

"In a way you are."

"Yeah, except I can't shake the weird feelings I have about Mark Hinton. About him having money and letting my biological mom struggle, especially when she was sick."

"Powerful men do things the rest of us don't understand."

"I suppose. But inheriting his money feels wrong…" She paused to think that through then said, "It feels sleazy."

"Sleazy?"

"It's almost like I'm so thrilled at the prospect of getting money that I'm letting him off the hook for abandoning me and my poor mom." She didn't mention that no one had seen her biological mom since she had given Leni up. Her mother knew that. When Leni was sixteen, they'd hired an investigator to look for her but never found her. They also never found a death certificate. That meant her mom had survived whatever illness she'd been fighting when she had to give up Leni. But she'd never come back for her. Hadn't even checked up on her as far as Leni knew.

That's the thing that haunted her sometimes. Her mother hadn't seemed to want her any more than her biological father had.

"But we need this money for dad. It's the worst rock and a hard place. Taking this money feels like I absolve everybody of not wanting me."

Her mom's soft sigh drifted through the phone. "Oh, Leni. Don't you remember how much your dad and I wanted you? We'd tried for years to have a child and couldn't. When the social workers put your little hand in mine, my heart melted. You brought so much joy into our lives."

She did remember. Mostly because she was eight, not a toddler, not an infant but a kid who understood what was going on. "You guys made me very happy, too."

"Because we were so grateful to get you. Your biological parents might have left you, but we were desperately happy for the privilege of raising you."

As always, her soft-spoken mother's words were like a magic balm. Still, there was something very basic about being rejected not just by a mother who didn't come looking for her after she got well, but by a guy who didn't want her at all.

And the money felt like the key. Almost as if, if she refused it, she would shake off her feelings of rejection forever. But just when she would convince herself that walking away was the right thing to do, she'd remember her sick dad and hesitate.

Would she be selling her soul, the way she viewed herself, the code of honor she didn't even realize was so strong, if she took that cash—even if it was for her dad, not herself?

Nick knocked on Leni's hotel room door that afternoon to take her for a stroll through the Metropolitan Museum of Art. Danny had called to say his trial had not ended, and when Nick asked for specifics, Danny mumbled about the length of testimony of witnesses being way over what Danny had thought they should be. But he swore the trial would finish up the next morning.

Nick had sighed and agreed to entertain Leni. Not because he felt for Danny but because he felt for *her*. She was a nice woman in a strange city, here to ascertain whether she was the heir of a huge estate, but the vetting process hadn't started because Danny wasn't available to do his job.

Nick was positive that after a morning of being cooped up, she'd be eager for even his company, but when she opened the door, she wouldn't meet his gaze.

His heart stuttered. They were right back where they were when he'd brought her to the door the night before. One minute they were practicing safe silence walking down the hall to her suite, and the next they were making flirty comments and gazing into each other's eyes. Then she'd broken the contact and run into her room.

While he'd been standing there thinking about kissing her.

What was it about being in front of a door, saying good-night, that brought out that instinct? Or longing. What had trembled through him wasn't just a desire for a kiss. It was more. Something part of him wanted but the other part knew he couldn't have.

But she'd raced off. She'd handled the moment perfectly—getting them both off the hook.

So why wouldn't she look at him now? And why wasn't she talking? She always talked. Even when he reminded her that they shouldn't.

"Where are we going?"

Her quiet, impersonal question might be talking, but it wasn't typical Leni chitchat.

Maybe she finally realized it really was better if they didn't get to know each other? Didn't veer off into conversations that tempted him to kiss her—

"I thought I'd take you to the Metropolitan Museum."

She slid her purse strap onto her shoulder as she faced him. She wore her scruffy jacket and jeans, but the Met was filled with all kinds of people. And she looked nice. She didn't need fancy clothes to be attractive.

"That sounds great."

"I think you'll enjoy it." And they could talk as much as she wanted—about art. The Met was the best way to allow her to be chatty and use up a lot of time happily, neutrally. He was a genius for coming up with it.

Silence reigned as they rode the elevator to the lobby and walked out onto the street and into his limo.

Accustomed to her talking, the quiet enveloping them felt wrong. But he told himself not to worry. She wouldn't be able to contain herself at the Met. Plus, her not talking on the drive worked to his advantage. The questions she asked always drew him in even though he knew it was wrong. He kept falling into the feelings he'd had at the diner, the instant connection. The almost-kiss at her door the night before proved it.

She didn't say a word on the limo ride, while she climbed out of the car or even on the busy street in front of the Met. But she also didn't look around the way she normally did. She kept her eyes fixed on her old boots as they ascended the steps into the museum. Her gaze stayed lowered as they walked inside.

He hated this.

She was much too perky and sunny to keep her head down and herself quiet. But that was why he'd brought her to this enormous museum. There was plenty to talk about without once getting personal. He just had to nudge her to recognize it.

He glanced around, saw the exhibit housing the Christmas tree and smiled. That would get her talking.

He guided her to the Medieval Sculpture Hall. Her head came up slowly and she gasped at the enormous Christmas tree. "Oh, my…"

"It's a twenty-foot blue spruce." Glad he'd skimmed the information as they'd walked in, he directed her to the base of the tree where a full nativity scene was arranged beneath the lower boughs.

But her gaze stayed on the upper branches. "The angels look like they're climbing to the sky."

Proud he'd realized she wouldn't be able to resist talking about the gorgeous Christmas tree, he rocked back on his heels. "Or coming down to earth."

She stepped a few feet to the right, examining the figures scattered about the tree and shook her head. "It's the most beautiful thing I've ever seen."

He angled his head toward the door. "There's a whole building full of wonderful things. There's even an armor room. Egyptian art. Modern art. What do you like?"

Her smile returned. "I don't know. I've never been any-place like this."

He motioned to the exit. "We have five hours to look your fill."

She headed for the door. "What happens in five hours?"

"I take you back to the hotel to get ready for dinner."

"Out?"

"Sure. If you're worried about what to wear, the account at the boutique has been set up for you. All you have to do walk in and give your name."

Her spine stiffened. "No, thank you."

"Seriously? You have access to money while you're here. Just take the limo to the boutique and use the account."

"You make it sound so easy."

"It is."

"When you have money."

Her statement was flat with a hint of bitterness, and he almost stopped walking. Locked in those few words was the reason for her unhappiness. He was certain of it. But he didn't want to be curious about her life any more than he wanted her to ask about his. He had parents to please, a brother who was gone and sorely missed, a difficult life that a good person like Leni shouldn't get dragged into.

He squelched the troublesome questions about why she might be so sad through two exhibits, but eventually he began going over everything she'd said the day before until he remembered how she'd reacted to his misleading his parents, especially her reasoning. She'd been confused by him distancing himself from his mom and dad because she'd spent a year in foster care—

That nagged at him until he couldn't stand it anymore, and his question was out before he could stop it. "Were you really in foster care?"

She turned away from a bright painting. "Yes. I was seven when my mom put me in. Eight when the Longs found me and adopted me."

Her answer brought him up short. *She'd been abandoned by her mom? In foster care for an entire year before she'd met the Longs?*

"That's tough."

"My mom couldn't keep me because she was sick. Her choice was to feed me or buy medicine." She shook her head. "My dad was a billionaire, but my mom was too broke to save herself and care for me, and she made the only choice she could. I ended up living in three different homes with three families I didn't know." She paused, caught his gaze. "It was the worst year of my life."

His heart hurt for her. There was so much sadness in that simple explanation that a longing to comfort her rose up in him.

But that was a slippery slope.

He shoved his hands into his pockets. "You know what? Let's just move along. Maybe work our way to the Egyptian exhibit."

"Okay."

The cloudiness was back in her eyes and Nick sucked in a deep breath. He'd probably been a little too abrupt changing the subject. But if he hugged her to comfort her, his brain wouldn't stop there. He'd feel her softness. Her curves. Get drawn into the strange connection he'd had in the diner, the feeling of warmth and comfort and rightness that had washed over him. He'd want things he couldn't have. Romance and connection required honesty, and he couldn't be honest with anyone, couldn't talk about his mistakes, didn't want anyone to see or know the real him.

Out of necessity, his life was nothing but business but hers could be about to change dramatically. In a very good way. And maybe he should help her realize that?

"You know, you might be surprised when you talk about the estate with the lawyer. If you're an heir, your life will change so much for the better."

She said, "You think so?" Then she peeked at him. "Is *your* life better?"

Though the question hit him right in the heart, he laughed. "Better than what?"

"The average person's?"

His little white lie was automatic. "Of course."

"Really?" She frowned. "You barely talk to your parents or your staff. I'm guessing you live alone. And the one thing you do that seems like fun—plan a ball—is probably organized by your assistant."

He scowled. "Do you always have to question everything?"

"Hey, I took a lot of psychology courses. I know what I see."

"I'm happy." In his own little way, he was. He'd built this life, this world, this persona to protect himself. And as long as he was safe, he was fine.

"No. You're not. Not even close. Take this museum," she said, motioning around them as they headed for the next exhibit. "While I'm actually looking at things, enjoying them, you're watching me. But not because you're interested in me. Because you're responsible for me and you think I'm a ticking bomb. Like any minute you expect me to explode."

"You have done some pretty weird things."

She stopped so she could stare him down. "Such as?"

"Tell my mom I'm funny."

She laughed. "Has it really been so long since you've made normal conversation that you've forgotten what it sounds like?"

"I talked to you at the diner."

"Yeah, you told me Mannington seemed like a nice town. That led me into talking about my job search. Which led you to tell me about your family business—and having a rebellious streak." She stopped, gave him a quick once-over. "Huh. I guess you do know how to hold a conversation after all."

She walked away, heading for a set of stairs. "There's an exhibit up here I really want to see. Because that's what people in museums do. They examine things. Then they discuss them. You should try it."

His footsteps echoing around him, he scrambled after her. Not to talk, though she was right. Talking about the exhibits was why he'd brought her here. But now that she'd pointed it out, he felt odd about talking. Every time he was around her, his reasoning got jumbled. His best intentions went straight to hell. His safe little world shook a bit. She didn't have the power to tear it down, but she could sure shake it.

She led him to the European paintings exhibit and honestly even if he'd wanted to talk, he wouldn't have. A reverent hush fell over them as they looked at work dating back to the thirteenth century. His breathing slowed as he studied landscapes and sunsets, blue skies and children. Knowing artists painted what they saw, he recognized he was looking at the world as it was hundreds of years ago.

"You're feeling better now, aren't you?"

He glanced at Leni. How was she so damned right all the time? "Yes."

She shrugged. "I'm really good at what I do."

And now she read minds? Answering questions he hadn't asked out loud? The woman was going to drive him insane.

Leni walked away glad she'd said her piece, but also enjoying the art. For as much as she knew the European exhibit would have a calming effect on Nick, she'd also known it would center her. She didn't want to rush her decisions about Mark Hinton's estate or jump to conclusions, and with the lawyer unavailable she had nothing but time to think about things.

She was glad Nick had brought her here. Not just for something they could discuss without consequences, but because sometimes all it took to get perspective was seeing the world through another person's eyes. Especially if that person lived in another century and their world was so different from her own.

They walked around the museum for the promised five hours, commenting on the exhibits sometimes but mostly staying silent, then Nick said it was time to go. She surreptitiously glanced at her watch. Five hours exactly.

She almost sighed. She didn't mind a person who loved precision, but he would take her to the hotel and then return to pick her up for dinner and he'd be careful about everything he said. If fun Nick did make an appearance, it would be short-lived.

It was getting old.

Just as she predicted, they stayed quiet on the ride to her hotel, and even on the walk to her room. With fun Nick nowhere to be seen, she didn't even think about a kiss good-night. But it wasn't really night. It was late afternoon. He had the entirety of their dinner that evening to sit stonily beside her. It was getting kind of insulting that he wouldn't talk because he didn't think it was appropriate for them to get to know each other.

Well, guess what? Neither did she. She had absolutely no desire to get to know grumpy Nick.

Frankly, she'd rather read a book.

She slid the key card over the lock, but as the door clicked open, she faced Nick again.

"I know you'd mentioned going out to dinner tonight, but I'm tired."

He frowned. "What?"

"I'm tired. It's what happens to people when they walk around for five hours straight. I'm going to order room service, put on my pajamas and watch some TV. Maybe I'll call that concierge guy and see if he can get me a book."

He stepped back, seeming totally confused. "Okay."

She supposed she didn't blame him. She had the whole of New York City at her disposal and she'd rather stay in. Not because she didn't want to see the city but because she didn't want to see it with a guy who didn't want to risk getting to know her.

It was weird, tiresome. Who the heck did he think he was, anyway? Did he think if he talked to her, she'd instantly fall at his feet in adoration?

She might be from a small town, but she wasn't brainless.

"I'm fine. Just in the mood for some me time. Don't worry. I'll be here tomorrow."

She entered her room feeling like herself for the first time in days. Not just because seeing the wonderful exhibits had centered her, but because she'd made a logical choice.

She didn't have to be bored with gorgeous Nick Kourakis. She could read a book.

Nick stared at her closed door. Okay. He had to admit his ego took a direct hit when she'd said she'd rather stay in and read a book than go somewhere with him. There had been a time when he was the most fun, most interesting guy on the planet. Women lined up to spend time with him. Not one of them would have preferred a book.

Walking to the limo, seeing the Christmas decorations that signaled the season of peace on earth, he stopped, glanced around. They *were* amazing.

He hadn't noticed things like Christmas decorations since Joe died. Being with Leni was opening his eyes again. Not because she was pretty, though that certainly didn't hurt. But because she was so damned transparent and honest. He knew her experience in foster care and then being raised by two loving parents played into that. Not to mention small-town living. He supposed if there were only fifteen hundred people in your entire town, life would be very different. She'd seen the good and bad side of the world, of people. Comprehended things only someone who'd gone through trouble could appreciate. And she had a degree in psychology.

Actually, she'd probably understand *him* if he told her about his situation.

Shaking his head, he started toward the door of his limo again. She'd love that. She'd already evaluated him in the museum, basically told him he was boring then refused dinner with him.

He hated that that bothered him so much.

But it did, and he wasn't sure why. He'd think it was because he didn't like being rejected. Except, this wasn't personal. They'd already decided to keep their personal feelings out of this. He only had to babysit her, entertain her, when she'd been left alone too long.

So why did her rejection skim along his nerve endings, a constant reminder that wouldn't go away?

He got into the limo and stared out the window at the lights and people on the drive to his Park Avenue penthouse. He rode the quiet elevator that opened onto his stunning open-plan home, stripped off his scarf and tossed his overcoat on the sofa to the sounds of silence. Cold, hollow silence. The same silence that greeted him every night.

She was right. New Wolf of Wall Street or not, he had become boring.

He walked past the seating arrangement, pool table and bar to the windows in the back and looked out at the city dressed for the holiday. Now that he was noticing the decorations again, he remembered how much his brother had loved Christmas, remembered their childhood Christmases. How Joe had spent months finding the right gifts for everyone, wrapped them with care and sat with bated breath while everyone opened their presents—

The cold, hollow silence morphed into sadness. He missed his brother. He'd never felt it before because the guilt was always stronger. But tonight, he missed Joe.

Missed him with the kind of ache that took ahold of his heart and squeezed until his eyes drifted closed.

He wondered what Joe would be like now, and knew they'd still be best friends. He felt the loss again. Thick and all-consuming. The weight of it on his shoulders made him pull in a long breath. In some ways, the guilt was better. Guilt pushed him to work, to not let their parents down. This sadness only hurt.

The ring of his phone burst into the quiet. He considered not answering, but knew he had to. He was his parents' only child now. If something was wrong, he had to be there.

He yanked it from his pocket, scowled at the caller ID and said, "Hello, Danny."

"Hey, Nick."

"I hope you're calling to tell me your trial ended today."

"No."

Nick sighed. He'd suspected as much, but it had been worth a shot.

"There are two more witnesses." Danny's voice wobbled in that weird way voices sometimes do when someone has something difficult to say. "We should wrap up tomorrow but if not tomorrow definitely on Friday. No one will want this thing on hold over the weekend."

"But that's not a guarantee."

"No. Sorry. Honestly, this opposing counsel has confused me at every turn. I have no idea what she's going to do next. For all I know, she might only have one question for each of the last two witnesses. But even if the trial is still going on Monday, I'll have the weekend off and I'll be able to talk to Elenore on Saturday. You'll be off the hook with her."

Relief poured through him, but he winced. Leni was one of the nicest people he'd ever met, and he was acting as if being with her was a chore.

It wasn't. Fighting his attraction to her was the chore.

He sat on the edge of the pool table. He'd told her that. Told her they shouldn't talk. Been a real jackass about reminding her of that.

All because he liked her.

Danny broke into his thoughts. "So, can you give Leni a little time out of the hotel room tomorrow?"

He'd never had a problem like this with a woman before. If he wanted someone he usually went after her. But Leni was different. She would soon be a client if she decided to keep her share of her dad's money with his management firm. And she was a nice woman who didn't deserve a broken heart from a man who only did one-night stands.

But that didn't mean he had to be a jerk. When he'd told her that they shouldn't talk, shouldn't try to get to know each other, he hadn't realized they'd be together so much. Now that he knew, he needed to shift his strategy.

And maybe he should be glad he had another day or two to make up for being an idiot.

He thought for a minute about how he'd go about doing that, then smiled.

"Yeah. I can entertain her tomorrow."

"Okay," Dany said. "Just remember not to talk about the will or the estate."

Nick laughed. The woman had called him boring. The last thing he wanted to discuss with her was a will, an estate or his job. "I can promise you the will and the estate will not come up in conversation."

He hung up the phone feeling much better. He'd taken the no-talking thing a step too far, but now that he'd figured that out, he could make it up to her.

Tomorrow he'd show her he could be a fun guy.

CHAPTER SIX

THE NEXT MORNING, the ring of her cell phone edged its way into Leni's dream about waiting tables at the Family Diner, giving out free Christmas cookies, getting big tips and saying "Merry Christmas" as she waved to customers walking out the door.

The phone rang again.

With a gasp, she sprang up, off her pillow. Confused to be out of the dream so suddenly, it took another ring before she grabbed her phone. "Hello?"

"Good morning, Leni."

Nick.

She couldn't stop the happiness at hearing his voice any more than she could stop the ripple of annoyance. She could spend 24/7 with the Nick who made her laugh, but she didn't want to spend another long, boring day with the guy who didn't want to talk.

She carefully said, "Good morning, Nick."

"Danny's stuck in his trial for another day."

And she and Nick were stuck together for another day—unless she could sway him into thinking she didn't need to be entertained? "I haven't even gotten out of bed yet. It could be a lazy day for me. It's fine that Danny's not available."

"No. It's not. It's incredibly unfair that we're keeping you in New York and not getting on with the reasons we brought you here."

Who was this guy? The Nick she knew was either funny

or grouchy. Never accommodating. "Don't worry about it. I can read a book today."

"No, your being stuck here is an imposition. So, to make up for that, I thought we'd do something really fun today."

"I'm okay with getting a book and just vegging today."

"You vegged last night. Today, I thought we'd go skating at Rockefeller Center."

Her breath hitched. She sat up a little farther on the bed. *"Rockefeller Center?"*

"It's gorgeous when it's decorated for Christmas. And they have an enormous tree."

Her entire body longed to do something physical, but more than that she loved to skate. With her busy schedule and her dad's troubles, she hadn't skated in the past two years.

Excitement filled her blood, boosted her mood, made her not care that Nick Kourakis wouldn't say a word beyond what he had to. As long as she had skates on her feet, it didn't matter.

"I love to skate."

"Good. Get your breakfast and put on something warm. I'll pick you up around ten."

"I'll be ready."

She threw aside the covers, called room service and got her shower. By the time she had herself wrapped in one of the hotel's big white robes, her breakfast had arrived. She tried not to gobble because she had until ten, but it was useless. Everything she'd done since arriving in New York had been foreign to her. Today, she would do something she loved.

In the bedroom, she pulled out two pairs of socks, her warmest jeans, a T-shirt and a sweater for over it. She applied a little lip gloss and mascara, but when it came time to do her hair, she decided against pulling it into a bun or a ponytail. She loved the feeling of her hair floating around her when she skated. She curled it but kept it down.

She returned to the sitting room just as there was a knock on the door. Opening it, she found Nick.

"Ready to skate?"

Instead of his usual suit, today he wore jeans, a thick sweater and a dark parka. With his hair just a little messed and his eyes bright, he looked young and carefree.

And happy.

If she didn't know better, she'd think he was as excited to go skating as she was.

Maybe ditching him the night before had made him realize he needed to loosen up? Maybe because he liked her?

Remembering that's exactly why he didn't want to talk to her, she stopped that wishful thinking. There was something between them. Attraction, sure. But it was more. There had been a connection that he didn't want. If she called his attention to it, he'd turn back into grumpy Nick. The guy she didn't want to be around.

On the way down in the elevator, he said, "Did you sleep well?"

"I'm finally getting accustomed to not being in my own bed."

"Good. I slept well, too."

His unexpected small talk caused her to give him the side-eye, but the elevator door opened, and he guided her outside to his limo. They seated themselves and the long car slid into traffic.

"How was your breakfast?"

She frowned. The guy who didn't want her to be chatty was chatting. Again. Still, she wouldn't be rude or, worse, call attention to it.

"I had toast and eggs. Hard to screw that up."

"That hotel is known for its restaurants." He glanced at her and smiled "Maybe we should eat there tonight?"

The smile jump-started her heart and scrambled her

pulse. She told herself to settle down because this kind of reaction was exactly what Nick didn't want.

Schooling her face into complete neutrality, she said, "Yeah. Eating at the hotel would be great."

The limo fell silent, but within a few minutes, they arrived at Rockefeller Center.

As Nick had said, the huge Christmas tree dominated the area, and she had to stifle a gasp. Lit by what looked to be millions of lights, it sat in front of the Rockefeller Center building, with a backdrop of other tall buildings. Angel statues with trumpets sat by the tree. A row of flags created a wall. At least fifty people were already on the ice.

She stepped out of the limo feeling like she was stepping into a fairy tale. "It's beautiful."

It was also a perfect day, cold but not freezing. A blue, cloudless sky smiled down on them. No wind. No snow and lots of sunshine.

"I think this is my favorite place in New York City."

No longer surprised that Nick had spoken, she sneaked a peek at him. He glanced around the space as if seeing it for the first time. She could tell from the expression on his face that he didn't intend to be a spectator. He wouldn't stand behind her watching her like a bodyguard or stalker. He wanted to be here.

But not for *her*. He was only entertaining her. If he liked this place it was because it was gorgeous and filled with fun. And she was desperate for a little fun.

Maybe he was, too?

"I can understand why it would be your favorite place. It's wonderful."

"It is."

They paid the fee, rented skates and were on the ice in what felt like seconds. With a quick push off, she skated in a big circle to get the feel of things, then eased back to him. He clearly liked this place. She liked to skate. Having something physical to do was exactly what they needed.

"Come on! Skate with me."

He stood there, looking gorgeous in his parka and jeans, but also unsure. "I haven't skated since my teens."

When he'd bring his brother.

The thought shot through Nick's brain as bright as the sun glistening off the ice. Joe had loved skating nearly as much as he'd loved Christmas.

Nick almost groaned, thinking it had been a mistake to bring Leni here—except he wanted her to have fun. Real fun. This was a place to have fun.

"You came here as a kid?"

He shrugged. "Yeah. By the time I was a teenager I was a great skater."

That made her laugh. "Conceited much?"

"It's only conceited if you talk about it all the time." Finally feeling comfortable enough on his skates to try them out, he eased his way to the far wall then back again. When he reached her, he skated a ring around her.

"Very funny."

"I keep telling you I'm not funny."

"So that was a sarcastic ring you just skated around me?"

"It was more of a proof ring." He grinned at her. The sky was blue. The world was dressed up for Christmas. And he was on skates.

For the first time in five years he felt Christmas in the air. The wonder of it swirled around him, along with a magic he didn't quite understand. Maybe because Leni was back to teasing him? Maybe because she no longer seemed quiet or careful? Maybe because she was back to her old self?

Tonight, he would nurse his remorse about his brother, but this afternoon he would not think about Joe. He would show Leni a good time and demonstrate to her that he was a fun guy in an unromantic way that would ease both of their nerves about what a jerk he'd been about not getting to know each other.

"Wanna race?"

He took off before she had a chance to answer, bobbing and weaving around other skaters. She saw a clearer path and took it, beating him to the wall.

"Ha! I win."

"You probably skated last week. So, you're on your game."

"Nope. Haven't skated in two years."

He shrugged as he made a small circle around her. "Give me another ten minutes and no one on this ice will beat me."

"How do you get through doors with that big head?"

He laughed, breathed in the air again and something inside him stilled. He'd brought her here to have fun and instead he was the one laughing.

"Race you to that wall." The second the words were out of her mouth she was skating away.

A lover of competition, he pushed off immediately and his longer legs had him beside her in seconds. "I'm going to beat you."

"Who says?" She blew past him and was at the wall before he drew three breaths.

He reached her and said, "One more time," before he shot off.

She burst after him, passed him and stood with her arms folded on her chest when he finally caught up to her.

"How do you do that?"

"What? Beat you?"

"You have short legs."

She laughed. "You have a fat coat." She caught a chunk of the material stuffed with down, but when she looked up at him to say, "It's not aerodynamically sound," they both realized she was touching him. Like a friend, sure. But they weren't friends. They barely knew each other—

Except they had that damned connection they'd made at the diner the day they met. She'd been cute and funny, and he'd been instantly smitten. They'd spent two days together and she'd made him laugh as well as made him crazy. And after Danny talked to her on Saturday, he'd only see her in his capacity as her money manager.

That didn't sit right. She was too different to like, a part of his job and a royal pain in the butt with her honesty, but the thought of never laughing with her again, casually, naturally, seemed so wrong it sent confusion rippling through him. He wanted this day, maybe *needed* this day to laugh with her, as much as she did.

She let go of her grip on his parka and jerked her hand away, but he caught it before she could put it down to her side. "Let's just do a few laps."

"Why?" Shielding her eyes from the sun with a hand nestled in bright green mitten, she said, "So, you can get your form back?"

That was as good of a reason as any. "Yeah." Was it so wrong to want to have fun with her? He hadn't had fun since Joe died and maybe that's why his subconscious had brought them here. He'd missed Joe the night before. And being here now made him remember his brother in a good way. Not the painful way that had enveloped him before Danny called.

She pulled her hand out of his, skated a circle around him. "When you were a kid, did you do tricks?"

He sniffed. "Like a trained dog?"

"Like someone imitating Olympic skaters."

She executed a perfect toe loop.

He applauded.

"Now, you do a trick."

"I didn't do tricks when I skated. I just raced."

"Raced?"

"My brother. So, I'd win, and girls would like me."

She frowned. "Your brother?"

His mention of Joe stunned him as much as it stunned her. He would have pulled back the words if he could, but they were out there now, and he wasn't sure why.

"He was only a year younger than me." He said it easily, casually, so she wouldn't make a big deal out of it, testing the words, trying to figure out why he suddenly wanted to talk about Joe. "We'd race. I'd beat him. And girls would flock after me."

She shook her head. "You have really got to do something about your ego."

She did another two toe loops and pushed off to get speed enough for an edge jump.

Nick watched her, his heart in his throat. He'd skated to get girls, but she skated for the pleasure of it and watching her was pure joy. Nothing he'd ever experienced. Something as mesmerizing as it was wonderful.

He eased over to her and took her hands, so they could skate sideways in a circle.

"This is your big trick?"

"I told you. I don't do tricks. I only skated to get girls."

She chuckled, let go of his hands and raced off. He followed her, caught her and grabbed her hand again. This time he twirled her under his arm. She spun gracefully, tilting her head back, letting her long hair fall behind her and looking like poetry on ice.

His heart swelled with longing. Of all the women in the world, why did he have to like the one he wasn't supposed to like?

She owned a big chunk of the money his company was managing. But more than that, she was one of the nicest people in the world and he was a man filled with guilt and remorse.

He didn't deserve her.

When she stopped, she said, "So tell me more about your brother."

His chest pinched. He longed to tell her about Joe. Years

had passed with him holding all this inside, and she was the one person who would understand.

Actually, that was the point. Her sweetness, her honesty made him want to open up. And he shouldn't. A man like him should let a nice girl like her alone.

"I'd rather race."

At first, she looked confused, then she smiled. "Okay." She pointed at a spot on the wall. "I'll be there two seconds before you."

He laughed and pushed off after her. He might not be the right guy for her, but that didn't mean he couldn't enjoy her company.

Just this one day.

CHAPTER SEVEN

HAVING MISSED LUNCH, they decided to have an early dinner at an Irish pub rather than at her hotel. Happy from skating, Leni glanced around excitedly as they entered. The place was dark, partially because of low lighting, but also the walls were paneled with dark wood. The floors were dark. Blinds covered the windows. Even the shiny bar was dark wood.

"It's like a hideaway."

Nick laughed. "You have a weird way of looking at things."

"Oh, I don't know. Maybe I look at things the right way and you're the one whose perception is skewed."

He shook his head as they approached the hostess. The restaurant was empty except for an older couple at a table in front and two men at the bar. The bartender, a beefy guy with dark hair and a ready smile, gave them a quick once-over and Leni suspected he was also the bouncer. She didn't miss the glance that passed between him and the hostess and she realized they were in love.

Her heart stuttered as she saw they both wore simple gold wedding bands. Without saying a word, they communicated the kind of love and commitment that anyone who looked at them would know would last a lifetime.

The hostess guided them to a little table in the back and Leni smiled her thanks before the young woman made her way back to the bar area. Leni caught the bartender's wink and the hostess's smile and her heart could have melted into a big pile of goo.

She peeked at Nick, who was engrossed in his menu, realizing he hadn't seen any of it. Two things hit her immediately. First, she was in some sort of fanciful mood because of skating. Second, a few hours of fun had changed him. He laughed easily. Held her gaze when they spoke. And suggested this lovely little bar for dinner. Like friends. Not a guy stuck with babysitting her.

They sat with their menus for only a few seconds before a waitress appeared. They both ordered a beer and she scurried away.

"See anything you like?"

She lowered her menu to the table and winced. "Just fries."

"You can't live on fries."

"So, my mother says but I've always wanted to test that theory."

"You shouldn't. You need protein, too."

She grinned devilishly. "I had protein at breakfast. This isn't a permanent rebellion. Just a little skirmish."

"I'm feeling a little skirmishy myself."

She'd already figured that out and peeked at him. "Really?"

"Yeah. You get the loaded fries. I'll get the classic margherita flatbread."

"And we can share!"

"My thought exactly."

The waitress arrived with their drafts and they ordered their appetizers. She walked away, and Leni leaned back in her chair. Fun Nick was here and better than usual. The weird connection that had popped up at the oddest times since their meeting at the diner seemed to be gone, but happy Nick was much better.

"I like it here. It's sort of like a bar back home but it's cleaner."

He laughed. "Did you go there a lot?"

"I thought I wasn't supposed to talk about my life?

You know, because it's pointless for us to get to know each other."

"Let's just say that things changed a bit. Besides, we've spent so much time together that we have to start talking about something or we'll die of boredom."

Totally onboard with that assessment, she sat up. "What do you want to know?"

He shrugged. "I don't care. Tell me about school."

"Well, scraping the money together was hard but I didn't want to be one of those people who graduated owing more money than I'd ever be able to pay back."

He smiled and nodded, and she shook her head. "Look who I'm telling. You don't understand debt."

He winced. "Sorry. I don't."

"I like that you're honest about that."

"I think you're starting to rub off on me."

She laughed. "Wouldn't that be something."

"Yeah. I just can't figure out if it's a good or bad something."

"What kinds of things are you picking up from me?"

"Your over-the-top honesty, for one."

She took a sip of beer. "That's a good thing. What else?"

"Saying things that pop into my head."

"That's all part of being honest."

He shook his head, but he also took a breath and glanced around. "It *is* comfortable in here. Reminds me of my old life."

"Old life?"

He looked down, played with his silverware. "Yeah, before I took over the family business, I traveled a lot. Went to places like this."

She might have wondered about why he seemed to be avoiding her gaze, except she'd never traveled, and she gasped excitedly. "Like Irish pubs in Ireland?"

"Exactly like that."

"Is that why you don't notice your surroundings or the

people?" She waited a beat then said, "You've been so many places that this is dull to you?"

"Not dull. But I've lived in this city my entire life. I've seen every restaurant and street. I'm kind of accustomed to it. Going to Yale was a nice change of pace."

Happiness filled her. When he was normal like this, she could just take his cheeks between her palms and kiss him. She reminded herself that she shouldn't. Not merely because grumpy Nick could make an appearance any second but because he'd warned her he didn't want a relationship. Though she could enjoy herself, she would keep her emotions under control.

"You went to Yale?" Having expected Harvard, Yale was a pleasant surprise. "Really?"

"Nothing wrong with Yale."

"No. No. Yale's a great school. So, what was your rank?"

He winced. "I was the top of my class."

She didn't doubt that for a second. "Then you went to…"

"The Navy."

Expecting him to tell her about post-grad work, she flopped back on her chair. "What?"

"By the time I was twenty-one I had had it with sitting in classrooms and writing papers. I joined the Navy, discovered the SEALs and the challenge was too hard to resist."

"The challenge?"

"I love a challenge."

"I want to save the world and you love a challenge."

He laughed at her. "You think saving the world isn't going to be a challenge?"

"I wasn't planning on making any big moves. Just saving one person at a time."

"That's nice."

"I thought for sure you were going to say that's naive."

"I've known you long enough, Leni, to realize that you probably get just about anything you set your mind to."

"My dad always said I was like a little dog with a bone." Thoughts of her dad struggling at home hurt her heart, so she said, "Tell me about being a SEAL."

"It was amazing." He caught her gaze. "Changed my life. Everyone thinks of the world through a specific set of beliefs. Going into the military shows you just how big and how troubled the world really is."

"And?"

"And?"

"Is that what made you unhappy?"

He shook his head. "Being a SEAL, being on active duty, gave me a sense of purpose. But when my time was up, I knew I'd seen things that messed up my thinking a bit. I wasn't ready to go home, but I couldn't shirk my family responsibility anymore."

She gaped at him. "Are you telling me becoming a SEAL was your *rebellious* streak?"

"Yes."

She shook her head. "And you tell me I have a skewed vision of life."

"You do. And I don't. Not really. My parents wanted me involved with the firm. Becoming a SEAL only delayed that, but it was a rebellion."

She nodded thoughtfully. "So, after the SEALs you settled down and took over the family business."

"No. After the SEALs, I was antsy and couldn't stay in one place long, so I had to figure out a way to do my duty and give myself a chance to process my time in the military. In the end, I told my parents I'd be something like a recruiter. I traveled the globe and looked for investors like your dad. After a few years of bungee jumping and skydiving with risk takers like myself, I grew the firm from being moderately successful to being one of the top firms on the planet."

She could only stare at him. She'd never in a million years have believed he'd done so much. And most of it dangerous. "Wow."

The waitress came with their food. The conversation died as they poured ketchup, cut the flatbread, asked for refills of their drafts.

She took a bite of flatbread and groaned. "Oh, this is fabulous."

"My fabulous girl is back."

Her heart skittered. He'd called her his. Even if he meant it in the most generic of ways, those words tumbling off his tongue filled her with joy. Which was ridiculous. She'd known him only a few days. And he'd very clearly warned her that he didn't think it was a good idea for them to even consider a relationship. She told her heart to settle down, but the reminder was good. Fun Nick was very hard to resist, but she had to.

They ate and laughed some more. The bar got darker, as if reflecting night falling on the street outside.

The waitress brought two more drafts. Nick talked a bit more about the jet-setting he'd done to find new clients, and she stared at him. He had to be the most interesting person she'd ever met. He knew and was friends with kings, princes, billionaires, tech geniuses.

He could have talked down to her. He could have bragged. Instead, he just talked. As if they were friends.

The power of it made her breath catch. He was better educated, more experienced, more refined, cultured, sophisticated than she could ever dream of being. And it was pretty damned hard to remind herself that she was nowhere near a match for him when her overeager heart just wanted to be with him. Even if it wasn't forever. Even if it was just for tonight.

After one more draft, they slid into their coats, walked past the busy hostess and bartender who still had time to exchange smiles and stepped onto the street. With the sun down, the brisk air had chilled even further. It seeped through her coat and made her shiver.

She slid her arm beneath Nick's and huddled next to him for warmth. "I hope the walk to the hotel isn't a long one."

He laughed. "It's not."

He tucked her hand against his chest and she all but melted. He might not mean anything by what he was doing, might not even notice what he was doing, but he was stealing her breath, changing her idea of Prince Charming and making her wish she could be the kind of woman he'd be interested in.

They walked through the hotel lobby laughing but drifted apart in the elevator.

At her door, the distance between them annoyed her. But what was she going to do? Fix his collar just so she could keep her hands on him?

"Thank you for a really great day."

"Figured I had to do something since you all but called me boring yesterday." He shook his head. "You'd rather read a book than spend another two hours with me?"

A laugh escaped. "I didn't mean it like that."

"Of course, you did." He stepped close, put his hands on her shoulders and slid them up her neck, under her hair. "You have such beautiful hair."

And him touching it sent a rain of glittery awareness from her scalp, down her spine. "Thank you. I always figured my hair was God's way of making it up to me that the first few years of my childhood were awful."

Her voice had come out soft and breathless. She didn't care. She wanted him to hear the shiver of awareness, wanted him to bend down and kiss her. She wanted their mouths to meet, their tongues to twine and the glittery sprinkles to go from a gentle rain to a torrential downpour.

"I had a good time today, too."

She smiled, giving him as much of a hint as she possibly could that he should kiss her—without embarrassing herself or ruining something about this night, this minute.

He closed his eyes and took a breath before pulling his hands away. "Thank you for today."

"You're welcome."

He could probably see the disappointment in her eyes because he'd stepped away from her. "Depending on Danny's schedule, I might see you again tomorrow."

And he didn't want to kiss her tonight if they had another day together. She understood that. Kisses were acknowledgments, invitations or endings. An acknowledgment kiss was a way of saying *I like you*. The invitation kiss said *I like you and this might go somewhere*. The ending kiss said *we had fun, I like you, but this can't go anywhere*.

He could have given her the acknowledgment kiss.

He could have given her the invitation kiss, knowing her inheritance could ease her into his world and, even if Danny was free the next day, they could see each other again on their own—if he wanted to.

The only kiss he couldn't give her was the goodbye kiss. Especially not if they had another day with him entertaining her.

No matter how much he liked her. No matter how much fun they'd had that day. No matter how right they seemed when they were together—

He didn't feel the same way about her as she felt about him. Otherwise, he would have kissed her.

She took the step back this time. She'd already realized that, though he was attracted to her, she probably wasn't his type. She wasn't a sophisticate. She hadn't been top of her class. She hadn't traveled the globe. A smart woman didn't long for a man so different from herself, a man with secrets.

And she knew he had them. She'd guessed it all along. The fact that he wouldn't tell her was a proof of sorts that what she felt pulsing between them wasn't going anywhere.

She slid her key card along the pad. "Good night."

"Good night."

In her room, she shrugged out of her jacket, tossed it on a chair and then peeled off her sweater.

She was so disappointed that her heart felt bruised. That confused her. She had accepted that she wasn't right for him—

So why did she still want that kiss?

One kiss.

It might not be good to wish for a lifetime with a guy whose world was so different than hers. But there was nothing wrong with wanting a kiss.

Was there?

Hell, no.

The guy was great, gorgeous…fun. She was allowed to want a kiss.

Tomorrow night, at her door, he wouldn't have to wonder if he'd see her again, wonder if she'd still be in his charge. No matter what happened, Danny would take over on Saturday morning.

She had one more day to get that kiss.

Then she'd go back to being a client or a customer or nothing, if she wasn't an heir. In which case, she'd be returning to Kansas and she'd never see him again—

Yeah. She wanted that kiss.

CHAPTER EIGHT

THE FOLLOWING MORNING, Leni's cell phone rang while she was eating breakfast. Seeing the ID for Waters, Waters, and Montgomery, her heart sank.

Noooo.

If that was Danny Manelli calling, his trial was over. She wouldn't see Nick that day—maybe not until the estate was settled, when she'd be his client—if she decided to keep her share of the money with him. When things would be all business.

There'd be no kiss.

Taking a breath, she told herself not to jump to conclusions, clicked the screen and said, "Hello."

"Good morning, Leni. This is Danny Manelli. You and I haven't officially met, but I'm the lawyer for the Hinton estate."

Desperate hope quivered through her. Maybe he was calling because he had something to tell her? Maybe he wanted to apologize for not being available all week? She knew there could be nothing between her and Nick, but she'd wanted that one kiss.

"I know who you are. Nick gave your card to my parents. I saw your name. But Nick has also mentioned you."

"My trial is over. This morning we can finally begin the process of me explaining a few things to you. We'll also get the DNA samples."

Her throat closed. Damn it. This *was* it. The end. She'd never see fun Nick again. From here on out he'd be the boring businessman, if she saw him at all.

She worked to keep her voice even as she said, "Okay."

"I can have a limo there in forty-five minutes. Is that enough time to get ready?"

"Sure."

She disconnected the call and immediately went to the spa-like bathroom to shower. She refused to cry. Yes, a kiss would have been wonderful. But maybe that would have made things worse? Whatever his secrets, Nick obviously couldn't give her what she needed. A real relationship. A strong relationship with no guessing, no possibility of rejection. And maybe kissing him would have drawn her in so much she might have tried for more with him when more wasn't possible?

She had to let her fantasy of a kiss go.

This was for the best.

She had herself believing that until she pulled her black dress out of the closet. Pressing it to her face, she closed her eyes. She'd worn this to the Italian restaurant. They'd had wine, great food and she'd met his parents.

She popped open her eyes again. That had been one of the best nights of her life. But she wasn't a simpleton. Lots of things separated her and Nick. Including the fact that she didn't know his secret. No matter how sweet, how funny, how kind he could be…something in his life was terribly wrong. She'd known it even before he'd mentioned it.

In her internships, she'd counseled women to stay away from men with secrets. Bad boys. Wouldn't she be foolish to fall for one herself?

When the elevator doors opened on Danny's office, her suspicions about not seeing Nick were confirmed. The tall, dark-haired man wearing a white shirt, black tie and black suit pants was the only person in the room. As she stepped out of the elevator, he rose from the big desk, extending his hand to shake hers.

"I'm Danny Manelli, Leni. It's a pleasure to meet you."

She slid out of her old, worn coat. "It's nice to finally meet you, too."

After she was seated, Danny called in a lab tech who took three DNA samples. One for his lab and two for random labs. With that out of the way, the attorney went on to explain that she was potentially one of three heirs and the estate was in the process of looking for the other two. That was all she needed to know until they confirmed she was an heir.

"But once you're confirmed, you'll have access to your share of the money."

She thought of her adoptive dad's needs and nodded.

"So, now we wait for DNA to come back before you either go home if you're not an heir, or before I set up some bank accounts for you."

"Okay." She got quiet. With four days to think all of this through and acclimate, it wasn't as overwhelming as it had been on Monday or Tuesday. Refusing her dad's money wouldn't be cutting off her nose to spite her face. Especially since her new plan was to ask for the child support her dad had never paid. But this wasn't yet the time to talk about that.

"Do you have any questions?"

"Not about the estate."

"Good." Danny relaxed against his seat as if satisfied with her reaction. "Do you have something to ask that's not about the estate?"

"Yes." She glanced up at him. "Can I go home?"

Danny shook his head. "That's tricky. Do you want to go home and risk being mobbed?"

"Why would I be mobbed? My parents and I haven't told anyone about this. As far as I can tell no one knows who I am or why I'm here. So, I'm still anonymous."

Danny tossed his pencil to his desk. "It seems iffy to me."

"It doesn't to me, and I want to go home, to talk about

this with my parents. I don't want to sleep in a bed I don't know and run around Times Square looking like a bumpkin when I'm not. In Mannington, Kansas, I'm a normal person. I want to go home."

She also didn't want to miss Nick. To walk down the street and see things that reminded her of him. Once she got home, she'd be fine. She was sure of it. The whole time they were together, she'd been smart enough to keep her wits about her. Going home would be like wiping the slate clean.

Danny studied her for a few seconds. "All right. I'll arrange it."

Nick went to his office on Friday morning and was inundated with messages and meetings. With a little persistence and focus, he was able to clear the things that only he could handle before noon. Which left him with his usual work.

When he returned from lunch, his assistant closed the door to his office, giving him total privacy. He settled himself on his big desk chair intending to buckle down, but with his brain cleared, his thoughts jumped to Leni.

Skimming his hands through her hair the night before was a terrible luxury he couldn't resist. He'd really wanted a kiss, but that was one step too far. He'd known there was a chance Danny would be free today and he wouldn't see Leni again as anything other than a financial manager. Kissing her would only confuse her—especially since he didn't want anything growing between them. Then he'd touched her hair and tripped something inside himself. Not merely a sexual attraction, their connection. The feeling that there was something between them.

But he'd already decided this. She was a wonderful person and his life was dark, bleak. He had regrets that made him moody. Work that kept him sane. He wasn't right for a fun, happy person like Leni. Not even to date.

He forced his mind to the prospectus in front of him, knocking her out of his thoughts, but before ten minutes were up, she had tiptoed into his brain again. By now she would have spoken with Danny. He knew that because Danny had told him she'd be in his office that morning, they'd do a DNA sample and he'd explain some things about the estate to her.

He didn't think she'd be overwhelmed. If anything, she probably felt like she had some answers. So, she was fine.

He took a breath, put his attention on the prospectus and managed to work twenty minutes before he wondered what she was doing that afternoon.

Not that she needed a babysitter. It was just that the city could be intimidating—

No. He'd taken her around and watched her handle herself in some pretty weird situations this week, including meeting his parents.

That made him laugh, then he groaned. He had work to do.

He focused again and he made it until four o'clock when his phone rang. Seeing Danny's name in the caller ID, he jumped on the phone.

"Hey, Danny. How did it go with Leni?"

"Really well. She's very sweet and accommodating and smart, but we have a bigger problem."

Nick sat up. "Problem?"

"I got a call from her mom. Her dad's been taken to the hospital."

His breath stopped. "What?"

"Her dad's in the hospital, but that's not the worst of it. Leni asked if she could go home. After making her promise she'd keep a low profile, I got her a flight to Topeka."

Though his heart skipped a beat out of concern for her, Nick forced himself to relax. "She'll be home where her parents need her."

"Nick, her dad's in real trouble, but her plane has already boarded so her phone is off. She's going to fly to Kansas and go home to an empty house. Her mom said she didn't even have time to leave a note."

"She won't drive home. She'll call her mom when she lands."

"Phones aren't allowed in ICU. But even on the off chance that her mom would be in the cafeteria when Leni calls her, do we want her to find out that her dad's in ICU, maybe dying—in a phone call? When she's at an airport, with no car and no idea how to get to the hospital? We can't do that to her. Someone has to meet her at the airport and tell her this."

Leni was the sweetest, nicest person in the world. Nick absolutely could not let her go through that.

He scrubbed his hand across his mouth. "If I take my jet, I can beat her commercial flight to Topeka."

"I know. That's why I called."

"Then you also know I don't have a minute to spare."

He said that as he gathered work to shove into a briefcase. If he would be in the air for three hours, he could at least get some reading done.

And not obsess about seeing her again, or worse, acknowledge the way his heart lifted with relief that he'd get more time with her.

Leni deplaned, happily saying buh-bye to the flight attendants and heading up the ramp to the gate. She raced to baggage claim, her phone in her hand as she called her mom. Again.

It wasn't a surprise that no one answered at the house, but her mom should answer her cell phone—

Nope. It went straight to voice mail, as if she had it turned off.

After a few minutes, her small bag came down the chute and rolled along the conveyor belt. Before she could grab it, someone behind her did.

She spun around to tell the man he had the wrong suitcase but found herself face-to-face with Nick.

Her heart stumbled. Crazy scenarios filled her head. Like he'd heard she'd left New York without saying goodbye and he couldn't have that.

Not letting herself give into a foolish wish, she said, "What are you doing here?"

He drew a breath. His usually serious eyes were even darker than normal. "Your dad had a problem."

It was the last thing she expected him to say and she fell back a step. "What kind of problem?"

"A major seizure. That's all I know. Your mom called Danny when she couldn't get ahold of you because you'd already boarded your flight. Danny sent me to get to you before you rented a car and drove to your empty house." He nudged his head toward the exit. "I've got a car and we can drive straight to the hospital."

She stared at him. It was the second time in a week he'd given her news that simply couldn't connect to her brain.

But this news filled her eyes with tears. "Is he all right?"

Nick solemnly shook his head. "I don't know. Let's not think the worst. Let's drive to the hospital, talk to your mom and see what's going on."

She nodded and they headed in the direction of his rental. Using GPS, they found the hospital. The information desk told them that her dad was in ICU and her mom was with him.

When they arrived on the floor, her mom came out of his room and fell into Leni's arms.

"It was the worst thing. One minute he was laughing and the next he had zoned out. I thought it was a longer-than-normal small seizure but then he started shaking and he fell to the floor. I called the ambulance immediately."

"You did the right thing," Leni said soothingly. "How is he now? Can I see him?"

"You can see him, but it took so long to get the seizure under control that he's heavily sedated and sleeping. He hasn't even moved in hours."

"I'll feel better if I see him."

Her mom nodded and turned to walk Leni into the ICU, but she noticed Nick and stopped. "I'm sorry. I didn't even see you there. Nick, right?"

"Yes. It's okay, Mrs. Long. I'm fine. I'll find a seat out here. You two go ahead."

Leni's mom nodded and guided Leni back to the ICU. In a hospital bed, with an IV and hooked up to several monitors, her dad looked awful.

Leni's mom put her arm around Leni's shoulders. "They told me that a grand mal seizure like that takes a lot out of a person and with the sedatives he could sleep through the night."

Desperate for confirmation, Leni looked at her mom. "They're sure he's okay?"

She pointed at the monitors. "That's what all those bells and whistles are for. As long as none of these alarms sound, he's fine and he's not having another seizure."

They stayed in the room and watched her dad sleep for at least a half an hour. But sitting in the plastic chair, the stress of the day caught up with Leni. She yawned.

"You should go home."

"No, I'm fine."

"You're not fine. You're tired." Her mother's head tilted. "Didn't you have a meeting with the lawyer today?"

"Yeah. He told me the bare bones about the estate. That everything had to be so hush-hush because there's tons of money and then said he couldn't tell me anything more until they got the results of the DNA test that prove I'm an heir."

"You don't seem to be upset anymore so it must have been good news."

"Yeah, mostly good." She still had the decision about

how much of this money she'd take, if any, but she wouldn't share that with her mom until her dad was home and healthy. "The thing of it is, if I am an heir, I think have to hire my own lawyer because Danny stressed that he's the lawyer for the *estate*. I know that means he's not looking out for me but for the estate.

"He also said my DNA samples had to go to the labs blind. Meaning no one could know they were for the Hinton estate. Even though Waters, Waters and Montgomery put a rush on them, no one could say when the results would be back. So I asked if I could come home." She grimaced. "I'd wanted to surprise you."

"Instead, we surprised you."

Nodding, Leni looked lovingly at her dad. What she wouldn't give for him to wake up and make a corny comment.

"Still, there's no reason for you to be here. He won't be up till morning. Go home. Get some rest."

She glanced at her mom. "Are you staying?"

"Of course. There's a pullout bed I can sleep on."

"Then I'm staying, too."

"And sleep on one of those plastic chairs in the waiting room?"

"I'm too nervous to sleep." Then she remembered Nick was with her and she sighed. "I'll send Nick to a hotel. Better yet, I'll send him back to New York. Do you have your car?"

Her mother nodded. "I followed the ambulance."

"Good. He can take his rental back to the airport and fly home."

She walked out into the waiting room and Nick bounced from his chair. "How is he?"

"Sleeping. Heavily sedated, so they think he won't wake up until morning."

"Is that good or bad?"

"Mom said the doctors told her this kind of seizure takes a lot out of a person and sleep is what he needs."

"Then that's good," he said hopefully.

She drew in a long breath. "I guess."

"Sit down."

She lowered herself to a tall-back, padded double chair big enough for two. As he sat beside her, she said, "Now that I'm here, you can go."

He looked at her incredulously. "Fly back home?"

"Or just get a hotel."

"Are you going to a hotel?"

She gazed at the door separating the ICU from the waiting room. "No. I don't think so. Mom's staying until morning. I will, too."

"Then I will, too. The chairs aren't too bad. We might even be able to get a little sleep."

"I'm too drained to argue." She leaned back, relaxing a bit. "But at three o'clock in the morning when your back aches, you might change your mind about these chairs."

He laughed. She nestled into the seat, getting more comfortable. With only the two of them in the waiting room, it got incredibly quiet when they stopped talking.

Her mind going in a million directions, she steadied her breathing to settle herself. Then she sniffed a laugh. "I remember the day I met my parents."

Nick shifted to face her. "You do?"

"Sure. I was eight by the time they got me as a foster child, so I knew exactly what was going on."

"It must have been hard."

"Being in foster care at all is hard. But it was scary too, going with another set of 'parents.' The Longs explained that they wanted to adopt me, and I was shocked."

"Why? I bet you were a cute little kid."

"Every foster home I went to, I had the ridiculous belief that these people would love me enough that they'd keep me." She met his gaze. "No one had."

"You didn't want to get your hopes up."

"But the Longs were so eager to please me that they were actually funny. After a day or two of my dad bending over backward to make me laugh or feel comfortable, I realized my forever home *was* with them. These people who always made breakfast and liked to play Yahtzee were mine forever. I decided to be the best child ever and I had a wonderful life with them."

"That's a great story."

She smiled. "I know." But the truth of where she was and what was going on washed over her and she squeezed her eyes shut. "I could not handle it if my dad died."

"He's not going to die."

"We don't know that."

Her raw fear came through in her voice and helplessness overwhelmed Nick. He leaned forward, across the double chair, and wrapped his arms around her. "We might not *know* but we can hope."

She nestled into him for comfort and he held her close. He understood her fear of having someone she loved die. He could not bear watching her go through it.

They dozed a bit, woke around three o'clock and she checked on her dad. Ten minutes later, she came back to the waiting room.

"I talked to the nurse. Everything's the same. My mom is sleeping."

Nick stretched. "That's good."

She sat on her chair again. "Yeah." This time when she settled in, she used her jacket for a blanket. Nick did the same with his big gray overcoat. They must have dozed again because the next thing Nick knew, they were cuddled against each other, his big coat covering them both in the cold December air, and light was streaming in through the big windows of the waiting room.

He just held her for a few seconds, savoring the feel of

her. He might not deserve anyone as good as she was, but if he could give her strength or courage, he would. She was a tough person, but she'd already gone through too much in her short life to have her dad die—

He couldn't fathom it. He knew how death hurt, how it ruined things, how it raced like a scourge through a family.

He took a breath to stop his runaway train of thought and when he looked down, she was gazing up at him.

"Hey."

"Hey." He couldn't protect her from this, but he would do the one thing he could do. Support her.

"We should go into Dad's room to see how he is and if my mother survived the night on that rock-hard sofa bed."

He laughed and released her, but his silent vow remained intact. He would do whatever she needed.

They walked into her dad's room to find him sitting up in bed. Her mom sat on the edge of the foot of the bed, grinning from ear to ear.

Leni raced to her father and all but threw herself into him to hug him. "Dad!"

"Hey, Kitten. Better loosen the hold."

She jerked back. "I'm sorry! Did I hurt you?"

"No. But I am a bit stiff and sore." He winced. "Weirdly stiff and sore. When I get home, I'm going to have you research seizures so I can see what this one did to me."

"Or we can just do a few tests."

The doctor standing in the doorway walked into the room. "I'm Doctor Stevens. I'm your neurologist. I've been looking at your chart and see you had a work injury."

Leni's dad nodded. "Two years ago."

"And these seizures are just manifesting now?"

"I started having small seizures a few months ago." Her dad grimaced. "That might not be true. I'm told the smaller seizures could have started long before I noticed them."

The doctor made some notes. "Let's get some tests before we make any assumptions."

He left the room and a few minutes later a nurse appeared. "I hear you're getting some tests this morning."

She looked at his wristband, asking his name, double checking. "Tests will be at least two hours." She smiled at Leni's mom. "Go get some breakfast." Without waiting for an answer, she took Leni's dad away.

Leni said, "We should do that, Mom." She glanced at Nick, silently asking for his help convincing her mom. "I know I'm starving."

"I could use something myself," Nick agreed.

But Leni's mom sighed. "I couldn't eat."

"You should eat."

She shook her head. "No. You guys go. Bring me back a cup of coffee."

Leni argued a few seconds, but eventually gave up. "If you're not going, I'm not going."

Nick said, "How about if I go find coffee and maybe some doughnuts?"

Leni sent him a grateful smile. "That'd be great."

It took him fifteen minutes to find the cafeteria but only a few seconds to realize he didn't know if Leni or her mom wanted cream or sugar for their coffee. He got a cardboard container, put three disposable cups of coffee in the slots then filled the fourth slot with creams and sugar packets. The clerk put six doughnuts into a bag, and he headed back to ICU.

He found Leni and her mom in the waiting area, seated at a round table. He passed out coffee and opened the bag of doughnuts, letting Leni and her mom choose first.

"It's all so frustrating," Leni's mom said before she took a long drink of coffee. "One minute he was fine. The next he was gone. No warning."

"That's what the service dog is for," Leni reminded her mom.

"We can't afford—" Leni's mom paused, smiled at Nick. "Sorry, don't want to air our troubles in front of you."

Nick shook his head. "Hey, no worries here. Every family has troubles."

He thought of his mom, who'd thrown herself into charity work after Joe's death, and his dad, who'd thrown himself into checking up on Nick, making sure he stayed put, making sure he made money for the family—his silent way of reminding Nick he had to make up for losing his brother.

"Besides," Leni said, taking a napkin from the stack by the coffee container, "we might not have anything to worry about financially. Even if all I take is what my father should have paid in child support, it'll be enough for Dad's medical bills."

The conversation died after that and though Nick should have wanted to ask Leni a million questions about potentially walking away from billions of dollars, he felt oddly proud of her. She had principles and guts. But she also wouldn't abandon her father.

A strange feeling tingled through him. The certainty that he should be here collided with the knowledge that being with her wasn't right. What if he gave her the wrong impression? What if he influenced her—

He almost laughed. Leni would call that notion conceited. She'd ask him how he got his head through doors.

Helping her in her time of need would not give her the wrong impression. She was level-headed and smart.

And he could handle himself, too. Yes, they'd gravitated together in the middle of the night. Yes, it had felt wonderful to hold her. But half-asleep, he'd forgotten he needed to keep his distance. Now that he was remembering, he could help her without getting close.

When Joe died, he'd forced himself through some of the worst emotions a person could feel. He could help her while protecting himself.

CHAPTER NINE

WHEN HER FATHER returned from getting his tests, the nurse suggested that they all needed to be rested when the neurologist arrived that evening to discuss the results. Leni agreed and she convinced her mom to come home with her to get a nap.

She rode in the car with her mom and Nick followed them in his rented SUV. They arrived at the Long home an hour later. Though the day was cold, the house was toasty. A batch of sugar cookies, coated in frosting and covered in red and green sprinkles, sat on the counter as if her mom had just finished making them when her dad had his seizure.

Denise removed her coat and hung it on a coatrack by the door. "Let me make lunch."

Leni gaped at her mom. "No!"

"Absolutely not," Nick agreed. "You heard what the nurse said. She wants you rested when you come back."

Denise shook her head. "I'm too keyed up to sleep."

Leni put her hands on her mom's shoulders and turned her in the direction of the bedrooms. "Go lay down anyway."

"I'll tell you what," Nick said. "You get some rest and when you wake up lunch will be ready."

Leni faced him. She might not have seen Nick's life, but she would guess he had a maid or ate out most of the time. He certainly didn't look like a guy who knew how to make lunch. "You're going to cook?"

He laughed. "I'm not a great cook but I make a mean spaghetti."

Denise half smiled. "I like spaghetti."

"Good. Go rest."

As her mom walked away, Leni studied Nick. When he wanted to be, Nick Kourakis was the nicest guy in the world. He'd picked her up at the airport, taken her to see her dad and stayed with her and her mom, not just getting coffee and doughnuts but offering moral support. And she couldn't forget how they'd moved close together in the night, snuggling together for warmth. And how he'd been studying her face when she'd awakened—

But she remembered he also hadn't kissed her at her hotel room door the night he could have. The night it would have been the perfect ending to the perfect day, he'd walked away from the chance to kiss her. And despite the way they'd cuddled together in the chilly waiting room, he'd told her Danny had called him to let him know about her dad and asked him to fly to Kansas to intercept her. His being here was Danny's idea. Gravitating together for warmth meant nothing.

"I'm not sure we have spaghetti in the house."

He shrugged. "Does Mannington have a grocery store?"

"Of course, we have a grocery store!" Realizing she'd protested too much, she winced. "A small one."

"As long as it has spaghetti, I don't care if it's the size of a minivan."

She laughed, as she re-zipped her jacket. He really knew nothing about small towns. But her mom needed support and Nick was offering it.

Because Danny had sent him.

As long as she remembered he was only here because Danny had asked, she wouldn't make too much of him being here and wouldn't get stars in her eyes.

"Let's go."

They headed outside to the SUV. Leni got in the passenger's side and Nick slid behind the steering wheel. Understanding the significance of Danny having sent him, she wouldn't lean too heavily on him. She would accept help caring for her mom. But that was it.

Apparently misinterpreting her silence, he said, "Are you worried about your father?"

Thinking about her dad and everything he might have to go through made her tired suddenly. She put her head back and closed her eyes. "No. I'm coming to terms with everything. Remembering things."

"Remembering things?"

"When he first started having seizures, I looked them up."

He laughed.

She sniffed. "You laugh, but the internet can be very effective. Especially when it says that most seizures aren't life-threatening."

Nick waited a beat then said, "His new, longer ones might be."

"I don't think so."

"You sound pretty sure of yourself."

"Not sure of myself, but sure of my dad. He's like a bull when he wants to be. It was hard seeing him weak when he was injured, but now he's back to being himself or wanting to fight whatever is going on, and to me that's half the battle."

Nick tilted his head. "Maybe… Which way is this store?"

She pointed right. He made the turn. The Moe's Market sign appeared about a block down.

He pulled the SUV into a parking space and they went inside. Leni grabbed a cart. He smiled stupidly.

"What?"

"I've never been in a store like this."

"Like what?"

He pointed toward the seven aisles of food and household products. "You think this is small. To me it's enormous."

"You mustn't have ever been in a superstore." She pushed the cart toward the fresh produce. "How deprived you've been."

He chuckled. "I think you're the first person who's ever called me deprived." He glanced around in awe. "Look at all this food. Especially the Christmas candy."

She studied the bright red, green and gold boxes of chocolates, candy canes, right beside red felt stockings. "Giving candy as a Christmas gift is very big around here." When she saw he was still staring at the boxes, she laughed. "Do you want to take a box or two home?"

He nudged his chin to the right. "Not candy, but maybe a few bags of potato chips."

She chuckled as she stopped by the lettuce. "Are you making a salad?"

"Do you want a salad?"

"We always have salad with spaghetti."

"Good to know."

Her eyes narrowed. He'd said that as if he planned on remembering it. But why? "Are you taking notes?"

"No. I just like knowing things about people for future reference."

His words slid through her. She tried not to conclude that he might be staying in her life—especially with their differences so clearly spelled out as he looked at her town's very ordinary store with wonder in his eyes. But when he was so personal, so helpful, so easy with her, the thought drifted through her brain anyway.

He casually grabbed the handle and pushed the cart up the aisle, toward the tomatoes, while Leni stood frozen by the lettuce. To her, it felt like he belonged with her. Weird as it seemed, they were good together.

She shook her head to clear it. She could *not* think like that. If Danny hadn't called him about her dad, she wouldn't have seen Nick after Thursday night—until it came time for his company to make a pitch for her to keep her Hinton inheritance in his money management firm. She couldn't fool herself into thinking he had feelings for her.

For pity's sake, they'd known each other five days. Six if she counted the current day. She'd stayed at three different foster homes *for months* and each time she'd walked in one day after school to be told to pack her bags and get ready to move on. She could still feel the sting of it. The horrible sense that she wasn't loveable. And she'd vowed she'd never let herself feel that again.

If she could be rejected after months with foster parents whom she believed liked her, six days was nothing.

Especially not a reason to set herself up for a rejection.

Where was her pride?

Where was her spunk?

She wasn't one of those women who fell for a man who wanted nothing to do with her. She was independent and in her own little small-town way, savvy.

Still, she grabbed a few bags of the potato chips he liked and met him at the end of the aisle.

"Any chance there's fresh bread here?"

She motioned to the left. "There's a bakery section down there." Then she laughed. "I'll bet some of your clients would pay to see this. I'll bet your *mom* would pay to see this."

He scowled. "I'm not helpless at doing normal things because I'm wealthy."

"Sure. Sure."

"I'm serious. I was a Navy SEAL. I know how to do things."

Confused about how being a Navy SEAL would help him make spaghetti, she tilted her head as they walked to the bakery section. "Like what?"

"Do you want to hear about the killing-a-man-with-my-bare-hands part or the how-to-survive-just-about-anywhere part?"

She stopped, gaped at him. "Did you actually do those things?"

This time he gaped at her. "What do you think being in the SEALs means? That they let me sit on a couch and watch TV while the other guys went on missions? I passed muster. I was part of missions to capture people and part of missions to rescue people."

She knew her mouth hung open, but she couldn't stop staring at him.

He put his fingers under her chin and closed her mouth. "Seriously."

"I'm sorry but it just all seems impossible." Or did it? He was a big guy. When she'd first seen him, she'd thought he had the comportment of someone in the military. And he'd told her he liked adventure…danger.

"What else did you do?"

"Classified stuff. So, don't ask."

By this time, they had all the makings of salad, spaghetti and meatballs and two jars of sauce. "I'm going to start cooking as soon as we get to your house. I want the meatballs to be ready when your mom gets up and she might only sleep an hour or so."

She nodded casually but she was in awe of him, the way she'd been when they walked out of the Irish pub. The day she'd slid her arm under his and snuggled into him as they returned to her hotel.

After ringing up the sale, Tilly Montgomery, that day's cashier, gave her a thumbs-up when Nick bent down to use his bank card. Leni shook her head, letting her know there was nothing between them.

They left the shopping cart behind after pulling out the bags of groceries. The return trip to her house was quick. In minutes, they had all of Nick's supplies on the counter.

He washed his hands. "Meatballs first. Why don't you go check on your mom while I work?"

She agreed, tiptoed down the hall, opened the door a crack and saw her mom sleeping above the covers on the four-poster bed.

In the kitchen again, she asked, "What can I do to help?"

"I cook alone," he said, his hand up to the wrist in the hamburger meat. She could see he'd added onion and some breadcrumbs.

"Are those going to be good?"

"They're going to be fabulous."

She laughed. "Stop that!"

"Why?" He caught her gaze. "I like to hear your laugh."

Her heart warmed, even though she told herself it wasn't supposed to. The smooth, sophisticated Nick was charming and almost irresistible but shift to normal Nick and they were looking at irresistible in the rearview mirror. She could have melted at his feet.

And she couldn't do that. Even if she didn't have a sick father and decisions to be made about her biological father's estate, Nick did not have those kinds of feelings for her.

She walked around the center island of the kitchen to the sugar cookies her mom had abandoned. Taking note of how many there were, she went to the cabinet to get some containers.

"I used to make people laugh all the time."

His comment came out of nowhere and she leaned around to look at him. "Oh, yeah? I thought you said you weren't funny." She pulled two big containers and one small one from the cabinet and headed back to the island.

He glanced at the cookies, his eyes narrowing as if they confused him. But he said, "I wasn't funny, per se. All my life I'd been something of a daredevil. I bungee jumped before it was wise or popular."

She snorted, as she began stacking cookies in the containers.

"I did tricks on the Jet Ski."

"Like a dog?"

"No. Like a stuntman." He shook his head. "And the reason I was pretty good with the ladies was all about having a good time."

"You're sure it's not your money and good looks?"

"I never flaunted my family's wealth."

"You don't have to. Your clothes tell the story."

"Not when I'm wearing jeans and a hoodie."

"All right. I'll give you that."

They were quiet for a second before he said, "So, you think I'm good-looking?"

Oh, she *wasn't* going to give him *that* one. The man was vain enough. "You don't?"

He chuckled. "You're not one for straight answers today."

She snapped the lid on the final container of sugar cookies. "I'm not going to feed into your vanity."

He said nothing for a second, creating the last meatball and setting it on a tray to take to the stove and the frying pan.

"I guess there was a time when I was vain."

"You guess?"

"It never crossed my mind that being lucky, showing people a good time, having some looks—" he gave her the side-eye and she laughed "—made me vain."

"So, what happened?"

He didn't reply, busy with the frying pan for the meatballs. She would have thought it was a natural pause in the conversation because he was wrapped up in his creation for lunch—which was beginning to look more like dinner—except she remembered other things he'd said. Like he'd had a brother who'd followed him around. She didn't remember seeing anything about a brother in the articles she'd read online about Kourakis Money Management. But when they were skating, he'd mentioned him.

"Was your brother in on all this fun?"

"My brother died."

His words shocked her so much, she stopped dead in her tracks.

Remembering her feelings the day before, when she'd heard about her dad, seeing him sedated, hooked up to equipment that kept him alive, her chest hollowed out, helplessness and fear rose as strong and sharp as they had been in that minute. Nick had experienced all of that and more. His brother had *died.* Her dad was alive and strong. Whatever the doctors told him had to be done, her dad would fight to do it.

Nick's brother was gone.

She watched him roll the meatballs in the pan and place them on a tray to bake. His face wasn't solemn as it had been her first few days in New York, but now that she'd heard more of his past, she could see that he didn't have secrets as much as he held something of himself back.

Whether he was afraid of another loss or simply still tired from the grief, she didn't know. But she did know that asking him about his brother had changed him back into the guy who'd taken her to New York. The businesslike guy who didn't smile.

And maybe he needed a break?

"Tell me more about bungee jumping."

The expression on his face clearly said he knew she'd changed the subject and he was grateful. "It's exhilarating."

"You'd never get me to do something like that!"

"You think?" He laughed. "I never have a problem persuading people to do fun things."

Oh, she'd bet that was true. Gazing into his mischievous brown eyes, she saw the devilish guy who'd probably had his pick of adventures and his pick of women.

She sniffed a laugh. "You're such a con artist."

The last meatball on the tray and the tray in the oven, he faced her. "Not at all."

"Come on."

"I'm serious. I can tell when someone's genuinely afraid to bungee jump or skydive and I don't push."

"Right."

"I don't."

"And you never use that charm of yours on women?"

"I'm always honest. Especially with women."

When he looked at her like that, his dark eyes sincere and seductive, her chest pinched. Her breathing stuttered. Her eyes felt locked to his.

He'd been honest with her.

He put one hand on the counter beside her, so he could lean in, angling their faces inches from each other. "I don't have to be a con artist. Because I'm honest with women, they can be honest with me. Enjoy me while I enjoy them."

Oh...

The chest pinch tightened. She wasn't entirely sure she knew how to breathe.

"It always starts with a kiss…a light one…more like a brush to see if there are sparks."

Now for sure she couldn't breathe. Her entire body poised in anticipation of a kiss—the one she'd longed for— just one kiss to let her know she was more than a woman he'd babysat.

But he didn't move. Their eyes might be locked. He might have her trapped against the kitchen island, but he didn't move.

She stood frozen. Waiting. And feeling like an idiot for waiting. If he wanted to kiss her, he would.

But he didn't.

Just when she could have wiggled away from him, he bent his head and brushed his lips along hers. The sparks that flew could have set the kitchen on fire. Her nerves popped. The blood in her veins woke and exploded. Her lungs collapsed from lack of oxygen.

She expected him to pull away. After all, his demonstration was over. And she'd gotten her kiss. They could walk away now.

He did pull back a millimeter, but he paused. She opened her eyes to find herself inches away from his dark, dark gaze.

Nick knew he should pull back. God help him, he hadn't been able to resist shifting the conversation so far away from Joe that they'd never get back to it again, but the joke had been on him. The second his lips touched hers he knew he wanted more. He'd told himself that he could control any simple want but somehow that want became a need. Sharp and sensual, it wound through his blood, and after only five seconds of gazing into her eyes, he knew she felt it, too.

He leaned in again and took her mouth fully this time.

She put her hands on his cheeks and pushed off the counter, pressing herself against him. Need ricocheted through him. Her soft breasts met his chest, even as her hands kept him right where he was, as if she were afraid he would stop kissing her.

He wouldn't.

He yanked her tightly against him. He swore he could feel the frantic beating of her heart—

When that registered, he froze. He wasn't sure if her heart was beating that hard from excitement, or fear or the craziness of the whole thing, but whichever, it was wrong. She had a sick father and decisions to make about Mark Hinton's estate. She didn't need the likes of him seducing her, then dumping her. Because that's what he did. Moved on.

Leni was the kind of woman a man stayed with—

But he'd never stayed with a woman. Especially not a woman so sweet and sincere that he didn't deserve her.

He would hurt her.

He pulled away slowly, watched her eyes open and smiled at her. He could keep this uncomplicated. The past few years, he'd been a master at holding back his feelings, keeping things simple. He called on that gift.

"And that's just step one."

She licked her lips, held his gaze and whispered, "I'm not sure I'd survive step two."

Part of him yearned to believe he affected her as much as she affected him. To believe that kiss meant something. But he knew himself. He didn't make commitments. He couldn't. No woman should be saddled with a guy so riddled with guilt he buried himself in work.

Plus, like her, he wasn't sure *he'd* survive step two either. They had some powerful chemistry. But all that would do is lure her in and make it hurt worse when he left her.

He eased back, away from her. "Luckily, we don't have to worry about that."

"Yeah. Lucky." She pulled her hand through her shiny hair. "How much longer for the meatballs?"

"I usually give them a half hour."

"Okay."

She looked as confused and befuddled as he felt. They both needed a break. Leaning against the stove, he said, "Why don't you take a nap, too?"

"No. I'm fine."

"I know you are. But I have a few calls I'd like to make while I wait for the meatballs."

The relief on her face would have killed his ego if he hadn't known how much she'd enjoyed that kiss. "Maybe a rest is a good idea."

"We all want you and your mom sharp when you speak to the neurologist."

She pulled her hand through her hair one more time. "Yeah."

"Go."

She nodded and scrambled out of the kitchen.

Nick let his head fall. Holy hell. That kiss tempted him to do things that would only hurt Leni. Tempted him to believe in something he wasn't even sure he understood. When he looked at himself, his life, his regrets, he knew he had to stay away. But, oh, how he wanted her. Just one night.

If he thought he could take one night without hurting her, he would. But he couldn't. He'd seen so many glimpses into her heart that he knew how soft she was. Vulnerable, though she hid it with humor.

He had to get away and stay away.

CHAPTER TEN

LENI'S MOM WOKE about three o'clock. The meatballs were out of the oven and had been marinating in sauce. Nick put the spaghetti in a pot while Leni brought the salad out of the fridge and set the table.

When they sat down to eat, Denise said, "This is nice."

Glad her mom looked awake and normal, Leni reached for the salad bowl. "Did you have a good rest, Mom?"

"Yes." She laughed. "I must have needed it. If you don't mind, after we eat, I'd like to get a shower and go directly to the hospital."

Nick said, "Whatever you want."

Leni winced. "I'm sorry—" She carefully peeked at Nick. They hadn't really made eye contact since that kiss, but she knew why. The touch of their lips had been electric. Something neither one of them had expected. That led to the bigger kiss, the better kiss, the *real* kiss. It was a demonstration gone off the rails and they both knew it. "—I never gave you the chance to shower."

"I didn't bring anything to change into. I had to race to my jet to beat you to Topeka." He laughed. "I'm getting accustomed to wearing the same clothes for two days when I'm around you."

Denise looked horrified. "She's not trouble, is she?"

"No. She's very easy to get along with."

Leni's heart stumbled. Nick wouldn't look at her when he said it, but his ears got red.

He liked her.

He'd said it before, a couple different ways. And that

kiss more or less proved it. But they'd only known each other six days. If she wasn't an heir, she'd be returning to Mannington, never to see Nick Kourakis again.

She'd gotten her kiss. The one kiss she wanted. She should be content with that.

Except—

Nobody had ever kissed her like that, and she was about damned certain no one ever would again. It seemed wrong, absolutely positively wrong, to walk away without at least exploring that.

But he didn't want to. He'd warned her off. Still, he'd warned her off before they'd gotten to know each other. Now that she'd had a few glimpses into his life, she was willing to guess that his aloofness had something to do with the loss of his brother.

What if she could help him through that?

What if fate had brought them together because whatever they felt, it was strong enough to ease him out of his mourning and back to life again?

It was risky.

But she couldn't leave him stranded in the limbo he seemed to live. She'd seen him sullen and quiet in New York and happy here in Mannington. There was a connection. She knew it.

The question was, did she want to risk rejection and heartbreak for a man she'd known six days?

They finished eating. Denise left the kitchen to shower. When she was ready to go, they climbed into Nick's SUV and headed for the hospital.

It was dark when they reached it. The moon rose over the buildings and the trees around it. Christmas decorations at nurses' stations, over doorways and in windows went unnoticed as they walked through the corridors to the ICU.

They waited an hour for the doctor, but Leni gratefully

used the time to tease her dad and watch her mom relax degree by degree the more her dad teased and chatted.

The neurologist arrived with two younger men, one of them rolling a cart with a computer. He explained that there was scarring in her dad's brain, in a very good place. Which sounded like an oxymoron until he said, "It's a good place because we can remove it."

Her mom's eyes widened. "You're saying brain surgery?"

"Yes. And as with any surgery there are risks, especially when we enter the brain. But we're confident that once the scarring that's been building since his injury is removed, his seizures will disappear."

They asked the neurologist a million questions. Nick leaned against the windowsill, listening, adding a comment or question here and there.

Leni took it all in. But in the end, she felt the surgery had too much promise to ignore.

Except she wouldn't want it done in Kansas unless the best neurosurgeon in the world worked there. To hire the best neurosurgeon in the world, she'd need money.

And she might have money. Tons of it. If Mark Hinton was her biological dad.

The weirdness of it almost did her in. She wouldn't have the wonderful father she had now if her biological father had wanted her. But he hadn't wanted her, so she didn't want him either. Except she needed him to save the father she wouldn't have had if he hadn't abandoned her. The logic scrambled her brain.

They stayed with her dad after the neurologist left, discussing pros and cons, but when visiting hours were over, they went home.

Exhausted, talked out, Denise went to her room.

Nick faced Leni. "Are you okay?"

"Yeah, I'm fine. I just have a lot of thinking to do and

need time on the computer researching everything that doctor said."

Nick laughed. "You like to research."

"Smart people do." She took a breath. "I'm going to be looking for the best neurosurgeon on the planet. Someone who's done this surgery hundreds of times."

"Makes sense."

She caught Nick's gaze. "To employ him, I'm going to need tons of money."

He studied her for a second. "You need your inheritance."

"Yes."

"You don't seem very happy about it."

She sucked in a breath. "It's weird. To help the father who raised me, I have to accept the help of the man who abandoned me."

"Did you ever stop to think that this would be what Mark would want to do?"

She sniffed a laugh. "What?"

"Mark wasn't a bad guy. He was an overworked, very paranoid, fearful guy. He didn't abandon you as much as he counted on your mom to take care of you. I'll bet he hadn't even known your mother was in trouble."

"He never checked on us."

"He barely got himself to work some days. The only time he was happy and felt safe was fishing in the middle of the ocean. Hundreds of thousands of people depended on him for jobs. He knew the pressure of that."

"So much that he didn't have time for one little girl."

"Don't think of it like that. Think of the stress, the pressure."

She pressed her lips together.

"Leni, your father had very few happy days. You love life. I'll bet after your experience in foster care, it wasn't easy for you to get to that place emotionally. But the Longs helped you. They made you the person you are today.

Don't throw away your happiness over this. Take a deep breath, be glad for the money to save your father and forgive Mark. Otherwise this will ruin your life."

There was so much wisdom in what Nick said that she let it sink in. Especially since she almost felt herself forgiving Mark Hinton for abandoning her. Not only had his stepping aside resulted in her having the best parents in the world, but also his gift of money would save her dad. How could she stay angry with him after that?

A strange warmth filled her soul, a lightness, as if she'd done the right thing.

"I get it."

"It's difficult that your dad has to have the surgery, but I don't think you'll be sorry you're opting into the estate."

"I hope you're right."

"I am. Don't use my screwed-up life to judge what it's like to be wealthy. I had everything at my disposal as a child and I had choices about things like where I went to school, joining the Navy, even jet-setting after leaving the SEALs. I had the most amazing life."

"That's true."

"Had it not been for my brother dying, my life would have stayed very, very good and I'd probably be on a beach somewhere now."

She searched his eyes. He was telling her everything would turn out okay and she appreciated that. But there was more, a bigger story in his eyes, sadness over his brother's death. She simply didn't know how to get to it. Or even if she should try.

"You wouldn't have come home for Christmas?"

"I would have been home Christmas morning. I always made it in time for gift exchange with my family. But the big picture is I had a life I loved. I worked, just not in a conventional way. I wouldn't have been stuck in my office all day or doing Danny's bidding when he couldn't get out of a trial."

"Then you wouldn't have met me."

He looked away. "Yes, and how blissful it would have been not to know that I was a vain guy who lied to his parents."

She laughed. Every time the conversation became about him, he deflected. But she understood that. It was part of why she couldn't get to his sadness. He didn't want her to.

Before she could say anything, he pushed away from the counter. "Anyhow, if you don't need me, I'm going to leave you to your research. I've got some work I have to do, too."

"Okay. Give me a second to fix up the guest room."

He caught her arm as she turned to scamper away. "I said that wrong. I'm going back to the airport to hop in my jet, and work through the flight home."

"Oh."

Her brain stalled. Why would he want to leave? It was late. He was clearly tired. He shouldn't drive an hour to an airstrip and spend even more hours in the air before he got home. Of course, he did have a bedroom in his jet. And he'd given a week of his busy life to entertain her. He really could be behind in his work.

She opted to stay positive. He was a busy guy. He had to get back to his job. The man had kissed her like a guy so smitten he couldn't help himself. And he'd taken the time to help her see she needed to forgive Mark Hinton. Whatever was between them, it was growing.

His leaving had nothing to do with her and she would respect his choice.

"I can't thank you enough for your help."

"It was my pleasure. But it's time for me to get home."

"Okay. Sounds good."

Within minutes he was leaving, outside her parents' house, ready to climb into his rented SUV. She stood beside the vehicle door, handing him a plastic container of homemade Christmas cookies, not quite sure what to say or do.

In her heart of hearts, she hoped he'd catch her shoulders and lean down to kiss her goodbye. No preliminary kidding around this time. She wanted the invitation kiss. The one that said *I like you. There might be something here worth exploring.*

She wanted *that* kiss.

But he didn't catch her shoulders and lean in to touch his lips to hers. He looked at the container of cookies with the weirdest expression, as if no one had ever done anything nice for him, his lips kicking into a crooked smile.

"Are these the iced sugar cookies I saw on the counter?"

She stuffed her cold hands into the pockets of her old coat. "Yep."

"They looked wonderful."

"I saw you eyeing them."

He shook his head. "You don't miss anything."

She said, "No. I don't," hoping he realized she was telling him that she knew what was going on between them wasn't simple or easy. She was a small-town girl with the most basic of educations. He'd traveled the world, served in the military, had been raised in luxury. It probably wasn't wise for them to start a romance.

But after that kiss, how could they not?

He opened the SUV door, tucked the cookies on the passenger seat and turned to her.

"I probably won't see you until after Danny gets the DNA results."

Hope tingled through her. He could have easily gotten into the vehicle when he put the cookies inside. Instead here he was, only a few inches away from her. Close enough to touch. Close enough for him to kiss her.

"I need to be here anyway."

"Okay." He paused a few seconds, gave her a weak

smile, then slid behind the steering wheel. "See you in a couple of days."

He wasn't going to kiss her. He wasn't going to go in for seconds, after that amazing kiss?

He'd said the kiss had been a demonstration, and the first part might have been. But the second part had been real. She *knew* it.

She took a step back. "Yeah. See you then."

He closed the door and drove off. She stood shivering in the driveway, watching his taillights disappear in the darkness, vibrating with feelings she didn't understand. It had been the best two days and the worst two days. She'd forgiven her biological father because like it or not, his money would save her adoptive father. A father she loved.

But something else had happened. With that kiss, Nick admitted that he liked her, and driving away as he had, he'd admitted he wasn't going to do anything about it.

Rejection spiked. Sharp, miserable, edged with darkness.

She closed her eyes, telling herself not to be foolish. Today was Saturday. She'd met Nick the Monday before. They'd only known each other six days. She was foolish to be upset or even concerned that he hadn't kissed her again.

She took a breath, fighting the feeling of not being good enough, knowing why her mind had gone in that direction. She might have forgiven Mark Hinton for not wanting her, but that didn't mean her biological parents' rejections hadn't left a mark.

She needed to get over that, too. But a sense of unworthiness ran deep, and she had no idea how to let it go. Wash it away. Send it off into the universe.

But she would figure it out. She had to. She'd accepted her dad's money. She'd felt that lightness in her soul. Moving on was the right thing to do.

Now she just had to figure out how.

* * *

Her father came home from the hospital the next morning. He'd gotten some new meds and appeared to be totally back to being himself. After twenty-four hours of Leni and her mother watching him like two hawks, she'd returned to work at the diner. She *might* be inheriting tons of money, but they didn't have it now and they had bills to pay. And there was also the chance she wasn't an heir. Everyone was so sure Mark Hinton was her father. She had niggling doubts.

After the lunch rush and before the dinner rush, George went to the back steps to smoke and Leni found herself alone in the diner again. As she had been the day Nick arrived.

Longing swept through her. She let herself feel it but didn't get carried away. The confusion and emotions of potentially inheriting billions of dollars and her dad's illness could have made her crazy. She knew to control her feelings, her reactions. She'd done it before, when in foster care. She'd call on that discipline again.

The pocket of her apron buzzed, and she pulled out her cell phone. Seeing Waters, Waters and Montgomery in the caller ID, she had to sit.

This was it.

"Hello, Danny."

"And hello to you, Miss Leni Long…confirmed child of Mark Hinton."

Her breathing stopped. "Mark Hinton really was my dad?"

"Three DNA samples don't lie."

"Oh, my gosh." The truth of it rattled through her, not finding footing because she wasn't sure what it all meant. How her life would change. But Danny was right. DNA didn't lie. And though she hadn't been a hundred percent certain she wanted Mark Hinton to be her dad, she had made her peace with that, too.

Something *Nick* had encouraged *her* to do.

She told herself to stop thinking about him. They were good together. Sort of. At least she thought so. But right now, she had more important things to figure out.

Danny's voice brought her back to the present. "So, I'll need you in New York again to run through a few things. The estate can't be distributed until all the heirs are found, but with this proof you have access to your share of the money."

Meaning, she could get her dad the best neurosurgeon in the world.

Her heart sped up. That was her priority.

"When do you want me?"

"Tomorrow?"

"So, I'd fly out today?"

"Or I can arrange for Nick to come and get you."

No. The time for depending on Nick was over. She wanted to be smart Leni. The foster child who'd adapted to her surroundings, studied, put herself through university. So, he could stop thinking of her as a responsibility and start seeing her as…a friend, for now. The other stuff, the romantic stuff, would blossom if it was meant to be. But she wouldn't push or even think about it. It was time to put her best foot forward.

"I can fly commercial." She laughed. "Actually, I'll make my own reservations."

Danny said, "Okay. The estate will reimburse you. Since you wouldn't get here until this evening flying today, make the arrangements for early tomorrow morning and reservations at the hotel where you'd been staying. When you get to New York, you can come right to the office and we can get down to business."

"Thanks."

"You're welcome. And, Leni." He paused. "Congratulations. Your life is about to change in the best possible ways."

She said, "Thanks," but the doubts she'd been fighting all along flooded her brain again. She was a blue-collar woman entering a diamond-necklace world. And maybe that was another thing she needed to change? Nick only knew her as needy Leni. In her worn coat and scruffy jeans. With the sick dad.

But she wasn't needy anymore. She had billions of dollars at her disposal. She could start looking for a neurosurgeon and maybe get some new clothes, so she didn't always feel out of place.

It was time to step into her new life.

When they disconnected the call, she searched online for her hotel, called the number and made reservations. When that part of the call was complete, she asked for the concierge and within seconds he said, "Can I help you?"

"Yes. You probably don't remember me, but I stayed at your hotel last week." She winced at how stupid she sounded and pulled in a breath. "I'm going to be there again this week. Nick Kourakis told me that if I needed anything or needed to *find* anything in New York, you were the one to ask."

"Absolutely. How can I assist you?"

"I need some clothes. Really *nice* clothes. Good clothes. Clothes that scream *money.*"

He laughed and gave her the names of three shops near the hotel, eased her fears about looking like a grandma when one of them was the boutique Nick had suggested, and wished her a good day.

She immediately looked up the three stores and smiled. He really did know his job. All three offered private consultations and Leni made appointments for the following afternoon. She wasn't going to play this by ear. Her life was changing, and she couldn't pretend it wasn't.

She would more than step into her world. She would take control.

CHAPTER ELEVEN

LENI HAD BOOKED the earliest morning flight, but with the time difference she arrived in New York City after eleven o'clock. She got to Danny's building around noon, and she had her appointment at the first shop at two. She didn't have to rush.

She accepted the three no-limit credit cards Danny gave her and the checkbook with accompanying bank card. He explained there were three heirs, but there was wording in the will that might result in her only getting one quarter rather than one third of her dad's estate—still, billions of dollars.

She told him she couldn't understand why anybody would fight about that and Danny had laughed. Then he slid into a conversation about security. She would be getting a limo with a driver.

That part concerned her, but she kept it to herself. She was an heir now. There would be plenty of things about this life that would be different. She had decided not merely to accept that but to take control. Today was the day all that started.

With her briefing complete, she took off for her appointments at the stores. Her new driver—parked at the building entrance and waiting for her—drove to the address Leni gave him, a small shop on an out-of-the-way street.

She pushed open the etched-glass door and walked into a sea of merchandise showcased in a room with black woodwork, white walls, upside-down fishbowl light fixtures and bronze tin ceilings.

Leni held back a *Wow*.

"Can I help you?"

"Yes. I have an appointment at two."

The clerk smiled and pointed to a set of steps that had been painted black. "Upstairs. Third floor. With Iris."

On her way to find Iris, she noticed the first floor was filled with bohemian clothes. Things she could see herself wearing in her downtime. The second floor was filled with what she considered work clothes. Pants, soft sweaters, pencil skirts, shiny blouses and dresses. All of them beautiful.

She didn't see a person until she reached the top of the third flight of stairs. Two women and a man stood in a semicircle in front of three full-length mirrors. Except for two chairs near the mirrors, the room was empty.

"Elenore?" Dressed in a black sheath and pearls, the older woman walked over and took her hands before kissing both of her cheeks.

"You must be Iris." Leni pulled back, ignoring the cheek kisses which she thought a bit much, and examining the black sheath and pearls. Lovely and obviously expensive, but not quite the image she wanted to project.

"It's such a pleasure to have you at our store."

Okay. She knew the woman had no idea she was one of the Hinton heirs but apparently making an appointment came with certain assumptions. "I'm glad to be here."

"What are you looking for?" Iris asked. "Casual, business or formal?"

Leni said, "All of them."

Iris smiled and faced the young man and thirty-something woman in jeans standing next to her. "Bill, Mandy, let's start with casual clothes and work our way to formal."

When Iris and her team left, Leni glanced around the room. Though another person might consider a shopping trip oodles of fun, she was on a mission. She had to look like she belonged in her new world. And, yeah, buying a ton of clothes probably was going to be fun.

A few minutes later, Iris and her employees each brought an armload of jeans, shirts and sweaters. Leni instantly fell in love with a white silk blouse and pumpkin-colored wool pants, a green sweater and artificially aged jeans, with high-heel ankle booties. Still, not everything they brought was her style, so she went out to the floor and waded through racks of jeans and pants, dresses, skirts and blouses and matching jewelry.

That's when the joy of it hit her. She could have anything she wanted. It was both exciting and humbling, and in some ways confusing.

But Iris was always beside her, talking about fit and tailoring. Bill and Mandy went ahead of her, pulling things they recommended. Now that they had seen a bit of her taste in clothes, Bill had an eye for casual wear that screamed big money while still being comfortable and Mandy knew the colors Leni looked best in.

Just when she thought she was done and wouldn't even have to go to the other two stores, Iris said, "Now, let's talk formal wear."

"I don't plan on going anywhere formal."

Iris chuckled. "This is New York City, darling. You won't be going out to dinner on a Friday in anything less than a cocktail dress. And if you're staying through the holiday, you'll also be going to a Christmas ball or two."

Mandy scrambled over, carrying two gowns. One green velvet, which Leni knew would make her eyes look amazing. The other a red flowing thing that caused Leni's heart to chug to a stop. Bill brought an armload of shorter dresses, half of which sparkled.

She remembered Nick's mom mentioning a Christmas ball and a Christmas party at the children's ward for the hospital. She'd said she'd attend, so if she got an official invitation, she intended to be ready.

She tried on the shorter dresses and the green velvet, saving the red one for last. Everything worked. The soft, supple fabrics cruised along her skin like a lover's caress. Bill and Mandy pinned the waistlines of three of the cocktail dresses to perfect their fit.

Iris stood on the sidelines approving everything.

When they were done and Leni was back in her old jeans and worn T-shirt, she handed Iris one of the no-limit credit cards.

Though Leni waited nervously, the card was approved in seconds. Iris returned it to her, and she glanced at it. It didn't look any different than her own Mastercard, but it worked a hundred times better.

Walking to her limo, she cancelled her other two appointments and had her driver take her to the hotel where she'd reserved a suite, the same one where she'd stayed on her last trip. Less than an hour later, her purchases began arriving with bellboy after bellboy rolling carts of bags and boxes into her room.

She wanted to laugh—who wouldn't?—but the reality of having so much stuff stopped her cold. First off, she thought about buying luggage, so she could take it all home—then she realized she probably wouldn't wear a lot of these clothes in Mannington. Maybe the jeans. And the really cute boots. But most of this "stuff" she would wear in only New York. Danny had mentioned her serving on the board of one or more of her dad's companies and she liked the idea.

Really liked it.

She would see firsthand how businesses were run, have a part in the decision making, make sure employees were paid decently and no one harassed an injured employee the way her dad had been harassed.

She felt the reality of her new life clicking in. She

wasn't just a woman who was getting billions of dollars. She had responsibilities. Choices. Options. Power.

And she'd probably have to be in New York as much as she was in Mannington. So maybe she needed to get a condo? She couldn't move all these fabulous clothes to and from Mannington. It simply made more sense to have a home here. She'd spent her teen years thinking she'd be a social worker in Topeka, but with the newly inherited fortune, she could see herself doing so much more for her community.

That's when she knew she needed to sit, breathe. She called room service for tea and curled up on the red sofa, letting everything sink in, going over her quick decisions, making sure she wasn't reacting when she should be planning.

Feeling out of sorts, Nick left work early. Today had been the day when Leni met with Danny to discuss specifics. He told himself he didn't care. He told himself the Hinton money wasn't any of his business until the estate was settled and the time came to discuss where the heirs would put their money.

Entering his condo, he ignored the silence that greeted him, but after having been with chatty Leni for days, through some tough things, but also some fun things like skating and the Irish pub, the quiet of his home was deafening.

He tossed his briefcase to the sofa. But as he turned, he saw the little plastic container of cookies on his dining room table.

Christmas cookies. Homemade. Not cookies his mom had ordered from the exclusive bakery in Long Island. Not cookies made by her friend who'd studied pastry in Paris.

Just plain, iced sugar cookies with sprinkles.

He walked over, opened the container and took a

cookie. He bit into it and the soft, buttery confection melted in his mouth.

He groaned. He couldn't remember ever eating a cookie this good. He also couldn't remember the last time anybody had done something so simple, so thoughtful. Six cookies in a little plastic container had almost done him in. As she'd put it into his hand, he'd nearly melted.

He'd nearly kissed her again.

Which was wrong.

He shook his head, went into his bedroom to change into jeans and went to his kitchen to order takeout—

But he remembered that Leni had been through a difficult weekend with her dad in the hospital. Monday, Danny had called and told her she was an heir. This morning she'd flown to New York and had a meeting with Danny.

Her head was probably spinning.

He'd bet it was.

And she had no one in New York to talk to.

Concern for her filled him. But as much as he wanted to help her, he couldn't really ask her to dinner. That was too date-like.

He looked at the cookies. So full of Christmas cheer. The spirit of it filled him. Peace on earth. Being kind to each other. Helping each other—

He slid his phone from his jeans pocket. He hit her number in the contacts section and within seconds her phone was ringing.

"Hey."

Sounding totally surprised, she said, "Hey. What's up?"

"I know you had a busy day with Danny but—" Feeling like a sixteen-year-old asking for a date, he had to remind himself that he was calling for her. He wanted to hear how her dad was, but he also knew she was probably overwhelmed about the estate and would need to talk. If he had to stretch a truth to find a way to give her that time, so be it.

"I was thinking about going Christmas shopping tonight. For my mom," he clarified, to make the story work.
"Since you made fun of the boutique, I thought maybe
you'd like to come with me and help me find a more hip
store."

"I'd love to."

"Good. I'll be at your hotel in ten minutes. Is that
enough time?"

"Sure."

"And then maybe we could get a bite."

"Okay."

"Okay. My limo will be outside your hotel in ten."

He hung up feeling better. Infinitely better. But only
because he liked her enough that he wanted to be sure she
was okay. Not because it was a date, or anything close. He
just wanted to be sure she had someone to talk to.

Leni disconnected the call and stared at the phone, but only
for a few seconds. Nick's offer might have confused her
but she didn't have time to wonder if this was a date. She
had to change into one of her new pairs of jeans, a cashmere sweater and the hottest-of-hot black leather jacket.

Riding down the elevator to the lobby, she told herself
this wasn't anything special. He needed help shopping
and, after today, she felt like a shopping pro. She was a
perfect choice to help him.

It was all good.

She stepped out of the lobby onto the street and into
the falling snow. Though Nick stood by the door of his
limo, she tipped her face up, let herself enjoy the soft wet
snow and Christmas spirit that shuffled through the air
around her. Christmas in New York City might feel different than at home—shinier and more expensive—but it
was still Christmas.

As she reached the door, she said, "Hey! Thanks for

asking me to help you shop. The hotel really was starting to close in on me."

"You're welcome." He winced. "But I had an ulterior motive. And more than help with finding my mom a Christmas gift. I wanted to hear about your dad."

She slid into the limo and Nick followed her. "He's fine. Really good. New meds are keeping everything stable, but after a few hours of hunting for the world's best neurosurgeon, I realized I was out of my league and contacted his neurologist. He and I are now on a quest for the best neurosurgeon on the planet."

Nick sighed. "That's really good."

"It is. So, what are you thinking about getting your mom?"

He shook his head. "No idea. I just know that you dissing my favorite shop sent a shot of panic through me. If my mother hasn't liked my gifts all these years, I've failed."

She laughed as the limo pulled out into traffic. "Failed?"

"My brother used to buy the best gifts."

Her heart stilled at his mention of his brother, but she casually said, "Oh, yeah?"

"Yes. He'd find the cashmere sweater in that year's 'hot' color, when I didn't even know years had hot colors."

"Oh, they do. One year it's pink. The next year it's olive."

He peeked at her. "And you know this?"

"Of course, I know this. I might not live in New York, but I don't live under a rock." She pulled out her phone, searched *hot color*. "And speaking of living under rocks. I'm thinking I might need a place in New York."

His eyebrows rose. "Really."

"Yeah. I bought a bunch of clothes today." She stopped long enough to roll her eyes. "I mean a *bunch*. And I realized I wouldn't wear half of them in Mannington, and would only need them for board meetings for Mark Hinton's…" She paused and amended that to, "my dad's companies."

* * *

Nick heard the change in her voice. She really had begun to accept that Mark Hinton was her dad.

When he said, "I'm glad," he wasn't just talking about being glad that she'd be attending board meetings. He was glad she seemed to be adjusting to who she really was.

He'd also noticed the black leather jacket, the trendy jeans, the new boots and her own cashmere sweater. "You look good."

She looked *great*. She looked like someone stepping into her future, becoming herself.

"Thanks. Anyway, when I realized I shouldn't lug all this stuff to Mannington where I probably wouldn't wear it anyway, I thought about getting my own place."

She truly was moving into her role. Nick couldn't have been any prouder and he knew Mark would have been, too.

"I think it's a good idea."

"Yes. I'm sure Mark had a condo here, but Danny reminded me we don't want to use my dad's condos or houses or jets and alert the media that I've been found, so I thought, hey, I have billions of dollars at my disposal. I don't need to stay in a hotel."

He smiled, warmth filling him. She was so cute and so smart. "No. You don't."

"So, tomorrow I may call a real estate agent and start looking."

"I know a person or two. I could make a call. I'll tell them you are a friend from the Midwest and ask for discretion."

She peeked over at him. "And you'll get it?"

Making eye contact took the warmth that always filled him when she was around and turned it to the kind of heat that would be nothing but trouble for them. So, he glanced away. "The price you'll pay for a condo will result in a hefty commission. Remember how I told you about not kissing and telling?"

She nodded, but her face turned red. Reminding her of the kiss had been a bad idea. Not just for her. She might be embarrassed but the heat already in his system turned to molten lava.

He sucked in a quiet breath, hoping she didn't notice. "Well, it works the same for real estate agents. Wealthy people need discretion. Real estate agents provide it to get their return business. And their friends' business. Discretion is like currency to them."

She nodded and pulled her phone from her jacket pocket. "I got my things today from this great boutique. And they had a top that I'm positive your mother would like." She hit her screen a few times, then displayed the address.

Glad she got both their minds off that kiss, Nick texted it to his driver and in five minutes they were standing in front of the etched-glass door.

Snow fell around them. Leni's face glowed in the light of a streetlamp as they walked to the door. "I might get something for my mom, too."

"I thought you said this wasn't a mom store."

"It isn't." She led the way to the door. "My mom's very youthful. Your mom's a trendsetter."

He laughed, especially when he realized there was a difference. Leni really was rubbing off on him.

They walked into the shop and Nick noticed Christmas music playing softly in the background. Tinsel edged the front counter. A ring of poinsettias almost hid the cash register.

"Leni! You're back!"

"Here to Christmas shop, Mandy," Leni happily said.

Nick wasn't surprised Leni remembered the clerk's name or that the clerk remembered Leni's. She'd probably spent a hundred thousand dollars that afternoon.

"Looking for a sweater for my mom and something like a kimono for his."

Nick frowned. "Kimono?"

"Something long and luxurious. Almost a duster," Leni clarified, talking to the clerk. "I want her to be able to wear it with jeans when she's shopping and look like queen of the world."

An older woman came down the stairs talking. "I have just the thing."

"Hey, Iris!"

"Hey, Leni. Who's your friend?"

"Nick. His mom is New York high society. I want to put her in an outfit that will make her feel funky and cool."

Iris laughed. "For when she lunches with her friends, so she looks like the hip one?"

"Exactly."

Nick had no idea what a kimono was, but apparently it was a good choice because Leni didn't merely gasp when Iris led them to one in the back, she touched it reverently.

"Silk," Iris said.

"It's perfect."

Nick studied it. Pale blue like his mom's eyes, it didn't look like something she might wear, but it did look like something Joe would have bought her.

"I like it," he ventured uncertainly.

Iris said, "Are you sure?"

"I've just never bought my mother something that I haven't already seen her in."

"You mean something similar?" Leni said.

"Yes."

Sliding her hand beneath his arm and nestling against him, she laughed. "Well, she will love this."

After a quick squeeze, Leni headed for three rows of sweaters and chose four for her mother. Nick stood behind her, not quite uncomfortable because shopping with a purpose almost felt okay.

Actually, watching Leni ponder sweaters for her mom gave him a boost. He knew Denise would love them, but he also knew her mom needed them. Seeing the joy on Leni's face at being able to buy things for her mother filled him with that indescribable feeling again. The feeling he had when she savored the wine. The feeling he had when she gave him Christmas cookies.

When they stepped out into the street, into falling snow with Christmas lights and tinsel billowing in the wind, he recognized it. This was the feeling he'd had as a child, the breathless wish for a toy or a video game he wasn't even sure his parents knew existed, the childish wonder of a holiday made for parties and presents. A day his dad didn't work or talk about work. His mom beamed over roast turkey and pie. And he and his brother couldn't sleep for anticipation.

And he didn't want to lose it.

He wanted this feeling to last forever.

If Leni was the reason why he felt it, he wasn't letting her go yet.

"How about another trip to the Irish pub?"

Her eyes widened. "Absolutely."

He opened the limo door for her and she slid inside. In a few minutes, they were climbing out again and heading for the little bar.

Celtic Christmas music poured out as he yanked on the door to let her enter first. In the few days that had passed, the place had been decked out with lights and tinsel.

"Now it really looks like the bar back home."

He laughed as the hostess said, "Good evening."

"Good evening. There are just two of us."

She smiled. "Right this way."

They walked back to the same table they'd had the last time they were there, and Nick wondered if it was a coincidence or if she remembered them.

He didn't say anything as they sat, but he recalled that day after skating. How much fun they'd had. How Leni had cuddled against him in the cold on the walk back to her hotel.

Feelings buffeted him, nudging him to take some time to think this through, but he ignored them in favor of keeping the wonderful mood they'd created.

He made her laugh over hamburgers and fries and encouraged her to have a third draft when she would have stopped at two.

"Today's the day your world changed. In a way, we're celebrating."

"I certainly spent enough money."

He smiled. "And you don't even have to care." He called for the waitress to bring the check. He gave her a credit card and she returned it with the receipt.

After he'd signed, he and Leni rose and slid into their coats. But out on the street, when his limo driver opened their door, he hesitated.

"Feel like walking?"

Her head tilted and she smiled, as if she remembered the last time they'd made this walk. "Yeah." She tucked her arm under his as he signaled for the driver that they would be walking.

Their feet made imprints in the snow that had fallen while they ate. Cold air filled his nostrils and horns beeped around them, but somehow it added to the magic. Everyone seemed to be laughing and chatting, carrying packages, talking about holiday plans.

Two blocks never went by so quickly.

They stomped the snow off their shoes and entered the lobby of her hotel. Though he considered letting her walk to her room herself, he got a weird, uncomfortable feeling about the day.

She, Danny, Mary Catherine, Jace and Nick himself should be the only five people who knew she was an heir. But administrative assistants and clerks saw papers all the time. People passing office doors heard things they shouldn't.

Leni was a small, soft, big-eyed girl from the Midwest, and though he was sure she could care for herself in normal situations, nothing about this situation was normal.

He motioned to the elevator and she headed there. An older couple joined them on the ride to her floor, so they didn't say anything. But as they ambled to her suite door, he remembered walking into the diner the first time he'd seen her. The elf suit. Their small talk. That wash of instant connection.

If he let himself, he could drift back to those few minutes. He could see her smile. He could feel his heart tumble when their eyes met.

Need spiked, sharp and sweet, along with something simple and reverent. He had never felt like that. And the pull of it was so strong his fingers tingled with the need to touch her, to tell her he was crazy about her—

But that wasn't right. She was on the brink of a whole new life. And even if she wasn't, she deserved so much more than him. Somebody so much better. Somebody special.

Still, he didn't even try to stop himself when instinct had him bending to brush his lips across hers. Quickly. Just a taste. He couldn't have her, but one little goodnight kiss didn't hurt.

She blinked at him.

He could almost hear her saying *Wow*, even though she didn't utter a word. He saw the intensity in her eyes and wished for thirty seconds he was a better man.

But he wasn't.

He knew who he was.

Not a liar. Not really a con man. Just somebody with the gift of persuasion. He could kiss her a million times, maybe even get her into bed. He could give her the best Christmas she'd ever had.

And then what?

What happened when she discovered he was responsible for his brother's death? That he wasn't lily white or even dingy gray? His soul was black from narcissism and selfishness that had led to losing his best friend.

Then what?

He'd become who he was: a solitary, stoic workaholic because he didn't want to hurt anybody else, but he also didn't care to feel the pain of that kind of rejection.

He would not take that risk.

CHAPTER TWELVE

LENI WAS ON her way to Danny's office the next morning to talk about when and how she'd get on the boards of some of her dad's companies, when her phone buzzed. Looking at the caller ID, she saw Nick's name and her heart perked up. He'd kissed her again the night before. Not the deep, romantic kiss he'd given her in her mother's kitchen. But a nice, normal goodnight kiss.

In some ways, that one had been more powerful. Filled with the happiness of their evening together, that kiss and been exactly what it should have been. Soft and sweet.

Still, she wasn't going to be a lovesick puppy about this. She would be cool and sophisticated. She answered her phone with a very casual, "Hey, Nick."

"Hey. I got a call from my mom this morning. She reminded me about the party in the children's ward that was supposed to be Friday afternoon. It's been moved up to tomorrow because we're in for a blizzard on Friday. I know it's short notice, but she'd love for you to be there."

She'd love, not *he'd* love.

She closed her eyes, telling herself it was idiotic to make that kind of distinction. The point was, they were getting more time together. More time to get to know each other. More time to figure out what was happening between them.

Striving to sound normal, she said, "Okay. I can be there. I only have a meeting with Danny, then my afternoon is free."

"Have your driver bring you to the hospital around

one-thirty. Party starts at two o'clock, but if you get there a little early, I can show you around."

Her pulse kicked up. Just as he'd told her to come outside to his limo the day before, didn't come up to her hotel room to pick her up, he wasn't going to fetch her for the party either.

As if he were deliberately making the distinction that this wasn't a date.

She stopped that thought, too. They'd never get anywhere if she was so picky about everything. For all she knew, this was how dates happened in New York. Or maybe among rich people. Because everybody had a limo, nobody had to fetch anybody.

"Okay."

"Okay."

She hung up the phone, shaking her head, reminding herself she couldn't nitpick Nick's behavior. She had to roll with at least some things.

With the fundraiser only a day away, she could have gone shopping. But that seemed weird when she'd spent oodles of money the day before. Surely something in the eight tons of clothes she'd bought would be good enough.

In her suite, after her meeting with Danny, she looked up more information about the fundraiser and tons of articles popped onto her screen. She was only interested in seeing how people dressed, but then she saw a picture taken six years before—further back than she'd gone in her search of Kourakis Money Management the day she'd met Nick. The photo was of Nick and his parents and another man. The caption gave their names and the other man was Joe Kourakis.

His brother.

She stared at the picture. Nick looked like a kid. A bad kid. The kind of kid who stole cars for fun and broke the hearts of starry-eyed socialites. His brother didn't look old enough to be out of high school, but he was listed as CEO of Kourakis Money Management. Their mom's head was tilted back as she laughed. Even their dad was smiling.

She squeezed her eyes shut, thinking about how that little family had changed, reminded again that something about Nick's brother's death haunted him.

The temptation rose to ask him about his brother when she saw him the next day, but she couldn't bring up something so emotional at a public event and she also thought it wasn't right to ask. Nick should tell her. She should let him broach the subject.

Forcing her mind off that, she reminded herself she needed to figure out what to wear the next day. She shifted her focus to pictures of the women attending the function. Sheaths and sweaters, an occasional pantsuit. A picture of Nick's mom grinning over the success of the function. Her heart hurt for Amanda Kourakis.

But for Nick, too. He'd said his life would have been very different if his brother hadn't died. Now she saw how.

The next day, Nick arrived at the children's ward at one o'clock. His mother was already there, firing orders at the caterer and the three people sprucing up the ward's existing decorations. She had a photographer, of course. Her public relations firm would send a press release chronicling the event, complete with pictures. Kids would be kept in their rooms so the food, cookies, decorations and brightly wrapped gifts would all be a surprise when they stepped into the activities room.

When he hugged his mom, she said, "You're here early."

"I got antsy."

"Antsy?"

"Yeah. I was in my office, preoccupied with being here…" Picturing Leni in a new dress, trying to guess how she'd wear her hair, even though he knew that was wrong. "I was wondering how things were going and I figured I should just come down." So, he'd stop thinking about Leni and get his mind on the fundraiser.

"Well, I'm glad you're here!" She gave him another quick squeeze. "Why don't you walk around, take a look at things, make sure I'm not missing anything?"

He laughed. "You're not missing anything. You're too thorough. But I wouldn't mind sneaking a peek at what we have to eat."

He walked away, and his mom called, "You can look, but no picking! I want every tray to be perfect."

He glanced at the food and gifts, all beautifully displayed, and eventually found his way to the office of the director. She gave him a rundown of things that had happened in the ward in the past few months, purchases and the ward's wish list, which he tucked into his pocket as something to discuss with Leni. She had the kind of money that would allow her to be a benefactor. Talking to her about potential donations, responsibilities she might want to pick up, would get their relationship back on track. He shouldn't have kissed her the night they'd shopped, mostly because the sweet kiss had rocked him as much as the sexy one had.

Still, it wasn't himself he was worried about. It was Leni. He hadn't wanted to give her the wrong impression. But the kiss was an easy, natural goodbye kiss. Nothing to get excited about. So today he'd be cool. And she'd be cool, and they'd be fine.

But when he noticed it was one-thirty, his gaze drifted to the elevator. When she finally stepped out at almost a quarter till two, his breath stalled. Not because he was relieved that she'd come, but because she looked amazing.

She wore black high-heel boots and a green dress that exaggerated her eye color, with a black wool coat draped over her arm. Her hair had been left down to curl along her back and swirl around her when she moved. A man in a sedate suit stood beside her, but Nick recognized him as one of Jace's employees. Someone he could dismiss.

He walked over and, unable to stop himself, caught both of her hands. "You are stunning."

Leni's heart stuttered. She told it to stop, but how could she be neutral when he looked at her like that?

She laughed. "This is what a little money can do."

He laughed and addressed Chuck, the driver Jace had assigned to her. "I think we're good here."

Leni frowned. "Good?"

"Sure. Everybody here is in the same tax bracket. Jace has security at all the entrances and exits." He smiled at Chuck. "No sense in overkill."

Chuck stepped into the elevator and Leni faced Nick. "So, what's going to happen here?"

"First, my mom will give a little speech about the good work the hospital does, then kids sit on Santa's lap and get gifts. Then there's a light lunch."

Her heart warmed. This was exactly the kind of charity she was looking for to share her wealth, but businessman Nick seemed to be back. She'd thought they'd ditched him days ago. But here he was again.

She glanced around, searching to see if there was an obvious way to bring fun Nick back. But she remembered the picture of this event from six years ago. The shot of his laughing mom, smiling dad and handsome younger brother—with bad boy Nick, who even though he looked totally out of place, had been here supporting the children's wing.

Obviously, this charity, this event, had been a family thing. Now it seemed like only Nick and his mom were involved.

She would be kind, especially to businessman Nick. "Sounds good."

He motioned to the left and said, "Let me take your coat," as a man in a black suit approached them. Leni handed the coat to Nick and he handed it to the guy in the black suit.

Nick's mom walked over. She took Leni's hands, leaned in, kissed her cheeks and said, "Thank you for coming."

Leni's heart broke a bit. Knowing what she knew now about Amanda losing a child and how it had changed her family, her life, she could have hugged her forever. "It's my pleasure."

"My son told me you are now a client of the firm."

She had to give points to Nick for that one. Though he'd given his mother a good explanation for her presence in their lives, he hadn't told her Leni was a Hinton heir.

"Yes. It's official."

"Well, that's wonderful." Amanda peeked at her watch. "I've gotta run. It's time for my greeting. We have to start the program exactly at two o'clock or the thing will run too long and I'm sure everyone has dinner plans."

Leni smiled and nodded as Amanda bustled away. The short talk she gave was both heartrending and upbeat. Leni applauded with everyone else.

Nick motioned for her to walk down the hall. "Let's go to the activity room and watch the kids open gifts."

Leni and Nick followed his mom and stopped beside Santa, who told the kids to form a line.

Leni's heart shattered. There were children in casts and on crutches. Kids with shaved heads. Little children in wheelchairs.

As if reading her mind, Nick leaned in and whispered, "Most of these kids will be home for Christmas."

"Really?"

"Yes. Medicine is so different now. We're seeing more and more kids recover and go on to lead normal lives."

"That's fabulous."

"And something your dad was a part of."

She laughed. "Why, Nick Kourakis, are you trying to get into my pocketbook?"

He grinned at her. "You didn't bring a pocketbook."

"Well, it looks like I should have."

He laughed merrily. Her heart perked up and she was having a little trouble controlling it. How could she not like him more and more with each passing minute? Seeing the picture of his family before his brother died, she realized how difficult it must be for him. Not just because he was mourning, but because it was clear his family had suffered the kind of loss from which some families don't recover.

How could she not long to see him as happy as he had been six years ago?

Santa arrived, and she stood with Nick, enjoying the kids as they hopped on Santa's lap and gave their Christmas lists.

The wishes of the kids ran the gamut of silly and normal to sentimental and wonderful. One little girl wanted her grandmother to get a washer, so she didn't have to go to the Laundromat. From the corner of her eye, Leni watched Nick type her name into his phone.

She smiled at him and he smiled at her. That rush of adrenaline that she'd felt the first time she'd seen him raced through her. After last night's kiss and today's easy conversations, she didn't even try to stop it. He was a great-looking guy, who clearly loved these kids and his mom. He was good at his job. And thoughtful enough to fly to Kansas to help her and her mom through the worst day of their lives—even as he was clearly still struggling with his own loss.

There was no way in hell she could stop herself from falling in love with this man. If the situation ended with

him not feeling the same way about her, she was going
to end up with the biggest broken heart in recorded history. But today she just couldn't stop herself from letting
go and letting herself feel everything her heart wanted to
feel for him.

CHAPTER THIRTEEN

NICK SAW IT. She'd given him *that* smile, and he'd felt the same thing he'd felt the first time he saw her. Smitten.

He reminded himself that he didn't deserve her. But that didn't mean he couldn't fall for her. How could he not when she was light and simple, easy to be with? And real. So wonderfully real in a world that was filled with money and power and posturing.

Still, he'd have to be careful. He might long for the feelings she inspired in him. Might even want to indulge them if only in his own heart. But he couldn't really act on them.

So, he let her limo take her home and resisted the urge to call her that night. The next morning, despite the snow, he made it to the meeting Danny had set up for him to explain details of Mark Hinton's estate to her. Show her slides of houses, give her lists of companies and things like yachts and Jet Skis.

He hadn't expected he'd be needed this soon, but Danny had explained that Leni was smart and adjusting to everything quickly. The more information they could get out of the way before they found the next heir, the better.

She wore a pink sweater and jeans with boots made for snow and he smiled to himself about her practicality. Something he didn't see a lot of in his world.

When Danny suggested lunch, he bowed out, blaming work and got into the elevator which returned him to the lobby. His phone rang before he could get outside, and he paused to take the call. As he stood talking to one of his managers, the elevator to Danny's office opened again and Leni walked out.

Alone.

He squeezed his eyes shut. He had no idea why she hadn't taken Danny up on is offer of lunch, but watching her walk through the lobby, out the revolving door into the hellacious winter storm, his heart stuttered. All the same, he told himself to give her time. She'd easily make friends. She'd easily fit in. She just needed time.

His chest tightened when he thought about how quickly and how easily she'd also find dates. With her looks and down-home charm, men would flock to her. He pulled in a breath to loosen his chest but went back to his call.

Watching her fall in love with someone else would be part of his penance.

Leni took her limo back to her hotel and busied herself searching real estate listings on the internet and trying to decide which of the three real estate agents Nick had recommended she'd choose to help her.

Eventually, she chose an agent and contacted her by email. Saturday morning, the agent called her and Sunday afternoon, they met at the coffee shop across the street from her hotel to talk about what she needed. Using her phone, the agent pulled up six potential condos and Leni chose three to see the following day. And the agent left.

Bored at three o'clock in the afternoon on a lazy Sunday, she nearly called Nick. But she hesitated. Friday, Saturday and now Sunday had gone by without a word from him except a very professional overview of her dad's holdings at Danny's office.

Did she really want to be the one to call?

She got a second latte, settled in on one of the stools at the counter and used her phone to research Mark Hinton again. Really curious about him now that she was hearing how he lived, how much he had and how alone he was. He could have had anything he wanted—except friends. Extrapolating from things Nick and Danny had said in their meeting, she realized he hadn't trusted anyone.

She scrolled through three of the websites dedicated to him, including one where people tried to guess his whereabouts. She shook her head with wonder. Didn't people have anything better to do?

"Hey."

She glanced up to see a youngish woman, maybe twenty-four, smiling at her. "Mind if I sit here?"

Leni shifted over a bit on her stool, as if she needed to make room for her, then told herself not to be silly. "Sure. I just need one chair," she added, making fun of herself for the way she'd shifted over to make room.

The young woman laughed and tucked a strand of her long black hair behind her ear. "I'm Sandy Wojack."

"I'm Leni." She stopped a bubble of panic that formed in her chest. If Mannington had a coffee shop, people would sit with other people all the time. If they hadn't been introduced, they'd introduce themselves.

But she was an heir of a multibillion-dollar estate. And in the thirteen days since Nick had found her in Mannington, nine of which she'd spent in New York City, no one had introduced themselves to her. No one had come up to her.

Of course, she hadn't been out much.

"I saw you with the real estate agent and was trying to overhear the addresses of the condos you were looking at."

Leni stiffened. Nobody in Mannington would admit to eavesdropping like that. "Oh."

"Real estate is so tight here, right?"

She had no idea. "Absolutely."

"I was hoping I could get a lead from your agent." She laughed. "But you're buying out of my price range."

And that felt downright weird. Nobody talked money with a stranger. At least, no one from Mannington did.

She reached to pick up her phone to gather her things and leave, and realized it was side-by-side with Sandy Wojack's phone. Not where she had put it…at least eighteen inches away from her.

Fear washed through her. Wasn't that how people cloned phones?

Hell if she knew!

"How did this get here?"

Sandy blinked innocently.

And Leni felt like an idiot. Sort of. She slid her phone into her expensive designer purse, lifted her even more expensive coat from the back of her stool and let her ridiculously expensive black boots carry her outside.

For the love of all that was holy, she might as well be wearing a sign that she had more money than she knew what to do with.

She raced back to the hotel, jumped inside her room and leaned against the closed door, her heart pounding. Not sure if she was panicking for nothing or if she'd just been identified, she sucked in a breath, raced to her hotel room phone and dialed Nick's number.

"I think I'm in trouble."

His voice hardened. "What kind of trouble?"

She told him the story of Sandy Wojack, and after he cursed, she burst into tears. "I don't know why I'm crying, except that it all felt really wrong, really odd." She took a breath. *"Invasive."*

"I'm coming over. Call Danny, tell him what you told me and then call room service and get us a really good bottle of scotch."

By the time Nick made it to her hotel room, she'd called Danny and had also taken a quick shower. The whole damned encounter had felt wrong and though the shower didn't ease her apprehensions, the warmth of it eased her nerves some.

Nick entered carrying Chinese food. "You're okay?"

"Yes. And I'm sorry. I feel really stupid for crying. Danny's not okay, though. He's going to look up cloning phones to see if she could have done that and he's calling his media contacts."

"He'll figure this out." He held up the bag of Chinese food. "Hungry?"

"Starving."

"Good. Is Danny calling back?"

"If he finds anything."

"Okay, we'll eat Chinese food, find a movie on pay-per-view and wait for his call."

Having him in the room made her feel safer somehow and that's when she began feeling foolish. Someone had sat down beside her at a coffee shop and started talking real estate. There was no sin in that. Yes, her phone had been moved and the girl—Sandy Wojack—had seen the condos she would be looking at—

Damn. Even trying to make it sound innocent, it was bad.

"I'm not going to be able to buy any of the condos I saw today."

"Not if we find out Sandy Wojack is a reporter." He winced. "Or that she sold your story to a reporter."

"Damn."

"You'll know to be more careful the next time."

"I will." She picked up the container of fried rice and slid some onto a paper plate provided by the Chinese restaurant. By the time she had a whole plate of wonderful-smelling goodies, Nick had the remote in his hands, searching for movies.

They watched a comedy for forty minutes, alternately eating and chatting, but as the reality of what had happened with Sandy Wojack sunk in, her stomach soured.

"I know this."

Nick peeked over. "You know what?"

"How much my dad had. And even how money makes people a little crazy."

"It's going to be fine."

"No. It's not." Just as her instincts told her she and Nick were falling in love, her instincts were telling her Sandy Wojack was a bad person. And her instincts were never wrong.

The chime of Leni's hotel room phone burst into the room and she and Nick exchanged a glance. He picked it up and said, "Hello?"

"It's Danny."

"It's Danny, Leni."

Leni let out her breath. "Put it on speaker."

Nick clicked the speaker button and said, "Hey, Danny, you're on speaker with me and Leni. What did you find out?"

"That Sandy Wojack's already tried to sell her story to three papers."

Leni squeezed her eyes shut.

Nick said, "How'd she figure it out?"

"She didn't. She was watching Leni because her clothes were expensive, and she was considering a seven-million-dollar condo. When the real estate agent left, she saw Leni reading about Mark Hinton on her phone." Danny took a breath. "She secretly took a few pictures of you before she sat down to talk to you. The woman must be a professional con artist or something because she told two of the papers she had the spyware to clone your phone."

Nick sat back on the red sofa. "Then she knows everybody involved and all of our phone numbers."

Leni shook her head and walked over to the wall of windows, looking out at Times Square.

Danny said, "Yes and no. Leni didn't text much. Her mom. A few friends. So, all Sandy really has is information about Leni's friends in Mannington and your number and my number. As well as the hotel number."

"Then she's not staying here tonight."

"No. She can't."

"She can stay with me."

For that Leni turned. "No."

She would not stay overnight with him. She wouldn't risk tumbling into bed because she was scared and helpless and overemotional. "There are hundreds of hotels in this city. Pick one."

Danny said, "How about if we pick one closer to my office, Leni?"

"That would be great."

"Call your real estate agent and cancel those showings tomorrow."

"Yes," Nick agreed. "I gave you three names. We'll move on to the next one."

Leni pulled in a breath. "Okay."

"Give me ten minutes," Danny said. "I'll have you in a hotel so secure even Nick will have to check in with your bodyguards."

"Okay."

CHAPTER FOURTEEN

THE UPROAR THE next day was beyond Nick's wildest dreams. He couldn't imagine what Leni was feeling. Her picture graced the front page of several newspapers, including national newspapers. The New York City television news programs showed the crowd of reporters outside the entrance to her Times Square hotel.

Danny had gotten her a new phone and when she called her mother with the new number, she'd had to explain that she'd been discovered and things were about to get weird. Hearing that, Nick had called Jace and Jace had dispatched two people to Kansas to protect her parents.

Nick watched it all with a huge hole in his heart for Leni. When noon hit, and her stomach growled, he got the strangest idea.

"What do you say we go out for dinner?"

She turned to him, her green eyes as big as two plates. "Are you kidding? Go out in that?"

She pointed at the window and he shrugged. "You can wear big sunglasses."

"In a restaurant?"

"You won't need them in the restaurant."

"Yeah, well, I thought I was safe in a coffee shop, too."

"You'll be safe. We'll go somewhere no one will know or care who you are."

"Mars?"

"Paris."

She gaped at him. "Paris?"

"Why not? It could be fun." He gave her a coaxing smile. "More fun than sitting in a hotel room."

He could tell from the look on her face that she couldn't argue that.

"Okay. Should I pack?"

"For an overnight trip."

She headed for the bedroom of her new suite where everything was shades of brown and gray with big blue throw pillows on the sofa and chairs.

While she dressed, Nick ordered sandwiches from room service, then he called his pilot. They ate lunch while the pilot prepped for the flight. Before they left, she asked for a few minutes in her bedroom. When she came out, she was wearing her old jacket, white turtleneck and jeans.

"That Sandy woman said she'd gotten curious about me because of how expensive my clothes were."

Her voice held a sadness that broke his heart.

She shrugged. "This outfit kept people away from me for a whole week. I like to wear it."

"Sure."

They rode down in the elevator and got into her limo. She barely said anything on the drive to the airstrip. When they stepped into the plane, Jace's two men followed them.

"This is weird."

Nick shrugged out of his parka. "Not really. Things will eventually calm down. Like your dad, you may find places to stay where no one cares who you are. Like Idaho."

Taking a seat, she laughed. "I don't think they'll care in Mannington."

"Really? No one will extort money or threaten your future kids?"

"I don't think so."

Sitting beside her, he smiled at her naivete.

"I like Mannington. I trust the people in Mannington, and I've been giving this whole money thing some thought. I've decided that since I can't live out my dream of being a social worker, I should find something to do to satisfy that need. At first when I was talking to Danny, I'd thought being on the boards of my dad's companies would work, but now I don't think that's a good idea. I don't want to be the face of a multibillion-dollar fortune."

"So?"

"I've decided to fix my town."

He chuckled. "How do you fix a town?"

"First, I'd invest in all the businesses. You know, to kind of beef them up. Like new chairs and booths in the diner. A new oven for the bakery across the street because they're always complaining theirs is too small."

"Makes sense."

"Then I'd find a way to bring work to the town."

"Ah…so people don't have to move to Topeka to find work."

"Exactly. I don't think I'm trying to buy everybody's love because they already like me. But I do believe they will see that having me around will have its benefits."

He considered her idea—knowing that wouldn't even put a dent in the Hinton fortune—and finally said, "I like all your plans and I hope you won't be disappointed."

"I won't be."

He cut her a look. "You sound so sure."

"And you sound so cynical."

He laughed. "That's my old Leni."

"There is no old Leni or new Leni or nice Leni or sharp Leni. I am always going to be myself."

Relief whispered through him. Not because he was glad she would remain herself, but because she was back to being feisty. "That I believe."

"Good."

"Okay. Can I make a few suggestions for your plan?"

She gave him a confused look, but said, "Sure."

"Beef up your police department and fire companies."

Her face brightened as she thought that through. "That makes sense."

"Bring in a clinic. Staff it with enough doctors that it can be open at least sixteen hours a day."

"I like it. It means more jobs."

"True. But it's also a safety issue. You'll have a doctor available when you need one."

The reality of why she'd need that hit her and she sighed. "Yeah."

"Speaking of safety. How is your dad?"

"He's good. He and mom went online and looked up the doctors and hospitals his neurologist and I found for him. He has appointments with three neurosurgeons."

"Three?"

"The guy is looking at brain surgery. We want all the opinions we can get."

"Good idea."

They went back to discussing Mannington and Leni's ideas to make it cleaner, nicer, safer, with more jobs, but eventually her sleepless night took its toll and she drifted off. The peaceful expression on her face took his breath away. The longing to stay with her forever rippled through him.

But that was wrong. She deserved so much more.

Especially since she had a plan that made her feel safe. She hadn't said that was why she intended to spruce up her town, bring it life, but he knew that was at least part of it. She felt safe there, among people she knew. Still, if he accidentally let himself think of her being in his life, happiness filled him. The happiness of having her at his side, the male pride that she loved *him*. But he only let himself think like that for a second because it was wrong and when he remembered that, misery filled him.

He might not have been happy before he'd met her but at least he'd found purpose in growing the family business, living up to his dad's expectations. Now all that felt empty.

He didn't care. Empty. Not empty. It didn't matter. That was his life. All the life he deserved.

He called Marie who hustled to the front of the plane. He whispered, "Could you get us a blanket?"

She nodded and raced off, returning with a thick white wool blanket. He placed it over Leni, then yawned himself. It had been a long, miserable twenty-four hours. He reached over and took a section of the blanket to cover himself and within minutes was asleep.

Nick woke after three hours, but Leni didn't stir until they landed. Though it was seven o'clock at night in New York, it was two o'clock in the morning in France. And it was cold.

When the plane stopped completely, he signaled for Marie to take their blanket and bring their coats. "I'm sorry to tell you that it's a little chilly in France in December."

She blinked up at him. "I have my coat. It's not like we were planning on going to the beach."

"But we could. If you wanted to, we could simply tack a few days onto the trip and head for an island where it's warm enough to wear a bikini."

She chuckled. "Right. That's funny."

"No. That's your life now." But he saw what he was doing. Sadness and longing had him subtly trying to convince her to go somewhere they could be together. Somewhere her safety and his past wouldn't be an issue.

"And maybe that should be part of this trip. Maybe you should look around and realize you can go anywhere you want. Live anywhere you want."

She took a breath.

He told himself not to argue his case, but his mouth didn't listen. "I'm serious. You can be an island girl."

"I know. But I like my plan about Mannington."

He had to admit he did, too. And having her consider an island was just his stupid selfishness. He wanted her.

He wanted to be with her, but not as himself. He wanted to hide or run and forget everything.

But that was even more wrong than trying to persuade Leni to give up her life, her friends, her parents for him.

She had responsibilities now.

He rose from his seat, took their coats from Marie and helped Leni into hers. They deplaned into the dead of night.

"I'm guessing there's a time difference."

He winced. "Yeah, I added the seven hours travel time to noon in New York and figured we'd get here for dinner. But in all the confusion I forgot the time difference."

She took a deep breath of the frosty air and glanced around as they walked to a waiting limo. "I see that."

"In a few hours we can have breakfast. Yummy pastry and rich dark coffee."

She laughed. "Sounds great."

He winced. "But then we have to get home."

"Really?"

"I also forgot the charity ball on Friday."

She gasped. "For the children's ward."

"Yes."

"Your mom wanted me to go to that."

"I'd like you to go to that."

The peace and quiet of the French countryside must have worked its magic because she smiled her Leni smile. "Then I'll go."

The drive from the airstrip was long but when they got close to Paris, Leni could see the lights of the Eiffel Tower and the trip suddenly felt real.

She was in *France*. She really could go anywhere she wanted. Do anything she wanted. As long as she could protect herself.

Because it was so late, Nick checked them into a gorgeous hotel. She expected them to go to separate rooms, but he opened the door on a suite.

"I know you're fine. I know you're safe," he said as they entered the room, bellman on their heels. "But I'll just feel better if you're within yelling distance."

Her mouth went dry. She knew he'd put a blanket over her while she was sleeping, then crawled under with her. The extreme circumstances they were battling were definitely bringing out his protective instincts…but what if they were bringing out more than that? Sharing a room… Would they be sharing a bed?

She thought back to their kiss and even though she knew they'd be an explosive combination, she didn't want to end up in bed because he was afraid. She wanted more kisses. She wanted him to woo her.

It was stupid to be such a romantic. But she was. She always had been and Nick was, too. He'd hinted at it right before he'd kissed her the first time in her mom's kitchen.

"Anyway," Nick said, glancing around the room that was soft shades of yellow with white sofas and chairs and bowls of white roses on every flat surface. "Those two doors are to the bedrooms. You can pick the one you want."

Disappointment and relief collided and flooded her. But disappointment won. He hadn't even thought of sleeping with her.

Which could be considered gallant.

Or prove that he didn't have the same feelings for her as she had for him—

Then why the blanket? Why share the blanket? She knew damned well there had to be more than one blanket on that plane.

She shook her head to clear it of the idiocy. She was tired. "It doesn't matter which room." She pointed to the one on the left. "I'll take that one. I still need some sleep."

"And when you wake up, I know the perfect café for breakfast."

She smiled and nodded, went into the room and face-planted onto the thick white comforter covering the big bed.

Soon she wouldn't have to worry about reporters or charlatans following her around. This situation itself was going to drive her crazy.

He made good on his promise of a café the next morning. Though it was cold, they sat outside drinking rich black coffee and eating pastries with names like cream puff, croissant, madeleine, macaron. With her wearing her old coat, they walked to the Eiffel Tower, along the Seine and then they had to go home.

But the trip had refreshed her. She'd put on new jeans when she dressed that morning and one of her beautiful soft sweaters. But she'd also slid into her old jacket so that when they reached her New York City hotel and she got out of Nick's limo, she looked like an average tourist. Her bodyguards discreetly walked ten feet in front of her and at least ten behind. She didn't look at them. She didn't draw any attention to them or herself. She simply got into the elevator with the first one, climbed to the floor of her new hotel room and walked down the hall.

When she entered her room, the oddest sense filled her.

She hadn't been afraid in Paris and, damn it, she refused to be afraid now. This kind of sneaking around, pretending to be just an average person, walking into a hotel room while discreetly surrounded by bodyguards wasn't her.

She was stronger than this. Smarter than this. More easygoing than this. That's how she intended to behave from now on.

Nick checked on Leni over the next few days, but he didn't go to see her. He was already too tempted to do something that wasn't right, to change her mind about where she lived and how she lived. His selfishness was back and if he got too close, he'd want more and persuade her to give him more.

Because that's what he did best, persuade people to see things his way. The night his brother died he'd persuaded Joe to go out when he didn't want to. If he'd listened to Joe, his brother might still be alive now.

He couldn't forget that.

On Friday, he arrived at the ball early enough to ease his mother's fears about whether everything looked perfect. As opening time approached, he stood with his parents in an informal receiving line where they could welcome guests. He tried to tell himself he wasn't watching for Leni but when she appeared at the back of the line his heart stumbled.

Every time she walked into a room, she stole his breath, but tonight he wasn't sure he'd get it back. Her red gown clung to her breasts and tiny waist but belled out with layer after layer of soft, shiny red fabric. Her shoes must have had five-inch heels because she was taller than he'd ever seen her.

He laughed remembering the first time she'd worn high heels around him, thinking she was tall enough to kiss, and his heart twisted.

He'd never met anybody like her. Normal and fun, but tonight she looked like royalty. Her head high. Her smile real. Her face breathtaking.

As she inched her way toward him, he thanked his lucky stars that he'd already worked all this out in his head and wouldn't make a move on her. Then he realized something that stopped his heart.

This would be their last night together for weeks. Soon, she'd be leaving for Mannington for Christmas. She wouldn't return until she had to. He'd endure a quiet Christmas at his parents' where everybody thought about Joe but no one said a word. He'd feel it. He'd feel their anger and their loss. Then he'd go to work and avoid talking to anyone for weeks.

By the time she came back to New York, they'd both be so different they might not really like each other. Or, worse, their paths might only cross when Danny called them both into his office.

She finally reached his parents. His mother hugged her. His *father* hugged her. Probably because he now knew she was one of the three Hinton heirs.

Leni shifted away from his parents, and Nick held his breath. This was his last night with Leni as Leni. Their last night of being two people so attracted to each other they experienced an almost irresistible pull.

He didn't know how it would end, but suddenly he knew he couldn't let this opportunity pass.

Her eyes had been painted with green shadows that gave her a mystical air. Her hair was pulled up into something that looked like a ponytail of curls that cascaded to her shoulders. Her red dress sparkled as if someone had hidden glitter in the fabric that hugged her curves.

He took her hands. "You are stunning."

"Thanks. You don't look so bad yourself."

He glanced down at his tuxedo, then laughed. "I guess men are lucky. We don't have to figure out colors or styles. We just have to look good in black."

"Well, you are amazing in black."

Her heart could attest to that from the jump in her pulse when she saw him. Good God. Could a man be any sexier? From his height to his shiny hair to the way he held himself as if he'd been born in a tux.

He made being rich look really, really easy.

He caught her elbow and turned her toward the ballroom. "Why don't we get a glass of champagne?"

She motioned to the receiving line. "Don't you have duties?"

He shrugged. "I think I'm done."

Because he wanted to be with her? After days of a phone call or two to be sure she was okay, he wanted to be with her? Maybe just for one drink?

Probably. She wouldn't make a big deal of it. Wouldn't let her aching heart get too excited. He might look at her with longing in his eyes, but since Paris he'd treated her like a friend.

So, she smiled at him the way she would a friend. "I'd like a drink."

They walked into the room that had been filling with people. White poinsettias acted as centerpieces on tables covered in crisp white linen. But red and green accent lights added some whimsy, making the room festive. A string quartet played softly in a far corner.

Nick took two flutes of champagne from a passing waiter and handed one to her. "Merry Christmas."

She would have thought it odd that someone was wishing her Merry Christmas a week before the actual event. But that afternoon she'd been shopping for her parents, being told Merry Christmas by some very happy clerks.

They touched their glasses together with a soft clink and she took a sip of the most perfect champagne she'd ever tasted. She closed her eyes in ecstasy.

"So good."

He laughed. "I love that you close your eyes to savor."

And she loved that he used the word *love* because right now, in this moment, he wasn't looking at her like a friend. His gaze had softened and his smooth voice was velvety seduction.

Maybe he'd missed her? Maybe he'd decided to stop fighting?

He introduced her to a few friends and business associates who were extremely curious about her but too polite to ask the questions she could see shimmering in their eyes. She made conversation about their jobs and families and everyone eagerly joined in. She might not have been born to money, but she did know people, how to be kind and polite. That was her and she'd already decided she wasn't losing herself.

As Nick swept her away from the last group, he laughed. "You're getting really good at this."

"I just decided to stay myself." She caught his gaze. "This is me. I'm not letting a bunch of crazy curiosity seekers ruin my life."

His head tilted as he studied her. "You're really okay?"

"I'm really okay."

"I knew you would be. I knew you'd figure it out."

For him, she would figure out anything. But she suspected in his own way, he probably knew that too, so she only smiled.

When it came time for dinner, he led her to his family's table where his father rose as Nick seated her.

Extremely glad for the online videos she'd found on etiquette, she took her seat, sending Nick a smile of thanks as he sat on the seat next to her.

She suddenly felt like Cinderella. Not at her first ball—the one where she'd lost her shoe. But the next ball. The one after the Prince had found her and told her he loved her. The one where he showed her off.

Because that's what this felt like. Nick had introduced her to friends and business associates and now she was dining with his parents, like part of their circle. It was heady fun, but there was a deeper message. She fit. And he liked that she fit. He liked *her* and he was done fighting it.

After dinner, they listened to a few speeches of thanks to volunteers and benefactors of the children's ward of the hospital, then the band began to play. She and Nick danced to the first few songs. Then his friends began asking her to dance. Nick would let her dance with three friends, then he'd rescue her, and they'd dance again.

She swore she really was Cinderella.

The night passed in a blur of champagne and laughter. Giggling on their way to the street and their limos, Nick stopped them in front of hers.

"This was so great. You made a usually dull event tons of fun."

And champagne had made *her* tipsy enough that she flattened her hands against his chest, feeling the smooth silk of his white shirt.

She looked up into his shiny dark eyes. "I think we're a good team."

"I think we are, too. So, I was thinking maybe we'd both take your limo." He caught her gaze. "Say yes, because I already told my driver to go home."

Her chest tightened and breathing became difficult, the way it had the first time he kissed her. She knew this was it. He wasn't just going to kiss her again. He was coming home with her.

She worked not to sound nervous when she said, "Sure."

The driver opened her limo door and they slid inside. The door closed, cocooning them in a dark, silent world.

The limo pulled into traffic, but neither one of them said anything. Glad for the short trip, she stemmed her nervousness as Nick helped her out of the limo and led her to her suite.

The second the door closed behind them, he pulled her to face him. His head descended slowly, and she held his gaze, keeping her eyes open until the very last second. She wanted to see everything, every emotion that flickered in his dark, dark orbs. She wanted to remember everything on the night of the first time they'd make love.

CHAPTER FIFTEEN

EVERYTHING SUDDENLY FELT right in Nick's world. As he brushed his lips across Leni's, the sense of rightness morphed into pure pleasure. She tasted like champagne and happiness. Everything he wanted in this minute. Everything he needed to remember her by.

Because he would not sleep with her. It didn't matter that their luxurious kiss rolled through him like thunder or that his heartbeat pounded in anticipation of touching her. He would only take this so far.

He unbuttoned the silk jacket that matched her gown, knowing only thin fabric would separate his palm from her skin, but reminding himself that had to be enough. He wouldn't hurt her. He wouldn't edge his way into her world. He only wanted this taste.

So, he kissed her, her mouth eager beneath his desperate one. There was something hot and mysterious between them. There had been from the first second their eyes locked. Tonight, it rose like thick smoke from a raging fire.

A voice deep inside him told him this was it. Real love that offered peace and contentment. Maybe even a second chance. And he should grab it.

Another voice, the stronger voice, reminded him he didn't deserve it, but more than that *she* deserved better.

Still, he smoothed his hand along the silk of her bodice, knowing taut skin lie beneath. Temptation spiked, but his conscience tweaked again. He ached for this and he knew why. He wasn't looking for redemption that wasn't his to find. But a new start suddenly loomed on the horizon because everything about her was fresh and original. Unique. Wonderful. She would make his life an open door. He'd never want anyone else. Anything else.

But that was the point. He couldn't walk away from his life. He had commitments. Sins that couldn't be forgiven. A life that would drag her down.

Only a true sinner would drag someone like her into his private hell.

He pulled away from her. "I think I'd better get going."

Her gaze connected with his. "Why not stay?"

Her voice was soft, innocent. His walls yearned to crumble. Need tore through him.

Which was why he stepped back. He wouldn't hurt her, but he couldn't tell her that because he didn't want to get into a debate about his reasoning. He wasn't sure he'd win. So, he fudged a bit.

"It's late. I had a long day."

She walked her fingers up the buttons of his shirt. "I wouldn't make you do all the work."

He couldn't help it. He laughed. But he wouldn't let himself forget who he was and why he had to let her go.

He brushed a light kiss across her lips. "You're nuts."

"But I think that's why you like me."

He turned toward the door of her suite. "Yeah. You're probably right." He kept it light, simple, so she wouldn't spend the night wondering what she'd done wrong. But in that second, he vowed he would never see her again unless it was in his office or Danny's.

Leni woke the next morning dreamy happy. She yawned and stretched and could have stayed in bed all day, except she wanted to see Nick. It was Saturday, but that didn't guarantee he wasn't working.

The night before had been perfect. Though Nick had laughed when she'd said he liked her because she was a little crazy, she knew that was true. She'd sensed all along

that he needed more happiness—maybe more craziness—
in his life. Now he saw it, too.

The most amazing idea hit her. She threw back the
covers, climbed out of bed, ordered coffee and toast from
room service, then called the concierge.

"I need to find a small Christmas tree and decorations."

He told her she could order a tree and have it delivered,
then directed her to two nearby places where she could get
sparkly ornaments, some tinsel and lights. He again suggested she could have them delivered too but she wanted
to be the one delivering them.

After a quick shower, she called Jace and asked him for
Nick's address. When he asked why, she told him about
the Christmas tree and, though he hesitated, he told her
the driver knew the address.

Two hours later, she had a small tree in her limo trunk,
two bags of simple ornaments and happiness in her heart.
She and her bodyguard walked into the lobby. The doorman's eyebrows rose.

"I guess I have to be buzzed up to Mr. Kourakis's
condo."

His eyebrows rose even higher. "Mr. Kourakis?"

"Yes."

He hesitated a second, but said, "Let me call him."

He called, gave Leni's name and after a wince, he hung
up the phone. "He's on his way out for the day, but he'll
see you."

That struck her oddly. Still, Nick had always been a
difficult man. She knew he'd want to see her. He might
not like surprises, but he did like kissing her and she liked
kissing him. And whether he wanted to admit it, he needed
a Christmas tree.

Nick waited by the elevator for Leni. When the door
opened, she walked out holding two bags, with a body-

guard behind her carrying a three-foot Christmas tree. He nearly laughed.

But he couldn't. He'd given her the wrong impression the night before and now he had to fix it.

She set the bags down and slipped out of her coat. "I came here to spice up your condo, give you some Christmas cheer."

After instructing the bodyguard to set the tree, already in a small tree stand, on the table by the window, he dismissed him.

When the elevator door closed behind him, Nick folded his arms across his chest. "How do you know I didn't already have a tree?"

She laughed, rose to her tiptoes and brushed a quick kiss across his lips. "Lucky guess."

Something soft and warm floated through him when she kissed him. He longed to grab and savor it, but he couldn't. Leaving her the night before had been the hardest thing he'd ever done and now he'd have to say goodbye again.

Except this time, she had to understand this was the end of anything romantic between them.

She took the two bags of ornaments to the table, removed the boxes and put a bright red ball on one of the tiny limbs.

"Look, Leni. I think you and I have to talk."

"Talk while I decorate. Any chance you have coffee?"

"I can make you a cup, but… Listen." He nearly lost the struggle inside him. She looked so perfect in his home. And one by one, as the brightly colored balls filled the small tree, the spirit of Christmas, the memories of happier days and what the week before Christmas was supposed to feel like, filled him.

He reminded himself that he didn't want to hurt her, walked over, took the ornament from her hand and led her to the sofa.

She sat, but he didn't sit beside her. He lowered himself to the chair across from her, put his elbows on his knees and took a breath. He was going to have to tell her the truth. He didn't know why he hadn't realized that all along, but he saw it now.

"I'm not the nice guy you think I am."

"Yes, you are."

"No. See? That's what's wrong here. You have this vision of me being a nice guy that's not true. If I take what you're offering, I'm going to hurt you."

"I don't think so."

He leaned forward a bit more. "You know my brother died. What you don't know is that he died because of me. My father is angry. After five years, my mother is still confused about how we're supposed to go on without him. But we all know it's my fault he died. I all but dragged him out in an ice storm. I was home from my gallivanting and wanted to have some fun."

He pulled in a harsh breath, ran his hands down his face. "I see everything from that night in slow motion in my head. Him trying to talk sense into me. Me telling him I was a Navy SEAL. I'd done things that would amaze him. I could certainly drive in a little ice. My parents angry because they didn't want us to go out. But I kept insisting and, in the end, I won. The roads were worse than anything I'd ever seen. But I got it in my head that this was like a mission and I needed to do it."

Memories of that night froze his chest, filled him with self-loathing.

"The few cars on the road were slipping and sliding but I was okay. Then I lost control and I couldn't even tell you how many cars I hit or how many hit me. I banged my head and blacked out and when I came to, paramedics were shouting about Joe. I looked over and he was so still. So quiet."

He stopped. He couldn't level his breathing, as those

minutes came back full force. Paramedics scrambling. Firemen shouting. The fear that his brother was dead racing through him like a wildfire.

"You think you killed your brother?"

"I know I killed my brother. The accident might not have been my fault but going out was. Both of my parents warned me. Joe argued. My dad got mad." He shrugged. "I wouldn't listen. Now I have parents who look at me and see the guy who killed their son. It's all I can do to handle the burden of that.

"Losing my brother drained something from my soul. My family is never going to get over this because we can't blame fate. We can't come to terms with it because, when we try, all we have is the fact that I pushed when I shouldn't have. You're a good person. Too good for that kind of life. Too good for me."

"Nick…"

He rose from his chair. "No. Don't you get it? It's been five years and we can't move on. You do not know what it's like to look at your parents and realize you took away their good son. The son who stepped up to run the family business, when I refused to settle down and globe-trotted like the world owed me fun. He's the one who bought the best Christmas gifts and took Mom and Dad to brunch once a month. You don't know what it's like to have to try to be everything my brother would have been to make up for cockiness, arrogance." He shook his head and fell to his seat again. "You don't know what it's like to come home at night with that day's pressure morphing into the next day's stress, sprinkled with guilt and the grief of *my* loss. While everyone feels sorry for my parents. No one remembers I lost a brother, too."

"Oh, Nick…"

She rose and knelt in front of him, but he gently nudged her back, so he could stand, then help her stand.

"I won't drag you into that. But more than that, I know I don't have the mental energy to be the kind of man you deserve."

Leni nodded, the whole story swirling around in her head as she desperately worked to understand him. All along she'd known something was wrong. All along she'd known it somehow connected to his brother. But she'd never taken in the signs. She'd ploughed ahead, believing that something as strong as what stirred between them would conquer anything.

But she heard the pained resignation in his voice. He'd killed his brother. He was bruised and broken. And he was correct. That was the kind of emotional wound a family only got over with courage and work.

He'd been telling her that all along, pushing away all along and she hadn't listened.

She was an idiot.

No, she was the seven-year-old foster child, desperate for parents to love her, who always wished and hoped and saw things that weren't there because she so desperately wanted love. Wanted everyone to be happy. Wanted the world to work the way it should.

And she'd always ended up hurt. First, her dad didn't step up to help her sick mom. Then her mom dropped her off and never looked back. Three families had her as a foster kid and all three asked for her to be moved on to another home.

Not only did she know what it was like to be the star in a drama that was totally out of her control, she knew there were some things that didn't work out. Just as there were some wounds an outsider couldn't heal.

She slid her coat from the back of a chair, where Nick had laid it, but glanced back at the tree. She'd had such good intentions and worried that leaving it behind would only bring back bad memories for him, but in the end she decided to leave it.

Maybe it was time he faced some things. Maybe the tree would push him to do that?

Maybe then he'd realize they should be together...

In her head, she cursed herself for her wishful thinking. She was always like this. Hopeful. Positive. But the world wasn't always a positive place and not all answers were easy. She knew that. She had a mom who had abandoned her. A father who hadn't wanted her at all. She'd been *lucky* the Longs had found her.

Not everybody was so lucky. Not everybody's life worked out.

And she had no right to interfere. Despite her education and her longing to help him, she couldn't.

Horrible sadness rose in her. A combination of the grief she felt rolling from him in waves and her own grief for him.

As the elevator door closed behind her, sorrow for Nick rose in her. He should be the happiest guy on the face of the earth. Instead, he might actually be the most broken.

Tired, worn down, angry with herself for pushing Nick, Leni removed her coat in her suite, called Jace and told him she wanted to go home. Back to Mannington.

She almost called her mom to pick her up at the private airstrip, but she decided to rent a car instead. Her brand-new bank card was like a little miracle worker. She never had to ask the price of anything. She gave the card number to the clerk on the phone and she got anything she wanted.

Tonight, she wanted an SUV delivered to the airstrip to get her through the Kansas snow and home.

Home.

That's where she needed to be. That's where she was who she was supposed to be. Not some New York socialite who got herself involved in things that were over her head, things she couldn't fix. Kansas was where she belonged.

Evening arrived as she drove the hour to her parents' house. She pulled the big SUV into the driveway, grabbed one of the three suitcases with her new clothes in them and headed inside.

Opening the door, she called, "I'm home!"

Wearing an apron, her mom peeked out of the kitchen. "Leni! What are you doing here? We thought you weren't coming until Christmas Eve."

Not about to tell her mom she'd fallen in love with Nick and forced him to relive the worst night of his life as he told her he didn't want what she wanted, she fibbed just a little bit.

"I was sitting in my room and I thought, 'I should be making cookies right now,' and here I am."

"Because you want to bake cookies?"

"Because I do whatever I want now."

Her dad came up behind her mom. "Don't let that go to your head, Kitten."

Oh, she wouldn't. She'd learned her lesson with Nick Kourakis. He'd given her every sign, every hint, that his family was in real emotional trouble and she'd missed it.

She thought of Nick casually mentioning his brother when they were skating but not being able to elaborate and her eyes drifted shut. He'd been so wonderful. Every time she'd had a problem like her dad's hospitalization or when Sandy Wojack told the world she was an heir, he'd been there.

She'd genuinely believed he loved her because everything he did for her was so natural, so honest, as if it had come right from his heart.

But he was the one who'd been in real pain and though she'd seen it she hadn't realized the depth of it and she'd pushed him.

Remorse shivered through her, hurting her to her core.

She took a breath. Reminded herself that she couldn't do anything about what had happened between them and that she'd be careful from here on out, wouldn't barge ahead, would pay closer attention to people, the way she'd been taught at university.

She shrugged out of the big parka she'd bought on her spending spree and hung it on a hook by the door, then rubbed her hands together. If it killed her, she would be happy. She would not let her parents see how upset she was.

"So? What are we making?"

"The cutout cookies that you like so much."

The same cookies she'd given Nick the weekend her dad had been in the hospital.

She fought the urge to weep. He'd always been there when she needed him, and she'd missed the signs that he needed her more.

"We'll ice them," her dad said proudly. "Then decorate. Maybe with sprinkles."

Her dad's happiness being able to do such a simple thing like make cutout cookies made her laugh. She breathed again. Told herself this was where she needed to be until she sorted out everything in her head. But what was there to sort? Money hadn't bought Nick's family happiness. Her love hadn't healed Nick. Her pushing had hurt him.

Her mom made two big bowls of batter which they re-frigerated while she and her dad played a quick game of Yahtzee. When the dough had chilled, she reached for the first bowl of batter.

"Oh, sweetie, get an apron." Her mom motioned toward Leni's pink cashmere sweater. "You don't want to ruin that."

"Why? I can always buy another." The words came out choppy, mixed with tears and confusion.

Having money was such an odd thing. So much good, but so much bad.

"Kitten?"

The tears spilled over. "I found out some things today that broke my heart. Especially since I made things worse."

Her dad put his arm around her. "What? What happened?"

"Nick and I seemed to be getting involved romantically." She sniffed. "He always pulled back and I decided to push, and he told me that his brother died in an accident and he'd been driving and he's not over it. Neither are his parents. But I pushed, and he had to tell me, and I knew I'd done nothing but bring back bad memories."

Her parents exchanged a glance. Her mom said, "You didn't know."

"I realize that." She rubbed her hands down her face. "But I keep getting these odd, disjointed memories of us having fun and being happy and I feel like I missed something. Like there was something I should have done."

"Oh, honey." Her mom sat her down at one of the kitchen stools. "You always wanted to change the world. But there are things you can't fix."

"Not even with money," her dad quietly said. "But that doesn't mean you stop trying."

Her dad's words comforted her. Especially when she remembered her plans for Mannington. Jobs. Money for the diner, grocery store and bakery. A bigger police force. A clinic.

Calm flitted through her and took root. Keeping busy was exactly what she needed to do.

That and stay away from Nick. She'd really thought that whatever hummed between them was good. But all it seemed to do was remind him of what he couldn't have.

Her heart broke for him, but it broke for herself, too. She loved him and she'd hurt him.

Nick left the half-decorated tree exactly as it was on his dining room table. Every morning it mocked him. Every night it made him wish he could just walk over and hang the rest of the ornaments like a normal person.

By Wednesday, he couldn't go to work.

Thursday, he couldn't get out of bed.

Friday, he got up, made coffee and stared out the window at Central Park. None of the tricks he used to force himself back to life after his brother died were working. He was hungry. He was tired. But he was too broken to care.

The sound of his elevator doors opening turned him from the window. "Dad?"

"I heard you weren't at work."

Oh, God. Just what he didn't need: a lecture from his father. "I think I had a touch of the flu." Leni asking him if he lied to his parents a lot popped into his head and he didn't know whether to laugh or cry. He *missed* her. He felt that more than the grief and remorse over losing his brother, and then that brought new pain. New self-loathing. He had no right not to miss his brother. To push him aside. To forget him.

His dad strolled into the living area. "Your mother was sort of hoping you were holed up with that Long girl."

The preposterousness of his dad's statement made him hiss out a breath. "What?"

"You like her."

He did. So much. Too much. He walked from the window to the sofa. His sweatpants baggy after days of not eating. "What difference does it make?"

"It makes a lot of difference." His dad sat on the sofa. "You mother thought Leni was helping you get beyond some of your grief."

"I'll never get beyond this."

His dad's face grew solemn, so sad Nick couldn't remember ever seeing that expression before. "You have to get beyond this."

Nick sat on the chair he'd sat on to tell Leni to leave.

To explain why he couldn't love her. He tried to say something but nothing came out.

"You liked Leni, right?"

He groaned internally at having this conversation with the father who pushed him and yelled at him, but he was dutiful now. So, he didn't argue.

"Of course, I did."

"Your mother thinks she was nature's way of nudging you to finally get beyond all this."

He sniffed. "My mother thinks a lot."

"Yeah, well, I took the job in the beginning. I forced you to work. I pushed you and yelled at you and made you get up every day and go to the office and have a purpose."

Nick stilled. "You didn't boss me around because you were angry with me?"

"No! I didn't want you to sink into a depression so far we'd lose you. Do you think I wanted to force you to work? I knew how hard Joe's death was on you. I *knew* you blamed yourself. Suffered in silence. And I knew if we let you go on like that, you'd never recover."

Thinking back on those days, seeing them in a new light, brought tears to his eyes. Everything was so confused. "I'm not exactly recovered now."

"Actually, son, I think that's what's nagging at you. You *are* recovering. You want to move on. But part of you won't let you. Holding onto the guilt is your penance."

Nick took a breath. "Oh, yeah?"

"Your mom and I went to therapy. Not for us. To figure out how to help you. That was our therapist's conclusion. Your guilt is how you think you make amends. But all you're doing is losing your life, too. Your mom and I don't want to lose both of our sons. Now that we finally see this light of hope, we're not letting it pass." His dad rose. "I won't push. Neither will your mom. This has to be up to you. But you like her. Maybe even love her. And it's time. We miss Joe, but we miss you, too." He paused, put a hand on Nick's shoulder. "We want you back. The real you."

The real him? The happy-go-lucky guy who only wanted fun was gone.

And though his dad might think he wanted the old Nick back, Nick wasn't that guy anymore.

He didn't want to be. He liked who he was now.

Leni would tell him that was vain.

He laughed. Then sniffed as the elevator doors closed on his dad. Setting aside his grief was too much. Too, too much.

He thought of skating with Leni. He remembered how he'd thought of Joe in a good way and how he'd been able to think about him without dwelling on it.

He thought of the Irish pub, telling her about his real self and having her nestle against him as they walked back to her hotel.

He thought about kissing her, being drawn in, always thinking about a future with her because that's what he'd been fighting. The knowledge that he wanted more with her.

He'd sent her off in the worst possible time of year in the worst possible way. He'd ruined her Christmas with his bluntness.

But he also might have ruined his one chance with her. She was a smart woman. He'd told her to move on and she'd probably listened.

He rubbed his hands down his face. His horrible life collided with the possibility of a new one. Strength he never realized he had punched its way up from his soul.

He missed Leni with an ache that gave spark and breath to the new yearnings struggling for life. His life.

His dad was right. He had to move on.

But could he?

And if he did, would Leni even want him anymore?

* * *

It took far too long for Nick to get from New York to Mannington. And when he got there, he froze. The Long house
was dark. Still, he knocked. But no one answered.

It flitted through his mind that her dad might have had
a seizure, but their network was too strong. She'd have
called Danny and Danny would have called him.

So maybe they were at Christmas Eve services?

Suddenly a light came on in what Nick knew to be the
kitchen, so he knocked again.

With her parents on their way to bed, Leni finished the
last chapter of her book and almost turned out her light
but there was a knock at her door.

Emotionally and physically exhausted, she walked to
the kitchen to turn on the light, then into the living room
where she opened door to find Nick.

Her chest tightened and hope rose, but she reminded
herself of everything he'd told her. She'd pushed him into
admitting the worst secret anyone could have and he'd explained that was why he didn't want a relationship.

She'd done enough damage to this man. She wouldn't
do anymore. So, she smiled politely and said, "What are
you doing here? Did something happen with the estate?"

"No. I'm visiting you."

Her heart hurt just looking at him. His eyes were tired
as if he hadn't slept in days. His chin and cheeks had at
least three days' growth of beard. Now that she knew the
extent of his grief, his pain, everything inside her hurt
for him.

"Can I come in?"

"Sure. I'm sorry! I should have let you in right away."
She wouldn't be so foolish as to believe he'd come here
because he loved her. The things he'd told her were too
deep to be dismissed in a few days. But maybe he'd come

to talk. They'd always been able to talk. And maybe she *could* help him?

He stepped inside and shrugged out of his parka, which she hung on a hook by the door. "I missed you."

That broke her heart. She wanted it to mean a thousand different things, but knew it was merely proof she'd insinuated herself into his life. "I missed you, too."

She motioned for him to sit on the chair and she sat on the sofa across from him.

"I had a long talk with my dad. My parents would like me to fall in love with you."

She would have laughed at the second part of his confession, but the first part threw her. "You had a long talk with your dad?"

"He told me he'd pushed me after Joe died because he knew my grief and guilt were too much to handle. That if he hadn't given me a purpose with running the family business, I might not have ever recovered."

She pictured his gruff dad saying that, then realized she might have interpreted his dad all wrong. What she saw as gruffness might have been his desperate way of keeping Nick from crumbling.

"He's probably right."

Nick leaned forward, his elbows on his knees, his hands clasped. "They've watched me take the blame for Joe these past five years, wondering if I'd ever get beyond it."

"Oh." How sad for them. How sad for Nick.

"Then you came into the picture and they said I changed."

"You had." She'd seen him changing, loved that he could be so fun with her.

"Their thought is that you nudged me back into the real world because I really liked you."

Her heart stuttered. "What do you think?"

He met her gaze. "That they were right."

"So, all the pushing I did wasn't bad?"

"You didn't push."

"I wasn't the desperate foster kid once again looking for love?"

"First of all, you have love. Your parents adore you. But, second, we were drawn together. From the second our eyes met the first time, I felt it. You are the perfect woman for me. You make me laugh. You make me think. You got me out of my condo more than I'd been out in five years. And you pick good Christmas gifts. My mother loved that kimono thing. We did our Christmas this afternoon, so I could come here to see you."

A small laugh escaped. She didn't see the grief and pain that had been on his face the day he'd told her about his brother. Everything felt washed clean.

He sat back, ran his hands down his face. "I hope I didn't ruin what we had. My life was a mess. But I'm ready to move on. Though I'll never forget what happened, never forget Joe, he wouldn't want me to live the way I have been."

"From the things you'd said, he sounded like a good brother."

He shook his head. "He was."

They were quiet for a minute. Leni took a breath. She felt a nudge. An odd sensation that someone was telling her it was her move. That he'd dwelled enough on the past and she was the one helping him move into the future. "Want a cookie?"

He laughed. "The iced ones?"

"Made them myself with my dad and mom."

She led him into the kitchen. Pulled milk from the refrigerator and a container of cookies from the cupboard. Before she could open either, Nick caught her by the waist and spun her around.

He pressed his lips to hers, kissing her long and deep and she melted into him.

When he finally broke the kiss, he said, "I think I love you."

She slapped his arm playfully. "You goof. I know I love you."

"Even though you have more money than me now?"

She pretended to ponder that. "We'll see how it goes." Then she bounced to her tiptoes and kissed him this time.

"You know I expect you to woo me."

"Does anybody really woo anybody anymore?"

"I don't know. I don't care. But I want wine and roses, to be taken to dinner…"

"And trips to France?"

Her eyes widened. "Yes! More trips to France."

He kissed her again, not desperately, as he had before, but with a simple longing that matched the beating of her own heart, the buildup of hope that she wouldn't be alone anymore.

They really were a good pair. The best pair. Because they both understood that life wasn't always easy, but they could handle it.

Together.

EPILOGUE

As usual on Christmas Eve night, snow fell on Mannington, Kansas. One year after their first Christmas together, Nick and Leni left the totally remodeled Family Diner, which they now owned and which they paid George handsomely to manage. The old Christmas bells that typically hung from the streetlights had been cleaned up and repainted. Red ribbons graced the parking meters. The storefronts for the bakery, coffee shop, auto mechanic and grocery had been renovated. All the sidewalks had been repaved.

Wearing a black leather jacket and to-die-for black boots with jeans and a new white turtleneck sweater, Leni took a long drink of air. "Do you think your mom will like what we got her for Christmas?"

"I'm not exactly sure how you had time to shop when you were arranging to move one of Hinton Industries' manufacturing plants here."

"I had a little help from a special Santa."

Nick laughed. "I'm glad you figured out how to get help." He glanced at her. "It's been a busy year for you."

"And you."

"Yeah, but I didn't become wealthy overnight, meet a new brother and sister, go through a complicated surgery with my adoptive dad and singlehandedly become the redevelopment authority for one very happy small town."

She grinned. Becoming a Hinton heir had been one surprise after another. Fixing up her small town, making it somewhere everybody loved to live, had been the obvious thing to do. But finding real love with Nick, finding a partner, had made it all like a great adventure.

"It was a fabulous year."

As always when she said the word *fabulous*, they exchanged a glance and laughed.

"Now, you have to plan a wedding."

She took in a deep drink of air. "Is this a proposal?"

"Yes." He laughed. "Finally." He pulled a ring box from his jacket pocket, paused in the street and got down on one knee. "Leni Long, will you do me the honor of being my wife, my life partner, person destined to spend most of our money?"

Though she had been expecting the proposal, tears filled her eyes. "Yes."

He got up and kissed her. As always, her heart warmed, then her limbs warmed, then heat filled her. Somedays she couldn't believe this man loved her. Other days, she couldn't believe she'd managed so many years without him.

They broke the kiss and smiled at each other. Looking at her beautiful ring, she said, "Where should we get married?"

"Well, your dad loves the Key West house."

She pondered that, gazing around at the new storefronts as they walked through the snow on their way to the house they'd built as their home base. His New York penthouse was empty more than it was occupied these days.

Friends said hello and waved as they walked by. Snow sparkled in the glow of the streetlights. The sound of the choir rippled out from the well-lit church where Christmas Eve services were being held.

This was and always would be her home.

She stopped Nick. "I think I'd like to get married here."

He glanced around. "Here?"

"On Christmas Eve."

"Christmas Eve?"

"And I'd like to invite the whole town."

He gaped at her. "That's fifteen *hundred* people."

"I know!" She laughed merrily. "But we can afford it."

He shook his head, but when he looked around, he saw what she saw. Not merely a group of houses and businesses, but friends who sometimes felt like family. He saw hope. He saw the future.

He slid his arm across Leni's shoulders and began walking again. "I suppose you're going to want to build a hall big enough for fifteen hundred people to celebrate."

"And maybe expand the church."

He threw his head back and laughed. The minute Leni had entered his world, he'd gotten his life back.

As for his love of adventure? He had more than a feeling this woman was about to take him on the ride of his life.

* * * * *

MAVERICK
CHRISTMAS
SURPRISE

BRENDA HARLEN

To my MAC girls—Stacy, Freda, Elena & Jen—
with thanks for so many fabulous memories
(and in anticipation of many, many more!).

Prologue

Dallas, Texas
Christmas Eve

Beth Ames couldn't help but sing along with the holiday song on the radio. Christmas had always been her favorite time of the year, and she was even more excited this holiday season because it was her nephew's first. Four-month-old Cody was the love of her life, and she was grateful—if a little surprised—that her sister had invited her to celebrate the milestone occasion with them.

Over the years, the relationship between Beth and Leighton had been strained more often than not. While Beth might wish it wasn't so, she couldn't change the dynamic on her own, and her sister had always rebuffed her efforts to get closer. That had finally changed when Leighton confided to Beth that she was pregnant.

No doubt Leighton had been scared about the prospect of having and raising a child on her own, now that the baby's father was no longer a part of her life. Of course, Beth had questions about the man, but Leighton refused to answer them. And the more she pushed, the more her sister resisted.

"I appreciate your support, but I don't need your lectures," she'd said. "So if you want to be there with me when the baby is born, you'll stop asking about a guy who, I can assure you, has less than zero interest in being a dad."

Beth wondered how her sister could be so certain of his disinterest if she hadn't told him about her condition, but she bit her tongue. Because as much as she believed the father-to-be had a right to know, she didn't want to do anything to jeopardize their tentative truce.

Instead, Beth had focused on doing what she could to support Leighton throughout her pregnancy. She'd coached her during sixteen hours of labor, and she'd spent every free minute with the new mom and her baby during the first few weeks—until Leighton had recovered enough to demand some space.

Still, she understood that motherhood was a big adjustment for her usually vivacious and fun-loving sister, and she tried to help without stepping on the new mom's toes. But as the weeks turned into months, Leighton seemed increasingly worn out and unhappy.

Thankfully the onset of the Christmas season had revived her sister's good spirits. She'd been so genuinely filled with holiday spirit that she'd invited Beth to spend Christmas Eve at her apartment and even stay over to share in the morning celebration.

So now here she was, with her back seat full of festively wrapped presents and a box of groceries to prepare the holiday meal.

She didn't see her sister's car in its assigned parking spot, but it wouldn't be out of character for her to have forgotten something she needed to have before the stores closed. And since Leighton had given her a spare key, Beth didn't hesitate to let herself in so that she could put the perishables in the fridge.

After the groceries were away, she plugged in the Christmas tree lights and turned on the radio, tuning it to her favorite station that had been playing "all holiday music, all the time" since the first of December.

Feeling excited, and a little impatient, Beth decided to

call her sister to find out when she'd be home. She was surprised, when the phone started to ring, to hear an echo of the sound coming from the bedroom—where she discovered Leighton's cell plugged into the charger on the bedside table.

Shaking her head over her sister's forgetfulness, she started to turn away when she saw a note beside the charger with her name on it.

Beth,
Change of plans—sorry. I'll explain when I can.
Merry Christmas.
XO
L

Change of plans?
What the heck was *that* supposed to mean?
Where had her sister gone?
And, more important, *where was Cody?*

Chapter One

Rust Creek Falls, Montana
Christmas Day

And another one bites the dust, Wilder thought, listening to the excited chatter of conversation around the table as everyone congratulated Hunter and Merry on their engagement.

But he kept a smile on his face, because his brother was grinning, the bride-to-be was glowing and six-year-old Wren was ecstatic that her Christmas wish for a new mommy had come true. He was happy for Hunter and Merry and the new family they were making together, but he was also grateful that he wasn't shackled with the responsibilities of a wife or child.

Not that any of his siblings acted as if they were constrained by their relationships. In fact, his brothers Logan, Xander, Knox, Finn and now Hunter, too, seemed sincerely happy to have found a special someone to share their lives. But Wilder wasn't in any hurry to follow in their footsteps. He was perfectly happy with his life the way it was right now. As the old saying went, "if it ain't broke, don't fix it."

"I'm a lucky woman," Merry said, responding to a comment from one of her future brothers-in-law.

"And Hunter's a lucky man," Max said, about his newly engaged son.

Wilder couldn't help but notice that, in addition to the paternal pride on his father's face, there was a look of smug satisfaction. When the family had moved from Dallas to Rust Creek Falls six months earlier, Max had set out to find romantic matches for all of his sons—even going so far as to enlist the services of a local wedding planner to act as a matchmaker and offering her a million-dollar bonus if she succeeded. With the announcement of Hunter and Merry's engagement, he obviously felt as if he was well on his way to accomplishing his goal.

Five out of six was a pretty impressive success rate, Wilder acknowledged to himself. But his dad was doomed to disappointment if he expected to go six-for-six, because, at this point in his life, Wilder would rather be dead than wed.

"I'm lucky, too," Wren piped up, eager to be part of the conversation.

"You certainly are," Max agreed, and winked at his granddaughter before turning his attention back to the little girl's father and Hunter's fiancée. "And if there was any doubt about what was going on between you two, your daughter took care of that when she spilled the beans as soon as she ran into the house."

Wren's brow furrowed. "I didn't spill anything, Gramps," she said, obviously interpreting his remark literally. "I just said that Daddy's gonna marry Merry, and I get to be in the wedding and then she's gonna be my mom."

Yep, five out of six was impressive.

And now that five of his sons were happily settled, Max would no doubt focus all his attention on the sole remaining holdout.

Oh, hell.

Wilder didn't realize he'd spoken aloud until Hunter sternly admonished him with a single word: "Language."

"Sorry," he said, his apology automatic and sincere as he looked at each of the couples around the table.

"But I just realized that I'm the last Crawford bachelor standing."

His announcement of this uncomfortable truth was followed by several chuckles and teasing warnings from his siblings and their partners.

"I'm right there with you," Max pointed out to his youngest son.

"Says the man paying to get us all married off," Wilder noted dryly.

"Suck it up, kid," Finn said, with absolutely no sympathy in his tone. Because why should he feel sorry for his little brother? Finn was happily married to Avery and anticipating the birth of his first child with his bride of two months.

Then Finn shifted his attention to Hunter and Merry. "I guess this means that you two will be the next Crawford couple to take on the mysterious diary."

The book he was referring to had been discovered beneath a loose floorboard shortly after they'd moved into the two-story log home on the Ambling A Ranch. Apparently the "A" was for "Abernathy"—the name of the family who'd originally owned the property. A jewel-encrusted "A" was also on the front cover of the diary, suggesting the book had belonged to a member of the family.

Merry looked at her fiancé. "With everything going on, I almost forgot to tell you what I found out the night of Wren's play."

But whatever she'd learned would remain unknown to the rest of them a while longer, as an unexpected knock at the door interrupted her announcement.

Wilder's gaze moved around the table again, confirming that everyone who was supposed to be there for the family meal was present and accounted for.

So who the heck would be visiting on Christmas Day?

He pushed his chair away from the table to find out. Hunter stood at the same time, and the brothers made their way through the kitchen toward the source of the summons.

As Hunter opened the door, Wilder's attention was snagged by a blur of color on the driveway. By the time he registered that it was a red car, he was staring at tail-lights as the vehicle drove off. Fast. He squinted, trying to decipher the license plate, but the car was already too far away. The best he could do was to note that the plate was from Texas.

"I guess whoever knocked must have realized they were at the wrong place," he decided, despite a niggling feeling that he should have recognized the departing car.

"Or they did what they came here to do," his brother suggested.

Wilder glanced questioningly at Hunter, then followed the direction he was pointing and discovered an infant car seat on the porch—with a baby inside!

"What the—"

"There's a note." Hunter bent down to fish out a piece of paper pinned to the blue blanket wrapped around the sleeping baby.

He unfolded the page to reveal a handwritten message in a distinctly feminine scrawl and began to read aloud:

"'Wilder—'" he glanced up from the page to give his brother a quizzical look before continuing "'—this is your baby. I've done the best I could for four months and I can't do it anymore. A boy needs a dad and you're Cody's, so it's your turn now. Please take good care of him.' It's signed 'L.'"

He looked at Wilder again. "Well, little brother, looks like you got a baby for Christmas."

Wilder snatched the paper out of Hunter's hand to read it for himself.

His brother said something else, but Wilder didn't hear him.

He stared at the writing on the page, as if he could will the words to change—or at least make sense of them. But none of this made any sense to him. It simply wasn't possible that he was the father of this kid.

Was it?

"What's going on out here?" Max wanted to know, pushing his way between his sons. "Good Lord…it's a baby."

"Wilder's baby," Hunter said and, miming the act of washing his hands, retreated into the house where the rest of the family was gathered.

His father pinned Wilder with his gaze. "You want to explain this?"

"I wish I could," he said. "But I've never seen the kid before. I'm as shocked by this as you are."

"But it's yours," his father remarked.

It wasn't a question.

"That's what the note says," Wilder acknowledged.

"You don't believe it?" Max asked him.

"I don't know what to believe. What to think." He scrubbed a hand over his face, sincerely baffled by this turn of events. He wanted to believe it was a joke, though he wasn't the least bit amused. "Who would abandon their kid on somebody's doorstep in the middle of winter?"

"Not just *somebody's* doorstep," his father argued. "The baby's father's doorstep."

He shook his head. "It's not possible."

"You've never been intimate with a woman?" Max challenged.

It was, of course, a rhetorical question. Though Wilder didn't share details of his romantic encounters, he'd been caught—more than once—sneaking into the house the morning after he'd spent the night in a woman's bed.

"I'm careful," he assured his father. *"Always."*

"Accidents happen," Max said matter-of-factly.

It was a terrifying thought.

"The note says he's four months old," his father continued. "Adding nine months to that is thirteen, which means the baby would have been conceived sometime around November last year."

"Okay," Wilder said hesitantly.

"So who were you with last November?" Max pressed.

Last November? *Seriously?*

He shrugged. "How am I supposed to remember something that happened that far back?"

Which he immediately realized was *not* the right thing to say to his father under the circumstances.

"You should darn well remember a woman who shared your bed," Max said, the low tone of his voice doing nothing to disguise the underlying anger and disappointment. "I don't expect you to be in love with every woman you sleep with, but you should know and respect her enough to remember her name."

"Give me a break," Wilder pleaded. "My head's spinning so fast, it's a wonder I know my own name right now."

"Well, there's no doubt the baby looks like a Crawford."

"The baby looks like a baby," Wilder said. Because in his admittedly limited experience with infants, they all looked like bald, chubby-cheeked, squalling little monsters.

As if on cue, the one buckled into the car seat started to squirm and squall.

Wilder stepped back, an instinctive retreat.

"Pick him up and bring him inside," Max said.

"Me?" Wilder was horrified by the very thought.

With a sigh, his father reached down and grabbed the

car seat with one hand and the enormous diaper bag with the other.

"Hunter said there was a baby on the doorstep," Avery said, entering the kitchen from the dining room at the same time that Wilder and Max came in from the porch.

Then she spotted the carrier in Max's hand and her expression softened. "Ohmygod—it *is* a baby." Her gaze shifted to Wilder. "Why didn't you tell anyone you're a daddy?"

"Because I'm *not*," Wilder insisted. "There's no way that kid's mine."

"He's in denial," Genevieve, his brother Knox's wife, said. Because apparently Hunter's announcement had drawn everyone away from the table.

"I think the baby's hungry," Lily said worriedly.

"You just want to feed everyone," her husband Xander teased.

"He is gnawing on his fist," Hunter noted. "And that's a telltale sign of hunger."

As Hunter was the only one of his brothers with significant daddy experience, Wilder was willing to defer to his expertise. But having the problem identified didn't give him the first clue about how to solve it.

So when his brothers and their partners—and Wren—huddled around the baby, pushing Wilder and Max out of the way, Wilder didn't object.

"He's definitely hungry," Sarah said, as the baby's unhappy cries turned to sobs.

"Let's see if there's a bottle in the bag," Merry suggested.

There were, in fact, two bottles—one premixed and one empty, plus a can of powdered formula.

Avery unbuckled the harness and lifted the infant out of his seat. His plaintive cries immediately ceased.

Everyone seemed to be talking at once, speculating

about the note as they fussed over the little guy. Wilder took advantage of their preoccupation to study the baby—who didn't seem quite so intimidating now that he was quiet—and realized, a little uneasily, that the baby was staring back at him.

Is it possible? he wondered. *Can he be mine?*

"Where'd the baby come from?" Wren wanted to know.

"Someone left him on the doorstep," her dad explained.

"Maybe he's a gift from Santa," she suggested.

Hunter chuckled. "Unfortunately for Uncle Wilder, I don't think the baby came with a gift receipt."

"He does look a lot like Wilder's old baby photos," Logan, the eldest Crawford brother, noted.

"He does not," Wilder denied, though without much conviction.

But no one was paying any attention to him, anyway.

Except his father, who sidled closer. "The note was signed with the letter 'L,'" Max noted. "Does that jog your memory at all?"

He automatically started to shake his head, because he didn't want his memory jogged. And if he was in denial—well, he was quite happy to stay there. Because in denial, his life was easy and carefree and he didn't have the responsibility of an infant who'd been dumped into his lap—or, to be more precise, on his doorstep.

But somehow, in the midst of all the chaos going on around him, hazy memories slowly came into focus in Wilder's mind. Memories of an early holiday party at Reunion Tower in Dallas, a few too many cocktails and a pretty—and very adventurous—blonde named Leighton Ames. And no, he wasn't oblivious to the fact that her name started with the same letter that had been scrawled on the bottom of the note.

They'd had a good time together, not just that night, but

for several weeks afterward. And then, just as suddenly as their relationship had started, it ended.

Her decision, Wilder remembered now.

Just after the New Year, she'd abruptly called things off. He'd been a little disappointed at first, but there were plenty of other women in the world. And truthfully, he hadn't thought of her again—until now.

Was Leighton the baby's mother?

Was it possible that he *was* the father of this baby who'd been abandoned on the doorstep?

But if she believed that to be true, why hadn't she ever told him that she was pregnant?

Well, he could probably guess the answer to that one. Either Leighton wasn't sure about the baby's paternity, or she didn't trust him to step up.

He would have, of course. He would have undoubtedly felt panicked and trapped, but he would have done the right thing. Not that she could have known that, because they hadn't had the type of relationship where they talked about their future hopes and dreams. Their conversations had been more along the lines of "your place or mine?" And after that question had been answered, there had been even less talking.

But if she hadn't trusted him to step up, why would she dump the baby on him now?

And how did she even know where to find him?

He'd had no communication with her in almost a year. And the last time they were together, he didn't know that he'd be moving to Rust Creek Falls, so it was unlikely she could have tracked him down here.

Reassured by his own reasoning that it couldn't have been Leighton who dropped the baby off—and conveniently ignoring the fact that his name was on the note—Wilder breathed a sigh of relief, confident that he was off the hook. But his father would require additional proof, so as the rest of the family went back into the dining room, he scrolled through the contacts in his phone to see if he still had her number.

Amazingly, he did, and tapped it to initiate the call.

"Hello?"

The female voice that immediately answered sounded frantic.

"Um...hi," he said. "I'm trying to reach Leighton Ames."

"You and me both," she replied, sounding as if she was fighting tears.

He frowned at that. "Is this still her number?"

"Yes, but she forgot her phone when she left." The woman on the other end of the line sighed. "Or maybe she didn't forget it."

Which didn't make any sense to him, but all he said was: "Well, if you hear from her, can you ask her to call Wilder Crawford?"

"Why?" She sounded both curious and wary. "What business do you have with my sister?"

Sister?

He couldn't recall Leighton mentioning a sister, but surely a sister would know if Leighton had had a baby. And if this was Leighton's baby, that meant the woman on the phone was the baby's aunt.

Before he could ask, she spoke again. "Wait a minute—did you say Wilder Crawford?"

"I did," he confirmed.

"I found your name and a Montana address scrawled on a Post-it note in Leighton's apartment," she said. "I think she might be on her way to see you."

The knots in his stomach tightened. "She might have been here already...and left something."

He heard a sharp intake of breath. "What kind of something?"

"A baby," he admitted. "Did she—"

"Cody!" she immediately interjected, not giving him a chance to finish. "You have Cody?"

"That's the name in the note," he confirmed.

"Note?" she echoed.

"The baby was left on my doorstep with a note."

"I don't understand. Why would she leave her baby?"

"I wish I knew," he told her.

"Are you Cody's father?" she guessed.

"Obviously your sister thinks so."

"You haven't seen her or talked to her?"

"Not in the past year."

"But Cody's with you? At the Ambling A Ranch in Montana?"

"That's right," he confirmed.

"Okay. I'll be there as soon as I can," she promised.

"Wait—"

But she'd already disconnected the call.

"What did you find out?" Max asked, when Wilder returned to the table where Lily had resumed serving dessert and Avery rocked the now quiet baby.

"The kid's mom is Leighton Ames," he said. "I spoke to her sister, but she doesn't know where she is or why she left the baby here."

"Because she wanted him to be with his dad," Max suggested as an answer to the latter question.

Wilder hoped like hell his father was wrong.

"Do you want ice cream with your pie?" Merry asked him.

Because for the rest of the family gathered together, today was still a celebration—and it was time for dessert.

"Sure," he said.

Though he wasn't even sure he wanted the pie now, he didn't want his family to know how freaked out he was about the arrival of the baby they were all happy enough to assume was his and turning down dessert would be a definite red flag.

"I want ice cream," Wren piped up, pushing her bowl toward her soon-to-be-stepmother who was scooping it.

"You already had ice cream," her dad reminded her, pulling the bowl back again before Merry could indulge the little girl's request.

Wren pouted and dragged her spoon around the inside of the empty vessel.

Wilder took the plate Merry passed to him and murmured his thanks. Then he halved the scoop of ice cream with the side of his fork and slid half into his niece's bowl.

Wren beamed at him; Hunter scowled.

"There's a reason I'm the favorite uncle," he said, and winked at the little girl.

"I'm finished with my dessert," Finn said to his wife then, "if you want me to take the baby."

"I can manage the baby," Avery assured him. "If you want to be helpful, you can start clearing the table."

As Finn began gathering empty plates and glasses, Wilder dug his fork into his pie, giving up the pretense of an appetite.

"Did you ask for a baby for Christmas, Uncle Wilder?" his niece asked, around a mouthful of ice cream.

"No." His response was immediate and definitive.

"I guess you're just lucky then," Wren decided.

Lucky?

Oh yeah, he had a horseshoe so far up his butt he couldn't swallow the pie that was stuck in his throat.

The house emptied quickly after dessert was finished and the cleanup complete, leaving Wilder and his father alone with the baby. Then Max took off, too, to pick up a crib he'd arranged to borrow from one of their many Crawford relatives in town.

Wilder had offered to make the trip, but his dad had insisted that he stay at the Ambling A to watch the baby. For the first half hour, there weren't any major snags—because the kid slept. But when he woke up, he was not in a very good mood.

The baby didn't cry. Not really. But his face was all scrunched up and he was squirming in his seat, and Wilder braced himself for the crying to start.

"Avery promised that you would sleep for a few hours," Wilder said, trying to reason with the infant. "That was barely more than an hour ago."

His words got the kid's attention, though, and he fixed his big, blue eyes on Wilder.

"You can't be hungry already," he continued, in the same logical tone. "You sucked back a whole bottle before she left."

The baby continued to fuss, clearly unconvinced and unhappy.

And his lower lip was starting to do that quivering thing that warned Wilder real tears and sobs likely weren't too far behind.

"I'm sorry," he said. "But I don't know what to do."

"You could try picking him up."

Wilder turned to see Hunter standing in the doorway. "I thought you'd gone home."

"I did," his brother confirmed. "And then I came back."

"Why?"

"Because I thought you might want to talk to someone who's been where you are."

On another day, Wilder might have made a snarky comment about not remembering when a baby had been left on Hunter's doorstep, but right now, he was too grateful for his presence to risk saying anything that might prompt him to leave again.

"I think I need a manual more than a sounding board," he confided.

"A manual would be useless," Hunter said. "Because every baby is different."

"So how am I supposed to know what's wrong with this one?"

"He's probably out of sorts because he doesn't know where his mama is."

"That makes two of us," Wilder said.

"And when babies are out of sorts, they need to be comforted."

He gestured to the infant in his carrier. "Feel free."

But his brother shook his head. "You need to step up."

"I would have stepped up months ago if Leighton had told me she was pregnant," he said in his defense.

"So why are you hesitating now?" his brother challenged.

"Because I don't have the first clue what to do with a baby."

"No first-time parent has a clue in the beginning."

His brother's matter-of-fact statement was hardly reassuring.

And while they were talking, the baby was growing more distressed.

With a sigh of resignation, Wilder unhooked the strap and lifted him out of the seat.

The baby stopped fussing for a moment to stare at him, as if waiting for something else.

Something more.

Wilder looked at his brother. "I'm doing this wrong, aren't I?"

"Babies generally like to be held closer than arm's length," Hunter told him.

Wilder pulled his arms toward his chest, so that he was almost nose-to-nose with the kid.

Hunter started to chuckle, but quickly covered it with a cough when Wilder glared at him.

"Closer," he urged. "But to the side, with his head about level with your shoulder so he can see behind you. With newborns, you need to keep one hand on the bottom and the other on the head and neck, for support, but he's obviously strong enough to hold his head up just fine."

Wilder did his best to follow his brother's instructions.

"That's it," Hunter assured him.

"He feels so tiny." His whispered remark was filled with awe and wonder—and just a hint of the nerves that were tangled up inside him. "So fragile."

"It's normal to be scared. I was terrified the first time I held Wren in my arms," his brother confided. "And she was a lot smaller than Cody is."

"But you had nine months to prepare yourself for her arrival," Wilder pointed out, though he wasn't sure anything could have prepared him for this moment.

Hunter nodded. "True."

Wilder patted the baby's back gently, as he'd watched Sarah do, and was rewarded with a shockingly loud belch.

"Gas might have been another cause of his distress," Hunter noted then.

"You think?" Wilder asked dryly.

"And now that it's out of his system, you can try the cradle hold," he said, and talked him through shifting the baby's position so that he was tucked in the crook of Wilder's arm. "Now sit down and relax."

Relax? He wasn't sure he'd be able to relax so long as there was a baby under his roof.

And though Leighton's note had given no indication that she was planning to come back for the little guy, he had to believe that she would. After all, what kind of mom just left her kid?

Mine, he thought, then shoved the unpleasant twinge from his mind.

Hunter took another seat at the table, leaning back in the chair and stretching his legs out in front.

Obviously relaxing wasn't a problem for him.

"Where'd Dad go?" he asked.

"To pick up a crib," Wilder told him.

"Ah, right. He said he was going to try to rustle up some of the stuff you'd need from local relatives," his brother recalled.

"Unfortunately, I don't think one of those things is a nanny."

Hunter chuckled. "No, he's been pretty clear that your baby is your responsibility."

"But we don't even know for sure that he is my baby," Wilder felt compelled to point out again.

"Obviously his mom is sure. Though I have to wonder, if you haven't kept in touch with her, how did she know where to find you?"

"I've been wondering the same thing. My best guess is Malcolm," Wilder said, naming a close buddy from Dallas. "When I talked to him a few weeks back, he'd mentioned that one of the girls we'd met at the holiday party before Christmas last year had shown up at his office to ask about me. But he told me that before Thanksgiving, and since nothing came of it…"

"Until now," Hunter remarked.

"Until now," he agreed.

"So the who and the how have been answered," his brother noted. "But we still don't know the why—beyond the obvious, of course."

"What's the obvious?" Wilder wondered.

"What 'L' wrote in her note—a boy needs a dad."

"Which proves she doesn't know me at all, or she'd know I'm not dad material."

"Or maybe she knows you better than you know yourself," Hunter suggested. "But since I'm not completely without sympathy, I'll give you a crash course in diapering and feeding."

"I can hardly wait," he said dryly.

"Or I can let you figure it out on your own," his brother suggested as an alternative.

"Please don't," he said, immediately remorseful. "I need all the help I can get."

"You're doing okay so far," Hunter assured him.

"Because I'm not doing anything."

"You've managed to relax," his brother pointed out. "And that's allowed Cody to relax, too."

Wilder looked down at the little guy tucked in the crook of his arm, close to his body.

He did look relaxed. Content even, his eyelids heavy, as if he might—fingers crossed—drift off to sleep again. And Wilder felt a small measure of satisfaction that he'd been the one to put that look on his face, though the satisfaction wasn't nearly strong enough to quell the rising tide of panic within him.

"I'm not ready for this," he confided. "I figured I had another ten years of footloose and fancy-free living before I even thought about getting serious with a woman—and then a few more after that before I had to worry about becoming a dad."

"There's nothing more serious than parenthood, or more amazing and awe-inspiring," Hunter told him.

The baby turned his head then, rubbing his cheek against the soft plaid of Wilder's shirt, just about where he felt his heart swell inside his chest.

And Wilder knew that whatever happened next, he and the kid were in this together.

Chapter Two

Beth turned up the radio and lowered the window a couple of inches, just far enough to allow the icy December air to sweep through the interior of her car and jolt her weary brain and sleepy body awake. Eager to get to Rust Creek Falls, she'd left Dallas almost immediately after ending her telephone conversation with Wilder Crawford, making only brief stops to fill her gas tank and use the bathroom. Now, after almost twenty-eight hours on the road, she was tired and hungry but refused to give in to either before she reached her final destination—and Cody.

She'd looked into flights to Montana, but the last-minute airfares and required connections made it more logical to drive. And now her journey was finally nearing its end.

She couldn't wait to see Cody again, to hold his chubby little body in her arms and breathe in his sweet baby powder scent. She'd been so worried when she found Leighton's note, but after talking to Wilder Crawford, she had reason to believe the baby was okay. She had no clue about her sister. Though Leighton had always been adept at taking care of herself, she hadn't quite been herself since the baby was born. Maybe it wasn't Beth's place to worry about her sister, but of course she *was* worried. And she was concerned that her sweet and innocent nephew was being used as a pawn in whatever game his mother was playing.

When Beth realized her sister was gone—likely headed

to Montana, where one of the previously unidentified potential fathers of her baby apparently now resided—she'd
considered that Leighton might want to reconcile with
her ex. And she'd hoped, for Cody's sake, that was her
sister's plan.

But if what Wilder Crawford had told her was true,
Leighton hadn't even spoken to the man in almost a year.
So why would her sister travel all this way and then not
see him? And why would she abandon her baby on his
doorstep without any warning?

Maybe Leighton had decided that she needed a break
from the day-to-day responsibilities of caring for Cody.
But why not leave him in Dallas with his aunt? Why drive
all the way to Middle-of-Nowhere, Montana—in the middle of winter, no less—and leave him with a stranger?

Even more than those questions baffled Beth's brain,
the insult wounded her heart. She'd made every effort to be
there for Leighton since she'd learned of her sister's pregnancy. She'd tried to offer support without judgment, help
without expectation. And she'd cried tears of joy along
with her sister when Cody drew his first breath—and let
it out again as an indignant wail.

Beth would do anything for her nephew—including
driving through the night and all the next day to get to
him. Unfortunately she hadn't considered the changes in
weather that she would encounter en route, and the tires on
her fuel-efficient hatchback had been slipping and sliding
in protest against the snow and ice that had been her near
constant companion since Colorado Springs.

But according to the faded "Welcome to Rust Creek
Falls" sign posted at the side the highway, she had finally
arrived. She checked her speed as she drove down Cedar
Street, noting that the storefronts were all decked out for
the holidays with boughs of evergreen and big red bows
and twinkling lights. Of course, it was late on the day after

Christmas, so the stores were closed, the roads mostly empty. No doubt all the town's residents were huddled comfortably in their homes, basking in the holiday after-glow and enjoying time with family and friends.

Certainly that was how she'd anticipated spending her holiday—not driving 1700 miles on her own, worry growing with each tick of the odometer. But missing out on the holiday didn't matter right now. All that mattered was Cody.

Once she was reunited with her nephew, she would think about how to track down her sister. Or maybe—fingers crossed—Leighton had already decided to return to Rust Creek Falls to pick up her baby and Beth would find her sister at the Ambling A when she arrived.

Continuing to follow the directions on her phone, she finally pulled into a long, winding drive that would sup-posedly lead her to the Ambling A. Assuming, of course, that her GPS wasn't sending her into the middle of a field where she'd get stuck in the snow and find herself sur-rounded by angry cows.

The drive had been plowed, but it was still snow-covered, making everything appear blindingly white when her headlights cut through the blackness of the night. She drove slowly, carefully, following the tire tracks to ensure she didn't veer off the road and end up in a ditch.

The dash clock read 10:14 when she finally saw the two-story log home. Parking behind a dark pickup, she felt a slight twinge of disappointment that she didn't see Leighton's car, but right now her main focus was Cody.

Still, she gave herself a moment to close her eyes that were burning with strain and fatigue. But only a moment, because any longer than that and she wasn't sure she'd manage to open them again. And anyway, as exhausted as she was, her nephew was inside that house, and she couldn't wait a minute longer to see him.

Grabbing her purse, she pushed open the door. The blast of frigid air was a stark reminder that she wasn't in Dallas anymore. Stepping out of the car, she nearly lost her footing on the snow-covered ground as the short-heeled boots that were perfectly suitable for winter in Texas proved to be no match for the ice and snow of Montana.

She blinked in the sudden brightness as a floodlight activated. A motion sensor, she guessed, grateful for the illumination as she moved carefully over the frozen ground.

There were no lights on inside the house, but she wasn't going to let that stop her now.

She noted the pine boughs draped over the railing of the porch and an enormous evergreen wreath decorated with a fancy velvet bow on the door—more reminders of the holiday she'd missed celebrating. She climbed the porch steps and, after a moment's hesitation, bypassed the bell to knock on the door instead.

When there was no response, she knocked a little harder.

Then harder again.

Finally, a light came on overhead, the door was wrenched open from the other side, and Beth found herself face-to-face with an obviously irritated man.

Actually, she was face-to-chest with his gray T-shirt, so she didn't see the scowl that furrowed his brow until she took an instinctive step back and lifted her gaze to his face.

In addition to the scowl, he was wearing a pair of flannel pajama bottoms low on his hips and the previously noted T-shirt that stretched across his muscular torso. He folded strong arms over his broad chest now and pinned her with a dark, piercing gaze, causing her to belatedly question the wisdom of showing up at a stranger's door on an isolated ranch in the middle of the night.

Because she was certain that the sudden dryness of her throat and pounding of her heart were signs of fear and not an immediate and instinctive attraction to the prime male specimen in front of her.

"I don't know where you're from, honey, but 'round here, people don't come visiting in the middle of the night," he said.

The growly timbre of his voice made her shiver.

Or maybe it was just the frigid air temperature.

"Dallas," Beth heard herself respond to what was obviously a rhetorical question. "And I'm not visiting—I'm here for my nephew."

"You're the woman who answered Leighton's phone," he concluded.

"Lisbeth," she said. "But most people call me Beth. And you must be Wilder."

He nodded and, after only a moment's hesitation, stepped away from the door to allow her to enter.

She had a vague impression of a kitchen beyond the entranceway, though the interior was only dimly illuminated by the light that filtered through the window from the porch. She kicked off her boots and left them on the mat by the door and unbuttoned her thin coat as she followed Wilder further into a house that was toasty warm in contrast to the frigid air outside. "Where's Cody?"

She sensed more than saw his frown this time. "Did your sister send you to get him?"

In retrospect, Beth would acknowledge that she should have answered his question with a firm and decisive *yes*. But in her agitated and sleep-deprived state, she wasn't thinking clearly enough to see the obvious solution to her dilemma.

"No, I still haven't heard from Leighton," she admitted instead. "And I'm starting to worry that something might have happened to her."

"I think what happened is that she got tired of being

tied down by a baby," he said, and handed her a piece of paper that he'd retrieved from the table.

As she unfolded the page, he turned on the light over the stove so that she'd be able to read it. Beth immediately recognized her sister's handwriting, and her heart sank as she skimmed the brief words. Then she read them more carefully.

"I don't understand," she said, after she'd scanned the note a third time.

"That makes two of us."

She looked at him again, noting the stubble that darkened his jaw and the overlong and tousled hair that suggested he'd just crawled out of bed. He was undeniably sexy with a slightly dangerous edge—exactly her sister's type.

None of which explained why she felt a quiver low in her belly when she found him looking back at her. Of course, it was probably just that she was overtired and overwhelmed and worried about her nephew. It certainly wasn't a visceral response to his nearness. It couldn't be.

She cleared her throat as she refolded the note and handed it back to Wilder. "I want to see Cody now. Please."

He hesitated, and for a moment, she thought he might refuse. But maybe he sensed that she wouldn't be put off— and that, if he even tried, she'd raise enough ruckus to wake the whole house—because he finally nodded.

She followed him through the darkness, up a set of stairs, then down a hall until he finally paused in an open doorway. She glanced past him, into a room dimly illuminated by a nightlight plugged in beside a crib.

"It looks like maybe you were expecting him," she noted.

He shook his head. "Maggie and Jesse—distant but local relatives—loaned us the crib. And the rocking chair."

Beth tiptoed to the crib, exhaling a long, quiet sigh of relief when she gazed down at the sleeping baby.

"It's okay, Cody. I'm here to take you home now." She murmured the words softly as she reached down to lift him into her arms and cuddle him against her chest. He squirmed a little at first, but settled quickly again without making a sound of protest.

Wilder stepped in front of the door, as if to block her path, and crossed those strong arms over his impressive chest again. "What are you talking about?" Though he kept his volume low so as not to disturb the sleeping infant, there was no mistaking the steel in his words. "You're not going anywhere with that baby."

"Of course, I am," she said. "I'm his aunt. He belongs with me."

"If his mother believed that, why'd she drive halfway across the country to bring him to me?" he challenged.

Beth faltered. "I don't know. But my sister's done a lot of things in her life that I can't begin to fathom."

"Well, it seems obvious to me that there must be a reason Leighton didn't want you caring for her baby."

"*Her* baby?" she echoed. "You don't think he's your baby, too?"

"I don't know what to think," he admitted. "But I know that it's late and this conversation should be tabled until the morning."

"Morning?" she echoed. "I expected to be halfway back to Dallas by morning."

"When was the last time you slept, Lisbeth?"

"It's Beth," she corrected automatically. "And…I'm not sure."

He nodded. "That's what I figured." He pointed to the rocking chair beside the crib. "Sit there with the baby for a few minutes while I make up the bed in the spare room across the hall."

"Oh. Um…thank you."

She hadn't expected an invitation to stay. Of course,

his words had been more in the nature of a command than an offer, but still, she was grateful. So she lowered herself into the rocking chair and snuggled with her nephew.

There were no words to express how happy she was to have Cody in her arms again, how grateful she was to know that he was safe. Worry and desperation had fueled her throughout the trip from Dallas—along with regular infusions of caffeine. But now that she was here, she felt completely drained—physically and emotionally.

She was also relieved that she didn't have to drive any further tonight, even if it was just back into town to rent a room at a local motel. Assuming there was a motel in this town.

In any event, it probably wasn't a bad idea for her to catch some shut-eye before embarking on the return journey.

It didn't take Wilder long to put sheets on the bed in the guest room. And yet, he wasn't surprised to return to the spare room that had been turned into a temporary nursery to find Beth fast asleep in the rocking chair, her nephew still in her arms.

Though he had no reason to doubt her claim that she was Leighton's sister, he couldn't see any obvious family resemblance. Leighton was a spirited blonde, and his first impression of Lisbeth was of a solemn brunette. With her messy ponytail and shapeless coat, Beth bore no physical resemblance to her curvy sister with the infectious laugh and lust for life.

And yet, there was something about Beth that sparked an unexpected—and unwanted—awareness inside him. Or maybe it was her obvious connection to her nephew that tugged at him. She'd wasted no time in making the trip from Dallas to Rust Creek Falls when she learned that he was there, which made him wonder again why Leighton had made the same trip to leave her baby with him when she had a sister who obviously would have been happy to care for the kid.

Unfortunately, he wasn't going to get an answer to that question—or any other questions—tonight. So he reached for the baby, intending to return him to the crib. Beth's arms instinctively tightened around the baby and her eyes flew open—a warrior ready to battle.

"I'm just putting him back in his bed so that you can go to yours," he told her.

She blinked, and he noticed then that she had really pretty eyes—the color of dark chocolate and fringed by a sweep of long, dark lashes.

Those lashes fluttered again as the confusion slowly cleared from her gaze. "Oh. Okay." She whispered her response as she finally relinquished her hold. "I guess I'm more tired than I realized."

"You can sleep now," he said, as she rose from the chair.

She nodded. "Thank you. For letting me stay here tonight."

He didn't point out that the offer had been born of necessity rather than kindness, because he couldn't have her knocking on the door of Strickland's Boarding House at this late hour. And the only other option nearby was Maverick Manor, but he'd heard the owner proudly remark that the hotel was fully booked through the holidays.

"Go." He steered her toward the open doorway across the hall. "There's an unopened toothbrush and toothpaste in the adjoining bathroom, if you need them."

"Thank you," she said again.

He turned back to peek at the baby again, exhaling a weary sigh of relief that the little guy was still sleeping soundly—at least for the moment—before starting toward his own room.

Thanks to the attention and efforts of his family, the baby had been well cared for the previous day. But eventually they'd all headed back to their own homes, leaving Wilder and his dad alone with the infant.

As a father of six boys, Max had had more than his fair share of experience with diapers and bottles, but he'd insisted that this baby was his youngest son's responsibility. Wilder didn't think it was fair that his father was willing to assume that he was the kid's dad just because some woman had scrawled his name at the top of the note.

"And because you admitted that you had a relationship with the mother," Max had explained, when Wilder challenged the assumption of paternity.

He couldn't deny that argument had some merit. That it wasn't entirely outside the realm of possibility that he could be the father.

And that possibility scared the bejeezus out of him.

And if Leighton had paused long enough to consider the implications of that possibility before depositing her child at his door, it would have scared the bejeezus out of her, too.

What had she been thinking?

Unfortunately, the answer to that question was probably that she *hadn't* been thinking.

By her own admission, she wasn't much of a planner. It was more fun, she'd once told him, to live in the moment and embrace whatever surprises life had in store for her.

When Wilder had confided that he wasn't a big fan of surprises, she'd surprised the heck out of him by inviting him back to her place.

And yeah, he'd liked *that* surprise.

This "surprise, you're a daddy" thing—not so much.

And if he really was the kid's dad…well, he couldn't help but feel sorry for the little guy, because there was no chance Wilder was ever going to win a "Father of the Year" award.

Chapter Three

Beth didn't remember her head hitting the pillow.

She fell asleep quickly and slept deeply, and when she opened her eyes again, the clock on the bedside table read 12:48 p.m.

Certain that number couldn't be accurate, she pressed the button on the side of her watch to illuminate its face.

12:48.

She jolted upright, shocked to realize that she'd slept for almost fourteen hours!

Her first thought after that: *Cody.*

She immediately pushed back the covers and hurried across the hall. Her heart, which had been pounding furiously against her ribs, settled into a more normal rhythm when she found her nephew in the crib, sleeping soundly.

She didn't believe for a minute that he was *still* sleeping. More likely, Cody had been up at 6 a.m.—as was his habit—and was now down for his second nap of the day. And because he was napping, she decided to steal a few more minutes for herself and indulge in a hot shower.

And it was an indulgence. She had no idea how old or new the house was, but it was apparent that the bathroom had been recently renovated with a mosaic tile floor and glass-walled shower. She stood for a long time beneath the rainfall shower head, letting the warm water wash over her body, easing the tension and aches in her muscles.

She used the shampoo and bodywash in the enclosure, as her own toiletries were in the duffel bag that she'd left in her car. Which meant that the change of clothes she'd packed for her overnight stay at her sister's apartment was still in the car, too.

As she wrapped herself in a thick, fluffy towel from the heated rack, she considered that ranching was obviously a much more lucrative profession than teaching. Not that she'd ever trade her class of kindergarteners for a field of cows, but she suspected that her sister might not have been so quick to discount the idea of spending her life with a cowboy if she'd known Wilder was a wealthy cowboy.

Of course, thinking about Leighton led to worrying about Leighton, even though Beth knew it was an exercise in futility. She had no way of getting in touch with her sister, so all she could do was monitor her social media accounts, check in with her friends and wait for Leighton to contact her—and ensure that Cody was taken care of while he waited for his mom to come back.

Because Leighton *would* come back. Notwithstanding what she'd written in the note she'd left with Cody, Beth knew that her sister wouldn't abandon her baby. She loved him too much.

Reassured by this internal pep talk, Beth toweled off and got dressed in her old clothes. As she finished toweldrying her hair, she heard voices across the hall in her nephew's temporary bedroom.

No, only one voice, she realized.

Deep and masculine, murmuring in a quiet tone.

Wilder's voice.

Her heart skipped a beat then, as it had the night before when he'd appeared in the door: six-feet-plus of rugged masculinity that, even in her worried and sleep-deprived state, she couldn't help but respond to.

She'd had two brief conversations with him: the first on the telephone, when he'd called looking for Leighton, and the second last night, when she'd arrived at the ranch, unannounced and uninvited. Although she should have been expected, as she'd told him she'd be on her way to Rust Creek Falls to get her nephew as soon as possible. Regardless, Wilder had been more hospitable than she'd had any right to expect.

Or maybe he'd been relieved to see her. Because standing in the doorway of the room across the hall, it was obvious to Beth that this cowboy had absolutely no clue how to take care of a baby.

"I know you can't do this on your own," Wilder said to the baby. "But is it too much to ask for just a little bit of cooperation?"

Of course Cody didn't respond, and Beth stayed quiet, too, watching as Wilder struggled to get the baby's legs out of his sleeper, opting to stretch the fabric rather than attempt to bend his limbs.

When that was finally done, he unsnapped the fasteners of the onesie and peeled it back to reveal the diaper.

"Or maybe this is some kind of test that only someone worthy of being called Mommy or Daddy can figure out," Wilder considered, as he opened the Velcro tabs. "And I think it's pretty obvious to both of us by now that I'm not worthy."

Beth wanted to say something then, to reassure the handsome cowboy that everyone struggled with parenting tasks in the beginning. But before she could find the right words, he pulled the diaper away and reached down to retrieve a clean one from the bag on the floor.

Cody responded as most baby boys would when his private parts were exposed to the fresh air, and Wilder yelped in surprise at the stream that fountained into the air.

Beth couldn't help it—she laughed.

The sound caught the attention of Cody and Wilder, and they both turned to the doorway. But while the baby smiled in recognition, the man looked so miserably unhappy she couldn't help but feel sorry for him, at least a little.

She swallowed another chuckle as she stepped into the room. "Is this your first time changing a diaper?"

"No," he denied, and blew out a breath. "I just don't expect him to do that every single time."

"You need to keep baby boys covered," she told him.

"How am I supposed to keep him covered *and* change his diaper?" Wilder grumbled, rummaging through the bag again.

"It isn't that difficult," she said. "You just don't remove the wet diaper until you have a dry one ready."

He sighed wearily and shoved the diaper bag aside. "And apparently that was the last clean undershirt thing."

"I packed some things for Cody before I left Leighton's apartment," Beth said. "But the bag's still on the passenger seat in my car."

"If you don't mind keeping an eye on him for a few minutes, I'll go get it for you," Wilder said.

"The keys are in my coat pocket," she told him.

He nodded. "I'll be right back."

While he was gone, she stripped Cody out of his damp clothes and put a clean diaper on him, chatting with him the whole while. Or chatting *to* him, as her nephew didn't respond except with happy gurgles and excited kicks. But those were enough for Beth to know that he was glad to see her.

After wrapping Cody in a blanket to keep him warm until Wilder returned, she sat with him in the rocking chair and rummaged through the diaper bag.

"It doesn't look like your mama thought to pack you any toys or books," she remarked. "Hopefully that's because she doesn't plan on being gone for too long."

Although the note Leighton had written suggested otherwise, Beth refused to believe that her sister would leave

Cody for more than a few days. It was more likely, she reasoned, that her sister had made the trip to Montana so that Cody could meet his dad, and the long journey with the baby had pushed her beyond the limits of her patience.

But Beth still didn't understand what had compelled her sister to contact the man now. Or why she hadn't mentioned her plans to Beth. Especially when they'd made arrangements to celebrate Cody's first Christmas together.

"I couldn't imagine any reason she would want to bring you to Montana," Beth admitted. "But now that I've met the very handsome cowboy who might be your daddy, I think I'm beginning to understand."

"So you *do* think I'm handsome."

Beth glanced up then to see Wilder in the doorway, a cocky grin on his face, and felt her cheeks burn.

"It's not my opinion so much as a simple fact," she said, furiously attempting to backpedal from her own admission.

"But attraction is very much subjective," he pointed out.

"I didn't say I was attracted to you," she denied hotly. "I was merely commenting that I could understand why *my sister* was attracted to you."

"Sure. We'll go with that," he said, as he dropped the duffel bag on the floor beside the rocking chair. But the playful wink that followed his words told a different story.

She looked away to unzip the bag, then frowned as she rifled through the contents. "Everything is ice-cold."

"The bag was in your car, overnight, in the middle of winter," he pointed out reasonably.

"And, as I discovered yesterday, winter in Montana is a lot different than winter in Texas," she acknowledged, as she pulled out a onesie, a pair of socks and a two-piece outfit. "Can you put these in the clothes dryer for a few minutes?"

He took the items from her hand. "They're not wet."

"No, but they're cold," she said again. "And a quick tumble in the dryer will warm them up to a more comfortable temperature for Cody."

He shrugged but headed out to do her bidding. Or maybe he was grateful for any excuse to leave her with the baby that he didn't believe was his.

Maybe he was right to be skeptical.

Maybe Leighton had been mistaken.

And maybe, after having spent a couple of days with Cody, he understood now how much time and attention a baby needed and would willingly accede to her request to take her nephew back to Dallas.

When Wilder returned with the warm garments, Beth quickly dressed the baby in a red top that had an appliqué reindeer head with Christmas lights looped around its antlers and a pair of dark brown corduroy pants.

"Very festive," Wilder noted.

"He has a lot of holiday outfits," she confided. "Every time I was out shopping, I seemed to find another one that I just couldn't resist."

"And all those Christmas gifts in the back seat of your car—more things you couldn't resist?" he guessed.

"He's my only nephew," she said, by way of explanation. "And it's his first Christmas."

"Do you want me to bring the presents inside?"

She shook her head. "Thanks, but I'd rather celebrate with Cody at home. And since I'm rested now, thanks to you and your kind hospitality, we can be on our way."

Now it was Wilder who shook his head. "I don't think that's a good idea."

"You can't want us to stay here," she said.

"Nothing has been about what I want since Leighton left her baby on my doorstep," he acknowledged.

"And considering what an inconvenience that's obviously been for you, why would you object to us leaving?" she asked coolly.

"Because I still don't know why your sister brought her baby to Rust Creek Falls instead of leaving him in Dallas with you," he said.

"No one but Leighton knows what she was thinking," Beth said.

"Maybe you don't know, but you can probably guess," he suggested.

Beth didn't respond to that. Because yes, she probably could guess. But she had no intention of sharing her suppositions with this man who might or might not be Cody's father and who, in any event, had no right to pry into the painful details of her often difficult relationship with her sister.

A relationship that she'd been certain was turning a corner—before recent events proved otherwise.

"And until you can answer that question to my satisfaction, the baby isn't going anywhere," Wilder said.

An assertion that, of course, put her back up.

"Who put you—a cowboy who clearly doesn't have the first clue about parenting and might not even be Cody's biological father—in charge?" she demanded.

"Your sister," he answered. "When she left her kid with me."

"My sister obviously wasn't thinking clearly," Beth said.

"I don't disagree, but that doesn't change the fact that she brought the baby here."

She hated that he was right. Even more, she hated that Leighton hadn't trusted her enough to talk to her about her plans. Instead, she'd snuck away, leaving only a cryptic note that did nothing to alleviate Beth's worries. And thinking about it now only made her head hurt. She lifted a hand and pressed her fingertips to her temple, as if that might assuage the ache.

"You're probably hungry," Wilder said, his tone more conciliatory than confrontational now.

She frowned. "What?"

"I'm guessing that your head hurts because you haven't eaten," he clarified.

"How do you…oh." She dropped her hand away.

"When did you last have a meal?"

"I grabbed a burger last night when I fueled up my car outside of Bozeman." But she'd only managed to choke down a few bites of the tasteless patty before she'd wrapped it up again and tossed it back into the bag.

"Well, according to the schedule I was given, it's time for the baby to have a bottle, so let's get you something to eat, too," he suggested.

"I'll be down in a minute," she said, reaching for the duffel bag. "I just want to change my clothes first."

"Did you want me to warm yours in the dryer, too?"

Though she didn't relish the idea of wriggling into cold undergarments, it was preferable to handing her bra and panties to a stranger. Especially a sexy stranger who had undoubtedly removed sexier undergarments from her sister's body.

"Thanks, but I'll be fine," she told him.

"Okay, I'll get started fixing the bottle."

She didn't ask him to take Cody and he didn't offer. She did wonder if his reticence was a result of not knowing what to do to take care of a baby or not wanting to acknowledge that Cody might be his.

And she had no intention of pushing him outside of his comfort zone. As far as she was concerned, the sooner he realized that he couldn't handle taking care of an infant, the sooner she could be on her way back to Dallas with her nephew.

When she was changed, she retraced her steps—as best she could recall—from the night before. But it had been dark then, and she'd been focused on Wilder's form moving ahead of her, unable to see much of anything else. In the light of day, she could appreciate the warmth and design of the home that Wilder lived in with…well, she had no idea who else lived in this house. Obviously she had more questions about the man than answers, but hopefully that would change over lunch.

Her stomach growled in support of that plan.

She reached the bottom step and turned—apparently in the wrong direction. Because she found herself in a family room with a grouping of leather furniture around a stone fireplace and a towering Christmas tree that almost touched the vaulted beam ceiling.

"Look at that," she said to Cody, her voice a reverent whisper as she moved closer. "It's almost as big as the tree at the mall where we saw Santa."

Of course, Cody didn't understand what she was talking about and would have no memory of the event even if he did. By the time they'd got to the front of the line and it was his turn to see the jolly man in the red suit, he was fast asleep. Beth hadn't wanted to wake him and risk ending up with a photo of an unhappy or crying baby. Instead, she had a beautiful photo of her nephew, decked out in a red velvet Santa sleeper and matching hat, peacefully tucked into the crook of Santa's arm.

She'd bought two copies of the photo and had framed and wrapped the second one as a Christmas gift for her sister. Of course, she'd invited Leighton to go to the mall with them, but her sister had waved off the suggestion, insisting that Cody was too young to even care. It was undoubtedly true, and yet, Beth couldn't let the occasion of his first Christmas pass without a visit to Santa.

She pushed the memory aside to focus on the tree in

front of her now. It wasn't just big, it was beautifully decorated in what she would call "country chic," with burlap
ribbon, handcrafted wooden ornaments, home-sewn felt
shapes, crocheted snowflakes, tied clusters of dried fruit,
sprigs of berries and striped candy canes.

And unlike the plastic tree in the mall, this one was real.
She could smell the rich, fragrant scent of pine in the air.

"Did you get lost?"

She started, turned. "What?"

A smile twitched at the corners of Wilder's mouth,
somehow making him look even more unbelievably handsome, and making her wonder what was wrong with her
that she could be so immediately and undeniably attracted
to the man who might very well be her nephew's father.

"I asked if you got lost," he said.

"Oh, no. I mean, I took a wrong turn, and then…" She
shrugged. "I got distracted. You have a beautiful home."

"It's got good bones," he said, turning to exit the room,
no doubt expecting her to follow. Which, of course, she
did. "But it's also been a lot of work to renovate and up-
date."

"Have you done the work yourself?" she asked, glancing at the framed photos on the sideboard as they passed
through the dining room. She was tempted to pause and
examine the pictures more closely, but her empty stomach growled to remind her that she had other priorities at
the moment.

"Me, my brothers and our dad," he said, handing her a
ready-made bottle for the baby.

"Thanks," she said. "But I would have mixed up his
formula."

"I just followed the instructions on the label."

She nibbled on her bottom lip, not wanting to appear
ungrateful but needing to ask, "Did you use previously
boiled water?"

"That's what the instructions said to do," he pointed out. "Plus Hunter, one of my brothers, gave me a crash course on basic childcare."

"He has kids?" Beth guessed, testing the temperature of the formula by shaking a few drops onto the inside of her wrist.

"One. A six-and-a-half-year-old daughter."

"There's no better teacher than experience," Beth said. "But in the absence of experience, there are some good childcare books that help. Leighton had about half a dozen beside her bed when she was pregnant."

She didn't tell him that she'd bought the books for her sister, or admit that Leighton hadn't cracked the covers on most of them. Because her sister had never been a fan of book learning—preferring to figure things out as she went along.

"I have to admit, that surprises me a little," he told her. "The Leighton I knew wasn't really the maternal type."

"I wouldn't have thought so, either," she admitted, as she settled into a chair at the table to give Cody his bottle. "But everything changed when she found out she was pregnant."

Wilder grabbed a mug from the cupboard and filled it from the carafe on a warming burner. "Are you a coffee drinker?" he asked.

"Only on days ending in a 'y,'" she told him.

He chuckled at that as he reached for another mug, then filled it with the steaming brew.

"Cream? Sugar?"

"Cream, please."

He opened the fridge to retrieve the carton, then added a splash to her cup and set it in front of her.

"Thanks." She lifted the mug to her lips and sipped. "That's good and strong."

"It's the only way my dad knows how to make it."

"So this is his house?" she guessed.

Wilder nodded. "When we first moved to Rust Creek Falls, in the summer, Xander and Finn lived here, too. But Xander and Lily have their own place closer to town now, and Finn and Avery renovated a cabin on the far side of the property, so it's just me and my dad left."

"So you've got three brothers?" She wasn't just making conversation; she was genuinely curious to learn more about his family, who might prove to be her nephew's family, too.

"No, I've got five brothers."

"Five?"

He nodded.

"Wow. Six boys. Your mom obviously had her hands full," she remarked.

"Maybe that's why she took off before my first birthday," he noted.

Chapter Four

Beth winced. "I'm sorry."

Wilder immediately waved off her apology. "No reason to be. You couldn't know."

"All the more reason not to speak without thinking." Then, in an apparent effort to smooth over the awkwardness, she quickly changed the subject. "Tell me about your brothers."

He responded readily, happy not to delve any deeper into the details of his mother's abandonment—especially when he honestly didn't know most of them. "Logan, the oldest, is married to Sarah. Hunter's a year younger, the one with the six-and-a-half-year-old daughter, and now engaged to Merry—that's with a capital 'M' followed by an 'e,'" he clarified. "Although I suppose it's also accurate the other way, too.

"Anyway, next after Hunter is Xander, who's married to Lily. Then there's Finn, who's married to Avery and expecting a baby in the spring, and finally Knox, who's married to Gen."

"So all of your brothers are married or engaged," she mused.

He nodded.

"You're not feeling any pressure to follow in their footsteps?"

"Not at all. I'm perfectly happy with my life the way it is," he assured her.

Then his gaze slid in Cody's direction, and when it

shifted back again, the look on Beth's face told him she knew that what he really meant was that he'd been perfectly happy with his life the way it *was*.

He turned to the fridge, away from her knowing expression. "I promised you food," he said. "What are you in the mood for?"

"Oh, um, just some toast would be fine," she said, as she settled into a chair at the table and positioned the bottle close to the baby's mouth. Cody immediately latched onto the nipple and began sucking.

"How about a sandwich?" he suggested.

"That sounds even better," she agreed.

"Do you like turkey?"

"Almost as much as coffee."

He pulled a cellophane-covered platter from the refrigerator.

"That's a lot of turkey," she noted.

"We had a full house for the Christmas meal, so my dad insisted on two birds to ensure we'd have leftover for sandwiches," he explained.

"I'd love a turkey sandwich—if you're sure he wouldn't mind sharing," Beth said.

"There's plenty." He pulled the plastic wrap off the meat. "I guess you didn't get to enjoy Christmas dinner, did you?"

She shook her head. "I mostly fueled myself on coffee and doughnuts."

More coffee than doughnuts, Wilder guessed, with a glance at her thin frame. He generally preferred the women he dated to look like women, with curves rather than angles. Beth was all angles, and yet, there was something about her—an innate warmth and sweetness that appealed to him.

The observation made him frown. Because while he appreciated the female form in various shapes and sizes,

Beth wasn't a female to be ogled—she was Cody's aunt. Leighton's sister.

And definitely not his type.

"White or dark meat?" he asked, turning his attention back to his task.

"Either or," she said. "And I can make my own sandwich."

"You're feeding the baby," he noted. "And that's something I'm not so good at."

"Your brother didn't give you a tutorial?" she teased.

"Apparently I'm not a very quick learner."

Beth smiled at that. "You're lucky your family is so supportive."

"Is 'supportive' another word for 'nosy and interfering?'"

"When it comes to family relationships, there's often some overlap," she acknowledged.

"Is your family supportive?"

"There's just me and Leighton—and Cody—now," she told him. "Our parents were killed during a bank robbery gone wrong almost ten years ago. Innocent bystanders."

Though the words were spoken matter-of-factly, the flatness of her tone suggested that the passage of time had done little to dull the heartache. As someone who'd grown up without a mother, he understood how the pain of loss could linger and wished he could take back the question.

"I'm sorry," he said instead, sounding and feeling awkward.

"Thanks." She eased the nipple of the already empty bottle from the baby's mouth and turned him onto her shoulder, gently rubbing his back.

Was it a maternal instinct that allowed women to anticipate and respond to an infant's needs? Or was it, as his brother had suggested, a parenting instinct? In which case, it was an instinct that Wilder obviously lacked.

"He was hungry," he noted.

"He always is," Beth remarked.

"And so are you," he remembered, refocusing on his task. "Cranberry or mayo?"

"Both."

Wilder made a face but retrieved the condiments from the fridge.

"Coleslaw?" he asked, when he'd cut the sandwiches and set them on two plates.

Her stomach grumbled a response before she did. "Sure."

He spooned some onto the plate beside her sandwich and set it on the table. After Cody had burped, she put him in his car seat and picked up her sandwich.

Wilder expected her to nibble around the crust, pretending more than eating, so he was surprised to see her take a hearty bite. And even more so when she closed her eyes and let out a blissful sigh that he was more accustomed to hearing in the bedroom than the kitchen.

"Oh. My. Goodness." She chewed slowly, swallowed. "You make a really good turkey sandwich."

It wasn't the only thing he did really well. In fact, sandwich-making didn't even crack the top ten list of things he did to please a woman, but he'd be happy to show her—

No. He immediately cut off his wayward thought, unwilling to go there with Beth, who wasn't just a guest under his roof but the baby's aunt.

He cleared his throat along with his mind. "I only assembled the ingredients," he told her. "Lily worked her magic with the bird."

"Lily is…married to Knox?"

He shook his head. "Xander. She runs her own business—Lily's Home Cookin'—now, but she used to be a cook at Maverick Manor."

"What's Maverick Manor?"

"The only decent hotel between here and Kalispell. It was originally an enormous house, nicknamed Bledsoe's Folly in honor of the man who built it. When he died, it stood dark and empty for a lot of years until Nate Crawford bought it and turned it into a hotel."

"A relative of yours?" she guessed.

"Apparently."

"Do you have a lot of family in Rust Creek Falls?" she asked.

"You can't walk down Sawmill Street without bumping into a Crawford—or two or three," he told her. "I thought I'd miss the anonymity of living in a big city, but there's something about this place that makes it feel like home already."

"Maybe the fact that you can't walk down Sawmill Street without bumping into a Crawford," she said, echoing his own words.

He chuckled. "That might be part of it."

She picked up the second half of her sandwich. "I honestly can't remember the last time I had turkey," she told him. "But I'm sure I don't remember it tasting this good."

He popped the last bite of his own sandwich into his mouth. "Last Christmas?"

"What?"

"You said you couldn't remember the last time you had turkey," he reminded her. "I suggested that it was probably last Christmas."

She shook her head. "I cooked a ham. Leighton isn't a fan of turkey."

"Do you always cater to your sister's preferences?"

"Not always," she denied. "But I probably do give in to her more often than I should."

"And I'll bet the more you indulge her, the more she takes advantage."

Beth frowned at his blunt assessment, but she didn't contradict it.

Aware that he was edging toward sensitive territory, he shifted the topic of conversation again. "Do you want anything else to eat?"

She shook her head as she pushed her now empty plate aside. "No, that was more than enough, thanks."

"Are you sure? Because I'm going to have a piece of leftover apple pie."

"I'm sure," she said. "Although if you'd said pumpkin, I might have been tempted."

"We have that, too," he told her. "And bourbon whipped cream."

"You're the devil, aren't you?"

"'A handsome devil' is what the ladies usually say," he replied, with a flirtatious wink.

Beth didn't respond to Wilder's comment, not even with a hint of a smile. If anything, she looked…disapproving.

Well, perhaps his teasing remark hadn't been entirely appropriate considering that she was the sister of one of his former lovers who believed that he was the father of her nephew.

"Was that a 'yes' to the bourbon whipped cream?" he asked, as he plated a slice of pumpkin pie.

"That was a 'yes, please,'" she confirmed, rising from the table to retrieve the coffee carafe from the warmer.

He opened the lid of the container and scooped a generous spoonful of the creamy topping onto the pie. Then he cut a wedge of apple for himself, grabbed two forks from the drawer and carried the plates and cutlery to the table.

"Thanks," she said, topping up his mug with coffee before refilling her own.

He nodded and straddled the seat across from her.

"Are you older or younger than Leighton?" he asked, when she sat down again.

"Older, by twenty-two months," she said, picking up her fork.

His lips curved as he popped the first bite of pie into his mouth.

"What?" she asked, though he hadn't spoken a single word.

"Just the way you said 'twenty-two months,'" he remarked. "I'll bet you held that over her head when you were growing up together."

"I did not," she immediately denied, dipping her fork into her pie.

"Yes, you did," he said. "As the older sibling, you probably couldn't help yourself. I know my brothers always held their maturity over me."

She seemed to consider this comment as she chewed, then slowly nodded. "Maybe I did," she acknowledged. "Of course, that completely backfired on me a few years ago, after my twenty-fifth birthday, when she started to take pleasure in pointing out that she was twenty-two months younger."

He chuckled. "Just like I refer to my brothers as 'old men' now. 'Old' *and* 'married' if I'm talking about Logan, Finn, Xander or Knox—because that's two nails in the coffin."

She frowned at that. "Not everyone looks at marriage as a death sentence."

"It was a joke," he told her.

"Was it?" she countered.

"You know, now that I've had some time to think about it, I do recall Leighton mentioning a sister...and referring to her as a stick-in-the-mud."

"That would be me," Beth agreed.

Now *he* frowned. "It's no fun to take a shot at someone who doesn't shoot back."

"Why would you expect anything different from a stick-in-the-mud?" she asked him. "And, for the record, she's also referred to me as a worrywart, a spoilsport and a killjoy."

"And the one who always does the right thing," he added.

"What?"

"I forgot that," he said, speaking almost to himself. "I guess she talked about you more than I realized, because I can remember her telling me that you were the one who always did the right thing. 'Little Miss Perfect'—cleaning up the messes she made."

"Not a term of endearment," she acknowledged wryly.

"I'm not so sure," he mused. "I think she really looks up to you, her older-by-twenty-two-months sister."

That earned him a hint of a smile. And he couldn't help noticing how pretty she was when she smiled.

But apparently she'd said everything she intended to on the subject of her sister, because the next time Beth spoke, it was to ask a completely random question.

"Aren't you supposed to be ranching?"

The vagueness and broadness of the question proved to Wilder that she was as unfamiliar with the responsibilities of a rancher as he was those of a parent.

"I wish," he said.

At her lifted brow, he shrugged. "Although ranching is a year-round job, things slow down a little in winter. Aside from feeding the cattle and livestock every day, we mostly focus on maintenance of buildings and equipment and perimeter fence checks, cutting and collecting fire-wood, and clearing snow."

"That sounds busy enough to me," she remarked.

"It is," he agreed. "But my dad assured me that he had plenty of hands to do the chores that needed to be done and that my hands should be taking care of the baby."

"Obviously he hasn't seen you try to change a diaper," she teased.

"Kids aren't really my thing," he acknowledged. Not that there was any chance she might have assumed otherwise.

"You know there's an easy way out of your dilemma," she said. "You could let me take Cody back to Dallas and pretend the last forty-eight hours never happened."

"Don't think I'm not tempted, but I don't walk away from my mistakes."

Beth bristled. "Cody is *not* a mistake."

"I didn't mean that the way it sounded," he said, immediately regretting his unthinking response.

"Then what did you mean?" she challenged.

"Let me just say that I wasn't thrilled to learn that I might be a father to a baby I didn't know anything about," Wilder told her. "And your questions about his paternity make me wonder how many other men Leighton was dating while we were together."

"I don't know," Beth admitted. "She didn't share those kinds of details with me."

Except to point out that Leighton, unlike Beth, had a personal life. Or remark that Beth was such a killjoy no one would ever be interested in her.

Beth never let her sister know how much those comments hurt. Because as much as Leighton could be kind and generous at times, she could also be hard and cruel, and—like a shark scenting blood—any sign of weakness could escalate her attack.

Beth pushed those uncomfortable memories aside to refocus on her conversation with Wilder. "And I didn't mean to suggest that there were others...during the time that she was with you. She didn't juggle men like that."

"That's a relief, I guess," he noted.

But the glance he sent in the direction of the now sleeping baby suggested to Beth that he was still more wary than reassured.

"My dad seems convinced that he's a Crawford, but I'm not quite willing to let myself be put on the hook on the basis of his gut feeling."

"If that's your attitude, then I really hope you're not Cody's father," she said.

"You don't think I should want proof?"

"Of course you should want proof," she said. "But instead of worrying about whether you're 'on the hook,' you might consider fatherhood as an opportunity rather than an obligation."

"I guess there's only one way to decide our next step," he said, and reached for his cell phone.

"Who are you calling?" Beth asked, as she dipped her fork into her pie again.

"The medical clinic—as soon as I can find the number," he said, searching for the listing.

"For a paternity test?" she guessed.

He nodded.

She chewed as Wilder connected the call, but her attention was no longer on the pie.

"Okay," Wilder said, when he'd set his phone aside again. "We've got an appointment at eleven o'clock tomorrow morning."

"That was quick," she said, surprised.

"The sooner we get the test done, the sooner we can get the results," he pointed out.

She nodded her agreement, eager to know the truth and still a little bit worried about what that truth might be.

"If it turns out that the baby isn't mine, I won't object to you taking him back to Dallas," Wilder continued. "Until then, however, he isn't going anywhere."

"But…the results will probably take several days. Maybe even longer."

"I guess that's possible," he acknowledged.

"You can't expect me to stay in Rust Creek Falls that long," she protested.

"You can leave anytime you want," he said. "But you'll leave without the baby."

Chapter Five

Wilder could tell his statement had surprised her. It had surprised him, too. If Beth had shown up immediately after Leighton had left the baby on his doorstep, he would have happily turned the infant over to his aunt. But somehow, over the past forty-eight hours, he'd started to get attached to the little guy.

He wasn't quite ready to accept that the kid was his, and truthfully—for Cody's sake—he still hoped Leighton had been wrong in identifying him as the dad. But he was invested in discovering the truth now, and determined to have it before making any decisions about his future.

"But my job is in Dallas," Beth protested. "My *life* is in Dallas."

"What is your job?" Wilder asked.

"I teach kindergarten."

"Then it's your winter break right now, isn't it?" he pointed out logically.

"It is," she acknowledged. "And I didn't plan on spending my holidays in Montana."

He shrugged. "As I said, you can go anytime you want."

"But you won't let me take Cody with me."

"Nope," he confirmed.

She sighed. "Is there a hotel in town?"

"Only Maverick Manor, just off the highway. But it's booked through to the New Year."

"Motel, then? Or bed-and-breakfast?"

"There's Strickland's Boarding House in town," he told

her. "But if you plan on staying in Rust Creek Falls, there's no reason you can't stay here. The room you slept in last night has been empty since Finn moved out."

"Are you sure the rest of your family wouldn't mind?"

"It's just me and my dad here now," he said. "And truthfully, I wouldn't object to some help with the baby."

"Cody," she said.

He scowled. "What?"

"His name is Cody."

"I know his name."

"Do you? Because I haven't heard you say it—not even once."

His scowl deepened at that.

"It's only four letters. Just two short syllables. *Co-dy*," she said again, deliberately emphasizing each syllable.

"I know his name," Wilder repeated.

"But you won't get attached if you don't use it," she guessed. "If you continue to refer to him as 'the baby,' and it turns out that he's not *your* baby, it'll be easier for you to walk away."

Annoyed by her insightful assessment—though not necessarily willing to believe it was true—he hit back. "I think I'm beginning to see why Leighton brought her baby here rather than leaving him with you."

Surprise and hurt were clearly reflected in her eyes before she sucked in a breath and quickly looked away.

Wilder winced. "I'm sorry."

"Are you?" she challenged, her eyes shiny with what he suspected were tears.

"I sometimes lash out when I'm feeling defensive, and you got caught in the crossfire," he explained.

"And I can be overprotective of those I love," she said. "I want what's best for Cody, and apparently Leighton thought that was you, so you need to step up and act like his father."

"*If* I am his father," Wilder said, still not quite ready to believe it was possible.

Because in the brief time that he'd been with Leighton, there'd been no forgotten or broken condoms, no reason at all for him to suspect she might have been pregnant with his child when they parted ways.

Yet somehow, in the short time that the baby—*Cody,* he mentally amended—had been at the ranch, Wilder had started to accept that fatherhood might not be the worst thing that could happen to him. That maybe it was time for him to not just step up but grow up.

Beth nodded in acknowledgement of his point as a knock sounded.

Before he could get up to answer the summons, the door opened and Avery stepped inside, kicking snow off her boots.

"No babies on your doorstep today?" his sister-in-law teased in lieu of a greeting.

"No," he said. "And not funny."

"I don't know," Beth said, maybe trying to prove that she wasn't a complete stick-in-the-mud. "I thought it was pretty funny."

Avery grinned. "That's because you have a better sense of humor than my grumpy brother-in-law."

"I have reason to be grumpy," he told her. "I was up I-don't-know-how-many times in the night with the baby."

His brother's wife was immediately sympathetic. "I'm not surprised the little guy had a restless night, in an unfamiliar place with people he doesn't know."

"And, as a result of his restless night, *I* had a restless night," Wilder felt compelled to point out.

"Actually, that's why I stopped by," she said. "To see if you were managing okay with the baby. I wished we could have stayed later the other night, but we had to get back to Pumpkin."

"Pumpkin is a goat," Wilder explained to Beth.

"Goat?" she echoed, as if uncertain she'd heard him correctly.

"Don't ask," he warned. "Because if you do, she'll never stop talking about it."

Avery's narrowed gaze promised retribution for what she perceived as the slight of her beloved pet, but she refocused on the purpose of her visit to ask again, "So how are you managing with Cody?"

"Lucky for the kid, I've got some help now," he said.

His sister-in-law's attention shifted back to Beth. "You must be the owner of the car in the driveway with the Texas plates."

She nodded and offered her hand. "Beth Ames. I'm Cody's aunt."

"It's nice to meet you. I'm Avery, one of Wilder's sisters-in-law," she introduced herself. "And since I'm obviously not needed here, I'm going to head back to my place. The furniture for the nursery was delivered this morning, and I can't wait to get it set up."

"You mean you can't wait to nag Finn to set it up," Wilder said firmly, concerned that his sister-in-law might attempt to tackle the chore on her own.

"Finn's busy trying to rebuild the engine of some piece of equipment."

"The baler?" Wilder suggested.

"Maybe. I sometimes tune out when he's grumbling about stuff like that," she admitted. "And anyway, the point is that I know my way around a toolbox well enough to put the furniture together."

"You should wait for Finn to do it," Wilder insisted.

"I don't want to wait," Avery told him.

He sighed. "Fine. If Beth doesn't mind me leaving Cody in her capable hands, I'll go put your furniture together."

"Of course I don't mind taking care of *my nephew*," she said pointedly.

"And I'd be happy to keep Beth company while you're gone," Avery said.

"Why does that *not* reassure me?" he wondered aloud.

His sister-in-law grinned. "I won't spill all of your deepest, darkest secrets," she promised. "But only because I don't know them all."

"Lucky me," he said dryly.

"But Finn has shared enough stories that I can probably keep Beth entertained until you're back."

"I'm glad you stopped by," Beth said to Avery when Wilder had gone. "Because I wanted to thank you personally for helping take care of Cody. Wilder said you've been a big help."

"It was my pleasure," Avery said. "Your nephew is a real sweetie."

"I think so," she agreed, with a smile.

"Plus—" Avery rubbed a hand over her rounded belly "—it was good practice for my own little bundle of joy."

"Wilder said you're due in the spring?"

"Early March," the other woman confirmed. "I feel as if I've been pregnant forever, but now I can finally almost see the light at the end of the tunnel." Then she sighed. "What I can't see are my feet. But maybe that's a good thing, because I haven't had a pedicure in…forever."

"You should treat yourself," Beth said. "Because you'll have even less time for those kinds of indulgences once your baby comes."

"I'd love to treat myself," Avery agreed. "Unfortunately, there isn't a spa in Rust Creek Falls. It's one of the things I miss about living in Dallas."

"You're from Texas, too?"

"Born and raised," the expectant mom confirmed.

"So what brought you to Montana?"

"Finn," she said. "We'd known each other in Dallas, and when I heard he'd moved to Rust Creek Falls, I came here to see him and decided to stay."

"You know it's love when," Beth said.

Avery chuckled. "Yeah, it was a pretty big change," she acknowledged. "But Rust Creek Falls isn't so bad, once you get used to it."

"I don't plan on being here long enough to get used to it," Beth said.

"That's too bad. Because Wilder's going to need some help learning how to be a dad to Cody."

"Do you really think he's interested in being a dad?" she asked dubiously.

"I *know* he is," Avery said. "Even if *he* doesn't know it yet."

Beth frowned at that.

"He just needs some time to get used to the idea, especially considering how the happy news was delivered."

"I encouraged Leighton to get in touch with the father, as soon as she told me she was pregnant, but she insisted he wouldn't want to know," Beth confided.

"I'm not judging your sister," the other woman hastened to assure her. "I walked more than a few miles in her shoes."

Beth's confusion must have shown on her face, because Avery said, "You didn't know that I was pregnant with Finn's baby before we got married?"

She shook her head.

"Well, I was," Avery said. "And although I came to Rust Creek Falls specifically to tell him that we were going to have a baby, it still took me a long time to find the right words—or any words, really."

"But you did it," Beth noted.

"I did it," the other woman confirmed. "And then, as if I

wasn't freaked out enough about being pregnant, I freaked out even more when Finn suggested we get married."

"You didn't want to get married?"

"I didn't know what I wanted. I was scared and confused and everything just seemed to be happening so fast. We had a one-night stand, I got pregnant, I told him about the baby, he proposed, we got married—" she paused then, a smile curving her lips "—and then we fell in love."

Beth sighed, a little wistfully. "It sounds like a romance novel."

Avery chuckled. "There was enough drama between our families to fill a lot of pages, that's for sure."

"And now you're one big happy family."

"Or faking it," Avery said. "But I don't care if our respective fathers are just going through the motions, because I know that Finn loves me as much as I love him."

"I'm glad things worked out for you."

Avery rubbed her belly again. "Me, too."

And maybe Beth was guilty of reading too many fairy tales to her kindergarten class, but one of the reasons she'd continued to encourage—Leighton would probably say "nag"—her sister to reach out to Cody's father was that she wanted a happy ending for them, too.

Though leaving the baby at his door wasn't quite what she'd had in mind, Beth wanted to believe it was the first step toward a possible reconciliation of Cody's parents.

Assuming that Wilder was the little boy's father.

Of course, she had no reason to doubt the claim in her sister's letter. No reason except Leighton's confession that she wasn't 100 percent certain.

But if she was being honest, she'd suspected, even at the time, that her sister had only been pretending to be uncertain so that Beth would stop nagging. Because she couldn't be expected to contact the father if she wasn't sure who was the father. And the fact that Leighton had brought Cody here proved she wasn't uncertain at all.

But if Beth acknowledged that the hunky cowboy was her nephew's father, and if Wilder was willing to step up and be his father, where would that leave her?

On her way back to Dallas, alone.

And that scenario wasn't one she wanted to contemplate.

When Avery had gone, Beth took Cody into the family room with the giant Christmas tree for some playtime. The ranch house was so warm and homey, she'd been taken aback to learn that Max was an unmarried rancher with six sons.

Of course, it was possible that he'd had the house professionally furnished. Or maybe one or more of his daughters-in-law had helped with the finishing touches. In any event, Beth felt comfortable in the house, despite being an uninvited guest.

She sat Cody in her lap on the floor and played patty-cake with him, then she entertained him with "Itsy Bitsy Spider" and used his favorite blanket as a curtain for peekaboo.

As much as she always enjoyed playful interaction with her nephew, she understood the importance of alone time, too, to teach him independence. But considering that Cody hadn't seen his mother since Christmas Day, she opted to focus on play today so he wouldn't worry that she'd left him, too.

"How about some tummy time?" she suggested, spreading his blanket out on the carpet.

"This is supposed to help you build strength for sitting up and rolling over," she said, laying him down on his belly on top of the blanket.

Then she stretched out on the carpet facing him, her chin propped up on her folded arms.

Cody lifted his head to look at her, a wide, toothless smile spreading across his face.

"You're already such a strong boy, aren't you?" she said, wiping his drooly chin with the corner of the blanket. "You're going to be rolling over before we know it, then I won't be able to put you down for fear of losing you."

Cody pushed himself up higher, as if to prove he was ready to move on to bigger and better things.

"I lost track of the number of times I had to tell my kids to get their feet off the furniture," a deep voice said from behind her. "But I never objected to anyone sitting on it."

Embarrassed to have been caught in such an undignified position, Beth immediately rolled over and rose to her feet. If his reference to "kids" hadn't already identified him as Wilder's father, she would have guessed the relationship just from looking at him.

She gauged him to be in his midsixties. His handsome face, deeply tanned and lined, attesting to a life spent outdoors. Though she knew him to be a rancher and he was dressed in the cattleman's usual uniform of jeans and plaid shirt, his clothes looked more Rodeo Drive than rodeo.

"Um, hi," she said, scooping Cody up off the floor. "We were just having some tummy time."

He nodded. "I heard."

"Oh." Her cheeks flushed hotter as she wondered how long he'd been standing there, watching them, and if she'd said anything she shouldn't have. She tended to think out loud when she was with Cody, to help build his listening and vocabulary skills, and often didn't even realize she was doing it.

"To build strength for sitting up and rolling over," he noted.

She nodded. "It also reduces the risk of developing a flat spot on the back of the head as a result of spending too much time on his back."

"We didn't worry about that when my boys were babies," Max told her. "Because the conventional wisdom of the time was to put babies to sleep on their tummies."

"Now 'back to sleep' is the recommendation," Beth said.

"I learned that when my first granddaughter was born," he acknowledged. "She's six and a half now—and a total princess."

"Is this hers?" Beth asked, reaching under the sofa to retrieve the Princess Aurora doll she'd spotted earlier.

"It is," Max confirmed. "Hunter called last night, asking me to look for it, and I insisted it wasn't here. Obviously I was wrong."

She gave him the doll. "A fringe benefit of tummy time is finding things you didn't even know you'd lost."

"Well, Wren will certainly be happy that it was found."

"By the way, I'm Beth," she said.

"I guessed as much," he said. "Wilder said you arrived late last night."

Beth nodded. "I'm sorry for showing up unannounced and uninvited," she said. "When Wilder called and said that Cody was here, all I could think about was getting to him."

"You don't need to apologize for caring about your nephew," Max told her. "The kind of love and devotion that compelled you to drive straight through from Dallas is admirable."

"I'd do anything for Cody," she said sincerely.

"But you don't know why his mother left him here with his father?"

She frowned at his ready acceptance of the paternity claim. "You believe Wilder is Cody's dad?"

"Don't you?" he countered.

"I don't know what to believe," she confided.

"Well, having raised six sons of my own, I have no doubt that little boy is a Crawford."

"I'm afraid I'm going to need something a little more scientific than that to be convinced," she told him.

His lips twitched, as if he was fighting a smile. "You're a skeptic, are you?"

"I'd say cautious."

"Is that why you're not married with a family yet?" Max asked.

She was taken aback by both his assumption and the personal nature of the question. "How do you know I'm not?"

"You left Texas on Christmas Day to drive halfway across the country for your sister's son. That suggests to me that you weren't celebrating with your own family."

A valid point, she acknowledged. "I guess I'm still waiting to meet the right person," she said. "And anyway, my focus right now is on Cody—and finding my sister."

"You don't have any idea where she might have gone?"

"I had no idea even that she was coming here," Beth confided.

"You're not close."

It was more a statement than a question, but she responded anyway.

"Not as close as I'd like us to be," she acknowledged, and wondered why she felt guilty for something that wasn't her fault. Or at least not entirely her fault.

But she'd only just met this man and had no intention of opening up her heart—or family history—to him. She definitely wasn't going to say anything that might cause him to view her sister in a negative light. Of course, Leighton's abandonment of her child on his doorstep had likely taken care of that already.

"I had six kids," Max said again. "You don't need to tell me about sibling relationships."

"But we've grown closer since she told me she was

pregnant with Cody. And especially in the past four and a half months."

"And yet she still left Dallas without telling you where she was going," he noted.

She nodded, because yeah, there was no denying that.

And no pretending that it didn't hurt.

"Well, you're here now," Max said. "And it's obvious that your nephew is happy to see you, so can I assume you're planning to stay a while?"

"It's looking that way at the moment," she acknowledged. "I offered to go to the boarding house in town, but Wilder was kind enough to invite me to stay here. Assuming it's okay with you."

Max's lips twitched, as if he was fighting a smile. "I'm not sure it was kindness that motivated his offer. But we have plenty of space," he confirmed, before Beth could question his first statement. "And you're welcome to stay as long as you need to."

"I appreciate it," she said. "But if I'm going to stay, I'd like to help out in some way."

"That isn't necessary," Max said.

"I'm not a bad cook," she told him.

The rancher tilted his head, considering her offer. "Do you by any chance know how to make meatloaf?" he asked, with a twinkle in his eye.

"I've got my mother's recipe stored right here," she said, tapping a finger to her head. "And it's the best I've ever tasted."

"In that case, there's a package of ground beef in the fridge."

She smiled, grateful for the opportunity to repay him in some small way for his hospitality. "What time do you like to eat?"

Chapter Six

Wilder felt a little guilty about abandoning the baby in Beth's care while he went to his brother's cabin to put together the nursery furniture. A little guilty and a lot grateful, because the more time he spent with Cody, the more doubts he had that he'd ever figure out this daddy stuff.

He'd been making a sincere effort, but he didn't seem to have any kind of instincts when it came to interpreting the baby's needs. Logan claimed he could tell if Sophia was hungry or wet or tired by the sound of her cry. Wilder only wanted to stop the baby from crying, but his attempts weren't always successful.

He had made some progress, though. The baby had only peed on Wilder once. And he was getting pretty good at mixing formula and giving the baby a bottle. But feeding him cereal? He'd swear the kid spit out more than he took in. And when that stuff dried, it was like trying to wash off hardened cement.

Despite his incompetence and missteps, Cody was a pretty good sport about everything. And just last night—in the middle of the night, when he'd been summoned by the baby's cries and tried to rock him back to sleep, the little guy had stared at him for a long time and then, finally, he'd smiled at him.

And Wilder's heart had completely melted.

The reaction had both surprised and unnerved him. Because while he'd figured he would probably become a dad one day, that day was supposed to be in the distant future. So far down the road he couldn't even see a speck of it on the horizon. It wasn't supposed to be now. And it definitely wasn't supposed to happen without any warning or preparation.

So maybe he took his time with the furniture, checking and double-checking that every bolt and screw was securely fastened. Then he moved it into position in the room—or at least as he thought it should be positioned—and tidied up all the packaging. Only when he'd run out of tasks and couldn't imagine any more, did he leave his brother's cabin to return to the main house.

He hung his coat up on a hook inside the door, beside Beth's. Because of course she was still there—where would she have gone while he was out?

And even if she did want to go out, she shouldn't venture far in the lightweight coat and useless boots she'd brought from Dallas. If she planned to stay in Rust Creek Falls for any length of time—and apparently she did—she was going to need some proper winter clothing.

He wandered through the house until he found her, sitting in the rocking chair beside the crib, watching Cody sleep. He paused there for a moment, wondering why the image of woman and child suddenly seemed so appealing to him—and maybe wishing the smart and sexy woman wasn't completely off-limits to him.

"Why are you hiding up here?" he asked. Then, as a thought occurred to him, "Did my father scare you off?"

"I'm not hiding," she denied. "And your father isn't scary. A little opinionated and outspoken, perhaps, but not scary."

"So you did meet him?"

She nodded. "We had a brief but pleasant chat."

"Do you have any idea where he is now?"

"I think he went to… Hunter's house?"

"Are you telling me or asking me?"

"Which one of your brothers has the little girl who likes princesses?"

"Hunter," he confirmed.

She nodded. "Then I'm telling you. He went to Hunter's house to return the doll that Wren left here at Christmas."

"And if my father's not home, why are you hiding up here?"

"I'm not hiding," she said again. "I just wanted to be close when Cody wakes up."

"Trust me, you don't need to be close to hear him," Wilder said.

"I didn't hear him during the night," she noted, but rose from the chair to follow him out of the room now.

"Yeah, you were pretty dead to the world when you crashed."

She frowned. "How do you know?"

"Because I walked by the door and saw you passed out on top of the covers."

Apparently she didn't want to venture any further down that path, because she asked instead, "Did you get the crib put together for your sister-in-law?"

"The crib *and* the changing table *and* two dressers." He shook his head. "I don't have enough clothes to fill two dressers. I can't imagine an infant's going to need all that space."

"Your brother and sister-in-law are obviously excited about their first baby."

"You mean their first human baby," he remarked. "Because Avery babies that goat like it *is* a baby."

"They really do have a pet goat?"

"I would not make that up," he assured her.

"Do they keep it in the house?"

"No," he said. "And don't give Avery any ideas, or she'll be after Finn to build another addition."

"Or sweet-talk her brother-in-law into doing it," Beth remarked, tongue in cheek.

"You think she sweet-talked me into putting her furniture together?" he asked, reaching into the cupboard for a mug.

She lifted one slender shoulder in a half shrug, and he couldn't help but notice how her breast rose and fell with the motion.

Off-limits, he reminded himself.

"All I know is Avery got to hang out here with me and then go home to a nursery full of baby furniture without breaking a sweat," Beth said.

"She's almost seven months pregnant. She shouldn't be breaking a sweat," he said, reaching for the coffeepot.

"Are you really going to drink that?" Beth asked, as he filled his mug.

"What else would I do with it?"

"It's been on the warmer for hours. Let me make a fresh pot."

"It's fine," he said, and lifted the mug to his mouth to prove it.

Okay, it was a little stale and slightly burnt, but the hot liquid warmed his body and the caffeine jolted his brain, and that was what mattered. Or maybe it was the interaction with Cody's aunt that revved up his system.

Beth shuddered as she watched him swallow another mouthful.

"I'm guessing you don't want any?"

She shook her head. "I'm coffeed out."

"There are tea bags around here somewhere, if you prefer that. Or juice and soda in the fridge, if you want something cold."

"No, I'm fine, thanks."

He swallowed another mouthful of coffee, then lifted his head and sniffed the air. "What do I smell?"

"Burnt coffee?" she guessed.

"No. Something smells good."

"Oh, your dad wanted meatloaf for dinner."

He opened the oven door to peer inside.

"You're letting the heat out," Beth admonished.

He closed the door. "My dad wanted meatloaf?"

"Why do you sound surprised?"

"Because meatloaf isn't his favorite meal," Wilder admitted.

But it was one of Wilder's favorites, a fact of which his father was well aware. And the fact that Max had asked Beth to prepare one of Wilder's favorite meals started his internal alarms clanging.

Was it possible that his father was attempting to make a match between his youngest son and Cody's aunt? Would he dare?

Of course, the answer to both those questions was "yes." With Max, anything was possible, and he would dare almost anything.

It was also possible that Wilder was being a little bit paranoid.

Except that it wasn't paranoia if it was true, and there was no doubt that Max was on a quest to see each of his sons happily married—or that he would never be satisfied with five out of six.

"So...you know how to cook," he mused, remembering that Leighton had claimed she couldn't boil water without a recipe.

"I'm not a gourmet chef, but my mom taught me the basics."

"She taught you but not your sister?"

Beth shrugged. "Leighton wasn't interested in learning."

"Or maybe she was happier to let other people take care of her."

"That's a possibility," Beth acknowledged. "Although

not one that reflects favorably upon the woman who might be the mother of your child."

"I liked your sister well enough, but I wasn't blind to her ability to manipulate people."

"I didn't think you knew her for very long—or very well."

"The Leighton I knew wasn't big on subtlety."

"Fair enough," she decided.

He sensed that Beth, though aware of her sister's faults, would defend Leighton against anyone else's criticism, and decided to shift the focus of their conversation. "I'm curious to know how two sisters, born of the same parents, could grow up to be so different," he told her.

"You have five brothers," she noted. "Are you all cut from the same cloth?"

"Of course not," he acknowledged. "But we all share similar traits—one of which is that women find us irresistible."

Beth rolled her eyes at that.

Most women, he mentally amended.

"Leighton and I share similar traits, too," she said. "Although she was labeled 'the pretty one' and I was 'the smart one,' she's just as smart as me—maybe even smarter."

Wilder had some doubts about that. Not because he questioned Leighton's intelligence, but because Beth was pretty, too. Maybe she didn't play up her attributes the way her sister had done, but her unenhanced beauty was even more alluring because there was no doubt she was real.

"And I think that was part of the problem," Beth continued, drawing his focus back to their conversation. "No one knew she struggled to read because she so quickly memorized the books she was being tested on. She was also good at mental math, so when she transposed numbers on tests, her teachers accused her of not paying at-

tention to what she was doing. It wasn't until she was in
high school that her dyslexia was discovered."

"Better late than never," he said.

"You'd think," Beth agreed. "But Leighton balked at
being labeled. She wasn't interested in strategies to deal
with her learning disability—she preferred to pretend she
didn't care."

"Maybe she wasn't pretending," he suggested.

She frowned, as if that was a possibility she'd never
considered. "Anyway, I suspect one of the reasons she
never learned to cook is that she works at a bar in a restaurant and eats there most of the time."

"Well, I'm definitely glad you learned to cook, because
that meatloaf smells really good," he told her, his mouth
already watering.

In fact, he was starting to understand how a man could
get used to coming in from a hard day's work on the ranch
to a homecooked meal every night. Especially if that hot
meal was prepared by a hot wife.

Wait! Where the heck had *that* come from?

He frowned at the dregs left in the bottom of his mug,
as if the stale coffee was somehow responsible for the wayward idea. Yeah, a lot of things seemed to be changing in
his life, but his readiness to put his neck in the marriage
noose was *not* one of them.

Pushing the uneasy thought aside, he asked Beth: "So
when do we get to eat it?"

They ate forty-five minutes later.

And it *was* good.

If Beth had any doubts about that, they were assuaged
when both Wilder and his father refilled their plates. Max
even insisted that the men would do the dishes to show
their appreciation for "the delicious meal." Of course, Beth
had already washed up all the bowls and equipment she'd

used in the prep process, so they really only had to put the plates, cutlery and empty baking pan in the dishwasher. Still she was pleased to note that, despite his apparent wealth and status, the Crawford patriarch didn't expect to be waited on hand and foot.

When the men had finished cleaning up, Max headed into town to meet another rancher at the Ace in the Hole for a beer and a discussion about the potential sale of a piece of equipment, leaving Beth alone with Wilder and Cody.

"I forgot to ask earlier—do you have a bathtub?" She posed the question to Wilder after his father had gone.

"You want to take a bath?"

"Not for me," she said. "For Cody."

"There's one in my dad's bathroom," he told her.

"Do you think he'd mind if we used it?"

"Of course not."

"Great," she said. "If you can grab a couple of towels and a washcloth, I'll get Cody's baby shampoo and bodywash."

He went to get the requested towels while she retrieved the toiletries. Wilder had pointed out the door to Max's room earlier, but despite his assurance that his father wouldn't mind her making use of his en suite bath, she still hesitated to enter the Crawford patriarch's personal space.

"You can knock, if you want," he teased, when he found her hovering outside his father's room. "But he's not home, so he won't answer."

"I know," she admitted. "But it seems like a violation of his privacy to just walk right in."

"I'll go first," he said. "And kick aside any clothes he's left on the floor."

She followed in his wake, trying not to be too nosy but unable to resist a quick peek at Max's inner sanctum— which was furnished in a simple and masculine style and neat as a pin.

"You knew there wouldn't be any clothes lying around, didn't you?"

"Yeah," he admitted, leading the way to the en suite bath. "My dad has never tolerated messiness or clutter—which is inevitable with six kids under one roof. Not even the full-time housekeeper we had in Dallas could keep up with us."

"I can't imagine any one woman being able to keep up with six kids," she said sincerely. "But kudos to her for trying."

He grinned at that and hit the light switch on the wall, illuminating a bathroom that was half the size of the enormous bedroom and twice as luxurious.

"Wow," she said softly, grateful that he seemed to assume she was reacting to the revelation of the facilities rather than the curve of his lips.

"My dad spared no expense in here," he confirmed. "But his two priorities were a shower with body jets and a tub big enough for his horse."

She stared down at the oversize soaker tub and imagined sinking into steamy water filled with mountains of bubbles. Of course, the tub was more than big enough for two, and her traitorous imagination immediately invited Wilder's big, hard body to join her—

She blinked and quickly dispelled the tantalizing image.

"I wouldn't be surprised if you could get a horse in there," she agreed, not looking at him. "Because it's definitely too big for a baby."

"So what are you going to do?" he asked.

Since turning her bubble bath fantasy into a reality wasn't ever going to happen, she suggested, "Plan B."

"I thought you were joking when you said the kitchen sink," Wilder admitted.

Beth shook her head as she put the stopper in and

turned on the faucet, testing the water temperature with the inside of her wrist. When there was about six inches of water, she took one of the folded towels and set it in the bottom of the sink.

"I thought the towels were for drying the baby."

"The second towel is for drying the baby," she said. "This one is so he doesn't slip."

"Why do I think you've done this before?"

"Because I have." She rolled up the sleeves of her shirt. "One weekend when Cody stayed with me, I forgot to pack his baby tub along with the rest of his things, so…Plan B."

"*You* forgot to pack his tub?"

"That's what I said." She stripped the baby down to his diaper, then tested the temperature of the water again with her elbow before removing that final barrier and easing the little guy into the water.

"His mom didn't pack his stuff?" Wilder asked.

"Sometimes," Beth said.

It was a surprisingly vague response from a woman who usually seemed happy to talk about her nephew—and extol Leighton's maternal virtues. And though Wilder was tempted to press for more details, or at least inquire as to how many weekends she'd looked after a baby who was only four months old, he decided to let the topic slide— at least for now.

"What do you need me to do?" he asked instead.

"Why don't you wash him while I hold him?" she suggested.

"Because washing seems a lot more complicated than holding," he replied honestly.

She smiled but didn't offer to reassign tasks.

Of course, she was already up to her elbows in the water, holding the baby upright so he didn't topple over.

"Wet the washcloth, wring out the excess water and

gently clean his face and neck. And don't forget behind his ears," she said.

He followed her directions, feeling awkward and inept—and far too aware of the scent of his shampoo in her hair as he huddled close to her by the sink.

"Now squeeze a drop of bodywash onto the cloth and work up a lather," she said.

She patiently talked him through the process of washing and rinsing the baby's body, then his hair, while she held Cody in place.

"This will be a lot easier once he's able to sit up on his own," she promised.

"And a lot easier with help," he acknowledged. "I don't think I could have tackled this on my own."

"Sponge baths work in a pinch," she said. "But it's good to get babies accustomed to the water, and Cody always seems to enjoy his bath."

It was obvious to Wilder that she'd performed the same task dozens of times before, and he was grateful for her help and guidance. But her obvious ease with and affection for her nephew caused him to question again why Leighton, wanting a break from the demands of parenthood, hadn't chosen to leave the baby with Beth.

While he was mulling over these questions, she'd toweled off, diapered and dressed the baby.

"There's my sweet-smelling boy," she said, nuzzling him for a moment before setting him in his car seat.

"Only until he fills his diaper again," Wilder noted.

Beth shook her head as she turned back to the sink to drain the water.

It was then Wilder noticed that the front of her shirt was wet—and plastered against her like a second skin.

Though he knew he shouldn't stare, he couldn't tear his gaze away from the delicate lace pattern of her bra, clearly visible through the now-transparent fabric, and he couldn't help but admire the nicely rounded shape of the breasts inside the lace cups.

She lifted the sodden towel from the sink and twisted it in her hands to squeeze out the excess water, causing her breasts to lift and strain against the fabric, making his mouth go dry.

"—in the washing machine?"

He turned quickly, so that she wouldn't catch him staring. "I'm sorry, what did you say?"

"I asked if you could keep an eye on Cody while I go toss these towels in the washing machine," she said.

"I'll do it," he said, grabbing the towels from her and beating a hasty retreat, grateful for the opportunity to escape the temptation of her nearness.

Max found Beth waiting for the kettle to boil when he walked into the kitchen later that night.

"You couldn't sleep, either?" he guessed.

She shook her head. "I hope I didn't disturb you by moving around in here."

"I didn't hear anything but the leftover pumpkin pie calling my name," Max assured her.

"Are you sure it was pumpkin pie talking?" she asked. "Maybe it was apple."

"It was definitely pumpkin," he told her. "And bourbon whipped cream."

"I finished the pumpkin earlier," she confessed guiltily. "But I didn't know it was the last slice until I saw the empty pie plate after I'd eaten it."

"Was it good?"

"*Really* good," she admitted.

"Eva Stockton makes the best pies in Rust Creek Falls— maybe all of Montana," Max said, opening the door of the pantry. "Which is why I always order an extra one from

Daisy's Donuts in town." He winked at her then as he pulled a baker's box out of the back of the cupboard. "Or two."

She exhaled a sigh, apparently relieved to know that she hadn't deprived him of his coveted late-night snack.

"Do you want a cup of tea with your pie?" she asked, as the boiling kettle automatically shut off.

He cut a generous wedge and transferred it to a plate. "Thanks, but I prefer milk near bedtime."

She opened the fridge to retrieve the milk—and the container of bourbon whipped cream he craved.

"You should put a dollop of this in your tea," Max suggested, as he scooped up a mound of the alcohol-infused topping. "It might help you sleep."

"Maybe too well," she said. "I want to be able to hear Cody when he wakes up."

"Wilder will hear him," he said. "I had the crib set up in the room adjacent to his to ensure it."

"Clever," Beth acknowledged, as she carried her cup of tea to the table.

Max took a seat across from her with his pie and his glass of milk. "Wilder told me that he made an appointment at the clinic for a paternity test."

She nodded as she dunked her tea bag in the hot water. "Eleven o'clock tomorrow morning."

"Waste of time if you ask me," he said.

"I'd never heard your son's name before I saw it written on a sticky note in my sister's apartment." Beth admitted. "So when I did, I googled it."

"And?" Max prompted.

"And I'd think, considering your family's vast wealth, you'd want DNA proof before welcoming a random child into your home."

"Cody isn't a random child," Max said. "He's a Crawford."

"Well, if it's all the same to you, I'd like proof of that before I leave my nephew here."

"Ahh," Max said, and nodded. "This isn't really about Cody, it's about you."

She sipped her tea, perhaps considering his remark, before she responded. "I made a promise to my sister to always be there for him."

"And yet, she brought him here," he pointed out. "Abandoning him and abdicating her own responsibilities."

"She didn't abandon him," Beth denied. "She left Cody with the man she believes is his father."

Though Max could appreciate her wanting to defend her sister, facts were facts.

"She left him on the doorstep," he pointed out. "And I'm sorry if it seems as if I'm judging her too harshly, but I'd argue that a woman who can walk away from her children doesn't deserve to have them."

"Them?" Beth echoed.

"Him." Max cleared his throat. "She doesn't deserve *him.*"

She nodded slowly, as if she understood that they were no longer talking about her sister—or not just her sister.

He scowled, none too pleased to realize that his son had spoken to this woman—a virtual stranger—about their painful family history. But of course he had. There was no other reason for her to have picked up on the slip of his tongue except if she knew about Sheila's defection.

And though Beth had admitted to googling Wilder's name, Max wasn't worried that a cursory online search might turn up details of his marriage or divorce. Especially when he'd paid good money to ensure they stayed buried.

"Leighton made a mistake," Beth said now, as she put her empty mug in the dishwasher. "But she'll come back for Cody. You'll see."

Max hoped she was right.

But he sat at the kitchen table with only his disquieting thoughts for company for a long time after Beth had gone upstairs to bed.

He should hit the sack, too. Morning came early and there was a lot of work to be done—especially as he'd directed Wilder to take a break from his usual chores to spend time with Cody. Of course, now that Beth was staying at the Ambling A, Max suspected that she'd assumed primary responsibility for her nephew. But it was good for Wilder to watch and learn, even if he was still in denial about his relationship to the child.

A certain amount of denial was to be expected under the circumstances, but Max anticipated that it would be followed soon by a whole gamut of other emotions. He hoped one of those emotions was anger. Because Wilder should be mad. He should feel ripped off of all the experiences he'd missed because Cody's mother hadn't bothered to tell him that she was going to have his child. He should be furious he'd missed the first four months of the little boy's life. That Leighton had deprived him of the opportunity to be there for his son from the beginning.

Just as Max had deprived Sheila of the opportunity to be there for her children.

He remembered the night of their final confrontation as clearly as if it had just happened.

"I could never love anyone more than I love my children," she insisted, when he accused her of choosing her lover over her family.

"And yet you left here and went to him," he pointed out, his tone dripping with anger and bitterness—but not hurt. He wouldn't let her see the hurt. He would never admit how her betrayal had gutted him.

"You told me to leave. I had nowhere else to go."

He had told her to leave—to get out. But only after she'd confessed that she'd fallen in love with another man.

"You chose him," he said again, confident that he was

on the moral high ground. Maybe he hadn't been the perfect husband, but he hadn't cheated.

"No," she protested. "I didn't choose him. Not over my children. I couldn't. Please, Max, try to understand—"

But Max had been too hurt and angry to understand.

Maybe there had been a tiny part of him that wondered if he was making a mistake, but he didn't allow himself to show any hesitation or doubt. It wasn't in his nature to back down. And it sure as hell wasn't in his nature to give a second chance to the woman who'd betrayed not just him but their family.

But in the end, he was the one who'd been deprived of a second chance to make things right. Because Sheila had signed the divorce papers he sent to her, then died of a broken heart.

A myocardial infarction, actually.

The autopsy would later reveal a previously undiagnosed condition that explained how a thirty-two-year-old woman in otherwise good health could suffer such a tragic event.

But Max knew the truth—he'd killed her.

Chapter Seven

Beth was up early the next morning and feeding Cody his cereal when Wilder came into the kitchen for his first cup of coffee.

"And I thought ranchers were early risers," he remarked, rubbing a hand over his raspy cheek.

The handsome cowboy was dressed in a similar fashion to what he'd been wearing when she first showed up at the ranch—flannel pajama bottoms and a soft cotton T-shirt over hard muscles. His jaw was similarly stubbled, his hair equally tousled. And just like then, her blood hummed in response to his raw masculinity.

"Ranchers have nothing on babies," she told him, pointedly ignoring her body's totally inappropriate reaction.

"Yeah, I learned that yesterday. And the day before," he acknowledged, stifling a yawn. "But I didn't hear him this morning."

"I managed to get to him before he made too much noise," she said.

"I'm pretty sure my father put him in the room next to mine so that I'd have to deal with middle-of-the-night feedings and diaper changes," Wilder remarked.

"And you did all of that the night before," she pointed out. "So it only seemed fair that last night was my turn."

"Do you always try to be fair, Lisbeth?"

"Maybe," she said, wondering how he managed to make fairness sound like a character flaw.

Or maybe she was being overly sensitive—which was definitely one of her character flaws.

"Do you want me to make you some eggs?" she asked, when Wilder opened the refrigerator door and stood for a long moment staring at its contents.

He took out the carton and slammed the fridge door shut again before turning back to face her. "If I want eggs, I can make my own eggs," he snapped at her.

"O-kay," she said, and dipped the plastic spoon into Cody's cereal again.

Because if she was guilty of being overly sensitive, he was just as guilty of being an arrogant jerk.

And apparently he wasn't done being an arrogant jerk, because after pulling a frying pan out of the cupboard he said, "I don't know what you think is happening here, but I have no interest in playing house with you."

"Playing house?" she echoed, torn between bafflement and outrage. "Is that what you think I'm doing—*playing?* Do you honestly think any of this has been *fun* for me?"

Though she kept her voice low so as not to upset her nephew, she made no effort to disguise the fury beneath her words. And when she stood to carry Cody's now empty bowl and spoon to the sink, she felt a grim sense of satisfaction that Wilder actually took a step back, out of her path.

"Let's revisit the most fun parts," she suggested. "Maybe showing up at my sister's apartment and discovering she'd left town without telling me?" She unbuckled the harness that held Cody in his seat, then lifted the baby into her arms. "Or answering her phone and finding out that my infant nephew was in the care of a stranger almost seventeen hundred miles away? And then driving for twenty-eight hours through the darkness of night and all kinds of weather to make sure he was okay—but essentially being held hostage by a man who doesn't even want to believe he's his father?

"You know what? You're right—it's been *so much fun* I almost wish I was back in grade school so I could write an essay on how I spent my Christmas holidays."

And with that parting shot, she turned on her heel and walked out.

He could be a complete ass at times.

Today was apparently one of those times.

Wilder had no defense for his behavior. Sure, he could make excuses—and having a baby dumped on his doorstep would probably be at the top of the list—but his actions and accusations were indefensible.

And if he was truthful, he'd admit that his questions about Cody and his relationship to the kid weren't all that had kept him awake last night or caused his pissy mood today.

He'd been thinking about Leighton, too, as he'd tossed and turned. Wondering why she'd never told him that she was pregnant. Even if she'd had valid reasons then, why had she never reached out after the baby was born? And, if not then, how about when she decided to undertake the drive from Dallas to Rust Creek Falls with the baby in the back seat of her car? Because a phone call at any of those times would have been preferable to no phone call at all.

And though he'd been thinking about Leighton and all the reasons he had to be furious with her as he'd finally drifted off the sleep, he'd dreamed about her sister.

And how screwed up was that?

Sure, Beth was an attractive woman, but she wasn't at all his type.

Not to mention that she was the kid's aunt, and since there was a possibility that he might be the kid's father, imagining her naked just seemed wrong. Because yes, he hadn't just dreamed about her, he'd had a sex dream about her—and woken up with a raging hard-on.

And then, as if that wasn't awkward enough, he'd walked into the kitchen and she was there. All soft eyes and warm smiles and "Do you want me to make you some eggs?"

So of course he'd responded by acting like a complete ass.

Her anger had been completely justified.

And ass that he was, he couldn't help but notice how pretty her eyes were when they flashed with fire, how kissable her lips seemed even while they were berating him.

But now that the caffeine had started to work its way through his system, he at least had the wherewithal to recognize the inappropriateness of his behavior and acknowledge that he owed her an apology.

He looked at the eggs on the counter and wondered if scrambled or fried would taste better with a side of crow.

Then he rummaged through the fridge for bacon. Because everything was better with bacon.

By the time Beth had Cody changed and dressed, ready for his trip to the clinic, she was ready to acknowledge that she may have overreacted.

Not that she wasn't in the right to be mad at Wilder—because she was—but perhaps she could have expressed her feelings a little less forcefully. No doubt it was the uncertainty of the situation that had them both on edge. But they had an appointment at the clinic today, and though she knew they wouldn't get any immediate answers, it was at least a step in the right direction.

"Just to be clear," she said, when she ventured back into the kitchen as Wilder was finishing his breakfast, "I don't want to be here any more than you want me here."

"I know." He cleared his empty plate then pulled a chair away from the table. "Sit down. Please."

She strapped Cody into his car seat first, and then she sat. Her puzzled gaze shifted from the folded napkin and cutlery to the steaming mug of fresh coffee with a splash of cream—and finally the plate of food he set in front of her.

"What's this?" she asked warily, as if the crisp bacon and scrambled eggs might, in fact, be something else.

"An apology," he said, proving her suspicion was correct.

She lifted the fork and poked at the eggs, as if she didn't quite trust that his culinary offering was a sincere effort to make amends.

"We don't keep any arsenic in the kitchen," he assured her.

"Why are you apologizing?" she asked, after she'd nipped the end off a slice of bacon.

"Because I was mad at your sister and I took it out on you."

His honesty was as surprising as his apparent contrition, and equally appreciated. Beth sampled the eggs, then nodded. "Apology accepted."

"Really?" Now it was his turn to sound skeptical. "Just like that?"

"I'm not too happy with Leighton right now myself," she acknowledged, still unable to understand why, if her sister was finding parenting such a challenge, she hadn't reached out to Beth.

But even as the question formed in her mind, she ruefully acknowledged the answer. Because Leighton had always viewed Beth as the favorite child, a rule follower who did everything right, even following in their mother's footsteps and becoming a kindergarten teacher. Leighton, on the other hand, liked to break the rules and had even dropped out of high school when she was sixteen to sing in a band.

They'd traveled across the country, en route to Seattle, playing in bars that paid them in free drinks, not caring that most of the band members were underage. Leighton had made it as far as Twin Falls, Idaho, before deciding that she'd had enough of eating fast food and sleeping in a rusty van.

Of course, she didn't come home with her tail between her legs. Regret and remorse had never been her style. Instead, she'd regaled Beth with outrageous stories about the things she'd seen and done, taking pleasure in shocking her straitlaced sister.

Their parents had only heard about half of the stories, but that had been enough to shock them, too. Eager to create some distance between their younger daughter and her so-called friends, Alfred and Lucy Ames had encouraged Leighton to spend a few months traveling in Europe.

Such a trip was a luxury beyond the means of their solidly middle-class lifestyle, but they made it work by cashing in Leighton's college fund. Since she'd given no indication that she was interested in even graduating from high school at the time, it seemed a better use of the money.

As Beth had mentioned to Wilder, Leighton eventually got her GED but she was still happy to work as a bartender, boasting that she could make more money in tips in one night than Beth made in a week working with "snotty-nosed little kids."

And wasn't it ironic that Beth, who'd always dreamed of marrying and having a family, was still single and alone, while Leighton, who never wanted to be tied down, had been blessed with a beautiful, perfect baby?

"So we're good?" Wilder prompted, drawing her attention back to the present.

"We're good," she said. "But if we don't get a move on, we're going to be late."

She was a little nervous about taking the baby into a clinic potentially full of sick people. Though Cody was as up-to-date with his immunizations as he could be at four and a half months, Beth still worried about unnecessary exposure to germs and viruses.

The Rust Creek Falls Clinic was bright and clean with friendly and efficient staff. While Wilder filled out the necessary paperwork, Beth sat Cody on her knee, gently jiggling her leg to keep him moving so he wouldn't fuss while they waited.

Thankfully, they didn't have to wait long. When the doctor came in to the exam room, he explained how the test worked, asked if they had any questions, then completed the procedure.

Wilder volunteered to go first, so that Cody could see how it was done. He showed no outward hesitation, but Beth sensed his wariness, though she suspected it was related to the potential results rather than the requirements of the test itself.

The doctor opened the sterile package, the potential daddy opened his mouth, and the inside of his cheek was swabbed. The swab with the collected sample was then deposited in a tube and sealed up again.

Cody was less cooperative on his turn. He didn't understand the concept of keeping his mouth open for the doctor to complete his task, and he didn't seem to approve of either the taste or the texture of what was in his mouth. Several times he clamped his jaw down on the wooden stick, prompting the doctor to remark that it was a good thing the baby didn't yet have any teeth. Still, it didn't take long for the doctor to be satisfied that he had an adequate sample, and less than half an hour after entering the clinic, they were exiting again.

"That was almost anticlimactic," Beth remarked, as she walked beside Wilder to his truck.

"Now we just have to wait for some computer to analyze the spit on those sticks and decide whether or not I'm the kid's father."

"Something like that," she agreed.

"Doesn't seem like it should take seven to ten days," he grumbled.

"The doctor said it's usually less than a week, but the lab might be backed up because of the holidays."

"I guess that puts a snag in your plans."

She shrugged. "I can't really complain about spending the holidays with my favorite guy."

"I'm flattered," he said.

She shook her head. "You know I wasn't talking about you."

"Yeah," he admitted with a grin. "But I do like to see you blush."

"Am I blushing?" she asked. "I can't tell, because my whole face is frozen."

He chuckled as he opened the passenger-side door of his truck for her.

Of course, she didn't immediately buckle up, because she had to wait for him to set Cody's baby seat in place and double-check that it was securely locked in the base.

"Are you hungry?" he asked, when he slid behind the wheel.

"It seems as if breakfast wasn't that long ago," she said. "But actually, I am hungry."

"You want to grab a bite at the Gold Rush Diner?"

"Sure," she said.

The restaurant wasn't far from the clinic—but according to Wilder, nothing in Rust Creek Falls was too far from anything else. A cowbell rang overhead as they entered, no doubt intended to alert restaurant employees to the comings and goings of customers. Though she would have thought they were ahead of the lunch crowd, several booths and tables were occupied by diners already eating or even finishing their meals.

Beth decided on a booth because she knew Cody's seat

would fit snugly on the red vinyl bench. She wrangled the carrier into place, then unzipped the fleece cover-over top so the baby—who'd been lulled to sleep on the short drive—wouldn't get overheated while they were in the restaurant.

Menus were tucked against the wall, propped up by a tray of condiments. Wilder handed one across the table to her, then took one for himself.

She quickly scanned the offerings, then set the menu aside.

"That was fast," he noted.

"I've had a craving for a spicy chicken sandwich, so I was happy to see it on the menu."

"Sounds good," he decided, and tucked his menu away, too.

A server appeared almost right away. She introduced herself as Raina and started to relay the lunch specials, then she spotted the baby seat and completely lost track of what she was saying in favor of cooing over the sleeping infant.

"See?" Wilder said to Beth, after Raina had finally managed to pull herself together and take their orders.

"What am I supposed to see?"

"The way she oohed and aahed over the baby."

"It happens all the time," Beth said matter-of-factly. "Because he's too adorable for real words."

"Well, my dad would say that's just more proof he's a Crawford," he said immodestly.

"What do you think?"

He shrugged. "I guess we'll know for sure in seven to ten days, won't we?"

"I guess we will," she agreed, as Raina delivered their drinks to the table.

As she sipped her diet cola, she noted interesting details about the decor. But while she looked around the restaurant, she got the uneasy feeling that others were looking at her. Not that anyone was blatantly or obviously staring, but a couple of times, she caught a gaze being quickly averted before connecting with her own.

"Why do I get the feeling people are staring at me?" she asked, whispering across the table to Wilder.

He turned his head so that he had a view of the seating area. "Because they probably are."

"Thanks for the reassurance," she said dryly.

"Or they could be staring at me," he suggested as an alternative, shifting his attention back to her. "Rust Creek Falls is a small town, and newcomers and strangers are equally rare sightings. And there's been a fair amount of talk and speculation about the Texas Crawfords—as we've been dubbed by some members of the community—who plunked down a boatload of cash for the Ambling A."

"How much is a boatload?" she wondered aloud.

"Are you looking for the specific number?" Wilder asked.

Beth immediately shook her head. "No, I'm only pointing out that 'boatload' is an incredibly imprecise measure," she told him. "I mean, a boat filled with singles wouldn't necessarily be a lot of money—unless it was a really big boat. On the other hand, a smaller boat filled with C-notes could be a significant amount."

He chuckled at that. "Fair point."

"But if the other diners are staring at you—Wilder Crawford from Texas with boatloads of money—they're probably also speculating about your relationship to the baby that your father insists looks so much like a Crawford no one would guess he was anything else."

"No doubt the gossip is spreading like wildfire," he agreed.

"That doesn't bother you?"

He shrugged. "I try not to be bothered by things that are out of my control."

"That's a very Zen attitude," she noted.

"Plus, there is a silver lining," he said.

"What's that?"

"Rumors that I knocked up an old flame in Dallas and moved away to shirk the responsibility of fatherhood might discourage the local women who have set their sights on snagging the last Crawford bachelor from Texas."

"Are such rumors going around?" she asked, immediately concerned for his reputation.

"No," he admitted. "But I haven't given up hope yet."

She shook her head despairingly. "Is it really such a trial to be sought after by a few young ladies in the community?"

"It is when 'sought after' becomes 'hunted'—which is what happened my father put a bounty on my head."

"A bounty?" she echoed dubiously.

He nodded. "Max offered a ridiculous sum of money to a local matchmaker to find marriageable women for each of his sons."

She couldn't imagine that any of the Crawford brothers had ever needed help snagging a woman's attention. Though she hadn't yet met all of Wilder's siblings, there were enough photos around the house to prove they were a good-looking group. In her opinion, Wilder was the most handsome of the bunch, but none of them was hard on the eyes. And according to Avery, each one was as charming as he was good looking.

But her curiosity was piqued by his revelation, prompting her to ask, "An honest-to-goodness matchmaker?"

"Well, technically she's a wedding planner, but that didn't stop her from embracing the challenge. And though she hasn't had much success, every one of my brothers has gotten engaged or married since we moved to Rust Creek Falls."

"How long ago did you move here?" she asked him.

"Six months."

"You're kidding."

This time he shook his head. "Barely more than a month after a chance meeting at the matchmaker's office, Logan married Sarah at the Ace in the Hole and became an instant daddy to baby Sophia. Then Xander fell in love with Lily, though she was originally identified as a prospective match for Knox."

"Lily and Knox didn't hit it off?" she guessed.

"They never had a chance to hit it off. Knox decided to be a no-show for the blind date Vivienne had arranged, so Xander went in his place and the rest, as they say, is history. Very recent history, in this case."

"What happened next?" Beth wanted to know.

"Well, our dad was starting to feel pretty smug about two of his sons finding their matches in short order, so Knox married Gen to teach him a lesson about interfering in his life."

"That seems like an extreme response," she noted.

"And one with very unexpected consequences."

She held her breath, waiting for the reveal.

"They fell in love," he concluded.

"Unexpected but happy consequences," she decided.

"Maybe. Depending on your point of view."

"You don't think they're happy?"

"No, they are happy," he confirmed. "I just don't think falling in love is always a happy consequence."

"Have you ever been in love?"

"I'm too steady on my feet to fall," he told her, adding a cocky wink for good measure.

She rolled her eyes at that as she sipped her diet cola. "Okay, so that's three of your brothers."

He nodded before continuing his narrative. "Finn was the next—or maybe he was the first, because he'd actually hooked up with Avery in Dallas before we moved to Montana, but they only got married a couple months ago.

Their second wedding—after they'd already eloped—was a big, splashy affair in Rustler's Notch, Colorado. We convinced Hunter to bring a nanny along to help out with his daughter so he could have some grown-up fun, and now he's engaged to the nanny."

"But going back to Logan and Sarah, it all started with the visit to the matchmaker," Beth pointed out. "So maybe she's done a better job than you're giving her credit for."

And though it wasn't something she'd ever considered before, it occurred to her now that enlisting a professional to help her find a life partner might not be such a bad idea. Because as much as she wanted to believe that her perfect match was out there waiting for her, she was twenty-eight years old and starting to doubt her ability to find him on her own.

"Or she's secretly serving Homer Gilmore's spiked wedding punch to her clients," Wilder muttered.

"What?"

He waved a hand dismissively. "Never mind. That's another long story."

"So has this matchmaker turned her attention to finding a match for you now?"

"If she has, she's destined for failure there," he said. "Because I have no interest in being matched by her—and even less in being manipulated by my father."

"Leighton always balked at being told what to do, too," Beth noted. "Which is why I was so surprised to learn that she'd brought Cody to Montana, because from day one, I'd been urging her to contact his father."

"Why do you think she decided to listen to you now?"

"I don't know," Beth admitted. "But I don't doubt that she was doing what she thought was best for Cody."

"Do you really think she'll come back?" he asked, as Raina approached with their meals.

"I know she will," Beth said, attempting to project more

confidence in her voice than she actually felt. Because she wanted to believe it was true, though after five of days with no communication from her sister, she was beginning to have some doubts of her own.

Cody woke up when the server set their plates on the table, almost as if he expected there to be food for him, too. Instead, Beth gave him a pacifier to keep him busy— and quiet.

Still, his eyes followed her hand as she picked up a fry and moved it toward her mouth. Watching him, she chuckled softly. "Yeah, I bet you'd like to try these, wouldn't you? But you need a couple of teeth before you'll be ready to tackle something like this—although the way you've been gnawing on that pacifier, I wouldn't be surprised if the first ones aren't too far in the distance."

"When do babies usually get teeth?" Wilder asked.

"Usually around the six-month mark, but first teeth can show up as early as three months or as late as the first birthday."

"How do you know so much about these things?" he wondered.

"I read a lot."

"All those books you bought for Leighton?" he guessed.

She frowned. "Why do you assume I bought them?"

"Am I wrong?"

"No," she admitted. "I just wondered why you leaped to that conclusion."

"I won't pretend that I knew your sister very well, but based on what I did know about her, she wasn't the type to read about something if she could do it."

"I think that's why she asked me to be her birthing partner," Beth said. "Because she knew I'd study the course materials and take notes in childbirth classes, so it wouldn't matter if she didn't pay attention because I'd be there to talk her through it."

"So you were there—when she had the baby?"

"Yeah." She looked at Cody and smiled at the memory of his face all scrunched up and red as he screamed at the indignity of being born. "I was there."

He picked up his burger, bit into it.

She didn't offer any more detailed information, because she wasn't sure how much he'd want to know.

But when he'd finished chewing and swallowed, he asked, "What was it like?"

"The birth?"

He nodded.

"Long and sweaty and messy." She smiled again. "And the most amazing thing I've ever seen."

"How long?" he wondered.

"Sixteen hours," she said. "Leighton was a trouper through it all. There were a few scary moments when labor stalled and they considered a C-section, but she pushed through."

She'd thought her sister was afraid of being cut open— a not unreasonable fear—and only found out after the fact that what her sister had feared most was the possibility of a scar that might prevent her from wearing a bikini at the beach.

And though a lot of people might think it a shallow rationale, Beth understood the root of her sister's insecurities. Because while Leighton had struggled in school, she'd quickly learned that being "such a beautiful child" had a certain intrinsic value—and she'd capitalized on it. She wasn't just pretty, she was popular. While Lisbeth spent her evenings at home with her head stuck in a book, Leighton was usually out with friends.

Because she had been known as "Lisbeth" back then. After all, it was what her parents had always called her and the name they'd put on her birth certificate. But the summer before Lisbeth started high school, Leighton had suddenly started calling her "Beth."

The reason, she explained without apology, was that she didn't want it to be so obvious to her friends and the other popular kids at school that they were sisters. Even though Lisbeth would be in her junior year by the time her sister was a freshman, Leighton had no doubt that she'd be immediately accepted by the in-crowd and didn't want anyone to connect her with "Little Miss Perfect."

Beth could have protested, but dropping the first syllable of her name seemed like a small thing to help her sister. Or maybe she felt as if she owed her something, because learning had always come so easily to Beth while Leighton had struggled to attain good grades.

As a result, her sister had learned to exploit her other attributes. Unfortunately, those attributes were superficial, so that even when she was laboring to bring new life into the world, she wasn't able to embrace and celebrate that miracle without worrying about stretch marks and scars that might diminish her sense of self-worth.

"But Leighton battled through," Beth said, continuing her explanation of her sister's labor to Wilder. "And, a few hours later, Cody was born weighing seven pounds ten ounces and measuring nineteen and a half inches. He also had a sprinkling of dark hair and a very healthy set of lungs." She smiled at the memory of those lungs announcing his arrival to everyone in the maternity wing of the hospital, then her smile faded as she looked at Wilder across the table. "I'm sorry you weren't given the option to be there."

"So am I," he said.

"Would you have wanted to be there?" she asked, surprised by the sincere regret she heard in his tone.

"I would have stepped up," he assured her.

"That's not what I asked."

He took a long sip of his cola, then he nodded. "Yeah," he said. "I would have wanted to be there."

Before she could say anything else, Raina appeared to clear away their empty plates.

"Can I get you anything for dessert?" the server asked.

Wilder looked at Beth, who shook her head.

"No, thanks," he said. "Just the check."

He reached into his back pocket for his wallet as the server returned with the requested check.

But Beth was quicker, having already slid her credit card out of her wallet, and she immediately offered it as payment.

"What are you doing?" Wilder protested.

"Buying you lunch," she told him. "It's the least I can do, considering that I'm not paying to stay at your place."

"Fine, I'll let you buy lunch," he relented. "But you can't take out your wallet again for the rest of the day."

Chapter Eight

"You said you wanted to go to *the* General Store," Beth remarked as they entered. "You didn't mention that it was *Crawford's* General Store."

"But I did warn you about walking down Sawmill Street and bumping into my relatives," he reminded her, as they approached a pretty blonde at the checkout counter. "And this one is my third cousin twice removed, or something like that."

"But you can call me Natalie," the clerk said, with a warm smile.

"And this is Beth," Wilder said, continuing the introductions.

"It's nice to meet you," Beth said automatically.

But the other woman had already turned her attention to the car seat in Wilder's hand. "And I'm guessing this is Cody," she said, crouching for a closer look at the baby. "Maggie told me there was a new baby at the Ambling A."

Beth looked questioningly at Wilder.

"Maggie's married to Natalie's brother Jesse," he told her. "Maggie and Jesse loaned us the crib and rocking chair."

Beth nodded, recognizing the names now that she had a context.

"So what brings you in today?" Natalie asked. "Just making the rounds through town to meet the family?"

"Beth's having enough trouble adjusting to the Montana weather. I don't think she needs the shock of being subjected to our family."

"The Crawfords aren't so bad," Natalie said, then winked at Beth. "Although I've heard some rumors about the Dallas branch of the family tree."

Her warm smile and easy manner immediately put Beth at ease.

Wilder ignored Natalie's teasing remark. "We're here because Beth needs some underwear," he said.

And that quickly, Beth's feeling of ease vanished.

"What?" She squawked the question as her cheeks grew hot. She'd only had one extra pair of panties in her duffel bag, because she'd only planned on spending one night at her sister's, but how could Wilder know that?

"Long underwear," he clarified.

But Beth still couldn't look at him. Couldn't believe that this cowboy she'd known all of two days had brought her here to shop for underwear—even if only the thermal kind.

"Beth's from Dallas," he continued his explanation. "So she's ill-prepared for our winter."

"You're the little guy's mom?" the other woman guessed.

"His aunt," Beth clarified.

"Oooh, plot twist," Natalie said gleefully.

Wilder rolled his eyes.

"How long are you going to be in Rust Creek Falls?" Natalie asked Beth.

"Seven to ten days, apparently."

"Then you're going to need a real coat," the clerk told her. "And some decent footwear, too."

Beth's frigid toes automatically curled inside her unlined boots.

"Avery said she's got a down-filled jacket that Beth can borrow," Wilder said. "Since she can't get it zipped up over her belly right now, anyway."

"She's probably got a dozen pairs of boots, too," Natalie guessed.

"But her feet are bigger than Beth's."

"And how do you know that?" Beth demanded.

"Because I asked."

"You didn't ask me."

"No, I looked at the label inside your boots," he acknowledged. "You wear a seven, Avery's a nine. But Sarah said she's got a pair of size eights you can borrow."

"A pair of thick socks would make those work," Natalie noted.

"She's going to want some of those, too," Wilder said.

"*She* would very much appreciate being able to decide what she does and doesn't need," Beth said pointedly.

"I'm only trying to help."

"A coffee run would be helpful," Natalie said.

"I don't want coffee," he said.

"Well, I do," the clerk said. "More importantly, I don't think Beth wants you hovering while she picks out underwear."

"Thank you," Beth said when Wilder had finally gone.

The other woman smiled. "Sometimes men are so clueless, blunt is the only option."

"It was kind of Wilder to consider what I might need," Beth allowed. "But it is a little awkward to discuss undergarments with a man I barely know."

"Agreed," Natalie said. "Now the key to surviving a Montana winter is layers. Long underwear refers to thermal undergarments that you wear over your usual underwear and under your clothes."

"I know what long underwear is," Beth said. "I just—"

"Got flustered by a handsome cowboy talking about your underwear?" Natalie teased.

Beth's cheeks burned hotter. "Apparently."

The other woman grinned. "So you *do* think he's handsome?"

"I also need regular underwear," she confided, ignoring Natalie's question. She did not want to discuss Wilder's handsomeness or acknowledge—even to herself—that her knees turned to jelly every time he stood a little too close. "I didn't plan on being gone more than a single night, so I've only got one spare."

"We don't have a great selection," Natalie confided. "Anyone who wants sexy stuff either goes shopping in Kalispell or orders online from Victoria's Secret, but we do have some cotton bikinis with lace trim."

"I'm not looking for sexy," Beth hastened to assure her. "No one's going to see my underwear but me."

"Well, that's unfortunate," Natalie teased.

And Beth realized that she was right.

In fact, it wasn't just unfortunate but a little sad that she had no concerns about a man seeing her intimate apparel, because it meant that she had no prospects on the horizon for a relationship. But until she sorted out the situation with Cody, that was the way it was going to have to be.

Beth was standing at the checkout counter when Wilder returned to the store with Natalie's requested macchiato.

"What do you think you're doing?" he demanded, as she started to hand her credit card across the counter.

"Paying for my clothes," she said.

He shook his head. "You agreed to put your wallet away for the rest of the day."

"That was before I knew we were coming here."

"A deal's a deal," he insisted, handing the to-go cup to Natalie along with his platinum credit card.

"I wouldn't have agreed to get half this stuff if I'd known you were going to insist on paying for it," Beth felt compelled to protest.

"He can afford it," Natalie said, with a dismissive wave of her hand, obviously aware he had boatloads of money. "All of this and a lot more. In fact, you should get that other pair of jeans you tried on."

Beth shook her head. "I don't need more than one pair."

But Wilder vetoed her decision. "Add the other pair of jeans," he said to Natalie.

"I don't need them," Beth said again, even as they were added to the pile.

"At least this proves you're different from the other women Wilder has been seen with around town," Natalie said, processing the transaction.

"How so?" she asked, a little warily.

"Because he's buying clothes for you instead of taking them off you."

"Thanks for your help, Nat," Wilder said dryly, snatching his receipt out of her hand.

She winked. "Anytime."

When they got back to the Ambling A, Wilder mixed up a bottle of formula while Beth took her new clothes up to the guest room. She did feel a little strange, letting a man she barely knew—and a former lover of her sister—buy her clothes, but, as he'd argued on the drive, what he'd paid for today didn't begin to repay her for everything she'd done for Cody.

Not that she wanted repayment. Everything she'd done for her nephew had been done out of love. But equating the shopping trip today to packages of diapers and cans of formula, she felt a little less guilty about the money he'd spent.

When her new clothes were stored away, she crossed the hall to the makeshift nursery to ask Wilder a question. The query slipped from her mind, forgotten, as her gaze settled on the handsome cowboy giving a bottle to the baby cuddled against his chest.

She saw it then—not just the physical resemblance between the man and the child that Max kept insisting was obvious, but how right they looked together.

Father and son.

Wilder might be quick to point out that the familial relationship was yet unproven, but looking at them now, seeing how the baby was carefully cradled in the crook of his arm, seeing the earnestness of his expression, she no longer doubted that the man cared about her nephew. And in that moment, though she was still frustrated with her sister for the way she'd handled things, she had to consider that maybe Leighton had done the right thing in bringing Cody here.

She watched Wilder ease the bottle from the baby's mouth before shifting Cody to his shoulder, his big hand gently rubbing the tiny back, and her heart swelled inside her chest.

But even if Leighton had done the right thing, where was she now? And why hadn't she been in touch?

Because it was one thing for Leighton to invoke radio silence with respect to her sister, but she should want to reach out to the man with whom she'd left her baby.

Wasn't she the least bit worried about Cody?

And if she wasn't, she should be.

Because as Beth had discovered when she showed up at the Ambling A, the handsome cowboy could barely manage a diaper change.

Of course, he'd come a long way since then, but Leighton had no way of knowing that.

Leighton had no way of knowing anything because she hadn't been in communication with anyone.

Which Beth knew because she'd kept a close eye on her sister's social media accounts, messaged her friends and reached out to her boss—to no avail. She'd even contacted the authorities in Dallas to inquire about filing a missing person's report. But after summarizing the situation, she'd been told that since her sister had have left of her own free will, Beth should hire a private investigator if she really wanted to track her down—an idea that she was keeping in her back pocket for now.

Desperate for a distraction, she retreated to the kitchen to figure out something for the evening meal.

She'd been a little surprised to discover that the obviously wealthy family didn't have a full-time housekeeper-slash-cook. When she'd asked Wilder about it, he told her that the woman who'd filled those roles in Dallas had declined to make the move to Rust Creek Falls with them. Although she'd worked for Max for almost thirty years and had been like a surrogate mother to his six sons, she had children and grandchildren of her own in Texas and no desire to move so far away from them.

Max had promised to advertise for a cook when they moved into the Ambling A, but during the summer months, it had been easy enough to throw some meat on the grill. So while there was a housekeeper who came in twice a week to tidy up, the men of the Ambling A had mostly fended for themselves when it came to meals—or gone into town to eat.

Of course, now that five of his sons were married or headed in that direction, the responsibility for meals in the main house fell to the patriarch and his youngest son. As a result, they'd eaten a lot of steaks, burgers and pasta over the past several months—unless they were fortunate enough to have Lily prepare a meal for them.

With that thought in mind, Beth rummaged through the freezer looking for some inspiration.

She was chopping carrots and celery when Wilder came down to the kitchen with Cody's empty bottle in one hand

and the baby monitor he'd borrowed from another of his relatives in the other.

"We didn't have lunch all that long ago," he noted. "Are you hungry already?"

"Ha ha," she said. "I'm making stew for dinner."

"You know you don't have to cook for us, don't you?"

"I know," she agreed. "But I'm sleeping in your house and eating your food, so it seems the least I can do is put a meal on the table."

"You made meatloaf last night," he reminded her.

"Are you suggesting that because you had dinner last night you won't want to eat tonight?"

"Of course not," he said.

"Is it that you don't like stew?"

"Stew's basically meat and potatoes in gravy, right? What's not to like?"

"Good," she said, and gestured to the bag on the counter. "You can peel the potatoes."

Max came in a few hours later, stomping to knock the snow off his boots. "Forecast says we could get another four to six inches of the white stuff tonight," he remarked.

"Oh, goody," Beth said dryly.

The old man chuckled as he removed his boots. "Missing Dallas yet?"

"I was missing Dallas by the time I hit Colorado Springs."

"What's cooking?" Max asked, hanging his coat and hat on a hook by the door.

"Beef stew."

"It sure does smell good," he said.

"Hopefully it tastes as good."

"It does," Wilder said. At her questioning look, he shrugged. "I had to sample it for quality control purposes."

"Well, don't sample till it's done," Max said. "I'm hoping there will be some left over for my lunch tomorrow."

"You're not going to be here for dinner?" Beth guessed.

"No," he confirmed. "I've got other plans."

"What kind of plans?" his son wanted to know.

A hint of pink crept into Max's weathered cheeks. "I've got…a thing…in Kalispell."

"A thing?" Wilder echoed dubiously.

"I'm meeting someone for a bite to eat."

"A woman?"

"What's with the third degree?" his father challenged.

"A woman," Wilder said again, but it wasn't a question this time.

Max huffed out a breath. "Okay, fine. Yes. I'm meeting a woman."

"So you've got a date?"

"It's not a date," his father denied. "It's just…a thing."

"Dinner with a woman in Kalispell sounds like a date to me," Wilder remarked.

"I'm going to shower," was all Max said in response to that.

"You shouldn't tease him," Beth chided, when Wilder's father had gone.

"I wasn't really," he denied. "I was just…surprised to hear of his plans."

"He doesn't date very much?"

"It seemed like he had a new girlfriend every few months when we lived in Dallas, but since we moved to Rust Creek Falls, he's been so focused on getting the ranch up and running, I didn't think he'd had a chance to meet anyone."

"Maybe seeing his sons find love has made him want the same thing," she suggested.

"Maybe," he allowed, though his tone was doubtful.

"Does it bother you—your dad dating?" she asked.

He shrugged. "It's his life."

"So why do you seem worried?"

"Because it's not like him to be so secretive about his plans."

"Ah, so it's not really the dating but the possibility he might have met a woman he could really care about."

"Beneath that gruff exterior is a fragile heart," Wilder confided. "My mom leaving did a real number on him."

"Just on him?" she asked gently.

He shrugged. "I can't say that it really affected me, because I was just a baby when she left and honestly don't remember her ever being around."

Beth didn't know what to say to that, and she suspected any effort to delve deeper into the subject would only be brushed aside, so she remained silent.

"Is it just a strange coincidence, do you think, that Cody's mom took off when he was too young to remember her—like my mom did?"

"It's hardly the same situation," she said.

"It seems like the same situation to me," he argued.

She shook her head. "Leighton isn't gone forever."

He shrugged again. "I guess time will tell."

Before their conversation could devolve into another argument about her sister, Beth said, "Why don't you go check on Cody while I serve up dinner?"

As she opened the oven to take out the bread, his words about playing house from earlier that morning echoed in the back of her mind. And while she still maintained that nothing about the current situation was fun, all things considered, being here with Wilder and Cody wasn't so bad, either.

Wilder took a thick slice of warm bread from the basket and slathered it with butter.

"You know, most people run out to the store if they want bread," he said, still marveling over the fact that she'd made it. From scratch.

"Why would I venture outside in this ridiculous weather to buy something I could make right here?" she countered.

"It took me some time to adjust to the cold, too," he acknowledged. "But a rancher doesn't have the option of sheltering inside when there are animals to be tended to."

"Then it's a good thing I'm not a rancher."

"We'll get you out enjoying the snow yet," he said.

"Don't count on it," she said.

"Have you ever taken a ride in a horse-drawn sleigh?"

"No," she said. "And if your next question is, 'Have you ever wanted to ride in a horse-drawn sleigh?'—the answer would be 'no' again."

"I bet Cody would get a kick out of it," he said.

Her gaze narrowed. "Oh, now you're fighting dirty."

"I'm not fighting at all," he denied. "But I am surprised that you'd let your nephew miss out on an enjoyable activity just so that you can stay warm."

She huffed out a breath. "Fine," she relented. "We'll go tomorrow."

He grinned. "Don't forget your thermal underwear."

Chapter Nine

Beth stood at the window, looking out at the pristine landscape. The promised four to six inches had arrived overnight, so that everything was covered in a fresh blanket of white.

"It does look pretty," Beth said to Cody.

She was holding him with his back to her front, so he could see what she was seeing. He reached out to put his hand on the glass, then quickly pulled it back again.

"That's the problem," she said. "As pretty as it looks, it has to be cold for that white stuff not to melt."

"It's not that cold out today," Wilder said, joining their conversation as he entered the room.

"I don't see the snow melting," she remarked.

He smiled. "No, the snow's not melting," he agreed. "So go put on your coat and boots while I get Cody bundled up for his first sleigh ride."

She appreciated the way the words "first sleigh ride" rolled off his tongue. As if he anticipated there would be a second and a third. As if he wanted the little boy to spend more winters here in Rust Creek Falls with him. Maybe all the other seasons, too.

For herself, she expected that this would be her first and her last sleigh ride. And though she suspected she'd be too preoccupied with her frozen fingers and toes to enjoy it, a promise was a promise.

She'd put on a pair of thermal underwear that morning, as instructed, then added a long-sleeved shirt and a thick sweater, blue jeans and two pairs of socks. Cody was similarly dressed in layers, and Wilder had borrowed a down-filled bunting bag with built-in mittens and a faux fur-trimmed hood for the little guy.

In the foyer, she shoved her feet into the boots she'd borrowed from Sarah, wrapped herself in Avery's jacket, pulled a knitted hat over her head, wound a scarf around her neck, and slid her hands into fleece-lined mittens, all accessories courtesy of Lily.

Wilder chuckled. "You really are a tenderfoot, aren't you?"

"And not ashamed to admit it," she told him, her voice muffled through the scarf already pulled up to cover her mouth.

"Let's get out of here before you overheat," he suggested.

She nodded and followed Wilder and Cody out the door.

Though she braced herself for the cold air, she forgot about the weather altogether for a brief moment when she spotted the pair of enormous black horses harnessed to a fancy black sleigh with glossy-painted red runners, a tufted red velvet seat and collapsible roof.

"Did you steal Santa's ride?" she asked Wilder.

"I'm pretty sure that would get my name on the naughty list, so no," he said. "This is actually an antique doctor's sleigh."

"So you stole it from an old doctor?"

He chuckled. "That would be another no. My dad bought it, restored, at an auction."

"It's beautiful," she said, stroking a mittened hand over the curved side.

"And it rides incredibly smooth," he promised. "Of course, you have to actually get in the sleigh before we can go anywhere."

He offered his hand, and she stepped up into the sleigh.

"There aren't any seat belts," she realized, as she lowered herself onto the seat.

"Seat belts hadn't been invented when this sleigh was made," he pointed out, passing her the bundled baby. "But it's perfectly safe, I promise."

She nibbled on her lower lip as she hugged Cody close to her body, uneasy with the idea of taking her nephew for any kind of ride without him being secured in an NHTSA-approved child restraint system.

"You're not convinced?" he guessed.

"I'm a worrywart," she reminded him.

"There's nothing wrong with being cautious," he said. "But trust me, I wouldn't have suggested this ride if I wasn't one hundred percent certain that Cody would be safe. Although I can try to rig up some kind of anchor system for his car seat, if that would make you feel better."

It would make her feel better. But she couldn't imagine how they'd both fit in the sleigh with the baby's bulky car seat between them. And maybe she needed to learn to be a little less rigid all the time.

"You're one hundred percent certain?" she asked, seeking reassurance.

"One hundred percent," he confirmed.

"And you won't go too fast?"

"I'll go as slow as you need me to go," he said, with a teasing wink.

"Okay, then." She decided to ignore his double entendre as she tightened her arms around the baby. "Let's go for a ride."

He settled beside her and picked up the reins, and she felt a little niggle of fear as she shifted forward in her seat when the animals began to move. But their gait was slow and steady, the ride as smooth as Wilder had promised, and she soon relaxed again.

As the sleigh traveled over the snow-covered ground,

he identified the other buildings on the property and described their specific uses, pointed out the cabins belonging to his brothers, and answered her curious and numerous questions about raising the cattle she could see in the distance.

"Now are you willing to admit that this was worth leaving the house for?" he asked, as he paused the horses at the top of a hill for an overview of the sprawling property.

"More than," she agreed, as she turned her head to admire the pristine beauty of the land in every direction. "Is all of this really yours?"

He chuckled. "Not mine, but everything you can see, all the way to that fence—" he pointed to a barrier in the distance "—is the Ambling A."

"You really like it here, don't you?"

"I thought I'd miss being close to the city when we moved," Wilder confided. "And I did, at first. But it's amazing how quickly I adjusted to being out here."

"'Out here' being the middle of nowhere?" she guessed.

He grinned. "It's not so bad."

"There's not even a movie theater in town."

"They show movies in the high school gym on Friday and Saturday nights—so long as one of the sports teams isn't playing."

"Oh, well, I had no idea," she said. "Movies in the high school gym? This town is practically a booming metropolis."

"And for anyone who can't live without a real movie theater experience, Kalispell is only half an hour away."

"Kalispell isn't Dallas," she pointed out. "It isn't a quarter the size of Dallas."

"Life's about choices,' he said. "My dad chose to come here and, as much as he drives me crazy sometimes, I wanted to support that choice."

"You're a good son, Wilder Crawford."

"That's kind of you to say. Of course, being a good son doesn't necessarily equate to being a good father, does it?"

"Not necessarily," she agreed. "But it never hurts to have a positive role model."

"It couldn't have been easy for my dad, having to parent six rowdy sons on his own, but he did it," Wilder acknowledged. "I respect and admire that, but I wish he'd accept that we're grown-ups now and let us live our own lives."

"Is this about the matchmaker again?" she guessed.

"Among other things."

The cryptic response didn't invite further discussion, so she only said, "Well, thank you for bringing me and Cody out here. It really was an unforgettable experience."

"It was my pleasure," he said, then smiled as he glanced at the sleeping baby. "But I don't know that Cody got much out of it."

"If nothing else, he got some fresh air."

"One of my favorite things about being a rancher is working outdoors," Wilder confided. "I could never imagine myself stuck in an office from nine to five."

"But as a rancher, you often work longer hours than that, don't you?"

"And seven days a week," he agreed.

"So if it turns out that you are Cody's father, how would you juggle that schedule with the demands of parenting?" she asked.

"I don't know," he admitted. "But I know my family will help. And Cody's only one baby. There's another rancher in town—Jamie Stockton—who was widowed with infant triplets."

"That must have been overwhelming," she acknowledged.

"You'd think so," he agreed. "But that's the thing about a town like Rust Creek Falls—the community comes together to take care of its own."

"Didn't you just move here six months ago?"

"Yeah," he confirmed. "But I already feel as if I've lived here forever."

"Of course, that might have something to do with the fact that you share a last name with half the town's residents."

He chuckled. "Not quite half, but that's a valid point."

"So you don't have any doubts that you'd be able to handle it?"

"Are you kidding? I've got a ton of doubts. But I've never backed down in the face of a challenge."

Then, because he didn't want to think about all those doubts, he reached over and gently nudged her chin up. "Look."

"Oh." Her eyes sparkled with childlike excitement and her lips curved. "It's snowing again."

He studied her as she watched the big, fluffy flakes that seemed to be floating on the air rather than falling from the sky.

"I've never seen snow like this." She smiled again as a flake landed on her cheek. "It's so pretty."

Looking at her, watching her surprised joy at something as simple as a snowfall, he couldn't deny that she was right. It was pretty. And so was she.

"It's pretty—until you have to shovel it," he said.

"Now who's being a spoilsport?" she teased.

And the curve of those perfectly-shaped lips tempted him to taste them, to discover if they were as soft and sweet as they looked.

But, of course, he didn't. He couldn't.

Because she was Cody's aunt and completely off limits.

"Guilty," he acknowledged, and turned the horses back toward the house.

"Though white Christmases are an anomaly back home,

for some reason snow always makes me think of the holiday."

"'Tis the season."

"And since it doesn't look like Cody and I are going to be heading back to Texas anytime soon, would it be okay if I put his presents under the tree when we get back?"

"Of course," he agreed. "And while you're doing that, I'll make the hot chocolate."

Wilder stacked logs and built a fire in the hearth while Beth arranged Cody's presents under the tree, then he went to the kitchen to make the hot chocolate.

He returned to the family room with two steaming mugs topped with marshmallows just in time to catch her brushing an errant tear from her cheek.

"Everything okay?" he asked.

"Under the circumstances, everything is better than okay," she told him.

"So why are you crying?"

"I'm not," she denied, as she accepted the proffered mug.

"You just wiped away a tear."

"A single tear isn't crying," she said.

"So what is it?" he pressed.

"Proof that the holidays make me a little emotional," she confided. "Christmas is my favorite time of year, but it's a bittersweet time, too, because I can't help but remember all the happy Christmases of my childhood, which makes me think about my parents, and then I find myself missing them and—" she cut herself off then. "Oh, Wilder, I'm sorry."

"Why?"

"Because I know you lost your mom, too."

"I didn't lose her—she left," he reminded her.

"And she didn't stay in touch after the divorce?" she asked curiously.

"She died only a few months after the papers were signed."

She wanted to apologize again for bringing up such a difficult subject, but he would only deny it was difficult. Instead she said, "I'm sorry you don't have any memories of her."

He shrugged. "And since I don't, there's nothing for me to miss."

To Beth, that was just as sad.

"So what were your Christmases like?" she asked, hoping he might share some happy memories.

"Nothing out of the ordinary. Presents under the tree, a big turkey dinner. Christmas cookies," he said, and smiled then. "Our housekeeper made these amazing cookies decorated with icing and colored sugars.

"I thought we'd miss out this year, but she sent a box in the mail. There must have been six dozen cookies, and they were gone within two days."

"Not just between you and your dad?"

"No," he admitted. "The note said we had to share, so we did."

She smiled at the obvious regret in his tone. "What about your tree—have you always had a real one?"

"Is there another kind?"

She tapped a finger against one of the branches, watched the tip bob. "They do smell good," she confided.

"You don't get a real tree?" he guessed.

She shook her head. "My apartment's on the sixth floor, and it just seems like too much hassle to drag one into the building, cram it into an elevator, then haul it down the hall and into my apartment, leaving a path of needles along the way."

"A path of needles would make it easy for Santa to find you," he pointed out.

"Instead, I have a sign that goes in the window that says Santa, Please Stop Here!"

"You don't think Saint Nick knows where he's supposed to stop?"

"I don't like leaving some things to chance."

"And what was on your wish list for Santa this year?" Wilder asked her.

"Oh, um, just…you know…the usual stuff."

"You didn't make a list for Santa, did you?"

"Not exactly."

His gaze narrowed thoughtfully. "But there was something specific you wanted," he guessed.

"I just wanted to spend Christmas with Leighton and Cody—to be part of the happy memories of his first Christmas."

"You do know he's not going to remember his first Christmas when he's older?"

"I know," she admitted. "But I've been taking pictures of every event and milestone, to make a scrapbook of his first year, so that he'll be able to look back and know, even if he can't remember."

"You should have asked me to take a picture of the two of you in the sleigh," he told her.

"I was so mesmerized by the sleigh and the horses, I didn't even think about it," she confided.

"Next time," he promised.

But they both knew there might not be a next time, because Beth's days at the Ambling A were numbered—seven to ten—and the countdown was on.

She carefully sipped her hot chocolate and wondered why she didn't seem as excited to anticipate her return to Dallas as she'd been only three days earlier. Goodness knows, she would be happy enough to get back to a place where she didn't need long underwear to step out the front door. But when she did, she might actually miss interacting with Wilder and Max and the various other Crawfords who'd been in and out of the main house at the Ambling A during her brief time there.

She pushed the uncomfortable thought aside and sipped her drink again, savoring the warm sweetness as it slid down her throat. "This is really good," she told Wilder.

"The key ingredients are real cream and dark chocolate," he confided. "And marshmallows on top, of course."

"Of course," she agreed.

"Speaking of marshmallows, you've got some right here," he said, and indicated the location on his own lip.

"Oh." She instinctively sought out the sticky spot with the tip of her tongue. "Did I get it?"

Instead of answering, he reached over and brushed his thumb over the curve of her bottom lip. The callused pad scraped against her soft skin, causing her breath to back up in her lungs and sending tingles through her veins.

She lifted her gaze to find his fixed on her mouth, his head tilted toward her, and for the space of a single heartbeat, she actually thought he was going to kiss her.

And, oh, how she yearned for his kiss. Just the thought of his lips pressed against hers made her tummy feel tingly and her knees grow weak.

But instead of shifting closer, he abruptly pulled away.

"It's gone now," he told her.

And then Cody was awake, allowing her to focus on the baby and ignore the twinge of what might have been disappointment.

After she'd snapped a few pictures of Cody propped up against the pile of presents, Wilder took her cell phone and assumed photographer duties while she helped her nephew open his gifts.

There were sleepers and outfits, a pair of high-top running shoes (and of course Wilder questioned the purpose of running shoes for a kid who couldn't even walk), board books and bath books, wooden puzzles and cuddly toys, learning toys and silly toys.

"Let's try these on you," Beth said, tugging off Cody's socks and replacing them with the foot rattles he'd just opened.

One was red-and-orange and decorated to look like a giraffe; the other was black-and-white like a zebra; both had noisemakers sewn into their ears. She put them on his feet and helped him kick his legs to demonstrate how they could make sound.

Cody rewarded her with a gummy smile.

"What's this one?" Wilder asked, picking up a small-ish square box wrapped in Santa paper with a red bow.

She took the box from his hand and glanced at the tag that read: To Mommy Love Cody.

"Oh." She managed a smile. "It's a 'Mommy' Christmas ornament, dated for the year Cody was born."

She set it aside and reached for a bigger and flatter package. After carefully prying the tag off the wrapping, she handed the gift to Wilder.

"What's this?"

"A present."

"I know you didn't buy this for me."

"No, I didn't," she acknowledged. "But it's something I'd like you to have."

Curious, he slid a finger beneath the fold of paper to break the tape. The flat, unmarked box didn't give anything away, so he lifted the lid and peeled back the tissue inside to reveal a beautiful brushed silver-tone frame engraved with the words "Cody's First Christmas." Inside the frame was a photo of the baby, asleep in the crook of Santa's arm.

"What a great picture," he said, sincerely touched by her gesture. "This was another gift for your sister?"

"Yeah, but I can get another one made for her," Beth said.

"Is this because you now believe I'm Cody's father?" he asked.

"Do *you* believe it?" she countered.

He looked at the little guy now sitting between his outstretched legs.

Did he believe it?

Were his residual doubts simply a manifestation of his reluctance to take on the responsibilities of fatherhood? Responsibilities that he wouldn't be able to duck if and when he was confirmed to be the baby's father. Not that he'd had much success ducking anything since the baby had appeared on the doorstep and his father had made his own determination about paternity. But doubts aside, the more time he spent with Cody, the less terrifying he found the idea of being his father.

"Well," she said with a shrug, obviously having given up on waiting for an answer. "If it turns out you're not his dad, you can give the picture back to me."

"For now, I'm going to put it right here," he said, propping the frame up on the side table.

Beth looked at the picture there and smiled. "Good choice."

Then she stood up and began gathering the discarded wrapping.

"Somebody lost a sock," Wilder noted, tickling the baby's bare toes as he reached to pick up the giraffe.

Cody giggled.

Beth gasped and spun around, clutching an armload of crumpled paper against her chest. "What did you do?" she asked Wilder.

"Me?" Had he done something wrong? "I just tickled his toes." Then he did it again, to demonstrate for her.

Cody responded with more giggles.

"Oh." The word was barely a whisper from her lips as

her eyes filled with tears. "That's the first time I've heard him laugh."

"Really?" Wilder asked, surprised.

She nodded.

Wilder brushed his fingertips over the bottom of the baby's foot, to see if he was ticklish there. The baby answered with another giggle.

Beth sighed. "Is there anything as sweet as that sound?"

Though she probably wasn't expecting an answer to her question, he heard himself responding, "It's pretty great."

"It makes me happy to know he's happy," she said.

"Of course, he's four months old, so his biggest concerns are a hungry belly or wet diaper," Wilder pointed out.

"And sore gums," she reminded him.

"Still, he's not lying awake at night worrying about the market price of beef," he said, as he worked the sock onto the baby's foot, stroking his fingertip along his sole and sending the little guy into a fresh wave of giggles.

Beth laughed, too, and their gazes met and held for a long moment of shared understanding and unexpected connection.

Then Cody kicked his feet again, shaking the rattles, and the moment was broken.

Chapter Ten

Wilder lay awake in bed for a long time that night, thinking about the day he'd spent with Cody and Beth. He couldn't help but admire Beth's devotion to her nephew and the way she overcame her own reservations to embrace opportunities and new experiences for the little boy. Everything she did seemed to be motivated by his best interests, even before her own wants and needs, her actions a stark contrast to those of her sister, who'd apparently had no qualms about abandoning her child.

Of course, Wilder knew from experience that maternal instincts weren't really instincts in the true sense of the word. They weren't as universal as the compulsion of birds to build nests. While a lot of parents might instinctively bond with, nurture and protect their children, giving birth to a child didn't automatically create or foster such instincts. If it did, his mother never would have walked away, leaving Max to raise their six sons on his own.

Had his father had stronger instincts to care for his children? Or had he only done what needed to be done because his wife's abandonment had left him with no other option?

More important, would Wilder be able to learn everything he needed to know to raise his son—if it turned out that Cody was his son? And why didn't he share Max's conviction that the baby was a Crawford? Was it because he didn't want to be a father to the little guy? Or was he afraid that he would fail in his efforts to be what Cody needed?

"Fatherhood changes everything," Max had told Wilder, when they were alone at the Ambling A after everyone else had gone on Christmas night.

Apparently that was true whether he wanted anything to change or not. And even without any confirmation that he was a father.

At first, he'd been panicked at the idea the kid was his. Now, after spending only a few days with Cody…well, he wasn't quite ready to start handing out cigars with blue bands that proclaimed "It's a Boy," but he wasn't quite so terrified anymore, either. Of course, cigars might be premature, anyway, as he was still waiting on the results of the DNA test.

Maybe he'd feel more of a connection to the kid if he'd known that he existed before he was four months old. If he'd had the opportunity to help Leighton prepare for his arrival. If he'd been there when their baby was born.

He was angry that she'd taken that opportunity away from him. That *she'd* chosen not to tell him about the pregnancy, to cut him out of the life of his child—*if* Cody was his child.

And he was still angry the next morning, and continuing to mull over these thoughts, as he sipped his coffee.

"Are you okay?" Beth asked.

"Sure. Why?"

"Because you're gripping the handle of that mug so tight it's a wonder it hasn't snapped off in your hand."

He uncurled his fist and set the mug on the counter.

"Wilder?" she prompted.

"I guess I'm just realizing how much I missed out on, not knowing that Leighton was pregnant."

"I think, in the beginning, she didn't reach out to you because she wasn't sure she was going to keep the baby," she admitted.

He swallowed. "She considered ending her pregnancy?"

"No." Beth immediately shook her head. "*Never.* She always planned to have the baby, but she didn't know if she would keep him."

"You're talking about adoption," he realized.

Now she nodded.

"But…why?" he wondered.

"Because she wanted her baby to have a better life than she could give him as a single mother. She wanted him to have a family."

"She didn't have to be a single mother. If Leighton had told me she was pregnant, I would have offered to do the right thing."

"Because getting married for the sake of a baby is the right thing?" she asked dubiously.

"Sometimes it is," he said.

"Maybe that's why she didn't tell you," Beth remarked.

"What does that mean?" he challenged.

"I can't imagine any woman being swept off her feet by such an offer, and it definitely wouldn't have swayed my sister."

He scowled at that. "You think she would have said *no*?"

"I wouldn't presume to know how she might have responded," Beth said. "But I think the fact that she didn't tell you she was pregnant proves she didn't trust you would support her choices."

"But she trusted you?" he challenged.

"I did support her," she said.

"And yet, when she got to the point where she felt overwhelmed by her responsibilities, she brought the baby to me," he pointed out.

He was right, and that truth was like a slap to Beth's face.

She'd thought she was doing what was best for her sister. She'd offered her a sympathetic ear and a strong shoulder; she'd listened and counseled and encouraged. And all the while she'd been promising her support, she'd also been pushing her sister in the direction Beth wanted her to go. *Of course it's your choice if you want to give your baby up for adoption. But if you decide to keep him, I'll be there for you. Whatever you need. Whatever he needs.*

Leighton had been honest in expressing her reservations about working as a bartender and raising a child on her own. She'd wanted to do the best thing for her baby— to give him a real family. But Beth had pointed out that they were a family; she'd assured her that they could be everything he'd ever need. And so Leighton had been persuaded to keep her baby.

But sometime during the past four months, she'd apparently had a change of heart.

Or maybe she'd begun to suspect her sister was wrong.

Either way, there was one fact that Beth could no longer deny: it was *her* fault Cody had been left on a ranch in Montana.

"We were just talking about the big New Year's Eve party at Maverick Manor," Max said, when Beth returned to the main level after putting Cody down for his nap. "It's the fancy hotel off the highway owned by Nate Crawford—you might have seen it on your way into Rust Creek Falls."

"Isn't everything in this town owned by a Crawford?" Beth asked.

"Not quite everything," Max said. Then he winked. "At least, not yet."

Beth smiled, though she suspected he wasn't entirely joking. The Crawford patriarch struck her as a man capable of world—or at least small-town—domination.

"So what do you think?" he asked.

"About what?"

"The party."

She looked at Wilder, as if he might be able to give her a clue as to why his father was asking, but he only shrugged.

"Sounds like fun?" she said.

"Great. I'll tell Nate to add your name to the guest list."

"Oh," she said, startled by the suggestion. "I meant it would be fun for you—not for me."

"You don't like parties?" Max challenged.

"She doesn't know how to have fun," Wilder said.

And though the twinkle in his eye assured Beth that he was only teasing, the remark too closely echoed her sister's oft-repeated criticism for her to slough it off.

"That's true," she said, aware that her tone was as stiff as her smile. "So while it's thoughtful of you to invite me, I have to decline."

"Don't say no," Max protested.

But she didn't stick around to discuss the matter any further. There was no point, when she knew she wouldn't change her mind.

She instinctively headed toward the guest room, just as she'd retreated to her bedroom when she was a child, as if closing the door could shut out the taunting voices that called her names.

"Worrywart."

"Spoilsport."

"Killjoy."

"Little Miss Perfect."

Sticks and stones may break my bones...

The childhood rhyme echoed in her head as Beth reached the top of the stairs.

Maybe names didn't leave physical scars, but they did hurt. The barbs stung even more when they were tossed by her sister. For as long as she could remember, Beth had adored her little sister, but she'd also been aware that her affection wasn't returned. So she'd tried harder to be liked by her sibling, to be included in her activities, to be part of her life.

Every once in a while, Leighton would invite her into her inner circle, allow her to be included in her plans. It didn't take Beth long to realize that her sister wasn't trying to befriend her so much as she was testing her. But it wasn't in Beth's nature to go along with the crowd when what the crowd was doing was questionable, dangerous or illegal. And Leighton had stopped inviting her, further cementing her status as an outcast, widening the gap between the sisters' lives.

Wilder caught up to her in the hall, before she even reached her room.

"I'm sorry," he said.

She shook her head. "You didn't say anything that wasn't true."

"But I didn't mean it."

"Yes, you did. And it's true. Leighton's the fun sister. I'm the responsible one.

"And normally that wouldn't bother me so much, except that her latest actions have been beyond irresponsible."

"You're worried about her," Wilder guessed.

"Of course, I'm worried about her. And I'm worried about Cody. And I'm mad that she doesn't seem to be worried about Cody."

She stalked back and forth in the hall. "I mean—she just left him here without telling anyone where she was going or when she would be back," Beth continued her rant. "How could she do that? And what if something were to happen to his mom? Where would that leave him?"

"I can understand your concerns," Wilder said. "But even in such a worst-case scenario, I'm confident that Cody would be just fine."

She frowned. "How can you say that?"

"Because he'd still have his Aunt Beth," he pointed out

to her. "And she's a force to be reckoned with. Brave and strong. Loving and loyal."

Inexplicably, her eyes filled.

"Oh, crap," Wilder said. "What did I say wrong now?"

She shook her head, but she couldn't stop the tears from spilling onto her cheeks. And though Wilder looked as if he'd rather be anywhere else in that moment, he drew her close and held her while she cried.

Of course he was only trying to offer her comfort, but with her face pressed against his shirt, she couldn't help but notice how the soft flannel contrasted to his hard muscles. And that he smelled really good.

"You want to tell me now what caused you to go from spitting nails to a complete meltdown in the blink of an eye?" he asked, when her tears had finally dried up.

She shook her head again.

"You don't know?" he queried.

"I don't want to tell you," she admitted.

"Why not?"

"Because you'll think I'm ridiculous."

"I won't think you're ridiculous," he promised.

"The things you said…about me being strong and loving…they were nice."

"And?" he prompted.

"No one's ever said such nice things about me before."

"You need to get some better friends," he told her.

She managed to smile at that. "I have wonderful friends," she assured him. "But I don't tend to open up and dump my emotional baggage on them."

"So why me?" he wondered.

"I guess you're just lucky."

He chuckled at that. "Yeah, that's what my niece said when a baby was left on my doorstep. And though I was skeptical at first, I'm beginning to think maybe she was right."

In only four days, Beth had seen it—he'd not just grown more comfortable with the daily responsibilities of taking care of a baby, but he'd learned to interpret Cody's cries and anticipate his needs. She'd heard it, too, in the warmth in his voice when he talked not just to Cody but about him. Forcing Beth to acknowledge that this was one more thing her sister had lied about.

Or maybe Leighton hadn't been able to guess how he would respond to the news of her unexpected pregnancy. Maybe she really hadn't known him well enough to anticipate that he would step up.

"So…will you reconsider coming to the party?" he asked.

Beth appreciated the invitation. She was even a little tempted. She couldn't remember the last time she'd gone out to celebrate the arrival of a new year, and the idea held a certain appeal. But she had nothing appropriate in her wardrobe for a night out, and no intention of trekking into town to spend money on an outfit she'd probably never wear again. Not to mention that she had no desire to see Wilder live up to his reputation, flirting with all the pretty girls in town.

"Truthfully, I'm not keen on the idea of hanging out with a bunch of people I don't know."

"You know me and my brothers," he pointed out.

Yes, and they were all—aside from Wilder and his father—engaged or married. In other words, if she went, she'd be surrounded by happy couples. And when the clock counted down to midnight, they'd instinctively turn to their significant others to embrace and kiss, reminding her once again that she was alone in the world—as she'd always been.

"I do appreciate the invitation," she said. "But I want to stay home with Cody."

Not only was that kind of celebration much more her

speed, but she sincerely wanted to spend the time with her nephew. Because she was beginning to suspect that, if Wilder was the little boy's father, he would want Cody to stay in Rust Creek Falls, which meant that her days and nights with her nephew were numbered.

"Did you convince Beth to come to the party?" Max asked, when Wilder made his way back downstairs.

"It's not my place to try to change her mind," he said, conveniently ignoring the fact that he'd attempted to do just that.

"I'm sure if you used some of your legendary charm, she'd reconsider," his father said.

Wilder narrowed his gaze. "What are you up to?"

"I'm not up to anything," Max denied.

"Then why do you care whether or not Beth goes to the party?"

"I just think she deserves a night out," his father said.

"That's the only reason?"

"What other reason could there be?"

Wilder didn't buy his father's innocent act for a minute. "Just as long as you don't have any crazy ideas in your head about matchmaking," he said.

"Why would I waste my time when I paid good money to Vivienne Dalton to take care of that?" Max countered.

"I didn't think you'd paid her anything yet."

His father waved a hand dismissively. "You know what I mean."

"I know that you've avoided giving a direct answer to the question," Wilder pointed out.

"How's this for direct? You don't need to worry that I've got any illusions about you and our houseguest from Dallas," Max assured him. "It's obvious that Cody's aunt isn't at all your type."

"I'm glad you can see that," Wilder said, even as a part of him wondered if his father—and his own instincts—might be wrong.

When Wilder walked into the kitchen while Beth was preparing a bottle for Cody on New Year's Eve, her heart actually bumped against her ribs. Because as good as Wilder looked in his usual jeans and flannel, decked out in a suit and tie and dress boots, he was even more mouthwateringly delicious. And looking at him now, she had absolutely no difficulty understanding why her sister had been so eager to fall into bed with him.

Not that Beth would ever do the same thing.

Of course, she'd never have the chance.

Because she and Leighton were complete opposites, and though her heart might act a little crazy whenever Wilder was near, the handsome cowboy had given her ab- solutely no indication that the unwelcome attraction she felt was reciprocated.

Well, except for that one time, when he'd brushed the remnants of gooey marshmallow off her lip and looked at her in a way that made her feel all gooey inside. But again, that was probably only her overreaction to a casual gesture not intended to be anything else.

"You clean up good, cowboy." She kept her tone light, as if she was unaffected by his appearance and merely making an observation.

He took a moment to peruse her outfit in turn: a chunky knit sweater, black leggings and wool socks. "And you look comfortable and warm," he said, with a wink.

"Because I am," she agreed.

"It's not too late to change your mind and come with us," Max said, entering the room.

He was dressed in a similar fashion to his son, and look- ing at him now, Beth could easily imagine what Wilder would look like in another thirty-five years—and it was a good look.

"Hunter and Merry are staying home with Wren tonight and said they'd be happy to watch Cody if you wanted to go out," he explained.

"I don't want to go out," Beth said. "But thank you again."

"Well, Happy New Year then," Max said, nudging his son toward the door.

She wished both men a happy new year in return, then locked the door behind them and settled in for a quiet night with her nephew.

As always, the advent of a new year caused her to look back and reflect on all the wonderful things that had happened in the past twelve months—the most notable event being Cody's arrival. She wondered if Leighton was thinking about him today, too. Maybe even missing him a little.

Six days had passed since she'd left Cody at the Ambling A Ranch. Seven since Beth had arrived at her sister's apartment on Christmas Eve in eager anticipation of celebrating the holiday together. And in all that time, she hadn't heard anything from Leighton. Not a single word aside from that brief and cryptic message left by her phone.

Maybe she could understand her sister not reaching out to her—especially if Leighton didn't want to answer the questions she knew Beth would ask—but she couldn't understand her not being in communication with her friends. Or her boss. And a full week's absence from social media was unprecedented.

Beth picked up her cell now, as if she could will her sister to call, but it remained silent, the screen blank. Of course, wherever Leighton was—unless she'd left the country—it was December 31, so she was probably out celebrating. There was nothing Leighton loved more than a party. The wilder the better. And yes, it had crossed Beth's mind, when she found Wilder's name and address in her sister's apartment, that Leighton would have found his name as appealing as the rest of him.

Beth had always been attracted to a different kind of man. The kind who would prefer a simple "dinner and a movie" date over loud music and fancy cocktails in a trendy nightclub. The kind who aspired to obtain a wife and a family rather than fast cars and faster women. She wanted a simple man with simple dreams.

Which was why her attraction to Wilder wasn't just unexpected but unwelcome. Because if he was her sister's type, he was definitely *not* hers. Unfortunately that knowledge didn't stop her pulse from racing when he was near, or prevent butterflies from swirling in her belly when he smiled at her, or cool the blood that heated when he touched her.

Aside from the fact that he wasn't her type, he was quite possibly her nephew's father. And regardless of whether or not the DNA results proved he was Cody's dad, there was no denying that he'd had an intimate physical relationship with her sister. Yes, that relationship had ended a long time ago, but it still felt as if she was violating some kind of unwritten code.

Or maybe a written code, she acknowledged, as coveting thy sister's lover was undoubtedly the moral equivalent of coveting thy neighbor's spouse.

Thou shall not, she reminded herself sternly.

But even if she did covet, nothing would ever come of her desires, because Wilder would never be attracted to someone like her. His history with her sister proved that he preferred a very different kind of woman.

So really, any fantasies that played out in her head—or in her dreams—were just that. And fantasies aside, she was happy with her life. She had a great job, a nice apartment, good friends and friendly neighbors, and now she had Cody, too.

The birth of her nephew had filled her life in ways she couldn't have imagined. But now she had to face the very real possibility that, if Leighton didn't come back and the DNA test proved that Wilder was Cody's father, she could lose him.

She no longer had any doubts that the cowboy would pursue legal custody of his child. And the courts, taking into consideration the biological connection and Leighton's apparent abandonment of her child, would likely rubber-stamp his application.

Sure, Beth could put in a claim for guardianship and argue that she had a stronger bond with her nephew, who'd never even met Wilder until he was four months old. But the courts tended to favor placement of a child with a parent, and they certainly wouldn't hold it against Wilder that he'd had no contact with a child he'd known nothing about.

Even if she believed she was better equipped to deal with Cody's day-to-day needs, she couldn't deny that Wilder had a lot of family support in Montana. And though she'd had limited interactions with his siblings and their spouses, it was evident that they'd readily accepted Cody as part of the family.

So the most likely scenario was that Cody would stay in Rust Creek Falls and she would go back to Dallas, and maybe she'd get to see her nephew a few times a year. The prospect made her heart ache unbearably.

Of course, if Leighton came back to reclaim her baby and Wilder consented to her returning with him to Dallas, then the status quo of Beth's life would be restored. Or maybe Leighton would return and decide to give her relationship with the cowboy another chance—to give Cody a family. Which was what Beth wanted more than anything for her nephew, even if it meant she'd be left on the outside looking in.

But perhaps this was a lesson to her. A reminder that she needed to live her own life and let Leighton live hers. Whether or not she agreed with her sister's choices, she had to accept that they were hers to make. And if Leighton made mistakes, she would have to own them and learn from them.

And maybe it was time for Beth to make some mistakes, too. Or at least take some chances. She'd mostly given up on dating, having grown tired of putting herself out there in an effort to meet "the right guy" only to find that she didn't click with anyone. Or, when she thought she clicked, to realize she'd been duped by someone who'd only said and done the right things to get her into bed and then totally ghosted on her.

Maybe she should put herself out there again—say "yes" the next time Barry Kendrick asked her to go out with him. So what if the fifth-grade science teacher didn't make her heart race or her belly quiver? It was time to grow up and accept that those physiological reactions didn't exist outside the pages of the romance novels that she loved to read.

Except that her body's responses to Wilder Crawford proved otherwise.

Chapter Eleven

Looking around the festively decorated ballroom of Maverick Manor, it seemed to Wilder that after a lot of years and a lot of parties, they all started to look and feel the same. The glittery venues and beautiful women mixed with champagne bubbles and blurred together in his mind.

His memories of last year's celebration, being the most recent, were perhaps a little clearer. He and Leighton had been seeing each other for a few weeks by then, and he easily pictured the sparkly green dress that hugged her curves and the sexy skyscraper heels that put her mouth within easy reach of his. But the rest of the details remained fuzzy.

He knew she had pale blond hair and moss green eyes, but the image that teased his mind now was of dark hair and dark eyes. And as the features came more fully into focus, he noticed other inconsistencies: the lush mouth was a little too full, and instead of being painted glossy red, the lips were naturally pink. Naked. And somehow even more tempting.

Beth's lips.

The realization was as startling to Wilder as it was unsettling.

Scowling, he escaped to the outdoor terrace to get some air and clear his head.

Looking around at the crowd, everyone decked out in their holiday finest, it belatedly occurred to him that Beth might not have wanted to come to the party because she didn't have anything appropriate to wear. He would have been happy to take her shopping, if she'd asked, though the way she'd balked at shopping with him the last time, he wasn't surprised that she didn't. Which was too bad. He wouldn't mind seeing her in something other than the jeans or leggings and bulky sweaters she seemed to favor. Or maybe in nothing at all.

Uneasy with the direction of his thoughts—and uncomfortable outside without a coat—he returned to the gathering. After a quick stop at the bar, he stood on the periphery of the crowd and spotted his father in conversation with an older, petite blonde he didn't recognize.

Could this be the mystery woman his father had gone into Kalispell to have dinner with? Max had been uncharacteristically tight-lipped the day after his date, volunteering no details and refusing to respond to his son's questions. But whoever this woman was with the platinum curls and four-inch heels, she seemed to have Max's complete and undivided attention.

And because Wilder was watching them, he didn't notice the pretty brunette who'd sidled up to him until she spoke. "Can I buy you a drink?"

His smile was automatic as he turned. She had dark hair pinned up in some kind of fancy twist, with a few strands pulled loose to frame her heart-shaped face. Her eyes were as blue as the sapphires in her ears and sparkled with wicked promise.

She was beautiful and confident and not at all subtle about what she wanted—the type of woman who usually made his blood hum in his veins. And yet, when he looked at her, he felt nothing but a vague appreciation for her obvious attributes.

In response to her question, he held up the bottle of beer in his hand. "I've already got one."

"Then I guess you should buy me one," she said.

Even if he wasn't interested, it wasn't in his nature to be rude. So he put his hand on her back and led her to the bar, where she ordered some kind of froufrou cocktail that set him back twenty bucks. A small price to pay for a man interested in what she was obviously offering. But he wasn't that man. Not tonight.

She introduced herself as Simone and told him that she lived in Billings but had come to Rust Creek Falls to visit a friend from college who'd recently split from a longtime boyfriend. Except that the longtime boyfriend had apparently seen the error of his ways and showed up with an engagement ring in hand, leaving Simone to celebrate on her own.

"Or maybe not entirely alone," she said hopefully.

"You're never really alone in a crowd like this," he remarked, looking around for one of his brothers in the vague and futile hope someone might come to his rescue.

He caught a glimpse of Logan, snuggled up with Sarah, oblivious to the world around them. Of course, even if he managed to snag Logan's attention, his brother would never guess that Wilder wanted to be rescued.

"Is something wrong?" Simone asked, licking her lips to remove the pink sugar that had transferred from the rim of her glass.

"What?"

"You're frowning," she told him.

"Sorry." He smoothed his brow. "I guess my mind was wandering."

"Not something a woman wants to hear when she's flirting with a handsome man," she chided, stroking a long, painted fingernail down his arm.

"Sorry," he said again. "It's not you, it's me."

The warmth in those blue eyes immediately chilled. "Yeah, I've heard that one before. Too many times." She stepped back then. "Thanks for the drink."

Then she turned and walked away.

He could have called her back. He knew how to turn on the charm and, with a wink and a smile, he could have smoothed her ruffled feathers and been kissing her at the stroke of midnight.

But he didn't want her to come back. He had no interest in yet another meaningless encounter with a virtual stranger.

A movement caught the corner of his eye, and he glanced over to see his brother Knox flying his hand through the air like a makeshift plane, then tipping his fingers to dive down and spreading them apart.

Wilder lifted a brow. "Are you having fun?"

"As a matter of fact, I am," Knox said. "Because not only am I here with the sexiest woman in all of Rust Creek Falls, but I just watched my little brother—the one that no woman can apparently resist—crash and burn."

"I didn't crash and burn," he denied.

"What are you guys talking about?" Xander asked, unapologetically shoving his way into their conversation.

"Our baby brother just crashed and burned," Knox said.

"You wish," Wilder retorted.

"So the sexy brunette with the mile-long legs in the skintight dress didn't just walk away from you?" Knox challenged.

"She walked away," he confirmed. "But only because I didn't want her to stay."

Xander frowned, feigning concern. "Did you hit your head when you crashed?"

"I didn't—" Wilder huffed out a breath. "You know what? I don't care. If you want to believe I crashed and burned, fine."

His brothers exchanged a glance.

"Okay, now I'm seriously starting to worry that there's something wrong with you," Knox said.

"There's nothing wrong," Wilder assured them. "I'm just not in the mood to spend the night with a woman who doesn't mean anything to me."

"But isn't that your whole MO?" Xander asked.

"If you stop having sex with women who don't mean anything, you won't be having sex with anyone," Knox warned.

"Unless he's met a woman who could actually mean something," Xander mused thoughtfully.

"Wilder?" Knox snorted. "As if."

"If you'd focus your attention on your own woman, you might realize that she's trying to snag your attention before she waves her arm right out of its socket," he replied.

Thankfully, the distraction worked in shifting the topic of conversation, but his brothers flanked him and maneuvered him over to the big table occupied by his siblings and their partners.

"What's going on?" Knox asked, when he'd lowered himself into the vacant seat beside Gen.

"Lily was just telling us the most recent news about the mystery lover in the Abernathy diary," she said, referring to the jewel-encrusted book they'd found hidden in the floorboards shortly after moving to the Ambling A.

"Am I the only one who feels uncomfortable about reading someone's diary?" Avery wondered aloud.

"Yes," Lily said. "I mean, a person's privacy should be respected, of course, but this diary is practically a historical document. And I believe Josiah Abernathy put his innermost thoughts on paper because he expected—or maybe even hoped—that someone else would read his words someday."

"Maybe the mysterious 'W,'" Sarah chimed in.

"Plus, there are some really steamy passages," Xander noted.

"Not trashy," his wife hastened to clarify. "But definitely passionate."

"I think he really loved her," Knox said.

"Who?" Logan asked.

Knox shrugged. "Whoever 'W' is."

"Are there any clues about her identity?"

"Asks the person who didn't think we should be reading the diary," Finn noted dryly.

Avery shrugged. "But since it is being read, are there any clues?" she pressed.

"Actually, there *is* something," Lily said. "Whoever she was, she was apparently pregnant with Josiah's baby."

Avery gasped. "He had a child with his mystery lady?"

Lily shook her head. "Apparently the baby was stillborn."

"Oh." The expectant mom instinctively touched a hand to the slight curve of her belly, as if to protect her own unborn child from such a tragic fate. "That's so sad."

Lily winced. "I'm sorry. I wasn't thinking—"

Avery shook her head. "There's no need to apologize. And I am as curious as everyone else about Josiah and the history of the Ambling A."

"Well, apparently 'W' was so devastated by the loss of her child that she went crazy."

"Literally or figuratively crazy?" Sarah asked curiously.

Her friend and sister-in-law shrugged. "I can only tell you what's written in the book."

"I asked because I'd heard that Winona Cobbs apparently spent some time in an asylum after the Abernathys left town," Logan's wife explained.

"The definitely eccentric and questionably clairvoyant Winona Cobbs?"

"The one and only," Sarah confirmed.

"But I've lived in Rust Creek Falls my whole life and I've never heard so much as a whisper of a rumor that Winona Cobbs was ever pregnant," Gen said.

"She wouldn't be the first woman to keep an out-of-wedlock baby a secret," Sarah remarked. "Especially so many years ago."

"Except that Winona isn't exactly known for her ability to keep secrets," Lily commented.

"And if the diary is as old as we think, she would have been a teenager at the time," Knox chimed in.

"On the other hand, if she did lose a child, well, that might explain why she's always been a little...odd," Gen acknowledged.

The mystery was admittedly intriguing, but as Wilder had nothing to add to the conversation, he decided to abandon the party and return to the place where it all started.

Max watched his youngest son slip away from the gathering and head out alone. Though Wilder had always enjoyed a party, he wasn't surprised to see him go. His life had been turned upside down since he'd found Cody on the doorstep, and though he'd yet to acknowledge the child as his own, over the past week, Wilder's denials of paternity had become less frequent and less adamant.

Max didn't blame him for not embracing the baby with open arms, because he knew it wasn't just the responsibilities of fatherhood that Wilder found daunting. It was the memories that had been stirred up by the realization that Cody's mother had walked out on him. Just like Sheila had walked out on her children when Wilder wasn't much older than Cody was now.

Of course, his youngest son had no real recollection of Sheila leaving, but he'd grown up believing that she'd chosen a life with another man over her children. Because that was what Max had wanted him to believe. What he'd wanted all his children to believe. Because admitting the truth would mean admitting that it was his fault his six sons had grown up without their mother.

"That's gotta be one of your boys," his female companion said, following the direction of his gaze.

Max nodded. "My youngest."

"He's a lucky boy," she remarked, with a bold wink. "Because he's almost as handsome as his daddy."

He smiled, appreciating her company and her flattery.

Of course, Max had always appreciated beautiful women, and Estelle fit the bill well enough. Blond curls framed a flawless face with thickly lashed blue eyes, a pert nose and slickly painted lips. He suspected she'd paid a price to retain—or maybe even enhance—her natural attributes, but he had no objections to hair dyes or face paint or even a little nip and tuck. Not when the results were so appealing.

Though she was barely five feet tall without the skinny heels that added several inches to her height, and probably not more than ninety pounds, she would never be described as diminutive. She was bossy and opinionated and didn't know the meaning of the word *quit*.

Some eighteen months earlier, she'd sold her wedding planning business to Vivienne Dalton—the same woman he'd hired as a matchmaker for his sons, though she'd been Vivienne Shuster at the time and the business had been located in Kalispell. Then Estelle had moved down to Phoenix to work with her sister in the funeral business. Six months later, she'd decided that the Grand Canyon State wasn't for her and returned to Kalispell.

"I'm not overly fond of cowboys," she'd said at their first meeting—set up by Vivienne Dalton—at a bar in her neighborhood. "But you don't look like the kind who buys his jeans at the same place he gets feed for his horses."

"I'm not overly fond of outspoken women," he'd replied, more amused than insulted by her blunt assessment. "And you do look like the kind who has an opinion about everything and not enough sense to know when to keep it to herself."

She'd smiled then. "You going to buy me a drink?"

"You going to order something ridiculously girly?"

She asked the bartender for Jack Daniel's Single Barrel Select, straight up. He'd had the same, and they'd chatted some more while they'd sipped the smooth whiskey.

Tonight, she was drinking champagne, as most of the other guests in attendance were doing. She lifted her glass to her lips now and swallowed the last mouthful of bubbly, then opened the clasp of her handbag and frowned as she examined its contents.

"Did you lose something?" he asked.

"I keep forgetting that I don't smoke anymore," she confided.

"Smoking's a bad habit," he said.

"My doctor spent years telling me the same thing," she confided. "But it wasn't until my sister lost her husband to lung cancer that I finally managed to kick it."

He nodded, only half listening to what she was saying.

But apparently Estelle was more intuitive than he'd given her credit for, because she stopped rambling about the treatments that had taken as much of a toll on her brother-in-law as the disease and asked, "What's got you so worried about your son?"

"He's going through some stuff right now," Max answered vaguely.

"In other words, none of my business," she guessed.

"More that it's not my place to tell," he said.

"Well, then, why don't we take ourselves to my place where I'll be better able to help you forget your worries?"

Max wasn't convinced anything could make him forget his worries, but he was willing to let her try.

The house was quiet after Wilder and Max had gone. Too quiet.

Or maybe it was the isolation of the ranch that made Beth a little uneasy.

She was a city girl born and bred, accustomed to the lights and noises of an urban setting. Here, it was so quiet she'd be able to hear crickets if the insects hadn't entered into a state of complete dormancy to survive the frigid winter season.

She turned on the television to provide some background noise. Because being alone with the baby, she found herself jumping at every creak and groan of the big old house. She wouldn't be so uneasy if there was a dog around—and wasn't having a dog a prerequisite of being a rancher?

They'd had a German shepherd named Rowdy for almost thirteen years, Wilder had confided when she'd asked him the question. But they'd had to put him down only a few months before making the move from Dallas, and Max had vowed that he'd never get another dog. Wilder didn't really believe it was true, especially considering how Max fussed over Harry and Dobby—the two dachshunds that belonged to Xander and Lily, but for now, he was without a canine companion.

And Beth was a great big fraidycat, she acknowledged to herself as she plugged in the lights of the Christmas tree to enjoy the holiday display—and because she hoped more lights would make her less likely to jump at shadows.

Wilder had told her that they always went out to cut down a tree two weeks before Christmas and took it out of the house again on New Year's Day. Which reminded her that she'd have to deal with her own holiday decorations when she got home. So maybe it was fortunate that she didn't have a real tree. If she did, it would likely be nothing more than a bare trunk surrounded by a pile of dry needles by the time she returned.

After Cody had his cereal and his bath, Beth read him a couple of the books he'd got for Christmas. She guided his fingertips over the textured pages so he could feel soft and rough, bumpy and slippery, scaly and furry. By the time she closed the cover, his eyes were drifting shut.

"Look, Cody, they're having a big party in New York City. See all the people?" She pointed to the TV screen to direct his attention.

Though she knew television wasn't recommended for babies so young, she wasn't yet ready to take him upstairs and face the reality of spending yet another New Year's Eve alone. But Cody's eyes were closed before the ball dropped in Times Square, so she finally put him in his crib and turned on the baby monitor.

When she returned to the company of the television in the family room, she scrolled through the channels until she found another station that was counting down to the New Year, this time in Chicago. She'd just started to relax on the sofa when she heard what sounded like footsteps on the porch.

She froze, straining to hear over the thundering of her heart, even as she tried to assure herself it was nothing but her own overactive imagination.

But then she heard it again. A sound like feet stomping outside the door. Definitely *not* her imagination.

It might have occurred to her that an intruder wouldn't likely make so much noise, but at the moment, the rational part of her brain didn't seem to be communicating with the rest of her.

She pressed the mute button on the remote and strained her ears. It was a click this time, like the dead bolt being released, then a creak, as if the door had opened.

She dropped the remote to grab for her cell phone, ready to dial 9-1-1 and trying not to speculate about the length of time it would take the local police to arrive at her isolated location.

"Beth?"

All the air trapped in her lungs whooshed out in a single breath as she recognized Wilder's voice. She set her phone aside and willed her heart rate to return to something approximating normal.

"In the family room," she said, picking up the remote again to unmute the television so that she could pretend his unexpected early return hadn't scared ten years off her life.

"What are you doing home already?" she asked, when he appeared in the doorway.

He shrugged. "The party was a little too noisy and crowded for my liking."

"Aren't those the usual prerequisites of a party?" she asked.

"I guess so," he acknowledged. "But tonight I just wanted to be home."

"I'm not judging," she assured him.

He glanced at the baby monitor on the table beside her. "Cody asleep?"

She nodded. "He just went down."

He checked his watch. "It's a little late for him, isn't it?"

"Yeah, but it's New Year's Eve and he wanted to watch some of the celebration in New York City with me," she explained.

One side of his mouth tipped up in a half smile that never failed to do crazy things to her insides. "He did, did he?"

"He did," she confirmed, unwilling to admit that she'd deliberately tried to keep her nephew awake because she hadn't wanted to be alone.

But now she was alone *with* Wilder, and she wasn't sure if that was better or worse.

Then he loosened his tie and opened the top button of his shirt, and she decided it was both better *and* worse.

Chapter Twelve

As Beth watched Wilder unbutton his shirt, all rational thoughts slipped from her brain, her mouth went dry and her body got warm. His fingers deftly unfastened the second button and, imagining how those strong, calloused hands might feel against her skin, she felt a quiver low in her belly.

She wondered if he would open a third button, and then a fourth, so that she could discover if his broad chest and flat stomach were as chiseled in real life as they were in her imagination. Because yes, she'd imagined and fantasized about the handsome cowboy undressed. Dreamed about him—about his naked body entwined with her own. And woken up embarrassed and ashamed to realize that she could harbor such wanton feelings for a man who'd been her sister's lover—and was very likely the father of Leighton's baby.

Beth swallowed hard and tried to quash the lustful thoughts that teased her body and her brain.

"What?" she asked, when she realized he'd spoken but she hadn't heard a single word.

"I asked if it was okay for me to hang out here with you."

"It's your house," she reminded him.

"But you've got the remote."

"That means I'm in charge?"

He smiled at her dubious tone. "At least in charge of the TV."

She handed the controller to him. "I should probably head up to bed, anyway."

"It's not even ten thirty," he pointed out, his voice tinged with amusement.

"Oh," she said, feeling foolish. Because even a killjoy like her knew that going to bed at ten thirty on New Year's Eve was beyond lame. "I guess I could stay up a little longer. But I'm going to apologize in advance."

"For what?"

"The fact that I'll probably fall asleep before the clock strikes midnight."

He gasped, feigning shock. "On New Year's Eve?"

"Cody was up three times last night," she told him. "I'm convinced, by the way he's been gnawing and drooling, that a couple of teeth will be breaking through soon."

"Is that what the book says to watch for—gnawing and drooling?"

"There isn't one book that's the authority on everything, and every baby is different," she chided. "But yes, those are generally recognized as common signs of teething."

"If you don't think you'll make it to midnight, maybe we should crack open a bottle of champagne now and toast the New Year along with Chicago," he suggested.

"Sounds good to me," she said.

He retrieved a bottle of bubbly and a couple of glasses, popping the cork with an ease that attested to experience. And didn't that immediately highlight the differences in their lifestyles, that he could make an offhand suggestion and know the fancy wine would be chilling? If she ever expressed a spontaneous desire for champagne, the spontaneity would invariably be lost as she made a hurried trip to buy it, with her fingers crossed that the local store sold it already chilled.

He could have chosen to sit anywhere. There were plenty of options in the spacious room: the love seat adjacent to the couch she occupied, one of a trio of armchairs, or even the other end of the big sofa. For some reason, he chose to sit right beside her, so close that their thighs were touching.

He handed her a flute of champagne, tapped the rim of his own glass to hers and said, "Happy Almost New Year."

"Happy Almost New Year," she echoed, and took a tentative sip of the bubbly.

The cool and crisp liquid tickled as it slid down her throat, causing an almost irresistible urge to giggle. She swallowed the urge along with another sip of champagne.

"So how does this year compare to your last New Year's Eve?" Wilder asked her.

"It's almost a carbon copy," she admitted. "But with a much better bottle of wine." And the unexpected company of a very handsome cowboy—though she wisely kept that part to herself.

"You mean you sat at home watching other people celebrate the occasion?"

"I wasn't lying when I said parties aren't really my thing."

"Why not?"

She shrugged. "I've just never felt comfortable around a lot of people. I prefer more intimate gatherings." Then, realizing how her words might be misconstrued, she hastened to clarify, "I didn't mean *intimate* intimate. I only meant that I prefer smaller groups and quieter settings."

And then, to stop herself from babbling even more, she lifted her glass to her lips again.

"Intimate should definitely involve a smaller number," he agreed, with a wink. "My preference has always been two."

She couldn't agree, because he might interpret that as flirting. And she couldn't disagree, because if she suggested "or three or four," he might think she was advertising an adventurous spirit she did not have.

"Or one," she said, deciding that was a safe option and also a truer reflection of her status.

It wasn't until his lips curved that she realized her mistake.

"You like to go it alone sometimes, Beth?"

She could really use a blast of Montana wind to cool her cheeks right now. In the absence of that, she sipped more of the chilled wine.

"I'm going to stop talking now," she decided.

His warm chuckle skimmed over her like a caress. "I didn't mean to embarrass you," he said.

"I think I embarrassed myself," she acknowledged, and was grateful when Wilder steered the conversation to more neutral topics.

They talked about books and movies and the successes or failures of books turned into movies. Then they debated the merits of favorite sports teams, with Wilder insisting that the Cowboys would win another Super Bowl before the Stars took another run at the Stanley Cup and Beth confiding that she'd rather watch the Rangers over the Mavericks any day of the week.

He shook his head. "Clearly you know nothing about basketball."

She narrowed her gaze. "What's your foundation for that claim? The fact that I prefer baseball?"

"And that watching baseball is about as exciting as watching paint dry."

"Clearly you know nothing about baseball," she told him.

"What I do know is that it's almost midnight and you're still awake," he noted, tipping the bottle to pour more champagne into her glass.

"I'm as surprised as you are," she said.

"I'm glad I didn't bore you to sleep."

"You didn't bore me at all. In fact, I quite enjoyed your company tonight."

"Who would have guessed that we could spend an evening together without sniping at one another?" he mused.

"We've spent a lot of time together over the past few days without sniping at each other," she pointed out.

"Yeah, it turns out that you're not quite as uptight as I originally thought."

"And I've been pleasantly surprised to discover that you're not as immature and irresponsible as my first impressions led me to believe."

He smiled. "There it is."

Her brows drew together. "I think I missed something."

"Because you haven't been paying attention," he chided.

"To what?"

"You've got passion and spirit, Lisbeth Ames. But—one early-morning outburst aside—I usually only see it in defense of your sister or your nephew. I'm happy to know that you're also capable of fighting back in defense of yourself."

"I thought we were trying not to fight."

"It turns out I enjoy our verbal sparring," he admitted.

"Given the choice, I'd rather be a lover than a fighter," she said.

Wilder's brows lifted. "Is that so?"

"I didn't mean—" She huffed out a breath. "I always seem to be putting my foot in my mouth around you."

"Let's see if we can find a better use for your mouth," Wilder suggested, as he set both of their champagne glasses aside.

And then he kissed her.

It wasn't a deep or passionate kiss—more a tentative exploration. And yet, when his lips brushed over hers, a jolt of arousal surged through her body, leaving hot tingles in its wake.

She lifted her eyes and saw that he was looking as shaken by the chemistry as she felt. Then his gaze shifted to her mouth, as if he maybe wanted to try that again.

Because she wanted the same thing, she took the initiative this time and leaned forward to kiss him. And he responded. His arm snaked around her waist, pulling her onto his lap so that her knees straddled his hips and her breasts tingled where they touched his chest, her nipples stiffening to tight peaks.

She pressed herself closer, relishing the feel of his rock-hard body. She slid her hands over his taut, sculpted shoulders to link them behind his head, her fingertips tangling in the ends of his hair.

He opened her mouth to deepen the kiss, exploring the sensitive inner recesses with his oh-so-talented tongue. She rocked against him, subconsciously mimicking the rhythm of mating, until he clamped his hands on her hips, stifling her moments.

"I'm going to embarrass myself if you don't stop that," he warned.

"I don't want to stop," she said. "But—"

"Shh." He brushed his lips gently over hers now. "Let's not analyze all the reasons this might be a mistake."

Then he nuzzled her throat, and the erotic scrape of his stubble against her skin made her shiver.

"But it would be, wouldn't it? Getting naked together would further complicate an already complicated situation."

"Or maybe it would simplify it," he suggested.

"How do you figure?"

"Sex is simple—the most primal and essential connection between a man and a woman," he explained, as he slid his hands under her sweater and up her torso to cup her breasts.

And the feel of those calloused palms moving over her skin was even more delicious than she'd imagined.

She moaned softly.

"I really like those noises you make when I touch you," he told her.

"Then keep touching me," she suggested.

"I don't think I can stop."

He rose to his feet then, effortlessly lifting her with him. She wrapped her legs around his waist, hooking her ankles as he carried her toward the stairs.

She felt like a fairy-tale princess in the arms of her Prince Charming.

Except that Wilder wasn't *her* anything and there was no happily-ever-after with him in her future.

But would it be so wrong to enjoy this one magical night? A stolen moment in time before the realities of the world descended upon them once more?

He carried her to the guest room, then set her on her feet beside the bed to whisk her sweater over her head and strip away her leggings.

"You, too," she said, unfastening the remaining buttons of his shirt to reveal a strong chest and rippling abs. *Definitely as chiseled as I'd imagined.* She touched her lips to his taut, warm skin, then flicked out her tongue. *And every bit as delicious.*

While she explored his chest, he discarded the rest of his clothes, then eased her onto the mattress, bracing himself over her and capturing her mouth with his again.

He seemed to know just where and how to touch her to heighten her desire, maximize her pleasure. Eager to reciprocate, she tentatively reached between their bodies to wrap her hand around his hard, velvety length. He pulsed in her hand; a groan rumbled in his chest. Emboldened by his response, she stroked her hand toward the tip, then back down again.

He unclasped her bra, releasing her breasts from the restraint of the lacy cups. Her already peaked nipples drew tighter when the cool air whispered over her skin.

He drew one of the aching tips into his mouth, tugging gently with his teeth, until she moaned and arched beneath him. His mouth moved to her other breast, affording it the same attention as his hands stroked over her body in a teasing exploration that made her quiver and yearn.

He gently parted her thighs, opening her to a more intimate investigation. His fingertips skimmed the sensitive skin of her inner thighs and traced the lacy edge of her panties, making her muscles tremble. Then his thumb brushed over the aching nub at her center, through the thin fabric barrier, making her whimper.

His mouth moved lower, skimming over her torso, then he caught the narrow band of lace at her side in his teeth and dragged it down over her hip before switching to the other side. He continued to alternate from side to side, inching her panties downward until they were dangling around one ankle. Then he spread her legs wide and lowered his head between them.

She felt the scrape of his stubble against the sensitive skin of her thighs, a surprisingly erotic sensation. When he touched her with his tongue, she gasped, shocked by the unexpected intimacy. And again, because the pleasure was more than she'd anticipated. More than she'd imagined.

He nibbled and licked, tasting and teasing, driving her ever closer to the pinnacle of pleasure. Then holding her there, right on the edge, until she was desperate for release. She could hear herself whimpering, pleading.

Stop. Please. More.

She didn't seem to know what she wanted, what she needed.

But Wilder knew, and he gave it to her. More and more,

until she couldn't take it anymore. Until she was no longer on the edge, but falling, falling, falling…

Her body was still quivering with the aftereffects of her climax when Wilder retrieved a condom from his wallet, then tore open the foil packet and covered himself. Only then did he position himself over her again, and finally bury himself between her thighs.

She wrapped herself around him, her hands gripping his shoulders, her legs anchored around his torso, pulling him even deeper inside. He began to move, and she met him thrust for thrust, urging him to find the same release he'd given her.

As their bodies merged and mated, she found her own desire escalating again. He picked up the pace, driving faster, harder, deeper. Pushing her to new and even loftier heights. But this time, when she took the plunge, he went with her.

Wilder was jolted awake—and jarred out of a tantalizingly explicit and erotic dream—by the sound of a baby crying. It took him a moment to get his bearings, for his eyes to adjust to the darkness and recognize that he was in the guest room, where he'd fallen asleep after making love with Beth.

He closed his eyes again and swore quietly as the memories washed over him.

It never should have happened.

But it had happened—and it had been amazing.

He'd always preferred the company of women who were looking for short-term companionship rather than long-term commitment. Beth was all about hearth and home right down to the marrow of her bones. She was the type of woman a man would choose to marry, and Wilder had no intention of being that man—for any woman.

But, as usual last night, he'd been thinking about his

own desires, selfishly taking what he wanted with little regard for the consequences.

And now…

A soft murmur joined the sound of the baby's cries. He realized the sounds were coming through the baby monitor on the table beside the bed and that Beth was already up and tending to Cody.

Cody.

He swore again as a fresh wave of guilt washed over him.

Barely a week earlier, he'd been reflecting on how great his life was, how lucky he was that he wasn't tied down in any kind of relationship, and how he had no interest in being saddled with a kid at this point in his life.

Because a week earlier, he hadn't known of Cody's existence. Now that he did, his intentions and interests were irrelevant. The fact was, if Cody was his child, he was going to step up and be the best father that he could be to him.

But it didn't really matter whether or not the kid was his. He should never have seduced his aunt. Because the intimacies they'd shared added a whole other layer of complications to an already complicated situation. Which, now that he thought about it, was almost exactly what she'd warned him about the night before.

Asserting his parental rights and applying for legal custody would deal a devastating blow to Beth, who'd been helping to care for her nephew since his birth.

But there was no way Wilder could let the child go. He wouldn't ever abandon his son, as his mother had abandoned hers. He wouldn't let anything matter more than his child.

But wasn't that exactly what he'd done last night?

Selfishly, and not surprisingly, he'd been thinking only

about himself. About what *he* wanted. And last night, he'd wanted Beth.

Maybe the realization had surprised him a little.

Being intimate with Beth had surprised him even more.

Despite her rigid expectations and uptight manner, she was a surprisingly passionate and gloriously uninhibited woman. And if he was the type of man who did relationships, he might be willing to take a chance with her. But he wasn't, and he couldn't.

Because everything else aside, he had a history with her sister. And yes, that was probably something he should have thought about last night before he'd removed Beth's lace panties with his teeth. It didn't matter that Leighton had made it clear she was done with him. He doubted she'd be pleased to discover that he'd picked up with her sister.

But had he picked up with her sister?

Or had last night been the beginning and end?

Frustrated that all he had were questions without answers, he pushed back the covers and gathered his discarded clothes. He dressed quickly in the dark, intending to go across the hall to help with the baby.

But he paused in the hallway, watching Beth, silhouetted by the dim light, as she tended to the baby. She continued to murmur softly, soothing the child as she dealt with the wet diaper that was likely the cause of his distress. After she'd finished with that task, she'd go downstairs to prepare a bottle to fill his tummy so that he might sleep comfortably for a few more hours.

Or Wilder could take care of that for her. He'd mixed the formula enough times now that he didn't even have to read the label anymore. But as much as they took turns with feedings and diaper changes during the day, sharing such duties in the darkness of the night felt like something else. Something more.

Like something a dad and mom might do—if they were a family.

And since he didn't even know for sure if he was Cody's dad, and she for sure wasn't his mom, it would be a mistake—even bigger than the one they'd made last night—to pretend they were a family.

So instead of offering to help, he retreated to his own room like the coward that he was.

Chapter Thirteen

"Hey, big guy." Beth crooned the words softly as she unfastened the tabs of her nephew's diaper, hoping to soothe the baby but not wake the sexy cowboy asleep across the hall. "What's going on in here?"

Cody's big blue eyes were swimming with tears, his long, dark lashes wet and spikey. But his quivering lips curved, just a little.

"I bet you're not just wet but hungry," she said, as she slid a dry diaper under his bottom. "Because you've been down for almost six hours." She stifled a yawn as she wiped his bottom. "Unfortunately, I've only slept about half that amount of time, so if you could go back to sleep without too much fuss, I'd appreciate it."

Cody shoved a fist into his mouth.

"Yes, of course, I'll give you a snack first," she promised, as she fastened the new diaper, then snapped up his diaper shirt and sleeper again. "There. That's better, isn't it?"

Cody continued to gnaw on his fist as she carried him downstairs. Though she'd only been at the ranch five full days, she'd quickly learned her way around the house in the dark—a necessary skill considering the number of times she was up and down with her nephew each night.

She blinked at the light when she opened the refrigerator to retrieve one of the bottles she'd prepared earlier. She turned on the kettle to heat the water to warm the formula, then turned it off again as she recalled Sharleesa—

a colleague from work and mother of three—mentioning that her kids all preferred a cold bottle when they were teething.

"Okay, we're going to try something different tonight," she said to Cody, uncapping the bottle and lowering the nipple toward his mouth. "Let's see what you think of this."

Cody thought it was just fine, apparently, as he latched on and immediately began sucking.

"Apparently you're not afraid to try new things," Beth mused as she headed back up the stairs again. "Which proves you inherited your mama's adventurous spirit."

As usual, thinking about Leighton led to worrying about Leighton. She wished she could adopt Wilder's philosophy and not worry about things she couldn't control, but she didn't think that would ever apply to her sister.

"I didn't make any resolutions this year," she said, continuing to talk softly to Cody. "But maybe it's not too late. Maybe this year, if I make more of an effort, your mama and I will learn to communicate better and grow closer."

Of course, if she really wanted a better relationship with Leighton, she probably shouldn't have slept with her ex, Beth acknowledged ruefully.

But maybe her sister wouldn't ever find out what she'd done. Certainly Beth had no intention of telling her, and she couldn't imagine that Wilder would volunteer the information. And since she was pretty sure their impulsive lovemaking had been the result of proximity and champagne, she was confident it wouldn't ever happen again.

And that was for the best, because when Leighton came back and saw how good Wilder was with Cody, maybe she'd decide to give their relationship another chance—to give their son a real family.

It was what Beth had always wanted for Cody. So why,

then, did the idea of her sister sharing Wilder's life—and his bed—make her heart ache?

Was it somehow possible that, over the course of only five days, she'd developed real feelings for the cowboy?

Thinking about it now, she knew it wasn't just possible but true. Because during that time, she'd had plenty of opportunities to interact with him and discover his true character.

Maybe he didn't instinctively know how to be a father, but he'd proven that he was open to learning and willing to make the effort. And though she knew he had a reputation with the ladies, since she'd been at the ranch, he appeared to have made the little boy his priority over all else.

Even tonight, when he'd gone out to celebrate the New Year with his family, he'd come home early. He'd said he wasn't in the mood for the crowds, but she suspected he'd really wanted to check on Cody. Because she knew, even if Wilder wasn't ready to admit it, that the baby had already worked his way into his heart.

There was so much more to him than the picture of the wild and aimless cowboy her sister had painted. He was undeniably the most handsome man she'd ever met, but aside from his striking good looks and mouthwatering muscles, he was intelligent and charming, insightful and compassionate. He also had a good sense of humor and a strong sense of family loyalty.

And after only five days at the Ambling A and one night in Wilder's arms, she was in serious danger of losing her heart.

"Why didn't you tell me that Cody's teeth had come in?" Wilder demanded, when he returned to the house following an early ride with his brother—and after hearing the news from his father, who'd puffed up like a proud grandpa as he delivered it.

"You didn't stick around long enough for me to say anything," Beth said, pointedly referencing his quick exit earlier that morning.

"I had to ride out with Hunter to check the fence."

"I'm sure you did." She dipped the spoon into the cereal bowl again and moved it toward the baby's mouth.

When Cody opened up, she let him swallow the cereal, then used the rubber tip of the spoon to gently pull down his lower lip and reveal the bumpy ridges of white poking through his gums so that Wilder could see what all the fuss was about.

"Look at that," he said, feeling his own chest puff up with pride, as if he was somehow responsible for the baby's milestone. "He's got teeth."

"They've still got a way to go, but now that they've broken through the gums, he should be a little less cranky," she said.

"That's good," he agreed.

Now if only he could figure out why Beth seemed so cranky this morning. Or maybe he already knew—which her next words confirmed.

"Should we talk about what happened last night?" she asked.

"If you want to," he agreed cautiously.

"What I want is for things to not be awkward between us," she said.

"Do things seem awkward to you?"

"It's hard to tell when we haven't been in the same room together for more than five minutes. Or maybe that is the tell," she decided.

"I haven't been avoiding you," he promised. "Hunter texted this morning and asked me to ride out to the eastern boundary with him."

"Why you?" she wondered aloud.

"Probably because he knew all our other brothers would be snuggled up with their wives."

"Oh." She blew out a breath. "So I may have overreacted," she acknowledged. "I'm not very good at this. I don't have a lot of experience with mornings after."

"Just say whatever it is you want to say," he suggested.

"Okay," she agreed. "I think last night was a mistake. I mean, it was great, but it shouldn't have happened. We shouldn't have...gotten carried away."

"Is that what happened? We got carried away?" he asked, wondering why her dismissal of their lovemaking bothered him when he'd arrived at the same conclusion.

"Isn't it?"

"Sure," he finally agreed. "We got carried away, it never should have happened, it won't happen again."

"Okay, then," she said.

"If that's all, I'm going to make myself a sandwich and then head back out to help my brothers fix the fence."

"Of course," she agreed.

He nodded brusquely and walked out, leaving Beth to wonder why, after he'd said everything she wanted him to say, she was so unhappy.

"What's going on with you and Beth?" Max asked the following morning, when Wilder returned to the supply shed for the box of screws Knox had left behind.

"What do you mean?" Wilder asked cautiously.

"She put on boots and a coat to go out to the barn and ask Hunter to put Cody's car seat in her vehicle."

"And?"

"Why didn't she ask you?"

He shrugged. "Maybe she figured Hunter has more experience with such things."

His father acknowledged that possibility with a slow

nod. "It would have been even easier to ask you to give her a lift into town."

"She knows I'm still working with Xander and Knox to fix the fence," Wilder told him, reminding his father of the barrier that had been destroyed when someone skidded off the road and crashed through it.

They didn't know what kind of vehicle or who was responsible, as the driver hadn't contacted Max to own up to the incident. But considering the damage to the fence and the fact that the vehicle had driven away, they suspected Butch Ferrell, who owned a jacked-up Escalade and had been known to get behind the wheel after a few too many drinks at the Ace in the Hole.

"Logan or Finn could've taken your place," Max pointed out.

"And then accused me of skipping out on the hard work." Wilder shook his head. "I don't think so."

"You'd rather skip out on spending time with your son," his father remarked with obvious disapproval. "Or maybe it's Beth that you don't want to spend time with."

"If I had a choice between fixing fence and shopping, I'd go with the fence every time," he told his father.

"Are you sure that's all it is?"

"Why do you think it's anything more?"

"Because recently it seems that every time one of you walks into a room, the other one walks out."

"You ever consider that maybe we each have our own stuff to do in different places?" he suggested, because he couldn't deny the accuracy of his father's observation.

Or that, despite Beth's claim that she didn't want things to be awkward between them, they were.

His father sighed. "I thought the two of you were finally starting to get along."

"We were. We *are*," he corrected.

"Really?" Max challenged. "Because it doesn't look like it from where I'm standing."

"There's no reason for you to worry, Dad," he said, grabbing the box of nails.

"Has Beth mentioned when she plans to go back to Dallas?" Max asked, apparently not yet ready to let his son return to his duties.

Wilder shook his head. "Not before the DNA results are in. Why? Do you suddenly have an objection to her being here?"

"I don't," his dad assured him. "We've got plenty of space, and I've eaten more home-cooked meals in the past week than in the six weeks prior to her showing up."

"Which only proves that we need to hire a cook," Wilder said. "Because she's not going to be here forever."

"But she's here now," his father pointed out.

Beth obviously hadn't thought this through.

She'd just wanted to get away from the ranch and the awkward tension with Wilder for a little while, and a quick shopping trip into town seemed the perfect excuse. But she didn't have Cody's stroller—and even if she did, she wasn't sure it would navigate the snow-covered sidewalks—and it was awkward to wear his baby carrier over her coat and it didn't fit under. Which left her with no recourse but to carry him in his car seat.

At least when she got inside the store, she was able to sit his car seat in the cart while she did her shopping. She only needed a few things, but after paying for her groceries, she was faced with the logistical problem of having to cart the baby, his diaper bag and three bags of groceries out to her vehicle.

She might have asked Natalie for help, if the woman she'd met on her first trip into town had been working, but she hadn't seen her anywhere in the store. Thankfully today's clerk—identified as Nina by another customer—anticipated her dilemma and called a stock boy to carry Beth's purchases out to her car.

After all of that, she decided she deserved a treat and headed over to Daisy's Donuts, the reputed mecca of everything sweet and delicious in Rust Creek Falls. An examination of the offerings in the display case required several minutes of careful study, leading Beth to conclude that the reputation had not been exaggerated.

An opinion that was further bolstered by her first bite of chocolate silk pie.

"Hey, stranger."

Beth glanced up as Natalie Crawford slid into the seat across from her. She lifted a hand to wave, unable to offer a verbal reply because her mouth was full.

Natalie eyed the plate in front of her. "Mmm…is that Eva's chocolate silk pie?"

Beth nodded and swallowed. "Do you want me to ask for another fork?"

The other woman shook her head regretfully. "Don't think I'm not tempted, but I'm actually here to pick up a Neapolitan cake for my mom's birthday and if I let myself indulge in two desserts today, I'll never squeeze into my favorite jeans tomorrow."

"Your call," Beth said, as she dipped her fork into her pie again.

"So what brings you into town today?" Natalie asked.

"Cabin fever," she said.

"We all suffer from a bit of that during the winter," the other woman said sympathetically.

"And since I needed an excuse to go out, I decided to pick up a few groceries to make chicken and dumplings for dinner."

"You're going to spoil Max and Wilder with all your fancy cooking," Natalie warned.

"It's the least I can do," Beth said. "And I don't really do anything else."

"I would imagine this little guy keeps you plenty busy," Natalie said, glancing at the baby in his carrier on the bench seat beside his aunt. Then she smiled. "He's watching you move that fork from your plate to your mouth and wondering why you're not sharing with him."

"Because it's a little too sweet and rich for a baby who only recently started eating cereal," Beth said, directing her explanation to Cody. But she dipped the fork into the whipped cream on top of the pie, then touched the tines to his lips so that he could have a tiny taste.

He rubbed his lips together to sample the cream, then his eyes grew wide and his feet kicked.

"I think he likes it," Natalie said.

"Apparently he's got a sweet tooth like his aunt," Beth noted.

"Or maybe two of them," the other woman said. "When did he get those?"

"Just yesterday."

"New teeth for the New Year. Speaking of which... I didn't see you at the party at Maverick Manor."

"Because I wasn't there," Beth admitted.

"Surely Max invited you?"

"He did," she confirmed. "But I opted to stay home with Cody."

"Just with Cody?" Natalie teased.

"What do you mean?"

"Wilder skipped out early, causing much speculation about where he was going and who he was going to be with," Natalie confided. "Because everyone's waiting to see if Max's matchmaker goes six-for-six, and a lot of the local girls are hoping to be the sixth lucky bride."

"Is that what passes for entertainment in Rust Creek Falls?" Beth wondered, feigning only mild interest.

"Well, we've got to do something," the other woman said. "We don't even have a movie theater in town."

She smiled at that, remembering a similar discussion she'd had with Wilder on the same topic.

"In that case, I'd put my money on Max," Beth said. "He doesn't strike me as a man who ever gives up before he gets what he wants."

"And Wilder seems equally stubborn."

"Could be," she acknowledged.

"But if you were going to throw your hat in the ring…" Natalie let her words trail off suggestively.

"Me?" Beth immediately shook her head. "I'm only here because of Cody."

"That's too bad," Natalie said, sounding disappointed.

Maybe she thought so, but Beth knew it was for the best.

By three o'clock that afternoon, Wilder was rethinking his choices. Because a trip into town to do some shopping with Beth and Cody had to be better than freezing his ass off in single-digit temperatures trying to rebuild a fence.

"We should sue Ferrell for damages," he grumbled.

Though it wasn't the cost of the materials that annoyed him so much as the inconvenience of having to make the repair—and the shirking of responsibility by the idiot driver who'd crashed through the fence.

"Good luck proving it was him," Xander said.

"I heard he took his truck to a body shop in Kalispell for repairs," Knox chimed in. "Claimed someone hit his vehicle while it was parked."

"With a two-by-four?" Wilder asked facetiously, rubbing his hands on his thighs in an effort to restore some circulation to his numb digits. "Because you can bet whoever does the repair finds splinters of wood while banging out the dents."

Yeah, he definitely should have chosen to go into town with Beth—except that he hadn't been invited.

And what was that about?

They'd had the "morning after" talk she insisted on, and he'd agreed with everything she'd said—even if he didn't really agree that the night they'd spent together had been a mistake.

So why would she be mad at him?

He was tempted to ask his brothers for their take on the situation, but that would require telling them what had happened with Beth on New Year's Eve. And though he'd never shied away from talking about his past successes with the ladies, he didn't want Beth to become the object of their crude jokes.

Unless he's met a woman who could actually mean something.

As Xander's words from the night of the party echoed in his head, Wilder found himself wondering if his brother wasn't right.

Chapter Fourteen

Late the next morning, Beth was checking her email while she waited for a fresh pot of coffee to finish brewing. She scrolled through the usual ads for sales and the junk that had managed to sneak through her spam filter. There was a note from her friend Elysia, thanking Beth for the books that she'd given to Elysia's daughter for Christmas. Attached to the message was a picture of the nine-year-old on the sofa, still in her pajamas, with an open book in her hand. The photo was captioned: "And there were still presents to be opened!"

Beth smiled, pleased that her gift had been well received. After sending a quick reply, she resumed skimming through her inbox. Her heart jolted when, a little further down on the screen, she recognized Leighton's email address with a subject line that read "Wayward Sister Checking In."

She clicked on the message.

Beth—
I bet you were starting to wonder if you'd ever hear from me again. And no doubt you're pissed about my disappearing act. I know I promised to explain, but I'm not sure I can except to say that I was living a life I never thought I wanted, and it just got to be too much. And that I'm sorry.

In case you haven't figured it out by now (although I'm sure you have), I took Cody to his dad in Montana. (And I am at least 90% certain that Wilder Crawford is his dad.)

I wish I could say I took him there because I felt guilty that I'd deprived Wilder of the opportunity to know his son, and maybe I did. The truth is, I'm not sure what I was thinking in the last few days leading up to the holiday, what compelled me to pack him up and take him so far away and then leave him behind.

Yeah, Wilder's probably pissed at me, too. And I'm going to have to face up to that when I go back to Rust Creek Falls to get Cody. You don't need to worry—he's not the type of guy to take out his anger on a woman. In fact, he's a pretty good guy, and if he decides he wants Cody to visit sometime, I wouldn't mind. It might be good for him to spend time outdoors, maybe learn to ride a horse and stuff like that.

But I'm getting way ahead of myself now—those things can be figured out later. I just wanted to let you know that we'll be home soon and then we can celebrate Christmas together the way we planned.

XO

L

Reading her sister's words, Beth's initial response was relief, then happiness and hope, followed by frustration, anger and guilt. And while she could blame Leighton's actions for most of those conflicting feelings, the guilt was entirely her own.

"Do you want some of this?"

"What?" She glanced up to see Wilder holding the carafe of freshly brewed coffee over her mug. "Oh, um, yes. Please."

He filled the cup she held out, then returned the pot to the warmer. "Are you okay?"

"Yeah. Fine." But she set the mug down again without taking a sip. "I got an email from Leighton."

The surprise on Wilder's face mirrored her own response—as did the shadow of guilt that quickly followed. "You did? When?"

"Just now."

"What does it say?"

She looked at the message again. "That she's sorry for leaving the way she did and—" She cut herself off with a shake of her head. "Why don't you read it yourself?"

He took the cell from her hand and dropped his gaze to the screen.

She watched him as he scanned her sister's words, noting the flex of a muscle as he tightened his jaw—the only outward indication of any emotion, though she couldn't begin to decipher what that emotion was.

Then he handed the phone back to her. "So she's on her way back here to get Cody," he noted. "And apparently she expects me to just hand him over to her, despite the way she abandoned him."

"She is his mother," Beth pointed out.

"She abandoned him," he said again, his tone implacable.

"So…what are you planning to do?"

He swallowed a mouthful of coffee as he considered his response.

"I'll apply for custody," he decided. "I'll call Maggie right now and make an appointment to get the paperwork started."

She remembered him mentioning that he'd borrowed the crib from Maggie and Jesse, but she hadn't known the woman was a lawyer. "You don't even know for sure that you're his father," Beth reminded him gently.

"Do you really doubt it?" he challenged.

No, she didn't. Not anymore. But if she admitted as much, she might as well go back to Dallas, leaving her nephew with his dad. And maybe that was what she should do.

"I thought we agreed that no decisions would be made until we had the results of the DNA test."

"Well, if Leighton's on her way back, it doesn't really matter what you think," he pointed out. "It's between me and her and has nothing to do with you."

Though the words felt like a physical blow, she knew Wilder hadn't meant to be cruel. He was only speaking the truth as he saw it.

What really hurt was that he was right.

Any and all issues concerning Cody were for the little boy's parents to figure out.

It didn't matter that she'd dropped everything to drive halfway across the country. It didn't matter that she'd been the one helping Wilder care for Cody these past eight days. None of that mattered because he wasn't her child.

She was only a supporting player in this drama her sister had planned, and it was time for her to exit stage right.

Wilder knew his unthinking remark had hurt Beth. And as he watched her walk out of the room, he acknowledged that he might have chosen his words more carefully. Or maybe he'd wanted to put some distance between them. Because it had become increasingly evident to Wilder over the past several days that his feelings about the situation with Cody were being clouded by his feelings for Cody's aunt.

And if he was smart, he would stay where he was and maintain the distance.

Instead, he followed her path up the stairs and found her in the guest room, stuffing clothes into a duffel bag.

"What are you doing?"

"I assume that's a rhetorical question," she said, as she struggled with the zipper.

"Why are you packing, Beth?"

"Because I think it would be best for everyone if I was gone before my sister got here."

"Even for your nephew?" he challenged.

"You've proven you're more than capable of taking care of Cody."

"While I appreciate the vote of confidence, I'd argue that part of taking care of him is ensuring that he feels comfortable and secure," he said. "And I'm not sure that being abandoned by his aunt—barely more than a week after being abandoned by his mother—would do much in that regard."

"I would never abandon him," Beth said fiercely.

"You came here with the intention of taking him back to Dallas, and now you're preparing to leave without him— what would you call it?"

"Getting out of the way so that what happened between us won't be an obstacle to Cody's parents getting back together," she told him.

His brows drew together then. "Is that what you want?"

"I want what's best for Cody," she said, refusing to look at him.

"Me and Leighton together would *not* be best for Cody. And I can assure you, there is absolutely zero chance of that ever happening, anyway."

She swallowed. "Please don't say that. Don't close the door on—"

"Zero," he said again, his tone gentle but firm. "Because for me and Leighton to get back together, we would have had to be together in the first place."

She frowned at that. "You're saying you weren't together?"

"We had some good times and we had sex," he acknowledged bluntly.

"Oh."

"I'm not proud of it, but I'm not going to lie and pretend it was more than it was."

"I'm in no position to judge," she acknowledged. "I fell into bed with you, too, with no expectations of happily-ever-after…or even a kiss the morning after."

His gaze slid away. "I left your bed because I heard you talking to Cody over the baby monitor, saying you needed to get some sleep."

"How very considerate of you," she noted, her tone just a little bit cool.

"And maybe I didn't want to deal with my father's questions, if he found me leaving your room in the early hours of morning."

"Or my questions," she guessed.

"*You* told *me* it was a mistake," he reminded her.

"Because it was," she said again.

"So why are you giving me grief about it now?"

"Because I wanted you to say that it wasn't."

She looked as surprised by the blurted revelation as he felt.

"Beth," he began, then faltered.

She closed her eyes and sighed. "Sorry. Forget I said that."

"I'm not sure I even understand what you said," he admitted. "Are you saying that it *wasn't* a mistake?"

"No, it was," she said. "Of course, it was. I mean, you have a history with my sister—even if it was brief and apparently insignificant. And what happened between us… it was just two lonely people finding comfort together."

"Comfort?" he echoed, torn between insult and amusement. "When your body was shuddering with the aftereffects of multiple orgasms and you were panting my name, that was because you were feeling…comforted?"

Beth glanced away, her cheeks flushed with color. "It

doesn't matter," she decided. "We agreed it shouldn't have happened."

"Did we?" he asked.

But before she could answer, he lowered his mouth to hers.

There was no hesitation in his kiss this time. This was no tentative exploration but an insistent demand.

And she responded. She couldn't help herself. The whole time she'd been packing, she'd been recounting all the reasons that getting tangled up with Wilder was a bad idea. But somehow, with his mouth moving over hers, those reasons didn't matter. Nothing mattered but the way she felt when she was in his arms.

Her lips parted to allow him to deepen the kiss; their tongues danced in a slow and seductive rhythm that made her heart pound and her body yearn. And oh, how she yearned to experience the thrill and satisfaction of his lovemaking again.

Except that what they'd shared wasn't lovemaking but sex—a purely physical coupling with no emotional attachment required or desired. And Beth wasn't very good at keeping her emotions detached. Her feelings for Wilder were already stronger and deeper than she was willing to acknowledge.

She eased her lips from his, reluctant but determined. "Didn't we agree that what happened before was a mistake?"

"We agreed that *you said* it was a mistake," he said. "But I think you're trying to convince yourself of that so it won't happen again."

"Of course, it won't happen again."

"Because you're not attracted to me?" he challenged.

Before she could respond to that, he lifted a hand to tuck a stray hair behind her ear, skimming his fingertip over the shell of her ear, making her tremble. He smiled, letting her know that her physical reaction had not gone unnoticed, so that if she tried to claim she wasn't attracted to him, he'd know she was lying.

"Because it wouldn't be smart," she said instead.

"Attraction is rarely based on logic," he said. "And I'm very definitely attracted to you, Beth."

She swallowed. "You are?"

"After the night we spent together, how can you even ask that question?"

"We had sex—once," she reminded him. "We didn't spend the night together."

"And that's my fault," he acknowledged. "I snuck out of your bed because I wanted to stay. Because I wanted more."

"You wanted more?" she asked, doubt and hope warring inside her.

"But I don't know that I'm capable of anything more," he confided. "And you're the kind of woman who deserves a lot more. You deserve to be loved—and I don't do love. I don't know that I can."

She sighed. "So where does that leave us?"

"I don't know. But I'd like to try to figure it out."

"This really is complicated, isn't it?"

He nodded. "And likely to get even more complicated when Leighton shows up."

"That's why I think I should go," she told him.

"Even if I want you to stay?" And then, before she could reply to that, he played his trump card: "Even if Cody wants you to stay?"

She huffed out a breath. "You fight dirty."

"I fight to win," he said, unapologetic.

"Leighton will fight back," she warned.

"Are you worried that you'll get caught in the cross-fire?"

She shook her head. "I can take care of myself."

"I don't doubt it," he said sincerely. "You're one of the strongest women I've ever known."

She was taken aback by his matter-of-fact tone. "You really think so?"

"I do," he confirmed. "You are fierce and formidable."

"I think you've got me mixed up with someone else."

He shook his head. "*You* are an amazing woman, Beth Ames."

And the way he said it, the sincerity in his voice, almost made her believe it.

But if he truly believed it, why couldn't he love her? Was he truly incapable of falling in love, as he believed? Or was she not worthy of his love? And why was she even thinking about love after one night with a man she'd known for barely more than a week?

"You're just trying to sweet-talk me into staying so you won't have to do the middle-of-the-night feedings," she said, in an attempt to ease the seriousness of the moment.

"If you stay, I'll happily do the middle-of-the-night feedings," he promised.

"Okay," she finally relented. "I'll stay."

Beth was folding a load of laundry as she listened to Wilder read to Cody. Hearing the simple story of *Goodnight Moon* in the cowboy's deep voice, watching him point out the list of items in the great green room, warmed something deep inside her.

The ring of her cell came between "goodnight kittens" and "goodnight mittens," and though she didn't recognize the number, she connected the call immediately so the ringing wouldn't disturb the story.

"Hello?"

"Is this Lisbeth Ames?"

It wasn't until she heard the male voice and registered a

quick stab of disappointment that she realized she'd been hoping it might be her sister calling.

"Yes," she acknowledged, bracing herself for a sales pitch.

"Are you related to Leighton Ames?" the caller asked, surprising her again.

"Who is this?" she demanded.

"This is Sheriff Burke from Clearwater County," he said. "I'm afraid I've got some bad news."

"Clearwater County?" she echoed, preferring to latch onto that detail rather than contemplate the possibility of "bad news." "I'm sorry—I don't even know where that is."

"It's in Idaho, ma'am," he said patiently, as if giving her a moment to catch up. "I'm calling because there's been an accident and—"

"What kind of accident?" she interjected, suddenly chilled to the bone recalling that it had been the sheriff who showed up at the door when her parents were killed. "Has something happened to my sister?"

"Her car spun out on Harbinger Road and slid down an embankment."

"Ohmygod. Was she hurt? Is she at the hospital?"

"I'm sorry, Ms. Ames, but your sister suffered traumatic injuries in the crash and—" He paused to clear his throat. "She didn't make it."

"I don't understand, Sheriff. What do you mean?" she asked, her brain refusing to acknowledge and accept the meaning of his words.

If he was trying to tell her that her sister hadn't yet made it back to the Ambling A, she knew that already, because she was here and Leighton clearly wasn't.

"She emailed to tell me that she was on her way to Rust Creek Falls, to pick up Cody," Beth said, eager for him to understand how important it was that Leighton keep her promise. "He's only four and a half months old and he misses her like crazy."

"I'm sorry," the sheriff said again, sounding weary.

"Don't say you're sorry," Beth snapped at him. "Tell me when she's going to be here."

"Beth." She started at the sound of Wilder's voice, gentle but firm. "Give me the phone."

She shook her head, her fingers instinctively tightening on the device, desperately maintaining her grasp on this tenuous connection to the man who was talking to her about Leighton, wanting him to explain why her sister was late.

"Cody's ready for his nap," Wilder said. "Why don't you put him down while I talk to the sheriff?"

It sounded like a reasonable request. It made sense to her. Unlike the gibberish spouted by the sheriff.

And then Wilder cleverly shifted the sleepy baby into her arms, forcing her to relinquish her grip on the phone.

She started out of the room while he took over the call, introducing himself as a family friend.

As Beth carried her nephew up the stairs, the sheriff's words continued to echo in her head, but they still didn't make any sense to her.

Accident…injuries…sorry.

She was supposed to put Cody in his crib, so that he could sleep, but for some reason, she couldn't let him go. Instead, she lowered herself into the rocking chair and snuggled him close.

The baby rubbed his face against her shoulder—a telltale indicator that he was fighting sleep. She touched her lips to the top of his head as she rocked him gently, and his eyes drifted shut.

A few minutes later, she heard the slow, steady rhythm of Wilder's footsteps on the stairs. Then he appeared in the doorway, where he remained for a long moment as if uncertain what to say or do, before crossing the room and gently removing the sleeping baby from her arms.

When Cody was settled in his crib, Wilder returned to crouch by the rocking chair.

"Hey," he said.

She couldn't respond. Her throat was too tight for any words to squeeze through. He lifted his hands to cup her face, his thumbs brushing away tears she hadn't realized she was crying.

He straightened up again, lifting her from the chair as he did so, then taking the seat and settling her in his lap, cuddling her as she'd cuddled Cody.

She wanted to protest that she was too big to be held like a baby, but it felt good to be in his arms. As the strength and warmth of his embrace penetrated the ice that had encased her body, she began to tremble.

He tightened his hold as silent tears continued to spill down her cheeks. But he didn't say anything, because what was there to say?

"I want to wake up and discover it was only a bad dream, that there was no phone call from the sheriff of—" she sighed "—where did he say he was from?"

"Clearwater County."

"Do you think it's possible they made a mistake?" she asked, grasping for any explanation other than the one she knew in her heart to be true. "Maybe Leighton's car was stolen and—"

"She identified herself to the paramedics when they first arrived on scene," Wilder said. "And the sheriff confirmed that she had a constellation tattoo."

"But Leighton doesn't have a tattoo," Beth said.

"Actually, she does," he told her, a reminder that he'd been intimately acquainted with her sister's naked body. "The Leo constellation, in the middle of her back, between her shoulder blades."

"Oh." Leo was her sister's Zodiac sign. "So it really was her? She really is…gone?"

He nodded. "I'm sorry, Beth."

She was sorry, too. And sad and angry and filled with so many more emotions that she couldn't begin to identify.

But somehow she felt empty, too.

Her sister was gone.

Not on a whim.

Not for a while.

Forever.

"I need to make arrangements," she realized. "But I have no idea where to begin, what she'd want."

She was silent for a minute, trying to focus through the grief to think. "Her friends are in Dallas. Our parents are buried there."

And suddenly the answer was obvious: "I have to go home."

Chapter Fifteen

Wilder must have told his family about the call from the sheriff and Beth's plan to return to Texas to arrange her sister's funeral, because the next morning, when she was packing her car, they were all there.

She had tears in her eyes as she said goodbye to Wilder's brothers and sisters-in-law, present and future. She tried to return Avery's jacket, but the expectant mom told her to hold onto it for the journey home, since she wouldn't be able to wear it for the next few months anyway.

Everyone took turns hugging her, expressing their condolences, and promising to see her again soon. Obviously they were assuming she'd bring Cody back to visit. Or maybe she'd be the one coming back to visit Cody, if Wilder followed through on his plan to apply for legal custody of the baby after he had the results of the DNA test.

Over the past ten days, he'd proven that he was more than capable of being the father Cody needed. Equally important, at least from her perspective, was the support of his family. And Beth knew her nephew would be lucky to be part of the close-knit and loving Crawford family.

But she couldn't think about that now. She'd barely processed losing her sister—she couldn't bear to consider that her nephew might be taken from her, too.

It had been a long time since she'd been part of a family. Since the death of their parents almost ten years earlier, Beth and Leighton had only had one another to rely on. Though she'd hoped that reality would bring them closer, there remained a distance that she hadn't been able to breach. And now she never would.

She wished her sister had called instead of emailing. She would have liked to have spoken to her one last time. To tell her that she loved her, no matter what.

"Damn, it's quiet in here," Max remarked, when he entered the house at the end of the day.

Wilder nodded. "I thought the same thing when I came in."

"And there's nothing cooking in the oven for dinner, is there?"

"Not unless you put something in there. And if you did, you forgot to turn on the heat."

Max shook his head. "You want to go to the Ace to grab a burger?"

"Not really," Wilder admitted.

"You have to eat."

"I'm not feeling very sociable," he said. Truthfully, he wasn't feeling very hungry, either.

"Want to tell me what you are feeling?" Max prompted.

"Really? You want me to talk about my feelings?" Wilder asked skeptically.

His father shrugged. "I know I'm probably not your first choice of confidant, but I'm the only one left here."

And it was a testament to how raw his emotions were that Wilder found himself opening up. "I'm mad at her," he admitted.

"Who? Beth?"

"Leighton."

"Well, there's no point in being angry with a dead woman," Max said bluntly.

"I know," he acknowledged. "And yet—I can't deny that's how I feel."

"Why are you mad at her?"

"Where to begin?"

"At the beginning?" his father suggested.

He sighed. "Okay, I'm mad that she never even reached out to tell me that she was pregnant."

"Understandable," Max agreed.

"And then, after not telling me that she was pregnant and not telling me she had a baby, she just drops him at my door and expects me to take care of him."

"That's one way to look at it," his father allowed. "Another is that she trusted you to take care of him."

Wilder just shook his head. "I don't think I'll ever understand how a woman who supposedly loves her child could walk away from him."

There was a long silence as his father considered his response—or maybe he, too, was thinking of another woman who'd done the same thing.

"Are we still talking about Leighton?" Max asked.

"Of course," Wilder said.

Because he and his brothers had learned a long time ago that asking questions about their mother only resulted in upsetting their father.

"Not every woman is cut out to be a mother," Max said now.

"So why would she assume that I could do any better at parenting? And if she needed a break, why didn't she leave Cody with his aunt? Anyone with eyes can see how much she dotes on the little guy."

"You have enough siblings to know that those relationships are never simple," his father pointed out.

"It just doesn't make any sense to me," Wilder told him.

"Is that all?"

"What do you mean?"

"I think you need to consider why you're as outraged

on Beth's behalf as you are about everything else," Max suggested.

"And why do you think that is?" he asked, because it was apparent his father had already arrived at his own conclusions.

So he was more than a little surprised when Max shook his head and said, "That's something you need to figure out for yourself."

When Beth got back to Dallas, she drove straight to the funeral home. After she'd signed the paperwork and paid the bill—which pretty much depleted her savings account—she automatically turned her vehicle in the direction of her condo.

Only as she was getting Cody ready for bed did it occur to her that he might have been more comfortable in his crib at home rather than the portable playpen he slept in when he stayed with her. But she couldn't go to her sister's apartment. Not tonight. Not knowing that Leighton was never coming home again.

She blinked back the tears that burned her eyes as she snuggled with Cody on the sofa in the living room. She didn't know if he sensed her tension or if he'd spent too many hours in his car seat over the past two days, but he seemed as wired as she felt. Though it was well past his bedtime, his eyes remained stubbornly open and fixed on her.

"I don't know what to say to you," she admitted. "How to explain what I don't understand myself. But what I can tell you, with absolute certainty, is that your mama loved you. She might have been uncertain about a lot of things, but there's no doubt she loved you with her whole heart."

Cody couldn't possibly make any sense of what she was saying, but perhaps he understood that she needed him as much as he needed her. He laid his head on her shoulder, rubbing his cheek against her shirt as he snuggled in. He exhaled a shuddery sigh, his breath warm against her throat.

By the time she finally got him settled and crawled into her own bed, she was completely drained—physically and emotionally—but sleep eluded her. She couldn't help wondering what she might have done differently so that her sister might have made different choices along the line. Or even just one different choice so that she wouldn't have been behind the wheel on that icy patch of an unfamiliar road so far away from home.

Logically, she knew it wasn't her fault. Leighton had always made her own choices, and quite often risky ones. But now, because of her choices, Cody was going to grow up without his mother.

She would have to talk to Wilder about his plans, but since receiving the call from the sheriff, she'd been focused on doing what she needed to do for her sister. There would be plenty of time, after Leighton was finally laid to rest, to worry about custody of her nephew.

But she already knew in her heart that she wouldn't fight Wilder if he decided that he wanted to raise Cody on the Ambling A. Not just because that was a fight she knew she wouldn't win, but because she knew that Cody needed a father—and Wilder deserved the opportunity to raise his son.

Ranching was both exhausting and satisfying, and it wasn't often that the activity in Max's mind overruled the weariness of his body. But tonight, he couldn't stop thinking about the conversation he'd had with Wilder, the questions his son had asked about his mother—without admitting that he was asking about Sheila.

Max rarely let himself question the choices he'd made

in his life, but he had doubts now and they were keeping him awake when he really needed to sleep.

Had he done his kids a disservice by letting them believe their mother had chosen to walk away from them, choosing her lover over her family?

He'd been so hurt to learn of her affair. Furious with Sheila, devastated by her betrayal, he'd lashed out at her. She'd chosen someone else over him, and all he could think about was hurting her the way she'd hurt him.

And Logan, Hunter, Xander, Finn, Knox and Wilder had all been casualties in the battle between the two people who should have put their children's needs above all else.

Love truly was a double-edged sword, and his children had been cut deeply. Thankfully, time—and love—had healed their wounds. Of course, Max liked to think that his decision to bring them to Rust Creek Falls for a fresh start had played a part, too. And for his five oldest sons, it had.

But Wilder was still guarding his heart. Not that anyone who didn't know him as well as his father would see it. To the rest of the world, he was just another cowboy blessed with effortless charm and a cocky grin. Only Max knew how much hurt hid behind his smile and why he didn't let anyone get too close.

Watching his youngest son with his son had given Max hope that Wilder's shields were starting to come down. No matter how much he tried to hold back, he couldn't resist responding to the child's sweetness and innocence.

The child's aunt had made a connection with the reluctant daddy, too. And not the kind of superficial connection that Wilder was famous for, but something real and deep and meaningful. But now Beth was gone, and Cody with her, and Wilder's defenses weren't just back in place but actively being reinforced.

Which left Max with no choice. He was going to have

to tell him the truth. He was going to have to fess up to all his sons.

But he had to start with Wilder.

Wilder stumbled into the kitchen on a mission for one thing: coffee. He'd slept like crap for the past two nights—and no, he wasn't blind to the fact that was the same number of nights that Beth and Cody had been gone.

Not surprisingly, his father was there before him, sitting at the table with a steaming mug of coffee in his hands. Max waited until Wilder had poured himself a mug and taken a long swallow before he spoke.

"We need to talk."

"Can it wait?" Wilder asked. "I promised to ride out with Logan today. He thinks there've been coyotes prowling around the northern boundary."

"No, it can't wait," his father said. "It's already waited too long."

Wilder's brows rose in response to the cryptic comment. "Okay…so what is it that you think we need to talk about?"

"I'm worried about you," Max said. "That you've closed yourself off from the possibility of finding love."

"Seriously? That's what you want to talk about right now? Didn't we discuss enough touchy-feely stuff the other day?"

"This is important," his father insisted.

"I know my brothers all falling in love has created some kind of wedding fever, but just because I'm not in a hurry to follow in their footsteps doesn't mean I've closed myself off," he said.

"This has nothing to do with your brothers," Max told him. "Don't get me wrong—I'm overjoyed with the recent and future additions to our family, but right now I'm focused on you."

"Well, you don't need to focus on me," he said. "I'm fine. I'm happy. Life is good."

"So why did you let Beth take Cody away just when you were finally starting to connect with him?"

Wilder frowned. "I let Beth take Cody because she was going home to bury her sister—Cody's mother—and that little boy is the only family she has left."

"That little boy is your family, too."

"Did the DNA results come when I wasn't here?"

"I don't need a piece of paper to know Cody's your son," his father insisted.

"Well, I promised Beth that no decisions would be made about Cody's future until we had the results. So if we're done here, I'm going to—"

"We're not done." Max scrubbed his hands over his face and sighed wearily. "Not even close."

Wilder refilled his mug, because something in his dad's demeanor warned him that he was going to need it.

"I know Cody's situation struck a nerve with you because you think he was abandoned the same way you were abandoned."

"The coincidence is hard to ignore," he acknowledged.

"Except that your mother didn't abandon you."

Wilder wished the caffeine would kick-start his tired body and sluggish brain so that he could keep up with his father's thought processes. "One day she was there and the next day she was gone—what would you call it?"

"She didn't leave you and your brothers...she left me."

"She left *all of us*."

Max shook his head. "She planned to find a place of her own and then she was going to move out and take you kids with her."

Wilder swallowed another mouthful of coffee. "And yet that never happened."

"No," his father agreed. "I asked her not to go. I didn't

understand why she was so unhappy in our marriage, but I offered to go to marriage counseling. I promised to change.

"But she knew me better than I knew myself," Max acknowledged. "She called my bluff. We had one session with a couples' therapist and it was a complete waste of time."

"I can only imagine," Wilder said dryly.

"I was the same man she claimed to have fallen in love with, so I didn't understand what had changed, why she'd fallen out of love with me.

"I blamed her. She'd grown up out East, living a life of wealth and privilege. And while we were well enough off, she didn't know how hard I needed to work to ensure the ranch remained successful." His father stared into the bottom of his empty coffee mug. "But it was my fault. I wasn't a very good husband. I was so busy working the ranch, I didn't think about the fact that she was alone in the house taking care of six kids. I only cared that she was there for me when I came in at the end of the day.

"When your four oldest brothers went off to school, she started taking you and Knox into town for a story time program at the library. She said it would help you both develop social skills and make friends, but it was Sheila who met someone.

"Every week, after story time, she'd stop by the little café next door. That's where she met him. He was the owner of the café, and they became friends—at least that's what she told me. But over time, their friendship grew into love."

Wilder didn't know how to respond to any of this. He could only imagine how distraught Max had been to discover that his wife was in love with another man.

"And she told me that she couldn't stay married to me when she was in love with someone else."

In his father's words, Wilder heard not just bitterness

and anger but the heartache that remained after so many years. Because while no one would ever deny that Maximilian Crawford could be a real son of a bitch, there was also no doubting that he'd deeply and sincerely loved his wife.

"So I told her she was free to go," his dad confided now. "But no way in hell was she taking my sons."

"And she chose her lover over her family," Wilder concluded.

But Max shook his head. "She said that she loved him, but she would never love anyone more than her children."

"But she left," he said again.

"She left," his father confirmed. "Because I told her to get out. I sent her away."

"Why?"

Max pushed away from the table to refill his mug of coffee. "Because I loved her and she didn't love me back. Because I was selfish and angry and hurt. Because I wanted to hurt her the way she'd hurt me."

"Why didn't you ever tell us this before?" he asked, when his father was seated at the table again.

"Because I was afraid, if you boys knew the truth…"

"If we knew the truth *what*?" Wilder pressed.

"I was afraid you'd blame me," Max acknowledged. "And you should—because it was my fault. Even when I sent her away, I knew I was acting out of anger and spite and that I'd probably regret the things I said and did. But I always thought there'd be a chance to make things right."

"Then she died," Wilder said. Not that he remembered anything from that time, but he'd been told about her sudden passing soon after the divorce papers were signed.

His father nodded. "Then she died—and it was too late to undo what I'd done. And what was the point in telling you the truth then?"

"What was the point?" he asked incredulously. "Maybe

the point was that we'd know the truth rather than thinking she didn't want us."

"You're right," his dad agreed. "But it was hard enough, living with my own guilt. I couldn't bear having to live with my sons' anger and hate."

"You should have told us," Wilder said.

Max nodded again. "I've had plenty of time to think about the choices I made," he confided. "To regret the things I said and did. It was my fault she left. My fault you grew up without a mom." He looked up then, pinning Wilder with his gaze. "My fault you haven't let yourself open your heart because you don't trust a woman to stick around."

"I know you like to think you can control everything, Dad," Wilder said dryly, "but not even you can make me fall in love or not fall in love."

Max's expression wasn't unsympathetic as he shook his head. "And you're so determined to keep your heart closed off, you can't even see that you've already fallen."

Chapter Sixteen

Wilder stood on the porch and watched the white van disappear down the driveway. Only when it was gone from sight did he turn his attention to the envelope with the purple logo of the DNA Testing Center in the upper left corner.

This was it: the moment of truth.

When he opened the flap and read the results, he would know for certain that he was Cody's father—or that he wasn't. There would be no more questions or uncertainty.

He'd been waiting for this moment for twelve days, anxious and impatient for the knowledge he finally held in his hand.

So why was he suddenly so apprehensive?

Was he afraid that the results would confirm he was the little boy's father?

Certainly, when Hunter had first read Leighton's note aloud, Wilder had been blindsided by her accusation. He hadn't wanted to believe it, because if it was true, his life would change in ways he wasn't ready for it to change.

But somehow, over the span of less than two weeks with Cody, he'd realized that he was ready for it to change. Maybe, as Beth suggested, he was even ready to embrace fatherhood not as an obligation but an opportunity.

And now he didn't want that opportunity to be taken away. He didn't want to discover that there was no biological link between him and the little boy who'd already taken hold of his heart.

He was still angry with Leighton for abandoning her child. And now that she was gone, he'd never get answers to all the questions he had. But if it turned out that Cody was his child, too, he would forever be grateful to her for giving him the chance to be the little boy's father.

But what about Beth? What would the paternity results mean for her relationship with her nephew?

She would always be Cody's aunt, but as she'd pointed out to Wilder on her first day at the Ambling A, her life was in Dallas. And if he was Cody's father, he'd want to raise him here, in Rust Creek Falls.

But maybe—

He shook his head, dismissing the thought before it had a chance to fully form. There was no point in speculating about possibilities or imagining happy endings that he knew weren't in his future. Because she was a woman who deserved a lot more than he was capable of giving. She deserved love, and he didn't do love.

Except that he did love Cody. And the way his mind and heart had been preoccupied with missing Beth, he suspected that he was starting to fall for her, too.

Starting? A voice mocked inside his head.

He ignored the voice and tore open the flap of the envelope.

His fingers trembled as he pulled out the single sheet of paper.

"DNA Test Result" was printed in bold letters at the top. Beneath it was a chart with columns of numbers that didn't mean anything to him. He scrolled further down and finally found what he was looking for: Probability of Paternity.

He didn't realize he was crying until the numbers blurred in front of his eyes.

Blinking away the tears, he refolded the page and slid it back into the envelope.

* * *

The whole time that Beth was in Rust Creek Falls, she'd looked forward to the day that she could take Cody home. At no time had she imagined that it would be for her sister's funeral.

Four days after that fateful call from the sheriff of Clearwater County, her head and her heart were still reeling from the tragic and premature death of her sister. But as much as she grieved for Leighton, she grieved even more for Leighton's baby.

But she pushed those heavy thoughts to the back of her mind for another day. Today was about Leighton, and Beth was trying to focus on celebrating her sister's life rather than mourning her death. Thinking about what would happen next—

No, she couldn't do it.

One day at a time.

That was her new motto, and today was all she could handle right now. Or maybe more than she could handle. But she would get through it, because she had no other option.

You're one of the strongest women I've ever known... fierce and formidable.

Though she'd doubted the veracity of Wilder's words when he'd spoken them to her, she called on them to sustain her now. Because she knew she was going to need every ounce of that purported strength today.

Though Cody was too young to understand what was happening, she took him to the funeral home for the early visitation. She believed it was important for him to be there, to have a last chance to say goodbye. He'd held up pretty well. It was Beth who'd cried like a baby when she put Cody's Christmas gift to his mom—the still-wrapped "Mommy" ornament—in Leighton's hand inside the coffin.

But then she'd pulled herself together, dabbed some

concealer on the dark circles under her eyes, swiped some mascara over her lashes and slicked some gloss on her lips. Not because she cared how she looked, but because she could hear the echo of her sister's voice telling her that she should care how she looked, and she knew Leighton would appreciate that she'd made the effort.

After the first visitation was over, Beth took Cody back to her condo. Moira Owen—her neighbor across the hall—had offered to watch him for the afternoon, and she was grateful for the help. Though Moira had no kids of her own, her job as an auditor for a multinational corporation meant she was a stickler for details, and Beth knew her neighbor would ensure that the baby was fed and played with and read to and put down for a nap precisely on schedule.

As for the details of her own life, she'd already been in contact with her principal, and Rebecca had told her to take whatever time she needed to get Cody settled. Beth appreciated the offer and understanding, but she wanted to get back to the comfort of her own routines as soon as possible. She needed to be busy so she wouldn't dwell on the loss of her sister—or think about Wilder.

In the three days since she'd left Rust Creek Falls, she hadn't heard a single word from him. Well, aside from the OK he'd sent in reply to her text message telling him that she and Cody had arrived safely in Dallas.

It had now been thirteen days since the cheek swabs were sent off to the lab, and she expected that he'd have the results by now. But if he did, he hadn't shared them with her.

One day at a time, she reminded herself, as she returned to the funeral home to greet those who'd come to remember her sister. Several gathered in groups, sharing stories and memories and offering comfort to one another. Beth didn't know most of them—more proof that she'd existed on the periphery of Leighton's life. And though she would always regret that they hadn't been closer, she was pleased to know that her sister had so many people in her life who cared about her.

Glancing at the clock, she felt a niggle of unease as she tried to remember if she'd given Moira directions on how to prepare Cody's cereal. Maybe she could slip out to make a quick call…

The rest of the thought faded away when he walked through the door.

Wilder.

Her heart skipped a beat, then raced.

She'd wondered if he might show up. After all, he'd had a close and personal relationship with her sister—at least for a while. On the other hand, seventeen hundred miles seemed a long way to travel to say a final goodbye to a woman he hadn't seen in more than a year.

But maybe there was another reason he'd decided to make the trip. Maybe he did get the results of the DNA test and had confirmed that Cody was his child. And maybe, when he returned to Montana again, he intended to take his son with him.

That was something she definitely couldn't think about right now or she'd completely lose it.

"Hey," he said.

"Hi." She stood there awkwardly, not knowing whether to offer her hand or initiate a hug.

He made the decision for her, wrapping his arms around her and drawing her close. And during that all too brief moment, she felt such a sense of peace she wished she could stay in his arms forever.

But of course she couldn't. So she eased away and said, "It was nice of you to come all this way to pay your respects."

"I didn't come only for Leighton," he said. "I came for you, too."

His admission had her fighting against a fresh surge of emotion. "Why?"

"Because I didn't want you to be alone today."

Her eyes filled with tears then, but she refused to let them fall. "Thank you," she said, sincerely touched.

"How are you holding up?"

"I'm doing okay," she said.

"Of course, you are. Because who would keep everything together if you fell apart?" he mused.

"Believe me, I've had my moments."

She turned automatically to shake hands and exchange a few words with another visitor she didn't know, before shifting her attention back to Wilder.

"You got the test results," she guessed.

"Let's talk about that later," he suggested.

She nodded, because he was right—this wasn't the time or the place. And really, didn't she already know what the results were? The only question now was what Wilder intended to do, and that was definitely better left until later.

"Cody was here earlier," she said, certain he had to be wondering about the baby's whereabouts. "But I didn't think he needed to make the trip to the cemetery, so he's with my neighbor now. Plus, you know how cranky he gets if he misses a nap."

"Yeah." Wilder smiled. "I do know."

"But he's sleeping almost through the night now," she said.

"Are *you*?" he asked gently.

She just shook her head as the minister took his place at the podium. Wilder linked their hands and guided her to the front row, while the other mourners took seats around them.

She hadn't realized how much she dreaded having to

get through the service on her own until he was there and she was no longer alone.

Afterward, they rode together to the cemetery, then Wilder took her back to the funeral home where she'd left her vehicle.

"Do you want to come back to my place?" she asked, and immediately felt hot color rush into her cheeks. "I didn't mean that to sound like I was propositioning you."

"I didn't interpret it as a proposition," he said, then winked. "Unfortunately."

"I only meant that I'm sure you want to see Cody," she explained.

"I do," he confirmed. "But I'll come by in a couple hours, if that's okay. I've got a few things I need to do first."

"I'll see you in a couple hours then."

Beth had to buzz him into the building, so when the knock finally sounded on her door, she expected to find Wilder on the other side. Instead, she found Santa.

Though she couldn't have imagined anything would make her smile today, she felt her lips curve as she stood back to allow him entry. "You're a long way from the North Pole."

Her visitor responded with a hearty: "Ho! Ho! Ho!"

She lifted a brow. "And isn't Santa usually on holidays this time of year?"

"Usually," he agreed. "But Cody was out of town on Christmas Eve, so I had to take all his presents back to the North Pole with me. And then yesterday, Tracker—the elf who keeps track of all the good little girls and boys—told me that I could find Cody here."

"Tracker?" she echoed, amused by his elaborate narrative.

"Just go with it," he urged in a stage whisper.

"Well, Tracker was right," Beth confirmed. "Cody is here."

She led "Santa" to the living room, where the baby was propped up by a pillow on the floor, gnawing on the paw of the teddy bear that was one of the gifts she'd given to him at the Ambling A.

"Ho! Ho! Ho! Merry Christmas in January," Santa said.

Cody's eyes grew wide and wary as he looked at the stranger in the red suit, then his lower lip began to quiver.

"I should have reminded you that he slept through his visit with Saint Nick when I took him to the mall," Beth said. "So this is the first time he's actually seen Santa."

And if the terrified look in his eyes was any indication, Cody wasn't too impressed.

Sensing that a meltdown was imminent, Santa immediately pulled off his wig and beard, revealing his true identity to the little boy. "Hey, buddy."

Cody's lip stopped quivering and he offered a tentative smile, showing off his two teeth.

Wilder dropped his bag of presents onto the floor and picked up the baby. "I can't believe how much I missed this little guy," he confided to Beth.

"He missed you, too."

"How about you?" he asked. "Did you miss me?"

She was reluctant to answer the question. She didn't want to admit how very much she'd missed him, how much her heart ached whenever she thought about him— which was pretty much constantly. "Maybe," she said instead. "A little."

"Just a little, huh?" He sounded disappointed. "I missed you a lot from the moment you were gone—and then a little bit more each day."

She was surprised by his admission. "You did?"

He nodded. "As the youngest of six brothers raised by a single dad, I sometimes struggle to find the right words to express how I'm feeling," he confided to her now. "At other times, I struggle to even acknowledge that I have feelings.

"But I can't deny the way I feel about you any longer. I don't want to deny my feelings. I want a life with you, Beth. I want you and me and Cody to be together. A family."

It was what she wanted, too. More than anything. But she was afraid to trust that his feelings—and her own—were real. "We've only known each other a couple of weeks," she reminded him. "And our whole relationship, if it could even be called a relationship, revolved around Cody."

"Not our whole relationship," he said pointedly.

She knew he was referring to New Year's Eve—the night they'd enjoyed a very small and intimate celebration together—and she felt her cheeks flush with color. But as fabulous as that night had been, and as much as she might want to repeat it—over and over again—he was the one who'd told her that he didn't do relationships, that he wasn't capable of falling in love.

So this apparent turnaround was a little too sudden and abrupt to be believable. No matter how much she wanted to believe. Which led her to another, more logical conclusion. "I can appreciate that you're probably reeling from the DNA results," she said. "And now you're looking for someone to take care of your son, and I'm the obvious choice because—"

Wilder shook his head, cutting her off. "You have some serious insecurities, don't you?" he asked, seeming sincerely baffled by her speculation.

She shrugged. "Leighton was the beautiful one, the fun one," she said, though she doubted he needed the reminder. "I was always the other one."

"Leighton was beautiful and fun, and we had some good times together," he acknowledged. "But I was never in love with your sister."

She blinked, not sure she understood what he was saying.

"You, Lisbeth, are just as beautiful and just as much fun. You are also warm and kind, generous and loving, and I am head over heels in love with you."

For a long minute, she could only stare at him, stunned by his declaration. "You love me?"

"I love you, Lisbeth Ames," he confirmed.

"I didn't even think you *liked* me all that much."

He smiled. "I had some reservations at first, as I know you did about me, too."

She couldn't deny that was true.

"But over the past couple of weeks, everything changed. *You* changed everything for me," he told her. "And I can't imagine my life without you and Cody in it. Because, as it turns out, I've fallen head over heels for the little guy, too."

"I'm still waiting for you to confirm that you got the DNA results," she told him.

"I got them. And when I finally had the envelope in hand, I knew that whatever was written on the page didn't matter as much as what was in my heart." He looked at the baby in his arms. "And in my heart, Cody was already mine. The lab report only confirmed it."

She smiled then, her heart overflowing with happiness for her nephew and his daddy.

"You know, now would be a good time to tell me that you love me, too…if you do," Wilder said.

She lifted her gaze to his, so he would see in her eyes the truth that filled her heart. "I do love you, Wilder Crawford."

He kissed her then, long and slow and sweet.

And just when Beth had decided that she would be happy to go on kissing him forever, he eased his mouth from hers and said, "Now it's time for Cody's second first Christmas."

"Second first Christmas?" she asked, amused.

"Well, I didn't have any presents for him when you celebrated his first Christmas, so I brought these," he said, dumping the contents of the bag onto the floor.

She looked at the assortment of presents—small ones and big ones, hard ones and squishy ones—then at the man in the Santa suit. "Did you buy out The Toy Box?" she asked, referring to the local specialty store.

He grinned. "Not entirely."

"And you said I went overboard."

He shrugged, unrepentant. "I think I'm entitled to go a little overboard for my son's first Christmas."

"I think so, too," she agreed.

They both knelt on the floor to help Cody open his gifts. There were wooden puzzles and more books, a cuddly octopus learning toy, a ball that flashed colored lights, a miniature piano, a set of maracas, a drum, a xylophone and a tambourine.

"Are you trying to turn him into a one-baby band?" Beth teased.

"I read that there's a strong correlation between music and brain development," he explained.

"Was that in the book?" she asked, echoing the same question he'd once asked her.

"There isn't one book that's the authority on everything," he said, echoing her response. "And every baby is different."

"But most parents would probably agree that they're more interested in boxes and bows than presents at this age," she said, noting how intently Cody was focused on the shiny green bow in his hand.

"There's one more," Wilder said, setting the last small square box on the floor in front of her. "For you."

"For me?" Her heart pounded inside her chest as she tore off the paper to reveal a velvet jeweler's box. With unsteady hands, she opened the lid to reveal a dazzling diamond solitaire.

She lifted her stunned gaze from the ring to find Wilder watching her. His expression was intent, serious—and just a little bit uncertain.

He cleared his throat. "Maybe it's too soon," he allowed. "But—"

"No," she quickly interjected, shaking her head.

"No?" he echoed.

His bleak tone and grim expression immediately alerted her to his misinterpretation of her response.

"No, it's not too soon," she hastened to clarify. "But you can't just hand a woman a ring—you have to ask the question."

"Oh." He released an audible sigh of relief. "Okay, I can do that," he said. "Beth Ames, will you—"

"Yes," she said, interjecting again.

He chuckled softly and slid the ring on her finger. "A perfect fit—just like you and me and Cody."

Epilogue

Five months later

"I now pronounce you husband and wife." The minister nodded to the groom. "You may kiss your bride."

Wilder didn't need to be told twice. He lowered his head and touched his mouth to Beth's, lingering for just a moment—sealing their vows, promising his heart.

Then they turned to face their guests, and the bride lifted her skirt just enough to show off the cowboy boots she'd donned beneath her wedding gown. There were chuckles mixed in with the applause then, and the happy couple joined hands to exit along the aisle of their make-shift outdoor chapel—pausing first at the front row of chairs so the groom could take his now ten-month-old son from the boy's grandfather.

As Beth and Wilder mingled with their guests, she couldn't help but reflect on how much had changed in her life in just six months. And although she still missed her sister every day, she took comfort in knowing that Leighton lived on in her little boy, who demonstrated more and more each day that he had his mother's happy disposition and his father's effortless charm.

Those traits had been on full display as he enchanted the guests who'd come to the Ambling A for the wedding of his biological father to his maternal aunt. And there were a lot of guests. In addition to Wilder's immediate family and all the distant Rust Creek Falls Crawford relatives, there were Daltons, Traubs, Stocktons, Joneses and O'Reillys. Beth had heard more names today than she could ever be expected to remember, but she was happy to be starting a life and raising Cody in this close-knit community—even if it meant a wedding reception far bigger than she'd ever anticipated.

Thankfully the whole day had been planned with meticulous attention to detail by Vivienne Dalton, who continued to circulate to ensure that everything went according to plan. Her only failing was an inability to corral Hunter's seven-year-old daughter. Wren kept returning to the chapel to practice walking down the aisle and tossing flower petals, in preparation for her very important role as flower girl when her daddy finally married Merry in only a few more weeks.

After a delicious meal—interrupted by countless toasts to the happy couple—the bride and groom shared their first dance. As the song drew to a close, the rest of the guests were invited to join them, and Beth was pleased to see each of Wilder's brothers on the floor with their partners. Even Finn and Avery were dancing, having enlisted Max to keep an eye on their beautiful three-month-old daughter, Mabel.

Of course, the proud grandpa was happy to have his arms full of babies. And Wren, finally satisfied that she'd had sufficient practice being a flower girl, was helping mind her younger cousins.

When the bride and groom took a reprieve from dancing and returned to their table with Cody, Beth found an obviously old but beautiful jewel-encrusted book beside her bouquet.

"What's this?" she asked, as Cody reached out to touch the sparkly stones on the cover.

"My brothers believe it's Josiah Abernathy's diary," Wilder said, and proceeded to give her a brief history of the book and the writer's forbidden love affair with a mysterious woman.

"But why is it here?" she wondered.

"They've been passing it around for months, claiming it carries a love spell or something like that. I guess they've decided it's our turn to experience its powers."

"All true," Merry confirmed, as she joined them. "But there's more—a note hidden inside the cover confirmed the mystery writer as Josiah Abernathy and his girlfriend as Winona Cobbs.

"Even more shocking," she continued, as the rest of Wilder's siblings and their spouses gathered around, "is that their baby girl wasn't stillborn, as she believed. Beatrix was taken away and given to another family to raise."

A revelation that led to much speculation about whether it might be possible to find Beatrix after so much time had passed.

"This is all very fascinating," Wilder said, speaking quietly so that only his bride could hear him. "But what I really want to know is when we can steal away from this party."

"You're not having a good time?" she asked, surprised.

"The wedding was great," he acknowledged. "But now, Mrs. Crawford, I'm more than ready to start the honeymoon."

She tipped her head back to smile at him. "I like the sound of that, Mr. Crawford."

As if on cue, their wedding planner stepped up beside them to ask, "What are you still doing here when the honeymoon suite at Maverick Manor is waiting for you?"

"We're on our way," Wilder said. "We just wanted to thank you for giving us the perfect day."

"Well, I did have a little help from Mother Nature," Vivienne said, gesturing to the sun setting against a cloudless sky. "But I'm happy to take credit for all the rest."

"If only you'd had as much success as a matchmaker," Logan said to her.

"I think I did pretty well helping you and your brothers find your perfect matches."

"What are you talking about?" Xander asked. "We found our own matches."

Vivienne smiled. "Did you?"

The brothers exchanged puzzled glances.

"I might not have introduced Logan and Sarah, but they met at my office," she pointed out. "And Xander and Lily only got together because I'd set up a date between Knox and Lily, then Knox rushed to marry Genevieve because he didn't want any part of Max's scheme. I also knew Finn and Avery would be perfect together, even if I didn't know they'd already found one another, and it was because they were getting married that Hunter decided to hire a nanny and fell in love with Merry."

Wilder nodded his agreement. "It looks like you did have a hand in five out of six matches," he said to Vivienne.

"I might have found someone for you, too," she told him. "Except that you managed to find your perfect match without any help."

"Actually, *I* found *him*," Beth said, making her husband smile.

"Five out of six is an impressive stat," Finn acknowledged. "But still short of Max's target."

"And nothing less than one hundred percent is ever good enough for Maximilian Crawford," Knox remarked.

"I think I could make a case for six out of seven," the wedding planner–slash–matchmaker said, nodding toward the dance floor where the groom's father was slow dancing with the woman Wilder recognized from New Year's Eve.

"Who's that?" Beth asked, because she hadn't been at the party at Maverick Manor.

"Estelle, my former boss," Vivienne told them.

"I thought she moved to Phoenix," Lily remarked.

"And then she came back. She said she enjoyed the

more temperate climate, but planning funerals was as depressing as hell."

"Dad seems completely smitten with her," Logan remarked, apparently baffled that such a tiny woman could have captivated the larger-than-life cattleman.

"She's got a personality equal to his own," Vivienne assured him. "And Max is so happy with the way things worked out for everyone that he's agreed to honor the terms of our original contract. As a result, we'll be able to fix the roof at Sawmill Station *and* invest more money in the Thunder Canyon operation. Plus, with the way business is booming, I'm thinking of hiring extra help in Rust Creek Falls, too."

"What kind of experience is needed to work in the wedding planning business?" Beth wondered, her curiosity piqued.

"Are you looking for a job?" Vivienne asked hopefully.

"I am," the bride confirmed. "And there are no teaching positions currently available at the local elementary school."

"Do you believe in happy endings?"

Beth looked up at her new husband, and the love that filled her heart to overflowing shone through her eyes. "I do now."

Vivienne smiled. "That's a good start."

Cody apparently thought so, too, because he clapped his hands together.

Wilder's chuckle drew the little boy's attention to him. Then Cody reached his arms up toward his daddy and said his first word: "Da-da."

And Beth thought that was the perfect ending to a perfect day—and a very happy beginning for the start of their life together as a family.

* * * * *

COMING SOON!

We really hope you enjoyed reading this book. If you're looking for more romance, be sure to head to the shops when new books are available on

Thursday 12th December

To see which titles are coming soon, please visit

millsandboon.co.uk/nextmonth

MILLS & BOON

Coming next month

CRAZY ABOUT HER IMPOSSIBLE BOSS
Ally Blake

There was no way he wasn't fully aware she stood behind him. The man's ability to read a room was legendary. He noticed changes in temperature, pulse, breathing, tone of voice the way other people noticed being kicked in the shin.

Yet still Lucinda took a selfish moment to drink him in before making herself officially known.

For Angus Wolfe's profile was a study in staggering male beauty.

The man was all chiselled angles. Sharp jaw close shaven. Hair darkly curling and a mite overlong. Reading glasses he refused to admit he needed to wear did nothing to soften the impact of the most formidable pair of dark hazel eyes that had ever been seen.

Even the tendons in his neck were a sight to behold.

Then he shifted. Slowly. Like a big cat stretching in the sun. The lines of his charcoal suit moved with him, cut as they were to make the most of his…everything. Each one cost more than she'd spent on her car. She knew. She paid his bills.

Then she spotted his socks. Peeking out from the top of his custom-made dress shoes she saw the merest hint of a wolf motif. She'd given him those socks for Christmas.

Her heart gave a little flutter, releasing a gossamer

thread of lust that wafted from throat to belly to places less mentionable.

She squished the thing. Fast.

Angus Wolfe might be able to read a room, but if anyone dared claim that Lucinda Starling - his long-time Executive Assistant, his right-hand woman, his not-so-secret weapon – was a teeny tiny little bit in love with him, he'd have laughed till he split a kidney.

Either she kept her cards closer to her chest than she realised, or he had a blind spot when it came to her. The fact that he had no clue was a gift. And she planned to keep it that way…

Continue reading
CRAZY ABOUT HER IMPOSSIBLE BOSS
Ally Blake

Available next month
www.millsandboon.co.uk

JOIN US ON SOCIAL MEDIA!

Stay up to date with our latest releases, author news and gossip, special offers and discounts, and all the behind-the-scenes action from Mills & Boon...

 millsandboon

 millsandboonuk

 millsandboon

It might just be true love...

LET'S TALK
Romance

For exclusive extracts, competitions
and special offers, find us online:

- **f** facebook.com/millsandboon
- **🐦** @MillsandBoon
- **📷** @MillsandBoonUK

Get in touch on 01413 063232